THE LONG SUNSET

Also by Jack McDevitt

JACK McDEVITT

THE LONG SUNSET

AN ACADEMY NOVEL

SAGA PRESS

LONDON SYDNEY NEW YORK TORONTO NEW DELHI

SAGA PRESS

AN IMPRINT OF SIMON & SCHUSTER, INC.

1230 AVENUE OF THE AMERICAS, NEW YORK, NEW YORK 10020

SAGA PRESS and colophon are trademarks of Simon & Schuster, Inc.

For information about special discounts for bulk purchases, please contact Simon & Schuster Special Sales at 1-866-506-1949 or business@simonandschuster.com.

The Simon & Schuster Speakers Bureau can bring authors to your live event. For more information or to book an event, contact the Simon & Schuster Speakers Bureau at 1-866-248-3049 or visit our website at www.simonspeakers.com.

Interior design by Hilary Zarycky

The text for this book was set in ITC Veljovic.

Manufactured in the United States of America

First Edition

2 4 6 8 10 9 7 5 3 1

Library of Congress Cataloging-in-Publication Data

Names: McDevitt, Jack, author.

Title: The long sunset / Jack McDevitt.

Description: First edition hardcover. |
London ; New York : Saga Press, [2018]

Identifiers: LCCN 2017022020 | ISBN 9781481497930 (hardcover : alk. paper)
| ISBN 9781481497961 (eBook)

Subjects: | GSAFD: Science fiction.

Classification: LCC PS3563.C3556 L66 2018 | DDC 813/.54—dc23

LC record available at https://lccn.loc.gov/2017022020

For Holly McClure and Jack Gonzalez,
friends of a lifetime

Acknowledgments

I'm indebted to my son, Christopher McDevitt, who read and helped repair early drafts; to David DeGraff, Walter Cuirle, Larry Wasserman, Frank Manning, and Jonty and Deron Jackson for technical assistance; and to my agent, Chris Lotts.

THE LONG SUNSET

Prologue

We can make our lives sublime,
And, departing, leave behind us
Footprints on the sands of time.
—Henry W. Longfellow, "A Psalm of Life," 1838

Charlie looked up at Saturn and its dazzling rings. Iapetus was in tidal lock, so the giant planet was fixed over a distant ridge, permanently emplaced. The statue, which the first visitors had named *Jennifer*, never looked away from the gas giant. He wasn't sure whether it was the planet or the statue that commanded his attention. He stared first at one, then at the other. "You okay?" asked Hutch.

"Yeah. I'm fine, Mom." The sculpture depicted a creature with half-folded wings, ominous claws, and eyes that seemed almost alive. They were locked on that distant ridge, watching the planet that never moved. The thing was carved of rock, utterly alone on that barren plain, a product of unknown visitors who'd left this existential landmark thousands of years earlier.

Charlie's attention shifted again, to the ground module left behind by the Steinitz mission, which had come in on the first manned flight to Iapetus. It was open to visitors, revealing little other than a bare metal interior. Two of the cushions had been ripped from the seats and presumably taken home as souvenirs. If anything else had been left, it was gone. A US flag was painted on the hull.

He put his hands on his helmet, which was the lone piece of hard material the Flickinger suit allowed. Inside the force field, he was wearing fatigues and a Capital University pullover shirt. He looked as if he'd just arrived after a casual walk from the campus.

The statue was a self-portrait of one of the Monument Makers. It had been possible to make that determination from a set of footprints, which had matched the sculpture's feet. Three lines of symbols, which had defied all efforts at translation, were carved into the base. In later years it had been discovered that the mysterious race had left sculptures, shrines, cones, and pillars all over the Orion Arm. But no other statues of the creatures themselves had been found. Hutch wondered whether the creature who'd arrived there had been a loner of some sort. There'd been only one set of prints. If that were true, it seemed likely she'd been trying to send a message. There was something familiar in that alien figure, something in the eyes, in the way it stood looking out at Saturn. Intelligent beings were few in a wide universe that didn't give a damn for their welfare.

Maybe that was how the symbols translated.

"You know, Mom, you were right." Charlie bore such a close resemblance to his father, to Tor, that it was almost painful. Dark eyes, chiseled features, charming smile.

"About what?"

"The virtual stuff. Sitting in the living room at home looking at this doesn't work the same way." He raised a fist. "You have to be here. I wish Dotty could have seen this." Dotty was his current girlfriend. Hutch had offered to bring her along too, but her parents had declined. Too dangerous.

"Happy birthday, son."

"You've made it unforgettable. Maybe it's time I told you something."

"Uh-oh." She glanced around at the other tourists. There were eleven altogether. A couple were looking inside the ground module. The rest were standing on the viewing section in front of the statue, some pointing at the wings, others at the claws or trying to make something of the symbols. "Is there a problem?" She knew, of course, there wasn't. But she and Charlie played games whenever they could.

"When I get through school—"

"Yes?"

"I'm going to follow your career. Become a pilot."

That was news. He was majoring in art and seemed to have much of his dad's talent in that area. "Glad to hear it, Charlie. You'll be a good one. When did you decide that?"

"Well, actually, years ago."

"You never said anything."

"You've always been a tough act to follow." He came over to her and they embraced. The truth was, she had mixed feelings about it. There wasn't much need for pilots anymore. Not for the interstellars, anyhow. It was like the twentieth century, when we found out there were no canals on Mars and Venus was an oven. During that period enthusiasm had declined. There was nothing left to get excited about, funding got cut from NASA, and the space programs all but died. Then the Iapetus statue was discovered, and there was a second breakout movement, which led eventually to the development of the FTL drive. But in the long run, even that had gone nowhere. We traveled to other stars, but the vast majority of worlds located in the habitable zones were as desolate as Mars. We reached a point where the exciting finds consisted of occasional cellular life. For a time people wondered whether they were actually alone. Then, on Pinnacle and Quraqua and a few other places, ruins were discovered.

The big news came when a race of theoretically intelligent beings was discovered on a world whose name made it into English as *Nok*. They had primitive guns and cannons and spent most of their time killing one another. Except for that, they were boring. There was little art to speak of, virtually no literature, nothing to invite anyone's interest. Since then, a couple of other intelligent species had been found, but a decision was made to stay away from them to avoid causing any damage. And, of course, there had always been concern over the possibility of confronting an unfriendly civilization thousands or millions of years ahead of us. In the words of the celebrated comedienne Marla Wallace: *"The first flight to the nearest star found nothing. The smart thing for us would have been to travel no farther. To stay where we were and never go west of Centauri."*

Eventually, Hutch hoped, there'd be a change of heart somewhere. And the enthusiasm she'd seen in her early years would return. If for no other reason than the strides that had been made in life extension, which had seriously intensified the population problem. Humanity needed to expand.

Quraqua was one of three worlds now available for colonization. But politicians were arguing that we were reproducing faster than we could ever hope to move people off world. So why bother? It was an argument that made no sense to her. Anyhow, if we got serious about constructing interstellars, we could turn things around. Or at least stabilize the situation.

Charlie was taking pictures of the sculpture. Hutch had always thought that *Jennifer* was a pedestrian name for a creature that she thought of as an angel. "Kind of irrelevant, I suppose," he said, "since we already have one at home." It was framed and had a center place in Hutch's office, surrounded by acclamations and awards for services rendered as an Academy pilot, back in the days when there *was* an Academy.

"Best to have your own, son."

"I guess. What I'd really like to see is a picture of me on the bridge taking us back to Earth."

Priscilla's Journal

I'd have loved to meet that young woman. (And she is a woman. That she has wings and belongs to a different species are details.) Standing out there this most recent time, by her side, I couldn't help thinking that, in a very real sense, we have met. I know exactly what was going through her mind when she created that figure, and I suspect she knew precisely who her audience would be.

—Thursday, December 27, 2255

1.

Ah! Then, if mine had been the Painter's hand,
To express what then I saw; and add the gleam,
The light that never was, on sea or land,
The consecration, and the Poet's dream;
I would have planted thee, thou hoary Pile
Amid a world how different from this!
Beside a sea that could not cease to smile;
On tranquil land, beneath a sky of bliss.
—William Wordsworth, "Elegiac Stanzas Suggested by a
Picture of Peele Castle in a Storm," 1807

On the day that everything changed, it rained. Derek Blanchard's car eased into the faculty parking lot while precipitation poured down across the University of Pennsylvania. A few students were hurrying through the storm. Otherwise, the campus looked empty. Derek pulled on his raincoat, tugged the hood into place, grabbed his briefcase, and got out of the car.

Ten minutes later he was seated at a table in the Gateman Conference Room with a half dozen doctoral candidates. He was an African American, tall, with a close resemblance to Hollywood star Alan Parkman, and a baritone voice that people took seriously. Guessing ages during an era when almost no one looked more than thirty was tricky, but most of his students had done the research, so they knew he'd been around a long time.

They were discussing theses. Each was targeted on aspects of stellar evolution. Derek outlined the requirements for a reasonable analysis, laid out the time limits, and went over other technical details. The candidates, three men and three women, submitted their topics. Derek supported some, recommended a completely different approach for two, and added a few general suggestions. It was hard to keep focused because of what was coming next.

When they'd finished, he closed his notebook. "There's something else," he said. "For anyone who's free, we'll have access to the Van Entel this morning from eleven fifteen to twelve thirty." The Van Entel was the supertelescope, which was in solar orbit. "We'll not only be able to look through it, but we'll be controlling it. If you'd like to sit in, stop by the Data Collection Center. But come early. And I'm sorry about the last-minute notification, but none of us saw this coming."

Derek was an astronomer, a physicist, a mathematician, and a WSA consultant. The latter gave him a few benefits, like the Van Entel, which he enjoyed passing on to his students. He was also a frequent guest speaker at scientific conferences. When he got in front of a microphone and looked out across an audience, he almost changed character. No one would ever have called him reserved, but he was not inclined to take over a conversation. On stage, however, he held his listeners' attention, provoked laughter, and enjoyed himself immensely.

Of the students, Karen Blum had probably the most potential. She showed serious analytical capabilities, she was ambitious, and she had an IQ that topped 160. She followed him out of the room. "Professor Blanchard," she said, "may I ask what project you'll be working on? With the Van Entel?"

"I don't have a specific project, Karen," he said. "You might think of me more as an eavesdropper. They'll be looking out at the Kellerman Cluster today. At some stars nobody's ever paid much attention to. They're trying to get them cataloged."

Karen literally hugged herself. "How far are they?"

"Seven thousand light-years. Give or take."

"Beautiful. Is there anything special about them?"

"Not really. Actually, they're not so much interested in the stars as they are in the telescope. It's still in its testing phase."

"Oh yes, of course."

"We'll be using the Hynds as well."

"The ultra-radiotelescope."

"Right. It's in orbit too, and it's also aimed at the area. We'd like to see what else we can learn about what's going on out there."

Her eyes brightened. "You planning on taking a trip to the area anytime soon?"

That was a reference to Derek's background, which consisted of several interstellar missions. That was one of the reasons he retained his situation with the World Space Authority while simultaneously teaching at Penn. "Maybe next week," he said.

"That's a joke, right? They're closing down the interstellar flights, aren't they?"

"If we let them."

"Do you think the Centauri Initiative will really pass?"

"I hope not."

Karen's amicable expression turned hostile. "Why do

those idiots worry so much about alien invasions? There probably aren't any aliens who would be interested in bothering us. There are hardly any aliens at all."

He managed a pained smile. "It's an election year."

The Data Collection Center was almost filled when he arrived twenty minutes early. Linda DuBreuil, the director, was standing guard by the group of seats reserved for the faculty. They were in front of the main screen. An additional eighty chairs were there to accommodate students and a few instructors not connected with the astronomy department. They were filling up as he walked in. The event had gotten coverage in the media, and he expected it to be picked up by the Science Channel.

Linda saw him and got out of her chair. "Hello, Derek. You ready to go?"

"Oh, yes." He loved each new development in telescopes. Loved being part of the process, even when he was merely serving as a PR guy.

They sat down and she handed him a microphone and an ear pod. "You want to do the intro?"

"Sure," he said. "If you like."

Linda had a smile that could light up the entire room. "It's your party, Derek."

"Good enough." He put the pod in his right ear so he could hear Ben, the AI, and turned the microphone on. "Ben, you there?"

"I'm here, Professor. We're on schedule."

Linda looked to their right, where a couple of people he didn't know were getting seated with the science faculty. "We have some media," she said.

• • •

The center filled and they had to bring in extra chairs, and finally just leave the doors open for any who wanted to stand in the rear. At five after eleven Derek got to his feet, turned to face the audience, and made some introductory comments about the Kellerman Cluster and the capabilities of the Van Entel. He was almost finished when Ben cut in. *"Professor, we've received another alert from the Coordination Office."* The Coordination Office was located on the Union Space Station. *"Control system will be transferred to us in one minute."*

"Ladies and gentlemen, we're apparently ready to go." Derek lowered his voice. "Okay, Ben. Activate the display." The screen lit up, as did a couple of smaller displays around the room. Derek looked out over his audience. "We'll be handling the operation from here. You'll notice, incidentally, when we tell the control system what to do, there'll be a delay before it responds. You know why that is, of course?"

Hands went up all over the room. Everybody knew the Van Entel was approximately five million kilometers away, so the radio signal would need about eighteen seconds to reach it. And consequently thirty-six seconds before there could be a response.

One of his students, Bobby Dexter, raised his hand. "Really? Only half a minute?"

"It's pretty close right now, Bobby. Sometimes the process would take close to a half hour."

The screen filled with stars, two the size of small coins, the others no more than distant glimmers in the night. "Ben," Derek said, "you know the target system. Take us to it, please."

"Transmission on its way. Hynds also activated."

Derek did a mental countdown. He reached nineteen before the stars began to move. From right to left, across the screen. The two coins slipped off the side of the screen. People were shifting in their seats behind him. He'd gotten so excited, he'd lost track of the fact he was still on his feet, blocking everyone's view. He didn't want to sit down, so he moved to the side of the room where he was out of the way.

Derek loved this part of his profession, inflaming the passions of students. There might be another Polcrest or Sagan in the room. Somebody who'd lead the charge against the politicians who were trying to wreck everything humans had accomplished in space over the past three centuries. *We've been down this road before, damn it. Went to the moon and forgot how to do it. And here we go again with people, including scientists, claiming that interstellar travel is too dangerous. That it should be stopped. We don't know what's out there. And it has gone to the heart of the current presidential campaign. We've looked around the local area. But stop it there. Do not go west of Centauri. It had become a maxim for the Progressives.*

This wasn't the first time he'd been present for a demonstration of the capabilities of a supertelescope, but having his hand on the wheel added a dimension he hadn't experienced in the past. He watched the stars drift by, saw a configuration that might have been a wrench, and knew where they were. More or less. The wrench reached the side and was gone, and he was lost again. But no surprises there.

"Professor Blanchard," said the AI, *"Union advises we slow down so they can get the two telescopes in sync."*

"Do it, Ben. And let's also increase magnification."

The sky was still moving sidewise when a vast cloud of stars began to edge in on the right side. Students gasped. Somebody asked whether anyone living out there would ever see night. Derek was ecstatic.

A young man seated a few rows back jumped out of his seat and started jabbing his finger at the display. A planet had appeared in the foreground.

It was, Derek thought, a rogue world. But it was hard to be certain, and before he could get a good look, it had gone off the edge of the screen. The infamous thirty-six-second delay. Still more stars were going off the side. Damn. Well, forget the planet. They had bigger things to think about.

He wanted the cluster in the center of the display, but it was already almost halfway across the screen before he stopped gaping and gave the order to stop the rotation.

It continued to drift while he waited. Finally it stopped and they had a near-perfect perspective. It was spectacular. As breathtaking as anything he'd ever seen. He would have liked to inform everyone what they were looking at. But he didn't know anything more about the specifics of the cluster than his students. That was an issue with the giant telescopes: He could spend a substantial amount of time tracing star patterns, constellations, whatever, but when the telescope zeroed in, the patterns tended to disappear. He was simply, like everyone else, staring at a sky full of stars. And if he did recognize a group of stars, it became rapidly irrelevant because there was just too much to look at. Pity. It would have been nice to be able to show off a bit.

Ben's voice again: *"Derek, we are getting a signal from the Hynds."*

"They've picked up something?"

"Yes. It appears to be a telecast. From the edge of the cluster."

"A telecast?"

"That is correct. Do you wish it placed on the display?"

"Yes. Of course."

Derek had no idea what he expected. It would have to be a directional signal to make it this far. No standard telecast could come close to covering thousands of light-years. So it was probably what? A distress call? A mission report?

Ben reduced the telescopic image to about a quarter of its size and moved it into a corner. Then he replaced it with a waterfall. *"This,"* he said, *"is the telecast."*

A *waterfall*?

The audience froze and then broke into applause. Several wanted to know whether the system had gone off track somewhere. Linda reached over and grasped Derek's arm. "At least it's not Niagara."

It wasn't an expansive waterfall, but it appeared to be extremely high, with water plummeting from a ridge deep into a canyon. He was just beginning to breathe normally again when he became aware of background music. It was a soft and gentle rhythm, in perfect harmony with the falling water.

The applause faded and the room went silent, save for the music. Then suddenly everybody was talking. "What is that?"

"Professor Blanchard, what's going on?"

Linda was looking at him and just shaking her head.

"Ben," he said, "is that the signal that's coming in?" He adjusted the microphone so everyone could hear the answer. "Or have we picked up something local?"

"It was forwarded by the Hynds unit. I have no way to determine its validity beyond that."

"It must be a transmission problem," said Karl Michaels, the science department chairman.

He had to be right. The system had gotten screwed up. "Ben," said Derek, as the noise level began to rise again, "connect me with the Coordination unit."

People in the audience were getting out of their chairs. "That can't be real."

"Where's it coming from?"

A woman behind him seized his shoulder. "Professor Blanchard, are we really seeing that?"

Michaels was on his feet, staring at the waterfall. "Derek, any chance this is really happening?"

"Anything's possible, Karl."

A male voice came in over the circuit. "This is Coordination. You guys have a problem?"

"Have you seen what's coming in through the Hynds?"

"I haven't—" He broke off. "My God, that can't be right. Hold on." He broke away and Derek heard him talking in the background.

The music played on. Derek's feet pressed against the floor in a subconscious effort to stop it.

A woman's voice broke in. "Give us a minute. We're checking on it now." Then she was talking to someone else: "You have any idea where they are?"

Derek couldn't make out the response.

"Professor Blanchard. I can't explain this. We're not showing any technical issues."

"Okay. Could you check it out? If you find anything, get back to me?"

"Of course. The techs are looking at it now."

He signed off. "Ben, can you lock in on the star that's closest to the source of this?" Water was still spilling serenely over the edge while the music continued. "Get me a catalog number."

"For the star?"

"Yes. Of course."

"Working on it."

Derek covered the microphone and tried to laugh everything off with his audience. "One of the reasons astronomy is such a pleasure," he said. "You just never know."

Then Ben was back. *"It's KL37741."*

"What can you tell me about it?"

"It's a class G yellow dwarf. Range is approximately 7,300 light-years."

"Anything else?"

"I can give you spectroscopic details if you want. But nothing about them stands out."

"Can we get some additional magnification, Ben?"

"Negative. We are at maximum now."

"Does it have a planet within the Goldilocks Zone?" In the area that would allow liquid water to exist.

He needed several minutes to respond to that. Finally, he was back. *"It's too far to determine."*

Linda was staring at the display. She looked gloriously happy. "Aliens?" she asked. "Derek, did we just discover aliens? Who play music?"

"I don't know."

The reporters were waving, trying to get their attention.

"We don't need a planet," said Linda. "Somebody's out

there. That's all that matters. But we need a name for the star. This is going to be fairly big news, and we can't just run around, referring to it by a bunch of digits."

"I'm open to suggestions."

"I don't know, Derek. How about Clemmy?"

"That's your cat's name, isn't it?"

"Yeah." She giggled. "You don't like it?"

He was groping for a quick answer. Something that sounded respectable. Derek's cousin had just given birth to her first child. And the kid's name, he decided, would be perfect. "Calliope, maybe?"

"Okay. That's not bad."

It even gave him a chance to show off a little. "It's Greek origin. It means 'beautiful voice.'"

Then, as he was about to speak to the reporters, the waterfall faded and the music went silent.

It didn't come back. *"Don't know what happened, Derek,"* the woman at the control unit told him. *"If it was actually coming in from the target area, we should have been able to stay locked on to it. Best guess is that the source shut it down."*

"Do we have any vehicles out in that general direction? Anybody who might have sent the signal?"

"We're checking on it. But there aren't any I know of."

"We recorded that thing, right?"

"Oh yes. We have the entire transmission."

As a precaution, Derek directed the AI to run the waterfall against every known cataract on Earth. There was no match.

He reran the transmission several times. There was vegetation around the edges. Ben could find nothing of a terrestrial origin to match it. A substantial number of the attendees stayed while they searched, and all were excited by the results. They were, in fact, delighted.

And finally, it was time for lunch. Ordinarily, Derek would have picked up a snack at one of the vending machines on the first floor and returned to his office. He didn't socialize much. But this time, he didn't want to be alone with his thoughts. "Have you eaten yet, Linda?" he asked.

They went across the campus to the college cafeteria. Rain was still falling, but it wasn't much more than a drizzle now. They got in line, collected some food and Diet Cokes, and sat down at a table where everyone nearby seemed to be caught up in animated conversations. About Calliope. *The aliens like the same kind of music we do.* It was a good sign. Derek loved seeing students get excited about science. Even if this was a bit wild. And, of course, the fact that they'd been present at what everyone recognized as a historic occasion didn't hurt. He signaled that he needed catsup for his meatloaf, and Linda passed the bottle over. Then she leaned forward and lowered her voice. "I guess it wasn't such a good idea to bring everybody in."

Linda didn't talk much. She was sedate, with animated eyes and a manner that left no doubt who was in charge. People always knew when she was in the room. She treated her subordinates well, enjoyed giving them credit when they'd performed appropriately, and showed no reluctance about taking responsibility herself when they hadn't. She gave Derek credit with the bosses whenever she could, she always kept her word, she never hesitated to invite his opinion, and she was willing to change her mind when the evidence went in another direction. On this occasion, she looked amused.

"What makes you say that?" he said.

The amusement gave way to laughter. "Missed opportunities. If it had just been you and me in there, maybe we could have claimed the discovery for ourselves. We'd have been famous. Now we get to share it with a couple hundred people. Next time, when you're planning to make a discovery that will go global, let me know in advance. Okay?" She raised a glass of water to him.

NEWSDESK
Monday, February 11, 2256
MALAYSIAN FERRY RUNS AGROUND
Coast Guard Gets Everyone Off Safely

METEOR KILLS SIX IN VOLGOGRAD
They Knew It Was Coming; Evacuation Failed

POPE VISITS SYRIA
Vatican Hopes to Calm Emotions Following
Assassination of Al Kassam
Hunt Continues for Killers

MARKETS UP AROUND THE WORLD
Rousing Start Continues Through Fifth Month

EXTINCTION LEVELS DOWN
Only Three Species Lost in Past Year
The Bad News: Mongoose Among Them

JAMIE COLBAN DEAD AT 162
Passed Three Days After Joining Westboro Hall of Fame
Four of His Albums Among All-Time Top Sellers

MARIE BANNER RECEIVES PRESIDENTIAL CITATION
Medal for Service to Humanity Presented During
White House Ceremony
Led Food and Water Operations into Baghdad at
Height of Crisis

CORAGIO, WITH 14 ALL-FEMALE CREW, WINS ROUND-
THE-WORLD SAILING RACE
Peggy Freeman, Skipper, Makes UK in 42 days, 11
Hours, 7 Minutes
Receives Jules Verne Award

EARLY BLIZZARDS BURY MAINE, QUEBEC, ONTARIO
Schools, Roads Closed
Authorities Urge Everyone to Stay Home
Call 777 for Delivery of Emergency Rations

SOUTH GEORGIA LEAGUE TO END FOOTBALL
Last High Schools Abandon the Sport

VAN ENTEL SUPERTELESCOPE MAY HAVE SIGHTED
HIGH-TECH ALIENS
Travel TV Show from World in Distant Star Cluster

from their sun, where the temperatures are perfect, and they have oceans and a thick atmosphere, but there's no one there, it's kind of creepy. Some of them have molecular life, so if we go back in a billion years or so, we'll probably see forests and squirrels and maybe even someone in a motorboat. But that doesn't seem to matter. There's almost never anybody there."

"But isn't that a good thing?"

"How do you mean?"

"A substantial number of scientists, most recently Halley and Brackton and Margaret Evans, are saying that the safest situation for us would be if the universe was completely empty."

"That's probably true, Jack. But an empty universe sounds pretty boring. And we know that's not the case. It's not empty; it's just not crowded."

"I understand that, Priscilla. Still, I'm not sure we should be looking for excitement. How would a civilization, say, millions of years older than we are react to us if they found out we were here?"

"They'd probably say hello."

"You really think that would be the case?"

"Why not?"

"What if they were hostile?"

"What makes you think they would be? If they've been around a long time, they're probably not dummies."

"You sound like the ultimate optimist, Priscilla."

"I guess anything's possible. But it's hard to imagine a highly evolved species picking fights with anyone who shows up."

"But we could get unlucky, right? Why are you smiling?

Isn't it a bit unsettling to think about what could happen if things didn't go well? Suppose we encounter a civilization that enjoys blowing up other worlds, and they're much more technically advanced than we are. What kind of chance would we have to defend ourselves?"

"Probably not much. And you could be right. But it's just hard to believe that could happen. With all the stuff out there to look at, why would they want to waste their time fighting with neighbors?"

"But we're getting warnings from scientists."

"Well, maybe they're right. Who really knows? I suspect, though, they've been watching too many science fiction movies. The members of a society that's been around for a million years will probably have learned to get along with one another. And it's hard to see how they could have done that without developing an ethical code that would prevent them from attacking other intelligent species for no reason."

"I hope you're right, Priscilla. But, still, if we get it wrong, we'd have a terrible price to pay." He sat back in his chair. "I have to tell you, you talk about how empty the universe is. For me, it's not empty enough."

"I'm surprised to hear that, Jack. You don't look to me like a guy who scares easily."

"Ouch. That hurts."

Hutch laughed. "That's a natural reaction, I suppose. If there'd been Martians, they would probably have been scared of *us*."

"Well, let's get serious for a moment. We're into another election season, and the interstellars have already become a hot item. Proctor has said she'll support the Centauri

Initiative, the ban on interstellar travel. How do you think that'll play out? If she gets reelected, will she follow through?"

"I hope not. It'll be a serious step backward."

When they were off camera, Jack thanked her and shook her hand. "You're a great guest, Priscilla." He handed her his card with its Black Cat Network imprint. "In case you need to reach me. It's my commlink. If you get out there again, and you get some pictures or whatever, send them along. We'll be happy to see what you have. Anyhow, you're welcome here anytime. If you want to talk about the shutdown effort, or if, as I hope, they decide to go with at least one more mission, we'd like very much to have you back on the show to talk about it. I'd love to find out who's transmitting pictures of a waterfall."

"Thanks, Jack."

"Something I can't resist telling you. My boss is in step with the president on this. He didn't like my bringing you in to defend interstellar travel. He thinks it's a crazy idea."

"You mean Harold Billings?"

"Yes."

"So, why'd he allow it?"

"Ratings. You come on the show and the viewers go through the roof."

"You're kidding."

"I never kid, Priscilla. I shouldn't be telling you this, and if it goes any farther, I'll deny it. He had a hard time giving us a go-ahead. But at heart he's a good guy and he did the right thing. Next time, though, we should probably change the subject."

THE WORLD REVIEW

Wednesday, February 13, 2256

We've come a long way. A century ago famine was a global problem of monumental dimensions. Population continued to increase throughout the underdeveloped world; regional violence, spurred by desperation, and whatever political or religious differences that extremists could exploit, occurred with stunning regularity; and armies of people, fleeing lethal conditions, were beginning to destabilize China, Japan, Russia, and the Western world.

Next week, on February 26, we will celebrate the one hundredth anniversary of the launch of the Gehringer Project. Ahmad Gehringer spent his early years in desperate circumstances, but he has emerged as one of the great leaders of the twenty-third century. He understood that, in order to build a more reasonable world, we needed to find a way to eliminate famine, to replace ideology with open minds, to control the growth of world population, to prevent unfettered capitalism from wrecking the world. And to make liberal education possible around the planet. Not until people could question not only local dogma but also their own beliefs, and accept the possibility they may be wrong about some issues, not until we learn to consider whether someone else may have a valid point even when it conflicts with our own perspective, only when we reach that day can we hope for a peaceful planet.

Gehringer was confronted by a world that believed a widespread liberal education impossible. The notion of world peace was a joke. He argued that until we made the effort, we could not hope that people would put the guns down. That maybe it was impossible, but that we wouldn't know unless we tried. In his celebrated Berlin address in 2247, he argued that the general notion that the problems are not curable was poisoning us. If that was true, he said, all the advances of the previous century would prove short-lived. Extended life spans were futile; interstellar vehicles, once thought to be impossible, would be of no value even if they were developed. Communication technologies, artificial gravity, and modern energy production would not save us. Ironically, he pointed out, the conquest of disease in virtually all its forms, and the reversal of the aging process, which was then just on the horizon, had become part of the crisis.

There is no question, Gehringer said, that undeveloped areas desperately needed food shipments. And clean water. The stark reality was that they also needed open minds. Let us, on this happy anniversary, be aware that we also needed Ahmad Gehringer.

3.

O pilot! 'tis a fearful night,
There's danger on the deep.
—T. H. Bayly, "The Pilot," 1844

The Calliope transmission was all over the media. Hutch sat in her Woodbridge, Virginia, home watching it play again and again. The accompanying rhythm was perfect, capturing precisely the mood of a waterfall high in a mountain chain. The entire clip ran for just forty-seven seconds. It didn't feel like something she'd have expected from aliens. The music was precisely what *she* would have selected. The signal had bounced in from somewhere, and she had no doubt we'd figure it out, given a little time.

Jack Crispee's guest was Lauren Millani. Hutch had heard of her. She was a physicist, had won a couple of prizes, and Jack considered her an expert on the Hynds radiotelescope, or possibly on alien life forms. She'd tuned in late and Millani's specialty never quite became clear.

Millani did not share the idea that the transmission had originated from a human source. *"It's possible,"* she said, *"that we just intercepted an errant signal from a station or a ship somewhere. But I don't think it's likely. It almost had to originate from something orbiting that star—what did they call it? Calliope? I would have thought they'd be able to come up with a less flamboyant name. Just look at it, Jack."* It was playing onscreen, the water pouring into the canyon. *"The waterfall's not terrestrial, and nobody's been able to identify the vegetation. You ever see anything like those long stalks before?"* She was referring to a pair of oddly shaped trees on either side of the falls. *"This is very big news, Jack. What we need to do is get a mission together and go out there and see what's going on."*

"Do you think that's likely to happen, Lauren?"

"No. If we're dumb enough to reelect Proctor and she really does shut down the interstellars, twenty years from now we'll still be wondering what it was about."

"She's good," said Charlie. "She's got it right. Some of these people who want to shut everything down need to get off their rear ends and go take a look around."

"You're right, kid. She's on point."

He still hadn't calmed down from the Saturn trip. "I wish *we* had rings. Maybe we'd be a little more realistic about deep space travel." He sounded as if he could no longer take seriously anybody who hadn't gotten out past the atmosphere.

"It's the way we are, son. You might as well get used to it."

"It's not the way *you* are. Or the way Dad was." Charlie

was about an inch taller than his mother. He had his father's wide shoulders. "Why were you guys so different from everybody else, Mom?"

"We were not that different. I suspect we just got lucky. Your father used to claim he got started because he read a lot of science fiction. *My* dad worked for SETI, and I guess I caught the bug from him." She glanced at the notebook. "Did you get the assignment done?"

"Yes." It had been an essay for his history class. If given an opportunity to meet and talk with a historical character, who would he choose? And why?

"Who'd you pick?"

"George Washington."

"Why?"

"Are you kidding, Mom? He's the most important person in the country's history."

"Okay."

"You sound as if you think that's a dull choice."

"No. It's good."

"Who would you have gone with?"

"The Iapetus angel. The sculptor."

"I guess that's not a big surprise."

She looked up at the time. "It's getting a bit late."

"On my way." He slung his backpack over his shoulder and headed for the door.

She watched him go. He wanted to follow her career path. But it probably wasn't going to happen. Not that the interstellars could be shut down permanently. *Eventually,* she thought, *we'll have to leave the planet and move out. But it will probably take too long to come to our senses. By then, Charlie might have to settle for a career as an architect. Or a journalist.* She smiled, recalling her mom's efforts to talk her into a more rational course than the one she'd been bent on pursuing. Become a lawyer, she'd advised. Or maybe get into real estate. That was where the money was.

She wandered into her office. The wind was moving tree branches back and forth. She read for a half hour, and then turned on the news. Melinda Allen, a friend and associate, was scheduled as a guest on Cosmic Broadcasting's *The Morning Show.* Melinda was the director of astrophysics at the American Museum of Natural History.

"*—your take on all this?*" the moderator asked.

"*It's much too early to make a call,*" Melinda said. She seemed amused at the excitement the sighting had caused. But that was typical. She was the ultimate cynic. "*There's still a possibility that the whole thing is just a glitch in the telescope.*"

"*That doesn't seem likely, does it?*"

"*I can't think of a good explanation that sounds likely, Marvin. Look, we've seen things before that we thought were evidence of an advanced civilization, but they don't usually amount to much. One thing we're learning about the universe: Intelligence is rare. And when it does show up, it turns out not to be good at survival.*"

Cosmic went to commercial. When the show came back, Melinda had been replaced by the campaign director for one of the presidential candidates.

Her daughter, Maureen, called. "I thought with that water-fall in the news you'd be back on TV this morning. I haven't missed anything, have I?"

"No. How are the classes going?" She was in her first year as a high school history teacher.

"It's a challenge."

"Why?"

"We're doing the Civil War, and it's taken us back to talking again about the Founding Fathers. Nobody can understand all the talk about freedom from people who owned slaves."

"It was a different culture. I think most of them would have gotten rid of the slavery issue if they thought they could do it and still hold the union together. I suspect you've been a bit critical of them."

"It's hard not to be."

"You *might want to cut them some slack. They were trying to put a country together."

They talked for a couple of minutes before she saw an incoming call from Derek Blanchard. The guy who was connected with the Calliope sighting. Holy cats. She could only think of one reason he'd be calling. "Gotta go, Maureen," she said. "I'll get back to you." She switched over. "Hello, Professor Blanchard. What can I do for you?"

"Hi, Ms. Hutchins. I've wanted for a long time to find an excuse to meet you. You've been a singular asset for the WSA. I assume you're aware of what's been happening? The waterfall?"

"Sure. You have any information that hasn't been released?"

"No, we've put it all out there. But I'd like very much to talk with you. If you're free this evening, I wonder if I could stop by and say hello."

"Sure. What time's good?"

"How about eight o'clock?"

"I'll be here."

Blanchard was a major figure, an astrophysicist who'd been near the forefront of half a dozen breakthrough discoveries. He'd written thirteen books on various aspects of cosmology and astrophysics, had been science advisor to President Crandall, and was a consultant for the World Space Authority.

She looked up at the framed photo of the Iapetus angel that dominated the wall over her printer. "Here we go, kid."

Blanchard arrived precisely on time, with a smile and a bottle of champagne. She'd seen him once before, at an Academy conference. He'd been one of the people who had tried to salvage the Academy when it was going under. But the political forces were too strong.

"Hello, Priscilla. I doubt if you remember me, but we met a few years ago."

"I remember, Professor Blanchard. Please come in." He gave her the champagne. She led him to an armchair and sat down on the sofa. "It's good to see you again. What can I do for you?"

"Priscilla, please call me Derek. We need your help."

"The WSA?"

"Of course." If there'd been any doubt about the purpose for Derek's visit, it went away. He looked down at the champagne. "Look, before we get into this, how about a drink?"

"Sounds like a good idea."

She carried the champagne into the kitchen, opened it, and poured two glasses. Her trip to the galactic center the previous year had been the first actual mission performed with the Locarno drive. It had a capability to cover almost

286 light-years in a day. So travel time tended to be short. At least, shorter than it used to be. But there was a downside: The transdimensional world through which the ships had to pass was absolutely without light. There was no sense of movement by the vehicle. If he was going to extend an invitation to head out for Calliope, which seemed the only reasonable purpose for his visit, she'd be stuck inside the thing for almost the better part of a month with nothing to do but watch movies and read. That would get old pretty quickly. She sighed, took the glasses back into the living room, and handed one to Derek.

He raised it and smiled. "To the world's best interstellar pilot," he said.

Hutch allowed her discomfort to show. She touched his glass with her own, thanked him, and sipped the champagne. It was dry, with a slightly sour touch and a lot of bubbles. He'd spent some money on it. "So, what can I do for you, Derek?" she asked.

"I'm sure you know that the *Barry Eiferman* is out on a mission, but we expect it back in a few days. We'll need a little time to service it, and then we're going to turn it around."

"You're sending it out to look for the source of the waterfall?"

"Yes. We want you to be its captain." He glanced around the room. At pictures of her and Tor seated on the *Memphis* bridge. At pictures of Maureen at her college graduation and Charlie in a baseball uniform. "We'll make it worth your while."

"How much?"

"Three hundred thousand."

She tried not to let her surprise show. She'd never received anything remotely like that before. A sudden burst of wind rattled the windows. "They're expecting snow tonight," she said. Then: "When will it be leaving?"

"In a couple of weeks. Can we count on you? You're our first choice. We need somebody who's had experience with the Locarno."

"Derek, you have other people who've operated with it."

"Yes. We have. But it's more than that. You've had a few tricky encounters and come through them in pretty good shape. We have no idea what's out there at Calliope." He paused. "We need someone with a history of making the right calls under pressure."

"What actually would be the objective? Just find out what's there and come home?"

"That's it. Go take a look. We'd like to know whether there's an advanced civilization out there. Define *advanced* as anything with offworld technology. Considering that they had a pretty strong beam seven thousand years ago, we're expecting that they'll be far down the road by now. If there are some radio signals, we'll try to intercept them. Record them, of course. But we'll keep our distance. We do not want to make contact. Not with a civilization that's thousands of years ahead of us. If we get any sense that they've figured out we're there, we clear out. We want to make sure they don't follow us back here."

"You're going along?"

"Of course. I wouldn't miss this."

"How do we make sure they don't follow us home? We've assumed that nobody can track a ship in transdimensional space, but we don't really *know* that."

"We're working on it." He finished off his champagne and reached for the bottle. "Want more?"

They refilled both glasses. Okay. Hutch was interested in making the flight. And the money was far more than she'd make going around talking at luncheons. But it would mean a lot of time again away from Maureen and Charlie. "This place is seven thousand light-years out," she said. "So we're talking almost a month to get there."

"Yes. I'm sorry. I know this is kind of sudden."

"Why such a hurry?"

"You know the politics. There are a lot of people who think the mission is not a good idea. We want to get moving before somebody can shut us down."

"Can you give me a couple of days to think it over?"

"Sure. How's Monday sound?"

"All right."

"Priscilla?"

"Yes, Derek?"

"We need you on this."

Chances were that the news she'd been offered the assignment would get out, and she didn't want her mother to hear about it before Hutch could let her know. Mom still lived in Hutch's childhood home in Cherry Hill, New Jersey. She called within minutes after Derek had left. *"Hi, Priscilla,"* she said. *"Everything okay? You sound a bit tense."*

"I just had a visitor, Mom. You been watching the news?"

"You mean those crazy people who blew up that dam in Colorado?"

"Not exactly."

"I hope you're not going to tell me they want you to go out to that place with the waterfall."

"Yeah, that's pretty much what's happening."

"You're not going to do it, are you? Or am I being naïve?"

"It's hard to turn down, Mom."

"You don't spend a lot of time with your kids."

"They're adults now."

"How long? I mean, how long will you be gone?"

"A couple of months."

"Wonderful. I don't suppose it's occurred to you that, since nobody knows what's out there, it could be dangerous?"

"We'll be careful. In fact, they're telling us to take no chances. If there's actually somebody there, we won't be going anywhere near them. We'll just take a look and come home."

"Answer a question for me, Priscilla: Don't they have any other pilots? Why are they coming to you again?"

"Probably because I have the most experience with the drive unit. You don't need to worry, Mom. We won't take any chances."

"I hope so, Priscilla."

The kids weren't exactly excited about the prospect of her leaving again either. Charlie pointed out that she'd miss *Left at the Altar*, the comedy at Washington University in which he would be playing a supporting character. And Maureen reminded her that she'd promised to talk to a couple of her classes. *"When you get out there, you're probably going to stay awhile, right?"*

"Long enough to look around. I doubt we'll stay much more than that."

"I wish you wouldn't do this."

"I'll be fine, Maureen."

"Be careful, okay?"

"Of course."

"Do you think you could come in next week? Talk about your life in the space program?"

"Sure. Tuesday okay?"

"Good. Let's go with it." She did not sound happy.

Hutch's telomerase treatment, which kept her aging process inactive, was scheduled to happen in two months. It consisted of a single IV therapy given at ten-year intervals. It was a viral vector that delivered a plasmid to specific cells, directing them to reset telomere length, so that molecules were repaired and recycled at the same rate as in young cells. The process took thirty minutes.

It didn't make her immortal. There were biological parts that eventually would break down regardless of treatment. But in the meantime, life was good.

It was a routine she didn't want to play around with. She called her doctor's office. Annie, the desk clerk, answered. "Any problem," Hutch asked her, "if I miss a treatment by a few months? I'm going to be out of town for a while."

"Probably be best if you come in before you leave. We can fit you in Monday morning if you like."

"Good. Thanks, Annie."

"We're happy to help, Ms. Hutchins. But please be careful out there."

Hutch paused. "How'd you find out?"

"About the Calliope? *It was on* The Morning Show.*"*

She settled in to watch *Zero Sum*, a comedy about a pair

38

of physicists who are out of touch with the everyday world. Halfway through it, she got a call, but it was from Tom Axler. Tom was an occasional boyfriend, a police officer she'd met while singing in the church choir.

"Are you ever going to start living a normal existence?" he asked.

"I guess not for a few weeks, anyhow, Tom." He was a good guy, and she'd enjoyed the evenings they'd had together. But she still couldn't let go of Tor. His death, caused by a heart issue that they'd had no idea even existed, had blown a substantial hole in her life.

"I think it's a fight you're going to lose. Maybe when the election's over, things will change."

"Maybe."

They fell silent for a few moments. *"You ever think about becoming a talk show host yourself? You're good at it. And you wouldn't have to keep running off somewhere every few months."*

"I think long-term it would get boring."

"Not like sitting for weeks in an oversized tin can." He took a deep breath. *"Can I take you to lunch tomorrow?"*

A few minutes later, Blanchard called. *"I'm sorry your name got out, Priscilla. I don't know how that happened. As far as I can tell, nobody here said anything."*

"It may not have been one of your people, Derek. I haven't exactly sat on the story."

"Be careful what you say to the media."

"I will." She asked herself whether she really wanted to do this. And knew that was a joke. There'd never been any question in her mind. "When can I get a look at the *Eiferman?*"

NEWSDESK

Thursday, February 14, 2256

STACKHOUSE DECLARES CANDIDACY

*First Transgender Presidential Candidate of Major
Party Joins Race*

MYERS GUILTY ON ALL COUNTS

*Ontario Governor Faces Thirty Years on
Corruption Charges*

TIDAL WAVE HITS SOUTH GEORGIA, CAROLINAS

*Offshore Earthquake Causes 90-Foot Strike
Despite Evacuation and Early Warnings, Hundreds
Believed Lost
Seismologists Had Been Predicting Event for Decades*

HAUBRICH WINS BAKER AWARD

Walking on Air *Named Best Novel*

ALAN BANNER LEADS EARLY POLLING FOR
INDEPENDENTS

NANCY MOUNT BILL PASSES IN HOUSE

*Proposes "None of the Above" Be Added to Ballot
Thirty Percent of the Votes Would Trigger New
Election*

HIGH SCHOOL IN MEDUA ATTACKED BY TEEN GUNMAN

*Attacker Was Quiet, No Record, No Previous Incidents
Four Dead, 13 Injured*

RESEARCH INTO PROVIDING HIGH IQ FOR INFANTS
COMES UNDER ATTACK
*Experts Claim IQ Set Naturally at Optimal Point for
Psychological Health*
*Providing 200-plus Intelligence Level Might Cause
Emotional Damage*
Darwin Again? Does Ultra-High IQ Handicap Survival?

SCOUT TROOP RESCUES HIKERS AFTER LANDSLIDE
Twenty People Swept Away in Missouri Avalanche
Two Still Missing as Search Continues

PRISCILLA HUTCHINS TO PILOT CALLIOPE MISSION
Flight Hopes to Resolve Waterfall Issue

STUDY REVEALS HEALTH BENEFITS FROM BUDDHISM
Serious Benefits Derive from Serenity

BIRTH DEFECTS REACH ALL-TIME LOW
*Statistics for 2255: Only 1 Child in 925 Shows
Abnormal Condition*

CONCERNS ABOUT CALLIOPE FLIGHT RISING
High-Tech Aliens Might Be Dangerous

JACK CRISPEE LEAVES BLACK CAT
Didn't See This Coming, Says Network
"We Wish Him All the Best"

4.

Ships that pass in the night, and speak each other in passing,
Only a signal shown and a distant voice in the darkness,
So on the ocean of life, we pass and speak one another,
Only a look and a voice, then darkness again and a silence.
—Henry W. Longfellow, *Tales of a Wayside Inn*, 1863

Charlie was getting ready to leave for school when his mom came downstairs. "I see you're taking some heat already," he said.

"Heat about what, Charlie?"

"Going out with the *Eiferman*."

"Oh." No surprise there. It was perfect fodder for the talk shows. "What are they saying?"

"Jessie Hoffman was on *The Morning Show* today." Hoffman was the National Security Advisor. "He thinks you have a moral obligation to back off."

She stopped by Dr. Gordon's office and got her treatment. Then she headed for a lunch date with Tom Axler. In this difficult time he was exactly what she needed. His gift to Hutch was that he didn't live in the stars, the way every other male did with whom she'd had any kind of romantic entanglement. Tom was strictly two feet on the ground. He worried that football had effectively disappeared, that comedians weren't as funny as they used to be, that the initiative to revalue the dollar again was going to create havoc, that people needed to stop thinking of their house AIs as conscious entities, and that churches no longer had the support they did when he was a kid.

He knew that Hutch was uncertain whether God actually existed. She'd told him that the universe was so big that it just seemed impossible that a single functioning deity could have set it all up. But she admitted that she didn't want to let go of the idea. Her mother was a believer, had taken her to church every Sunday. And the reality was that the size of the cosmos also worked against any effort to deny His existence. It was a lonely place. Hutch knew that traveling among those distant stars was much more comfortable when you could focus on the possibility that someone out there knew about you and cared. It explained why she'd eventually joined a church choral group.

She got to Larry's Diner first, took a seat, and ordered a glass of apple juice. It wasn't quite noon yet, but the place was already beginning to fill. Tom walked in the door just as the juice arrived. He lit up when he saw her. It was one of the qualities about him that she especially liked. He enjoyed being with her, and he showed it without, unlike most guys, putting it on display. With him, it was somehow more *real* than simply a transparent way of trying to win her affection.

"You getting ready for the big trip?" he asked. Tom was just over six feet, with brown eyes that invariably showed where his mind was. Except probably, she suspected, when he was in uniform. He looked sometimes like a guy who would brook no nonsense and, at other times, who understood that the world was strictly for laughs.

"I'm trying to decide which shoes to take."

He looked at her uncertainly. "You know, when you're gone, which seems to be most of the time, I can't resist driving by your house and thinking how empty it looks."

"It's good to know the police are watching the place."

The waitress showed up, brought coffee for Tom, and took their orders.

"Hutch, you think maybe we could get out tonight? Have dinner and go to a show?"

"I'd like to, Tom. But I'm doing a speaking engagement at the Patriot Club. I'm free *Saturday* night."

Dismay clouded his eyes. "That won't work. I'm starting a shift Saturday."

"Evenings?"

"Yes. Unfortunately." He put his elbows on the table, clasped his hands together, and set his chin on them. "Well, it was nice having you around for a while. Long enough to have a couple of lunches."

"Come on, Tom, I've been back for a few months."

He laughed. "Yeah. Don't know how we could beat that. Maybe *next* week?"

"Things might get crowded by then. Let's play it by ear."

"Okay. You ever going to retire?"

"Eventually, I guess. The way things are going, I may not have much choice." Actually, she'd been thinking about it. Her life wasn't going the way she'd wanted. The passion for star flight was still there, still consumed her, but it had been largely a series of disappointments, empty worlds, occasionally planets with beaches whose only sounds emerged from incoming tides. The highlights of her career had been, with only a couple of exceptions, clusters of crumbling buildings from long-dead civilizations.

She'd missed a lot of time with her kids. Her mom had filled in, but Maureen and Charlie had spent as much time in Cherry Hill as in Virginia. Now they were getting ready to move on, and if she continued along this road, she'd miss the next round too.

So yes, maybe she *should* settle down. But she didn't want to tell Tom that. Didn't want to say anything that would encourage him. She doubted they had a future together. She liked him, but the chemistry simply wasn't there. "I can't imagine life without the interstellars," she said. The remark wasn't complete before she knew how dumb it sounded. But he just looked at her, nodded patiently, and smiled as if that was precisely what he expected and he was prepared to live with it.

Their lunches came. Tom liked red meat, steaks preferably. Hutch tended to stay with fruit and veggies and sometimes grilled chicken, which of course in that era, like the steaks, wasn't a product taken from live animals. Where health was concerned, it didn't really make much difference what anyone ate. Just don't eat too much.

"I don't suppose," Tom said, "that you could arrange for me to go with you?"

"I doubt they'd allow that, Tom." Then she saw he was kidding.

"Yeah, I'd probably have a problem making my rounds."

The conversation lightened. They talked about movies

and TV shows. Tom told her about a couple of arrests he'd made. One guy had gotten upset about a restaurant bill and thrown a tantrum, as well as a dish of broccoli and potatoes across the room. "He did this while Angie and I were sitting at one of the tables." Angie was his partner.

"Another guy got angry with his girlfriend and started breaking shop windows. We were parked across the street."

"I never thought of policing," said Hutch, "as a comical job." Her commlink vibrated. It was Blanchard. "Let me take this, Tom. Just be a second." She leaned down toward it. "Yes, Derek."

"Hi, Priscilla. Hope I'm not interrupting anything."

"I'm at lunch with a friend. Is everything okay?"

"I hope so. The project is getting more media attention than we'd like. There are a lot of people out there who are trying hard to shut us down. The media will probably want to talk to you. We just need you to be careful what you say. Okay?"

They got back to talking about some of the silly things people do while committing crimes, like waving at security cameras, leaving fingerprints on a counter at the bank, calling each other by names that allow detectives to trace them. "By the way," Tom said, "I don't know if I told you. I'm being promoted to detective." A wave of false humility brightened his eyes.

Hutch got up, walked around the table, and kissed him. "Congratulations. I suspect you'll be a natural." Her commlink vibrated again. She checked it as she returned to her seat.

"More starship people?" Tom asked.

"No. WCSM."

"Well, there's another interview for you."

She hesitated and decided finally not to answer. Minutes later there was another call, from the *Arlington Courant*. She shut it off.

"You know," said Tom, "they'll be waiting for you when you get home."

"Yeah. Probably."

"You can hide out at my place if you want."

She trusted him implicitly, but it still wasn't a good idea. "They'll catch up with me eventually."

Spring was still a few weeks away. But the Woodbridge area seldom got cold that time of year. Nevertheless, on that day, despite plenty of sunlight and only a scattering of clouds, it was frigid. A cluster of cars and vans was waiting when the car pulled up at her house. She tugged her jacket around her and opened the door. Reporters crowded around, taking pictures and asking questions. "What do you think is out there, Priscilla?"

"How do you feel about this flight? Is it scary?"

"Are you worried?"

"You guys have any idea what that waterfall is all about?"

"How can you be sure they won't follow you home?"

That one needed a reply. She wished she had one. "As far as we know, you can't track anything in transdimensional space. It's not possible."

"'As far as we know.'"

"That's correct." Hutch raised her left hand, trying to suppress the noise. Finally, they grew quiet. "Thank you. Look, guys, I'm just a pilot. But for what it's worth, we've spent the last hundred years traveling all over the Orion Arm. And we've been to the center of the galaxy. We have yet to find anybody anywhere who constitutes a threat to us. The only issue we've had was with the omega clouds, and that had nothing whatever to do with our missions."

A man with an ID indicating he was from CBS put up his hand. "But that's all past history, Priscilla. This is the first time we've seen something that we think is a high-tech civilization. And there are millions of places we *haven't* been to."

Hutch wanted to point out that there are never any guarantees, but she knew that would be the segment that would be on every news show an hour later. "That's all I've got," she said. "Listen, I have to go."

She tried to push through the crowd, but more questions came.

"If it were your call, Priscilla, would you send this mission out?"

"What do you think about the president's comment?"

She had no idea what the president had said, but it didn't sound good.

"How about Dale Foxworth?" Dale was a retired pilot. "He says going out there looking for inhabited worlds is crazy."

"What do *you* think, Priscilla?"

"Above my pay grade, guys. But you want my gut instincts?" The microphones moved closer. "We'll arrive at Calliope, the lights will have gone out, and that'll be the end of the show. In the long run, we'll be safer if we look around. If there *are* any threats out there, better we find them than the reverse."

"Why will the lights have gone out?"

"Because, whatever they are, we saw what that area looked like seven thousand years ago. Somebody, by this time, will have shut down the TV station."

Okay. So it was a joke and they got it. Cosmic wanted to

know if she had anything serious to add. "There's just not enough data right now," she said. "But there's certainly nothing that should alarm anyone." She got to her front door and was about to turn back to the reporters, wave, and ask them to "wish us luck." But she'd been around too long to make that mistake. "Hope you got what you need," she said. "Take care."

An hour later she got a surprise: Jack Crispee called.

"Hello, Jack," she said. "I see you left the Black Cat. Where are you headed now?"

"That wasn't voluntary, Priscilla." He was seated on a sofa, with a couple of cushions behind him. *"They terminated me."*

"Oh. I'm sorry. That's not exactly the way it was reported."

"The Cat was being polite."

"I hope it wasn't connected with my interview."

"They didn't want to go into details. They just said that I'd run my course."

"You had pretty good ratings."

"That was another world. But you've got this interstellar thing exactly right, Priscilla. Don't change your mind."

"Sorry, Jack. I should have kept my mouth shut."

"You're not listening to me. We did exactly what needed to be done."

"What are you going to do now?"

"I'm doing an interview with Cosmic Monday. They sound interested."

"Good luck, Jack. Let me know if I can be of any help." She stopped and laughed. "Well, maybe that wouldn't be a good idea."

• • •

President Emma Proctor, beginning the final year of what she hoped would be her first term, had lost none of the charm and credibility that had carried her into the White House. She sat in her chair in the Oval Office, which was now projected into Hutch's living room, and looked directly into her eyes. *"We can't continue,"* she said, *"with the WSA and even private entrepreneurs sending vehicles out to unknown territories. They like to pretend that we've visited the vast majority of stars in this section of the Orion Arm. That, of course, is nonsense. There are millions of stars out there, and at the moment, anyone with a ship is free to go take a look. And maybe bring back a disease, a horde of toxic aliens, or perhaps some other lethal surprises."*

She took a deep breath but kept her focus on her viewers. *"Letting the Academy go under was a serious mistake. It's true it wasn't a government operation, but it provided a degree of control that we no longer have. There's no serious need to worry about the several interstellar corporations. Their enterprises have always been aimed at developing revenues. And that derives from transportation of tourists or colonists. There's no risk there. They aren't going anywhere we haven't been to before. The sole area of concern is exploration.*

"Major scientists—Stephen Hawking, Marie Bradford, Eliot Thomas, Karl Unterkoefler—have been warning us for two and a half centuries about other places, about what might lie beyond the solar system. We may feel safe because we've been to a handful of worlds and so far encountered nothing resembling a threat. But there are countless worlds of which we know nothing. It's time we got smart. Time we listened. Time we decide to stay away from unknown places.

"Therefore, I have signed the Centauri Initiative. We will be submitting it to the World Council. If passed, it will require authorization by a special commission for travel to any star not previously visited and cataloged.

"Let me be clear. This is a vital matter. Once we reveal ourselves to an advanced, and potentially hostile, civilization, it will be too late to make adjustments. We have an opportunity now to step in, to safeguard the future. We do not wish to let it slip away." The laser gaze softened. *"Thank you. And God bless the North American Union."*

Twenty minutes later Hutch watched herself admitting that aliens couldn't follow her home "as far as we know."

The Mark Farmer Show
Friday, February 15, 2256

FARMER: Our guest this evening is Professor Teri Shaw, chairperson of the physics department at Oxford University. Teri has written numerous books on space exploration and on various aspects of interstellar life. Her latest is *At Home in the Milky Way*. Teri, welcome.

SHAW: Nice to be here, Mark.

FARMER: Well, I can't imagine who'd be better equipped to deal with some of these issues. Let's start with the question that's on everyone's mind. Are we looking at a spacefaring civilization out there? Near Calliope?

SHAW: It's impossible to say with the information we have, Mark. It certainly appears as if we are. But keep in mind, that signal passed through the

Calliope area seven thousand years ago. It may not even have originated there. If there's anybody there, they might have gotten the same surprise we did and tried to track down its source. But, sure, that was probably where the transmission originated. We're inclined to assume they would have kept evolving. If human history teaches us anything, though, it's that no civilization, no culture, ever manages to improve over an indefinite time period.

FARMER: Is it a good idea to go out there? And maybe reveal ourselves to whoever's there?

SHAW: Mark, I'll let you know after we see how things turn out.

FARMER: What would you recommend we do?

SHAW: Exactly what we are doing. Take a look. Find out what's going on. My gut tells me it's nothing. It'll turn out to have been a reflection or something. But we're going to find out, one way or the other. Let's just hope we're careful.

FARMER: But suppose they are hostile? And they have the technology to follow the *Eiferman* back here?

SHAW: That seems unlikely. Let's go get some answers. I was happy to see they put Hutchins on board to run things. Obviously, that's good news. If anybody can make the mission work and bring them home safely without being followed, she's the one.

5.

A brother may not be a friend, but a friend will always be a brother.

—Benjamin Franklin, *Poor Richard's Almanac*, 1752

Derek left a message: Her copilot would be Hugh Walcott. She knew him but had never been on a mission with him. He had a good reputation, and he'd been on the *Eiferman* a few months before for a short flight. And of course Blanchard was going. Three others would complete the team. She had no connection with any of them, who were identified as an MD, a technician, and a historian. The historian was Ken Squires, who'd written several bestsellers. So he was on board for obvious reasons.

Maureen was teaching at Westside High School, which stood atop a hill overlooking the Potomac. Hutch had been there before as a guest speaker at a dinner for a retiring teacher who'd served as a technician on the Union Space Station. And she'd handed out diplomas at a graduation ceremony. But on this occasion there was a painful dimension to the experience. Tor would have loved to see the young woman his daughter had become. He'd missed so much.

Hutch was scheduled to talk with Maureen's first-, second-, and fourth-period classes. She came early, arriving as the students headed toward their homerooms.

She went into the front office and signed in. A staff member escorted her to her daughter's room. She arrived just as the students were settling in to their seats. Some of them looked from her to Maureen, apparently trying to decide who was their teacher. Hutch's antiaging treatment had remarkable effects. She would have admitted it to no one, but she loved seeing the confusion. "See?" one of the girls said. "I told you so."

Her daughter gave her a big smile. "Hi, Mom." She came over and they embraced.

Then Maureen turned to the class. "Boys and girls, I'd like to introduce you to one of the great women of the space age, Priscilla Hutchins. My mother. She'll be explaining to us why space travel is so much fun."

One of the boys said, "Hello, Hutch." That brought a round of laughs.

It was an American history class, so she talked about the space program, how it had begun as a competition between two major powers near the beginning of the Cold War. "The United States made it to the moon, primarily as a political gesture. Then, when the Cold War ended two decades later, both sides discovered that manned flight was too expensive and, as far as the political leaders were concerned, it had no point."

She'd brought some visuals, pictures of distant stars

and worlds, of interstellars entering orbit, and of ruins from dead civilizations. And of course she had images of monuments left across the Orion Arm by an alien race that had been driven to make an artistic imprint. Those got more attention than any other aspect of the presentation. The species was famous and the students knew they'd lost everything, had devolved into primitives who now had no idea who their ancestors had been.

During their last few minutes the students asked her to describe what it was like to ride in an interstellar and to walk on another planet. And about this mission that *she* was going to lead; what did she think they would find?

At this point a boy near the front of the room waved his hand. "Ms. Hutchins," he said, "do you think maybe you should not do this?"

"You think because it's dangerous?"

"Yes. They're saying that you might get us all killed."

A small blond girl a couple of desks away turned toward him. "Oh, shut up, Roger."

"He's got it right," said a girl in back.

It would have devolved into a loud argument except that Maureen stepped in. "Ms. Hutchins has heard the debate. Mom, you want to respond?"

"Roger has a point," Hutch said. "But there's always a risk when we try something new. Where would we be now if Columbus had decided that looking for a shortcut to the Far East was too dangerous? If he'd never come to Americas?"

"I bet," said the girl in back, "that the Native Americans would be happy."

• • •

When the class ended and the students were on their way to the next period, Maureen told her she was still pure gold. "But they may be right," she said. "Don't you think we'd all be better off if you stayed home?" Her eyes acquired an appealing look. "Please, Mom." Then the kids for the second-period class were filing in.

It went much the same way, except that the issue of public safety surfaced more quickly and the kids got louder. There were a few tears, and they didn't buy Hutch's argument that safety was simply not an issue. "It's political," Hutch said.

When they'd finished, she got moderate applause. Several of the children gathered around her, looking angry and upset. "Please, Ms. Hutchins," said a boy who looked particularly rattled. "Don't go. Don't help them."

They filed out, and Maureen apologized. "I should have seen this coming," she said. "I'm sorry."

"You really think I shouldn't go?"

Maureen's eyes almost closed. She nodded. "Yeah."

Another teacher entered the room and came over to speak with Maureen. She listened, said thanks, and came back to Hutch. "Mom, do you know where the faculty room is?"

"I have no idea."

"Okay. I'd go with you, but I have another class." She collared a student. "George, would you take Ms. Hutchins to the teachers' lounge?"

"Sure," he said, and smiled at Hutch.

"You have a visitor, Mom. And don't forget to come back here for fourth period, okay? You won't duck, will you?"

"I'll be here. Who's the visitor?"

"I don't know. But I gotta get set up. He's waiting for you in the lounge."

The visitor was Gregory MacAllister, an old friend and a prize-winning journalist. There were only two other people in the room when she arrived, and they were just leaving. Mac showed her that familiar all's-well-with-the-world smile, got out of his chair, and held his arms out for her.

"Mac," she said, "what are you doing here?"

The smile widened. "Once I heard that you'd be here, I couldn't stay away." MacAllister was probably as influential as any journalist on the planet.

"Why'd you stay out here? You could have come into the classroom."

"I'm a little too big for the furniture. I assume you've had lunch?"

"It's a little early yet."

"How about we go for a drink?"

"I can't, Mac. I have another class to do."

"Well, okay. That limits our options. I've been meaning to call you."

"Running out of stuff to write about?"

"I wouldn't put it exactly that way. You've become the story of the week."

"It'll go away pretty quickly." A half-empty cup of coffee waited on a side table where MacAllister had been sitting. A basket holding a few muffins and buns rested on a counter beside a refrigerator. He reclaimed his seat. Hutch refilled his cup and got fresh coffee for herself. "It's good to see you again, Mac."

"You too, Hutch. We should get together once in a while."

"Sounds like a good idea if we could get the timing better."

"I know." MacAllister, when he wanted to, was able to make her feel that, no matter what was going on in the world, everything was okay. There was nothing to worry about. He was a big man in every sense of the word. He took up a lot of physical space. And he was an intellectual heavyweight. When he entered a room, everyone came to attention. Mac was an international figure, an editor and commentator whose connection with Hutch stretched back to when they were stranded together on Deepsix. "I wanted to talk with you about the Calliope flight."

"Well, that's a surprise."

"All right. Look, I know you too well to try to talk you out of doing it. In fact, I think you're precisely the right person for this idiot mission. And I don't mean that as an insult."

"Of course not."

"No, I mean that if anybody can make it turn out well, you're the person. And it's very likely a smart career move for you. If things go the way we hope they will, if you get there and discover intelligent squirrels or something cruising around in rockets, it'll provide another boost to the space program, which I know is what you live for. And you'll come home on top of the world. So, really, the only reason I'm here is to wish you luck. I hope everything goes according to plan."

"So why do you want me to pass on this?"

He got up and walked over to the muffins. "You want one?"

"No, thanks."

He picked one up and took a bite. "Hutch, you've become one of my favorite people. I don't want to see anything bad happen to you. And this business just feels *unsafe*. And not only for you but for the whole planet. Look,

I know you'll go out there and probably nothing bad will happen. But you might light the fire again, and if you do, somewhere down the road—" He shook his head.

They sat for a minute, staring at each other. "I've only said this to one other woman in my life, Hutch: I love you. I would not want to see you become known to history as a primal figure in a global catastrophe."

On the way home, she got a call from Derek. "Priscilla, the director's flying into DC tomorrow. He wants to talk to us. Eleven a.m. at the Truman Building. I'm not sure what this is about, but I assume it'll have something to do with the Centauri Initiative. You want me to have someone pick you up?"

SCIENCE DESK
Tuesday, February 19, 2256
QURAQUA READY FOR COLONIZATION
KOSMIK CEO Marie Dubois Announces
Terraforming Complete
Millions Around the Globe Apply

SIX CARRIERS WILL BEGIN MOVING SETTLERS IN MAY
Supply Stockpiles Already in Place at Quraqua

UN PROMISES FUNDING FOR MORE CARRIERS

COMMUNICATION IMPLANTS LOSING
POPULARITY IN NAU
Doctors for Common Sense: "I'd Rather
Carry a Commlink"

STUDY REVEALS DISADVANTAGES OF
EXTENDED LIFESPANS
*With Passing Years We Become Progressively
Wedded to Opinions*
*Research Suggests Exercises Designed to Maintain
Mental Flexibility*
Population Issues Grow

TIME TRAVEL EXPERIMENTS PROVIDE NO SURPRISES
*Some Particles Can Be Sent "Down Time,"
but Not People*

BREAKTHROUGH IMMINENT IN CLIMATE CONTROL
*Techniques Acquired from Terraforming Show
Terrestrial Applications*
Research: Polar Ice Caps May Be Restored by 2400

ALVIN CARMICHAEL DEAD AFTER FALL
FROM ROOFTOP
*"What's the Point of Being Alive," He Famously Asked,
"if You're a Tree?"*

ASTRONOMERS MAY HAVE FOUND THE EDGE OF THE
UNIVERSE
*Same Star Cluster Believed Sighted on Both
Sides of Sky*

SCIENTIFIC GROUP DEMANDS CANCELLATION OF
CALLIOPE MISSION
Unterkoefler Says Operation Invites Disaster
"Even if They Come Home Safely, We Are Setting a

Precedent. Eventually, This Type of Operation Will Wake a Sleeping Dragon and Get Us All Killed."

WSA COMMISSIONS LOCARNO UNITS FOR
THREE INTERSTELLARS
Eiferman *Only Vehicle Currently Available That Can Reach Calliope*
Move Intensifies Debate over Deep-Space Exploration

6.

The happiest moments of my life have been the few
which I have passed at home in the bosom of my family.
—Thomas Jefferson, Letters, 1790

The Truman Building is located in Foggy Bottom, just
north of the National Academy of Sciences in DC. For
more than a century it had housed the State Department. Now, of course, it provides accommodations for the
NAU branch of the World Space Authority. Hutch found
an escort waiting. She was taken to the second floor and
shown into an office, where a staff member asked her to be
seated, and informed her that the director would be with
her shortly. He arrived a few minutes later, accompanied
by Derek.

The World Space Authority, during that difficult period,
was being run by Zhang Chao. Zhang had a long background in government. He'd started as a prosecutor in the
Chinese Department of Justice, served in President Kai's
administration as secretary of commercial affairs, and had
been an advisor during Li Guying's successful presidential

campaign in 2251. Zhang gave her a brief smile and led the way into his office. He took his place behind the desk and waited while they seated themselves in two armchairs. The walls were covered with photos of interstellars, planetary rings, starship crews, and political leaders around the world. One depicted Emma Proctor and Zhang sharing a lectern in a crowded hall.

He was small, gray, with a receding hairline. Hutch's first impression was that he could easily have been lost in a crowd, except that he was capable of projecting not only a substantial level of authority but also a sense that, whatever the issue might be, he had the correct perspective. "Priscilla," he said, "I'm pleased to meet you." His accent had a slightly British flavor. "I assume you know Derek."

"Yes, Director Zhang, I do."

"Excellent. Then let's get to business."

Derek delivered a slightly uncomfortable smile but said nothing.

Zhang glanced toward one of the two windows, momentarily distracted as something fluttered past. "I've been intrigued by your career, Priscilla. To be honest, I've wanted to meet you ever since I heard about your connection to the omega clouds. You've performed at a remarkable level. I could not have been happier when Derek informed me that you would be serving as the pilot for the Calliope mission."

"Thank you, sir."

"The reason I asked you to come in here today is that, as you are aware, there is currently a rising concern about interstellar activity. I have encouraged Derek to try to hasten preparations for the launch of the *Eiferman*. But

I must reluctantly inform you that there is a very good chance the mission will not happen. I'm sorry to tell you this, but I don't want you to be disappointed. If the project is cancelled, we will pay you twenty percent of the promised amount to compensate for your time and whatever efforts you've already put into the operation."

"That's very kind of you, Director Zhang, but if there is a cancellation, we can let it go. The effort has cost me nothing."

His smile suggested the matter was of no real consequence. "We can debate the matter if and when it becomes an issue." He leaned back in his chair and joined his hands together. "Would you like some tea or coffee?"

Derek let her see that she should accept. "Tea would be good," Hutch said.

"Coffee for me, thank you," said Derek.

Zhang passed the requests to a secretary. "We have a matter of substance to consider." He got up, went over to the window, and looked out at sunlight and treetops. "There is more at stake here than simply getting the Calliope mission out before our more cautious associates can stop it. Our primary concern is the long term. Everything on this mission has to go smoothly. We don't want any more omega clouds. And we certainly don't want you going to the Kellerman Cluster and encountering a vicious species or anything else that would provide fuel to the talk shows and scare the voters. I'll be honest with you. I'm not sure those who think interstellar missions are just asking for trouble don't have it right. But who knows? A thousand years from now, this will very likely be remembered as a critical moment, not only in the development of spaceflight, but in our overall progress as a species. If anything goes wrong now, it may shut things down for the foreseeable future, and maybe forever.

"Something else to consider: You'll be getting back here in the middle of a presidential election. President Proctor is very likely to remain in office. And turning out the lights, as the antiflight people like to say, has become a major part of her platform. Screw something up and she'll come down even harder on us."

Derek's eyes narrowed. "Director Zhang, I understand what you're saying, but it's irritating to have a deranged politician opposing something so important to the human future for political reasons."

"I don't think you give her enough credit, Derek. Her attitude has nothing to do with politics. She thinks *we're* the ones who are deranged. We're the ones who are putting the human future at risk. I'm just not sure she's wrong. In any case, I want you—both of you—to exercise caution. Take no chances. Bring everybody back. And let's not have any bad news. Is that clear?"

It was. Zhang cautioned them on their relations with the press, primarily that they be careful not to say anything that could be used as ammunition against the project. He assured them of his confidence in their ability to log a successful effort and wished them well. The meeting ended and they all shook hands and said how they were looking forward to working together. But when Derek and Hutch had reached the lobby, she stopped him. "He put a lot of brakes on the mission, Derek. All that caution."

"You think I didn't notice?"

"So what's the mission really about? I can't believe we're going all the way out there to take a quick look for whoever sent the waterfall signal, and then we're going to turn around and come back home."

"Well, think what you like. That's the plan."

"Yeah." Of course it was. "Derek, I'd love to find out who's there, then sit down and talk with them. Maybe take them to lunch."

"I understand, Priscilla. I feel exactly the same way."

"But we don't get to do it. Why are we so scared, Derek?"

"I don't know. Maybe it's political. Maybe they're right and it's simply too dangerous. Zhang's rational. He feels the same way we do. But he doesn't want to take a chance. He doesn't want to support a project that could get everyone on the planet killed. Now, I know that's over the top, but a lot of people feel that way. Including a good many in the media. He's hoping everything will go quietly. And that attitudes might change while we're away. Possibly if we go out there and find a peaceful society with great music and good food." He grinned. "Maybe then they'll put together another mission and actually go out to say hello. Let's see if we can find something that would encourage that."

Hutch's mom called next morning. Her image blinked on in the living room, seated in the black leather armchair that still survived from Hutch's childhood days. She was worried and made no effort to conceal it. *"Hello, Priscilla,"* she said. *"I don't guess you're going to get up here before you leave?"* She looked pretty good. She'd started the telomerase reverse-aging process a few years earlier. And while

66

nobody would mistake her for a young woman, she was nevertheless making excellent ground. Her hair was black again, the wrinkles were gone, and her eyes had acquired a sparkle. Even when she was unhappy.

"I was planning on driving up tomorrow, Mom. If that works."

"Oh, yes," she said. *"Good."* She paused. *"Everything all right?"*

"Yes. I'm doing fine. Spent most of the day yesterday with Maureen. Helping with the classes."

"What does she think about this Calliope thing?"

"I assume you'd prefer I not go, right?"

"I don't want to lose you, Priscilla. And these missions scare the devil out of me. I thought this was supposed to be all over years ago. But you keep going back for more."

"I'm sorry, Mom. It's basically what I do for a living."

"There's a lot more to it than that."

"I suppose. I like the work."

"Did you see Unterkoefler's comment?"

Unterkoefler was probably the world's best-known physicist. "Yes," Hutch said. "I saw it."

"Don't you think it would be a better idea not to go to these places? Even if this one is safe, eventually somebody else will find something that follows him back here. You know, I try to stay out of your affairs, Priscilla. But this time I feel I have to speak up."

"I understand how you feel, Mom. I'd be nervous too if Maureen was off doing stuff that might have a bad ending. And you're right, I suppose. It would be safer, in the short term anyhow, to stay home. And keep our heads down. But do you really think we should do that forever? Hide here and keep quiet? Turn off all the radio and TV signals? That really what you want?"

"Of course not. I just want you to stay alive."

Calls came in from multiple journalists asking for interviews. The Internet was filled with comments on both sides of the issue. She was surprised at the anger showing up on some of the posts. A few people even made remarks along the lines of hoping that the shuttle carrying her to Union would go down.

They had a legitimate argument. Suppose they were followed back by an invisible fleet that proceeded to destroy everything? It struck her as being hopelessly silly, but it got into her head.

An ABC team arrived and was filming and asking questions when Charlie got in from school. As soon as she was able to finish with the reporters, she suggested they go out for dinner. Tina's Café on Sunrise Boulevard was a good place to lose themselves. She passed Charlie's number along to Derek and turned her own commlink off. It gave her the first quiet time she'd had since opening her eyes that morning.

Unfortunately, she couldn't take Charlie's commlink to South Jersey with her next day. So she gave Derek her mother's number and was consequently able to enjoy an uneventful ride.

A few minutes after she arrived, friends and family began showing up. Uncle Frank and Aunt Louise, two cousins, her mother's cousin Alice, and Hutch's younger brother, Jason. There were a few people she'd been in elementary and high school with, including a guy she'd fallen in love with at fifteen. Harry Collins. He still looked good. And though she'd done what she could to put him behind her, you never really forget a first love.

They came and went throughout the day and evening, commenting on her courage, admitting how they would never do it, and going on about how it would be a flight into the dark. "I think it's crazy," said Uncle Frank. "It just seems like asking for trouble."

In the morning they enjoyed a long breakfast of French toast and an assortment of fruit. Afterward they just sat and talked until Jason said how he had to be getting to work. He did public relations for Cranby & Fitch, a law firm. So, finally, it was time to say good-bye. There were lots of hugs and assurances from Hutch that when the mission was done, she would return to Cherry Hill and actually spend some serious time with the family.

"I will," she said. "Absolutely."

Mom's commlink sounded. She answered and listened for a moment. Then she grinned and covered the link. "This woman says she's calling from the White House." Her eyes sent the rest of the message: *The president wants to talk to you.*

Hutch's heart skipped a beat. Her mother handed her the link. Priscilla looked at one of the exits, signaling that it would be a good idea if she got some privacy. Mom and Jason looked awestruck, but they wasted no time leaving the room. Hutch stared at the phone for a long moment. Then: "This is Priscilla Hutchins."

"*Ms. Hutchins, the president wishes to speak with you. Please hold.*"

She heard a click at the other end. Then, after only a few seconds, Proctor's voice: *"Ms. Hutchins?"*

"Yes, Madam President. What can I do for you?" Dumb. She knew what was coming.

The president blinked on. She was standing beside a window, with rain beating down on the glass. Emma Proctor was tall and vibrant, with dark brown eyes that cast a look of frustration across features that usually reflected a sense that all was well in the world.

Hutch got to her feet and moved away from the table. *"Ms. Hutchins, I've been an admirer of yours for a long time. You've rendered major services to the country and to the world. You're in a position again, as much as ever before, to help.*

"What you've signed on for is a serious mistake. The Calliope mission, if it's allowed to take place, has the potential to cause immense damage. We have no idea who or what is out there. Even if we do not encounter a threat, it may set a precedent that will encourage more missions that will continue until the inevitable occurs. This may be our only opportunity to stop it. Please, back off. And do what you can to dissuade the people planning this operation to do the same."

She had to catch her breath. "Madam President—do you know something I don't?"

"Only that it's just a matter of time before one of these missions goes seriously wrong. We are playing with a wildcat here."

Hutch was having trouble with her voice. "I understand," she said. It wasn't what she'd wanted to say. It sounded too much like caving in. But she couldn't stop struggling.

The president came away from the window and walked

slowly toward her. *"So, what are you going to do?"*

"We've been traveling to other stars for a long time. It's never caused a problem. In fact, we've gotten some serious benefits from it."

"Priscilla, we've barely touched reality. The handful of stars we've visited is infinitesimal." She was towering over Hutch now. Her eyes had taken on a look of urgency. *"High-tech life is obviously rare. I grant you that. We have not yet encountered much of anything that operates at an advanced level. But the waterfall signal certifies that a high-tech civilization was out there seven thousand years ago. They've had seven thousand years to continue evolving. We cannot conceive what they might be capable of today."*

"They may not even be there anymore, Madam President. If things go the way they generally have in the past, they've been dead a long time."

"We don't yet know enough to have a grasp of the probabilities. This flight puts us all at risk. I understand you're at your mother's house?"

"Yes."

"Do you have any children?"

"Two."

"You understand you're putting them all at risk."

"I have no influence over the WSA Authority," said Hutch. "They're not going to pay attention to anything I have to say."

"I understand that. But you can refuse to pilot the mission."

"They'd just get somebody else."

"Of course. But you could make a public statement as well. Let everyone know why this is so dangerous. Priscilla, it's a potentially deadly project. We all know that." Proctor stood, not

moving, gazing at her with growing desperation in her eyes.

"No," Hutch said. "I can't do that. I made an agreement and I'll live by it. Maybe you're right, Madam President. Maybe the universe *is* full of lunatic aliens. But that's hard to believe. In any case, I don't think we'd be looking at a very bright future if we spend the rest of our existence sitting here hiding under a table."

"I see."

"I'm sorry."

"As am I." She hesitated. *"There's not much time to change your mind. If you need to reach me, you have my number."*

"Thank you."

"I understand this is difficult for you, Priscilla. But I'm your president, and I'm asking for your help."

The ride home was one of the longest of her life. She'd traveled more quickly between stars than she did that day in the automated car between Cherry Hill and Woodbridge. She couldn't make up her mind. Who should she betray? Her friends and her lifetime convictions of the necessity for interstellar travel, or the President of the North American Union? Was she so committed to her life's work that she could not look at the issue objectively? What if something lethal *did* accompany them back? The responsibility would be hers.

She got home midafternoon Sunday. Her commlink was crowded with calls, mostly from media types. One was from Unterkoefler. Derek and Tom had also tried to reach her. She called Blanchard first.

"The Eiferman's docked, Priscilla. We're going to turn this around as quickly as we can. Some of the guys from the Save

the Earth Foundation have been calling around, trying to put pressure on our people, hoping to shut us down. They got to your copilot. Walcott. He's passed on the project. I'm guessing they've talked to you too."

"More or less."

"Really? Please tell me you're not also bailing."

Last chance. She was still not sure what she should do. "No," she said after stalling a few moments. "Who's going to replace Walcott?"

"Clay Clairveau."

She'd heard his name but couldn't recall ever having met him. "He have any experience with the Locarno?"

"Yes. It's okay. He'll be fine. If nobody gets to him and talks him out of going."

"So, when's liftoff?"

"We're trying for Wednesday. We have to get out of here as soon as possible. Can you manage that?"

Three days. "Okay."

"When can you be here?"

"When do you need me?"

"Tuesday would be good."

"I'll be there."

"Excellent. We'll send the lander down. You'd be coming from DC?"

"Yes."

"It'll be at the terminal at eleven a.m. Clay'll be coming up with you. And also Ken and Beth Squires. Beth is our medic. Ken's her husband. He's our PR guy. He's a historian, and he tells me he's going to be writing a book about this mission. But the real reason I wanted him along, other than that we also needed Beth, is that he's the best linguist I know. The guy

73

speaks a half dozen languages. If we actually meet someone we have to learn to talk to, he'll be just the guy to have on board." He laughed, trying to turn it into a joke.

She called Tom. *"I was afraid you'd left,"* he said.

"I was in South Jersey."

"I remember when that used to sound far away. Priscilla, are you available for lunch?"

They met at Larry's again. And it was exactly what Hutch needed: leisure time with a friend, pizza, nobody trying to talk her into anything, and of course her comm-link turned off.

"When does your promotion take effect?" she asked.

"Friday. This is my last week on the beat. I'd have enjoyed having you around to help me celebrate."

"I wish I could be, Tom. Everything's seriously busy right now. Maybe when I get home?"

"By then, I may be a lieutenant."

"Wouldn't be surprised." She sat chewing on the pizza, wanting to tell him about the president. But she knew how that would end. "It's good," she said.

"There's no such thing as pizza that isn't."

President Proctor was at her right hand, sipping Coke, staring at her. *There's still time to back off. To do the right thing.* What would her father have said if he'd lived to see this day? He'd been a naval officer at the start of his career. And protecting the NAU had been the consummate responsibility of every citizen. He'd have been horrified at what she was doing. The guy who, himself, had devoted his life to listening for signals from the sky.

"Priscilla," said Tom, "what's wrong?"

And she let go. She told him everything, what the president said, how she'd felt, and her own inability to come to a decision.

"But you *have* decided, right?"

"Yes."

Her voice went so low, he couldn't understand. "Say again, please."

"Yes, I've made up my mind."

"Well, I'm glad. Having you back away from that damned thing is the best news I can think of."

"I'm not backing away, Tom."

"You mean you're going? After the president asked you not to?"

"Yes. I'm going."

"You can't do that. The president's asked you to stop. You can't disobey her."

"She doesn't have the authority to give me orders."

He stared at her, stunned. "Priscilla, please. You'll regret it the rest of your life."

"How would *you* know that?"

He shook his head a few times and pushed the pizza away. He was finished. "It's your call." He sounded as if he was bestowing the privilege.

She called the White House from the car. "This is Priscilla Hutchins. Is President Proctor by any chance available?"

A female voice responded. *"Ms. Hutchins, I'm sorry but she's in conference at the moment. Do you wish to leave a message?"*

"Yes. Would you please tell her I wish I could help. But I can't manage it. I'm sorry."

Derek Blanchard, Extract from Notebook, Intended for Autobiography

The argument that the Calliope project presents an existential danger isn't absurd, but it's unlikely anything like that could happen. In any case, it's a step we're going to have to take eventually. Developing a society with technology sufficiently advanced to provide FTL travel requires cooperation on a level far beyond any that can be achieved in the presence of a primitive mind-set. Its members have to be smart enough to get along. Ultimately, a talent for cooperation may be the definition of intelligent life.

Burke, Unterkoefler, Nakata, and the others who are maintaining the position are pointing at the fact that savagery still exists across our world. And they are correct to the degree that we have not yet established a completely peaceful planet. But it might be helpful to point out that we no longer have governments threatening world order. Yes, there are small groups of hostile lunatics killing themselves periodically in the name of religion or politics. But all they can do is create havoc. They have no capability to design new technology, and we no longer have outlaw governments willing to deliver technology into their hands.

A bright future awaits us. But we have to possess the courage to move forward into it.

—Sunday, February 24, 2256

7.

Point me out the way
To any one particular beauteous star,
And I will flit into it with my lyre,
And make its silvery splendor pant with bliss.
                    —John Keats, "Hyperion III," 1819

Hutch put on a pair of sunglasses and her Washington Hawks baseball cap. Then she picked up her luggage, climbed into the car, and directed it to take her to the DC spaceport. People with signs were gathered around the entrance, apparently waiting for her.

STAY HOME AND BE SAFE

KEEP OUT OF THE HORNET'S NEST

MIND YOUR OWN BUSINESS

THEY'RE OUT THERE

DON'T BE CRAZY

YOU'LL KILL US ALL

They flew the blue-and-white banners of the recently organized Save the Earth Foundation. *"What do you want to do?"* asked the car, whose name was Molly.

"Pull up in front of them," she said.

"You sure, Priscilla? They look disorderly."

It didn't matter. The spaceport had no accessible back door. She climbed out, and catcalls started before she was even able to get to her luggage. "Take care on your way out, Molly," she said. "They might be mad at you too." She pulled her bags out of the trunk and started to walk toward the entrance. Ordinarily, the car would have driven away as soon as the luggage was clear, but Molly waited, giving her a chance to change her mind.

Security people were present, though substantially outnumbered. Nonetheless, when the demonstrators started toward her, they moved in and set up a restraining perimeter.

The demonstrators were mostly college age, the kind of kids who, in an earlier era, had been animal rights activists or who'd worked to get passage of government-funded elections. A young woman, carrying a sign that read simply: HUTCH, PLEASE BACK OFF, called out to her. "Captain Hutchins, please don't do this."

The officers cleared her path to the door.

Voices rose all around her: "Hutch, this is not you."

"Priscilla, how can you possibly help these people?"

"Is that really *her*? I never would have believed this."

There was no way to respond. Eye contact would have been potentially deadly, so she stayed focused on the side of the building, then on the doors, and finally on the security guards who got in the way of the more aggressive demonstrators.

Beth Squires and Clay Clairveau were already in the waiting area, talking. She joined them, and they shook hands and tried to laugh off their reactions to the crowd. But it *was* unnerving. "It's okay," said Clay. "We have a pretty good chance of making the history books."

"Let's hope," said Beth, "that it won't be because we get everybody blown up."

"I'll settle for that," said Clay with a grin that was almost malicious. "Maybe we could bring a few aliens back to say hello to these Save the Earth nitwits."

"They may have a point," said Hutch.

"You okay?" asked Beth. She had dark brown curly hair and hazel eyes and an expression that suggested she was a bit rattled.

"Yes, I'm fine. Just not sure which side I'm on."

"I know exactly what you mean."

"If we had people like those ding-dongs running things," said Clay, "we'd still be living in caves."

Beth smiled and her eyes softened. She checked the time and looked around, obviously not happy. "My husband always runs late."

"He working on another book?" asked Hutch.

"He's always working on one. But he was a guest on *The Public Square* this morning. Threw his schedule off a bit. He's on his way, but that's all I have."

Hutch couldn't remember having met Clay before, but something about him rang bells. "Clay," she said, "are you related to Marcel Clairveau?"

He grinned. "My dad."

He was one of the guys who'd rescued her when she was dangling over Maleiva III. Clay resembled him, congenial eyes, lantern jaw, thick black hair, the kind of guy you felt instinctively you wanted at your back if you were headed for trouble. "How's he doing? I owe him."

"He's fine. Still with TransGalactic. He asked me to say hello."

"Give him my best."

"I will, Hutch. I should tell you that I owe *you* as well."

"Why's that, Clay?"

"You're the reason I got into this business. You've set a serious example for the rest of us."

They embraced, shared a few more jokes about their reactions to the anger around them, and after a few minutes were joined by Ken, Beth's husband. "Sorry," he told them. "Traffic jam." He was even bigger than Clay.

Derek was waiting when they docked at Union. "Glad to see you guys," he said. "They're still working on the ship, so we'll be staying in the Starview tonight. Don't worry about your luggage. They know where it's going. I take it you've all been introduced to one another?"

Hutch was happy to see there were no more demonstrators. They all shook hands with Derek while he suggested they have dinner and relax for a while. "I heard about the problem on the ground," he said. "I wish we could have kept all this quiet until we got clear. We're just not very good at keeping secrets." He glanced at Ken. "How's the book coming?"

Ken had been a catcher with the Boston Red Sox, and he looked it. He'd stayed in shape and moved with the ease of a track and field athlete. Hutch had watched a couple of his presentations and been struck by the degree to which his amiable features could clash with the sudden intensity that showed up periodically in his blue eyes. "I'll let you know," he said, "when we get back."

"I hope it has a happy ending." Derek had obviously wanted a more upbeat response. "Somebody want to pick a restaurant?" They had arrived in front of Big Bang Burgers, and everybody looked in its direction. "All right, why do any unnecessary walking? Let's go over there and chow down, and then we'll get checked into the Starview."

The Union Space Station ran on GMT, which was approaching six forty-five p.m. when they arrived at the hotel. "So we're all together on the details," said Derek after they'd signed in, "we're going to try to get out of here by nine tomorrow morning. We've been hearing about a last-minute effort to close us down, so we want to go as soon as the service people give us the ship. Meet in the lobby. Nobody be late, okay?"

He got assurances, wished them good night, and headed out the door.

Hutch had brought three suitcases with her, but only one was waiting in the hotel room when she walked in. She'd marked the others for the *Eiferman*. Everything she needed for the overnight was in the lone bag. She opened it and took out a change of clothes. Then she showered, dressed, and went back downstairs to the bar, where everyone except Derek eventually showed up. They settled into a corner and spent the balance of the evening getting to know one another. It was, she had learned, one of the most important aspects of prepping for a long mission.

All except Ken were veterans of interstellar flight. He'd been out only once, to take a look at Quraqua. It was becoming Earth's first real colony, he said, and consequently it would occupy a major position in his upcoming history. Mars, he explained, didn't count. It was an outpost. Nothing more. "I almost got left behind," he said. "Blanchard apparently got bad information on me. He thought I'd been out on a few flights. When he found out there'd been just one, he was going to back off. He could have gone with either Yakata or Keller. Both would have been happy to provide the history he wanted. And they'd been out several times."

"So why," asked Clay, "did he stay with you?"

Ken grinned at Beth. "He also needed an MD. She let him see she wasn't going without me."

"Why would he care about the number of flights?" asked Walter. Walter Esmeraldo, introduced as Wally, was the final member of the team. "I mean, you're not the pilot or anything." Wally was two inches shorter than Hutch, with red hair and an easy smile. He'd been out on missions with her several times, and her overall impression was that if the drive unit or the life support system gave out, he was the guy you wanted on board.

"I think he was worried I might develop psychological problems. I guess he didn't want to take a chance on some-body getting homesick."

"How about you, Wally?" asked Clay. "Are you the Jack McGuire of interstellar techs?" Jack McGuire was the hero of an adventure series, a guy who was always able to defeat the bad guys and solve mechanical problems by coming up with duct-tape solutions.

"You could say that." Wally delivered a wide smile. "Were you out on that earlier flight with your husband before, Beth?"

"Nope. This is the first time we've been together. I'm looking forward to it."

"How'd *you* get the assignment?" said Wally.

"I'm not sure. I think Ken has the wrong side of this. I suspect they wanted him for the PR, and he probably cut a deal." She flashed a smile in his direction while he managed to look shocked. "They needed an MD anyhow, so I guess that part of it was an easy call."

"Beth," said Hutch, "you worked for TransGalactic, right?"

"Until a couple of years ago. I liked life at Union and an opening developed here, so I made the change. It made life a bit easier for us. I got to see my husband once in a while."

"Do you guys actually live here? On the station?"

"Oh, no. We have two kids, and this is just not a good place for them. I do occasional missions, but I'm not out constantly running all over the universe like it was before we got married."

Somebody snickered. "So now you're leaving town with us?"

"Yeah. I know. We talked about it before I got on board. This could be a historic mission. I almost passed, but the kids will be okay and I know Ken wanted to do this."

"And it pays pretty well," said Clay.

Eventually, Hutch excused herself and walked over to the docking area. Two vehicles that she'd taken out, the *Phyllis Preston* and the *Harold Wildside*, were in view. There was no sign of the *Eiferman*, but the docking area was big. The roof was open allowing her to see a slice of the moon.

She missed the old days, when there were more missions than she could handle.

She slept soundly, got up with the alarm, and was checking out at the desk when her commlink sounded. *"Gotta move,"* said Derek. *"They're waking people up to get a stop order signed. As we speak. Get over here right away. Where are you now, Priscilla?"*

"Just leaving the hotel."

"Okay. Hustle it up. The others with you?"

"No. I'm alone at the moment."

"All right. Just get here. I'll call everybody."

Hutch grabbed her bag and hurried out through the front doors. But she'd only taken two steps onto the concourse when she realized she didn't know where the *Eiferman* was docked. She dug out her commlink again. "Ops," she said.

A male voice replied, *"This is Operations. What do you need, Captain Hutchins?"*

"Where's the *Eiferman*?"

"One second, please." He clicked off, then came back. *"Romeo."*

On the far side. There were no transport vehicles in the station, but it had a moving walkway. She carried her bag over to it—there was no time for the delivery service—and got on it. As she moved forward along the concourse and the Starview started to curve out of sight, she saw Beth and Ken charge out through the front doors and look wildly in both directions. Then Beth was on her commlink.

She needed fifteen minutes to get to the Romeo boarding area, where she hurried into the connecting tube. The *Eiferman*, locked in place by magnetic clamps, was visible through transparent walls. The Union docking system was capable of holding eighteen vehicles. In Hutch's early days it had usually been crowded. She could remember once having to settle for an emergency quay on the roof of the station. Now the bay was almost empty.

Beth and Ken caught up with her as she approached the airlock. It was open, and they passed through into the passenger cabin. "Touch and go," said Beth. She and Ken sat down. The luggage from the terminal had arrived and was piled in a corner.

"You guys," said Hutch, "can go back and pick your cabin if you like. But be back up here when we get ready to leave." She heard movement on the bridge. Wally was there, standing in the door and talking with Barry, the AI, checking the maintenance report. "How we doing?" she asked.

He wiggled a hand. "We haven't been cancelled yet."

"Are we ready to go?"

"More or less. I'd like to have a little more time to look around, but the reports are okay. And our luggage is on the way from the hotel. As far as I can tell, we'll be ready in a few minutes."

"Is Derek here yet?"

"He's in back somewhere."

She returned to the passenger cabin. They'd installed eight chairs, which could be locked into the deck. There was a large display screen, and a group of lamps, one positioned to service each of the chairs. She passed through into the corridor, which led aft along the cabins to the galley, storage, and workout areas. Beth and Ken had just opened the door to their cabin and were carrying luggage inside. Derek came out of the captain's cabin. "Good morning, ladies," he said. "Glad to see you. Hello, Ken."

He gave Hutch a hand with her bag. Then he pushed open one of the doors. "In here," he said. She watched while he hauled her suitcase into the wrong room. There was no difference between the cabin reserved for the captain and those set aside for the other occupants, except for a private line in from the AI for emergency use. The cabin was not expressly marked in any way, other than a star at eye level. On all ships it was located on the port side, nearest the passenger area and bridge.

Once they were inside, Derek closed the door. "Priscilla," he said, "we want to get moving as soon as Clay gets here."

Hutch nodded. "Have we locked in all the numbers yet? For Calliope?"

"Of course," he said, sounding annoyed. "Barry has everything."

"Good. Just playing it safe. I wasn't trying to insult anybody."

She left the cabin and headed for the bridge. *"Hello, Captain Hutchins,"* said the AI as she walked through the door. *"I've heard a lot about you. Welcome aboard."*

"Hi, Barry." She lowered herself into her seat. "It's a pleasure to be here. You have the range and direction for Calliope?"

"I do, Captain. Seven thousand two hundred and forty-seven light-years. That is, of course, an estimate."

"Of course. So we'll be under—?"

"Twenty-six days, three hours."

A commlink sounded behind her. She turned to see Derek standing by the door. He took the call and listened for a minute. Then: "Okay, Janet. Thanks for letting me know." He paused. "The stop order's been signed."

Outside, other than the presence of a few lights along some of the docks, the dome seemed suddenly dark. Hutch began going over the check-off list with the AI.

Derek leaned dismayed against the doorway. "Janet got the word from one of her contacts. They haven't let us know officially yet. But unless the contact's got it screwed up, they should be calling it in now."

"Well, what do you want to do, Derek? Give it up, or start the engines?"

"You know the answer to that." He looked away from her, staring at the windows. "Do it."

It was the reply she wanted. "Go, Barry."

Lights came on across the instrument board, and the soft murmur of power rose out of the bulkheads.

"I've got to tell you, Priscilla, we didn't quite complete the inspection. But we should be okay."

"That's not good, Derek." Her training was clear on the issue: You don't go anywhere until inspection and mainte-nance are complete.

"We don't have much of a choice, do we? Stay or go."

"Where's Clay?"

"He's coming." Derek checked the time and looked out through the windows, but there was no sign of him. He opened his commlink, glared at it, and grumbled Clay's name.

"On my way, Derek," Clay said. *"I was in the shower when you called."*

"Where are you now?"

"Outside the hotel. I'll only be a few minutes."

Derek shut it off and rubbed the back of his hand against his mouth. "Great," he said.

His commlink buzzed. "It's Janet again." He turned the volume up so Hutch could hear.

"A message just came in from Director Zhang. I haven't looked at it yet."

"Don't go near it," said Derek. "Priscilla, get us out of here."

"What about Clay?"

"Can you manage without him?"

"As long as nothing happens to me. Or Barry."

"Then leave him. Let's go."

She connected with Ops. *"Eiferman* ready for departure."

Derek was talking to Janet again. "We're pulling out now."

"You want me to ignore the message until you're gone?"

That would get her in trouble. "Give us a couple minutes. Then try to relay it. Meantime, we'll have a communications breakdown." He turned to Hutch. "How long before we can make the jump?"

Across the bay the launch doors were opening. "Derek, we'll need thirty minutes after we get out of here."

"That's not good. What happens if we just make the jump as soon as we get clear of the station?"

"We'd probably melt the drive unit."

"Okay. Just get us moving. But keep the radio off. We're having a breakdown until we get clear."

"Derek, I can't do that."

"If you answer, it puts the thing on record. We'd have to go back."

"If we block communications, there's a possibility of a collision with an incoming vehicle."

"What are the chances of that?"

She began wondering again if she was on the wrong side of this. "Unfortunately, there *is* a possibility. I'm sorry, Derek. But we can't do it."

"I'll take the responsibility if anything happens."

"If anything happens, we'll all be dead. They probably don't have the word yet, anyhow."

"Eiferman, this is comm-ops. You are clear to—wait one."

"They're getting the shutdown now, Derek. But there's nothing incoming."

"Then go. Disconnect and go." He produced a frustrated grunt, the kind that suggests the world is full of idiots. He switched back to Janet. "You might as well pick it up, kid. We can't shut the comm system down."

"Okay, Derek. The mission is cancelled."

Hutch broke in: "But there's no traffic, Janet?"

"Negative, Captain."

Hutch directed everyone to belt down. She disconnected from the magnetic clamps that locked them to the pier, and released the *Eiferman* to the station, which assumed control, eased the ship away from the dock, angled them toward the launch doors, and took them forward.

"Why are they doing this?" said Derek.

"They're probably a little nervous about changing course inside the bay. Or maybe they're just not good at communicating with one another. There's nothing coming in, so if I have to, I can assume control and take us outside."

Nothing changed and they cleared the station. Somebody, probably Wally, shouted *"Yay!"* as they began to accelerate.

"Incoming message," said Hutch.

Derek was on the bridge with her, seated in the copilot's chair. "Don't touch it," he growled.

"It's okay. It's from Clay."

"Oh, Lord. Okay, put him on."

Hutch pressed the button.

"Hey, guys. What the hell's going on? You left without me?"

Derek took it. "Sorry, Clay. We ran out of time."

"You said nine. It's only a little after eight."

"I can't explain now, Clay. I apologize, but we had no choice. You'll be reimbursed. And I'll see that you get some compensation."

"Great. Thanks a lot, Derek." He broke off.

Derek grumbled something. "Those idiots will never know," he said, "how much trouble they've caused." He didn't explain which idiots he was referring to, but it wasn't hard to guess. "Priscilla, we need to get clear as quickly as we can. When can we make the jump?"

"It's still thirty minutes, Derek."

"All right. Just go."

"Ops is tracking us. But they released control to us. Janet seems pretty good, by the way."

"She's only a staff assistant. I don't think we pay her enough."

"I suspect you're right. Oh, one other thing."

"Yes?"

"We need to talk about the cabin arrangements."

They sat watching the moon approach on their port side. "I hate this," Derek said. "The real problem here is that some of the politicians got involved. Nobody really listens to physicists, but when the politicians started talking about alien invasions, everybody got nervous. Hard to believe they could do this. Where are we now?"

"Fifteen minutes."

Barry began blinking. *"Incoming transmission, Captain. From the Collier Center."* That was the administrative offices of the WSA.

"Don't pick up," said Derek.

Their eyes locked. "I can't do that," Hutch said.

"Are we going to go through that again? We don't have a choice."

"If I ignore it, we're talking about my career."

"You worry too much, Priscilla." She said nothing and kept her eyes on the moon. "Come on. It's *me* they'll come after."

"They'll come after you too. But that would be *your* problem."

"We're only talking about a transmission. We could claim we didn't receive it. Communication breakdown."

"All transmissions are logged."

"You can change the log, right? Delete the damned thing?"

She shook her head. No. "Put them through, Barry," she said. "But block any visuals."

Derek folded his arms and glared at her.

"Eiferman, this is WSA. Be advised your mission is cancelled. Return to Union." It was a female voice. Not Janet's.

Derek held up a hand, signaling that he'd take it. "This is Blanchard," he said. "Who am I speaking to?"

"You know damn well who you're talking to, Derek. Now shut that thing down and turn it around."

"It's too late. We're about to make our jump."

"Derek, I'm not going to say it again. Come back. Or you'll face prosecution when you do *get back here."*

"I'm sorry, Anna. I can't do that."

"Where's Hutchins?"

Hutch shut down the mike. "Who is she?"

"Anna Capleton. My boss."

She reopened the channel. "This is Captain Hutchins, Ms. Capleton."

"Just for the record, Captain, I'm Doctor Capleton. Now turn around and return to the space station. Immediately."

"I can't do that, *Doctor*."

"You don't have any choice, Captain."

It was getting personal. "I have no idea who you are other than somebody on the other end of the circuit. I take direction from Dr. Blanchard. If you want me to go back—"

"Hutchins, be aware that you will also be subject to prosecution. Now do as I say."

Derek was standing and watching her with a desperate expression taking over his face, signaling, *No, please don't cooperate.*

"I'm sorry, Doctor. My obligation is to Dr. Blanchard." She paused a moment, making up her mind. And finally: *"Eiferman* out." She signaled Barry to shut the comm system down.

"Thank you, Priscilla," said Derek. "I know that wasn't easy for you. But you'll be okay. I have friends in high places."

"Well, at the moment, I think you have one less."

UNIVERSAL NEWS NETWORK
Wednesday, February 27, 2256

BLIZZARD THREATENS NORTHEAST NAU
Complete Coverage on The Weather Channel

ZIENKOW SAYS IMMORTALITY NOT OUT OF REACH
Two Species on Oracle III Apparently Live
Indefinitely

CONSERVATIVE DEBATES SEEK TO MEND
PARTY FRACTURES
Leah Aronda Hosts First Round

RUSSIAN-INDIAN COLLABORATION HELPS
ETHIOPIAN CHILDREN
Brackov Humanity Awards This Weekend
Thousands of African Kids Benefit from
Electronic Schools

A YOUNG WINSTON CHURCHILL FALLS INTO THE
HANDS OF PROFESSOR MORIARTY ON
THE WATSON FILES
Tomorrow at Eight on Mystery Channel

LOOK OUT, LOUIE STARTS NEW SEASON MONDAY
Award-Winning Comedy Back for
Sixteenth Season

WILLIAM CASTOR RETURNS TO *SATURDAY NIGHT
FOLLIES*
Repeats Iconic Role as First Gentleman

DOSTOYEVSKY IN THE MODERN AGE
Harry Corbin Stars in *The Brothers Karamazov*
Twelve-Episode Series Starts Tomorrow

LIFE ON OTHER WORLDS
Science Wednesday Visits Teegarden III
Say Hello to the Dragons

DESTROY EARTH: TWELVE WAYS ALIENS
MIGHT ATTACK
Documentary on Black Cat Tonight at Nine

EIFERMAN ON WAY TO CALLIOPE
Effort to Cancel Deep-Space Mission Fails

8.

Granting that we had both the will and the sense to choose our friends well, how few of us have the power . . . Nearly all our associations are determined by chance, or necessity; and restricted within a narrow circle.
—John Ruskin, "Sesame and Lilies, I," 1865

They were adrift in the unbounded jet-black night that was the natural realm of the Locarno drive. No stars, no light of any kind, not even a sense of movement. The windows were dark with no impression of depth, no suggestion that they were traveling through a vacuum with any hope of arriving somewhere. The void simply seemed to wrap itself around the *Eiferman*. When Hutch turned on the navigation lights, they did not penetrate as far as they should have. The darkness seemed more than simply an absence of light. It was a tangible force.

She saw no reason to sit on the bridge for extended periods, although that was where she felt most at home. But it separated her from everyone and would have suggested she was antisocial. That wasn't at all true. There was, however, no way the others could have understood.

In fact, it made no sense to *her*. Except that it was her station, and even though she could have easily controlled the *Eiferman* from the galley or the workout area, the bridge was her assigned post. The technology had changed over the years, and she had no doubt that pilot training was different now. She suspected the instructors were no longer especially concerned about where the command officer was located.

The most numbing effect, as far as Hutch was concerned, was the utter lack of movement. When you rode the Locarno, you went nowhere. The drive put out a barely audible murmur. And you were in a vehicle that simply floated in the dark. In fact, it didn't even *float*. Rather, it was fixed on a foundation. The Hazeltine system, which the Locarno had replaced, which they'd been using for the better part of a century, had at least provided a sense of going somewhere. You drifted through starless skies, but you passed through mist. And you knew you were in a *ship*. It had been no big deal, but now it seemed like a much better way to travel. She could have been sitting in an office building. The Locarno would never appeal to tourists. Except that it gave the flights a radically shorter duration.

After about twenty minutes she joined the others in the passenger cabin. They'd released the chairs from their magnetic clamps since there was no longer a concern about movement, and put them in a circle. They were talking mostly about the mission, discussing what they should do if they arrived at Calliope and found a fleet of interstellars filling the sky. Turn around? Try to talk to them? "Invite them in for dinner," said Beth, with no indication she was joking.

"Lots of interstellars?" said Derek. "These people, whoever they are, *whatever* they are, had lights in the sky when we were still living in caves. I'd be surprised if we don't find them with a Dyson sphere around their sun, scooping off all that energy instead of just watching it get wasted the way ours does at home."

"You actually think," said Wally, "that's possible?"

"I'm not aware that it would violate any of the basic laws of physics."

Hutch couldn't imagine it would ever be possible to erect that kind of structure, but physics wasn't her strong suit. She was reacting strictly from her gut. And she knew how much she could trust that.

"I was sorry we had to leave Clay behind," said Wally. "He was pretty excited about the mission."

Hutch also felt uncomfortable about the decision. They all did. "He would have been the right guy to have around if we have serious trouble," she said.

"Maybe," said Ken, "if nobody has any pressing business, we should have some breakfast." That sounded like a good idea, something to change the mood. They followed him into the galley and discovered a broad selection of eggs, potatoes, waffles, French toast, pancakes, hash brown casserole, country ham, muffins, strawberries, and apples. It was the first time any of them had seen the menu.

They sat down at the table, ordered from Barry, and waited for the bell to ring. Derek thanked everybody for their response to the shutdown attempt. "In the end," he said, "they'll be glad we did this."

"Let's hope we find something," said Ken.

Hutch became aware that Derek was watching her with concern. Was she okay?

She nodded. *I'm fine.*

Barry announced that the coffee was ready. Everybody took a cup, and they commented on how good it smelled. And tasted. They struggled to find a subject other than the mission, which, at that moment, had a dark side. They talked about the comfort of their cabins, the layout of the workout room, the shows and books that were available through the library. And finally, the bell dinged. They got up and collected their breakfasts at the server. The food looked good, so *it* became the center of discussion.

Life in a Locarno interstellar, completely cut off from the outside world, quickly becomes a bubble. For Hutch, who had been through this before, twenty-six days suddenly seemed like an extraordinarily long time.

Hutch knew it was smart to eat slowly on extended missions. There was an inclination to eat too much, to put away a packaged meal and go after a second one. If she followed her instincts, she'd come home with an extra twenty pounds. "You know," she said, "we get all these scientific advances, communication implants, life extensions, lightbenders, avatars, and I'm not sure what else. I wonder when we'll get a breakthrough that lets us eat whatever we feel like without gaining weight."

When they'd finished eating, they returned to the passenger cabin and looked up at the display. They were all in the habit of watching news reports periodically through the day. "Sorry," said Derek. "But we have a million shows."

They put on a comedy that everyone had enjoyed back home. But here, it didn't work unless you could start with, say, the Jack Crispee Show. If you couldn't get the latest report on the presidential election campaign, there was no way to avoid feeling isolated. "It makes me wonder," said Beth, "how people managed at all before we got electricity. You know, in those days, the country could get into a major war and you might not know about it for weeks."

Hutch watched as the lead character discovered his highly touted blind date turned out to be his sister. The room stayed silent. "I'm reluctant to mention this," she said, "but this is only Wednesday." The first day.

She normally read herself to sleep every night. She'd been saving Anthony Pagden's classic analysis, *The Enlightenment: and why it still matters*, for the mission. She easily lost herself in it.

In the morning, Derek showed no sign of getting past his confrontation with Anna Capleton. "She's been on both sides of this issue from the beginning," he said. "She has a ton of political connections. Everybody's scared of her." Including, apparently, Derek. But he didn't seem worried for himself. Rather, he was concerned about Hutch and Wally.

"The truth is," he continued, "that she doesn't really care about anything except her career. She was all for going to Calliope when we first saw the waterfall. In fact, I think it was the music that actually got her curiosity aroused. But then some of the heavyweights jumped into it, and the president. She developed cold feet and started talking out of both sides of her mouth. The last few days she's been telling people she tried to warn everybody right from the start that sending a mission out was a bad idea."

Wally jumped in. "I'm not so sure she doesn't have a point. There's really no way to know what kind of technology somebody out there might have."

"I know," said Derek. "Maybe if they'd turned us loose, we might have been able to take some of that advanced tech home. Assuming we found some."

Early on, Ken became entranced by a book he'd brought with him. Hutch wandered into the mess area Sunday morning, where he sat alone with his notebook propped up in front of an empty plate. "What are you reading?"

"*The Evolution of the Rational Mind*. By Hal Carter."

"You say that as if you know him."

"I do. We went to school together."

"How is it? The book?"

"It's good."

"So, who gets the credit?"

"Probably Plato and Aristotle. Hal tends to wonder how they would react to the modern world. That they are in large degree responsible for. He loves to think about how enjoyable it would be to go back in a time machine, bring them forward, and take them to the moon."

"That's in the book?"

"Oh, no. I'm talking about private moments. Before we left home, I had a chance to talk with him, and I asked where he thought those guys would come down on the starship debate."

"What did he say?"

"That they both thought that curiosity is what life is all about. They would both have cringed at the thought of a society that had an interstellar and didn't use it."

"They'd have accepted the risk?"

"He doesn't think there's any question about it, Hutch. It's curiosity that made us who we are. Unfortunately, we've been living pretty much since the beginning of recorded history in a world that has become increasingly dangerous. The downside of improving technology. And he says it loads us down with an excessive degree of caution."

"So we scare too easily?"

"Correct. It's why a few scientists or politicians can show up on the Black Cat and terrify everybody. Five years ago, most of the world was demanding that we get the interstellars moving, that we get out and look around. Wednesday, they had demonstrators waiting for us at the spaceport."

"Well, Ken, it's certainly true people seem to be nervous."

"If Unterkoefler and his crowd keep talking about the hazards of this flight, if guys like MacAllister keep going on about it, they'll have everybody in a panic by the time we get home. Hell, they've already won over Wally."

"Maybe he's right."

"You too, Hutch?"

"No. All I'm saying—" She sighed. "You know, the living conditions on this kind of flight tend to encourage arguments."

"I know. If Plato were around today, I think he'd look at this whole fiasco about whether we should or shouldn't go to Calliope as a demonstration of our inability to think for ourselves, rather than to react to external forces, like nitwits on TV and the Internet. The ironic part of all this is that there are some serious advantages we could get from visiting an advanced alien species, and we haven't even considered them."

"You're talking about technology?"

"Oh, come on, Hutch," said Ken. "More technology's the last thing we need. No. I'd be more interested in getting a handle on finding out how an advanced species looks at the universe. Do they believe it has a purpose? Are we just monkeys who got lucky? Do they have intelligence beyond our level? What would it be like to talk with someone who has a three hundred IQ? What is consciousness?"

"If you had a chance to sit down with a guy who has a three hundred IQ, what would be your first question?"

He pushed his notebook out of the way, put both elbows on the table, clasped his hands, and rested his jaw on them. "I guess I'd go for the old classic."

"Which is?"

"Does life really have a meaning? Does it have significance beyond what we can see? Or is it just a ride through Darwinian sunlight and ultimately good-bye baby?"

"So the major practical advantage we might get from this kind of mission is purely making a social connection?"

He grinned. "Yes. I think it would be. Make new friends. Sit down and talk with them, if we can find a way to do that. And I don't mean talking with their physicists. I mean ordinary people. These guys at Calliope: If they really had television seven thousand years ago, I'd love to get a few history books from them. Find out what matters to them. Whether they've been able to put together a peaceful existence."

Hutch smiled. "It all comes down to hanging out with them in a bar."

"I think you could say that, Hutch."

"I think Jack Crispee should get you on his show."

• • •

They left the mess area and strolled back into the passenger cabin, where the conversation had shifted to politics. Wally supported Proctor; Beth and Derek thought any of the candidates on the other side would be a distinct improvement. They were all nursing drinks. Hutch's intention was to cruise straight through and go onto the bridge. Not that there was any point in sitting up there, but she didn't want to listen to another debate. "Wait, Hutch," said Wally. "I've got a surprise for you."

"Oh?" The remark caught everyone's attention. Surprises were generally not something you wanted to encounter on a starship.

"What's the surprise?" asked Hutch.

He glanced around at the others. "We've all been on long-range runs before, right? Well, that means everybody can remember sitting in here for weeks, wishing you could get out of this damned room and go somewhere? Just get some fresh air? Well, I'm happy to announce there's been an upgrade in the technology. Barry, you listening?"

"I'm right here, Wally."

"Good. Make it happen."

"Wally, you know I can't do that. The only person here who can give me instructions is the captain."

"All right. Hutch, I guess you'll have to tell him to proceed."

"Proceed with what, Wally?"

"Just tell him to go ahead. Trust me."

Hutch knew Wally well enough that trusting him was not a problem. Still, she didn't want the others to get the impression she was weak. She glanced over at Derek, who was seated beside him, signaling that she should go ahead.

She was about to do it when her instincts cut in. "What's going to happen?"

"Hutch," he said, "where would you like to be at this moment?"

"I don't know. Maybe in New York, headed for one of the shows."

"Good. I don't think we can quite manage that, but we can get close. Tell Barry to run the program."

She didn't see how that could go wrong. "Okay, Barry. Do what Wally set up."

The overhead light and two of the lamps were on. But they faded and the room grew dark. Then a panorama of lights blinked on outside a virtual window that was longer and wider than the two windows that looked out into the unending dark. The blackness had been replaced by a night sky. Among the lights she could see trees and bushes and a stream. It was a park. People were walking, some relaxed on benches, some standing on a small bridge looking down at the water. A couple of kids were running with balloons trailing.

"Beautiful," she said. They rearranged their chairs so they were sitting in a straight line. "Where are we?"

"We're in the second-floor gallery of the Grady Hotel."

"That's Central Park," said Derek.

"That's correct." Wally wore a wide grin. "Over on your left is the American Museum of Natural History. And if you'd like to go to a show, we can't actually walk to the theater, but we can put ourselves into a box seat and watch the performance. We have some of the stuff that's now running on Broadway. Anything anybody would like to see?"

"Maybe later," said Derek. "What else is there?"

"Barry, would you run whatever's next on the program?"

The AI beeped. *"Wally, I need Captain Hutchins to give the directive."*

"I'm sorry. I keep forgetting that when we're actually in flight, I can't control anything. Hutch?"

"Do it, Barry," she said.

The virtual windows disappeared and they were seated behind a handrail under a roof. The park vanished, the star-swept night shifted to midafternoon, and a loud roar filled the room as the park morphed into a massive waterfall.

"Welcome to Niagara," said Barry. *"We're on the Canadian side, on the front porch of the Brookwell Hotel."*

"Brilliant," said Beth.

"If you prefer it at night, Beth," said Barry, *"I can take care of it. And I can also put a full moon in the sky if you wish."*

"The times, they are a-changing," said Hutch. "I have a question."

"Go ahead."

"How come you didn't mention this until now? We've been sitting in here watching TV shows for three days."

"It took me a while to set it up. And anyhow, I think it has a better effect now after all that other stuff."

"What else do you have?" asked Ken.

The waterfall faded, blinked out, and was replaced by a towering snow-capped mountain. It was pure rock and snow. *"The Matterhorn,"* Barry said. Near the top they saw a campfire.

The porch did not change. "We can move the porch around wherever we want," said Wally. "Barry and I both liked the Brookwell. We also have access to Fujiyama, the Eiffel Tower, the Great Wall, the Thames, the Moscow Memorial. We can go to Cuba and sit on a front porch across from where Manuel Octiva used to live." Octiva, of course, was the classical novelist from the previous century.

Hutch was never going to forget the compressed passenger cabin that they'd lived in for the first three days. They'd had a VR tank that provided TV shows and converted the place into a kind of living room. But the black envelope that surrounded the *Eiferman* had never really gone away. They were sitting someplace, watching a high-tech TV. This was different. They were out on a front porch, feeling a soft breeze, watching the moon rise, and listening to birds sing. Wally was beaming.

Barry took them to a beach but put them on a deck with windows this time. Rain was pouring down, and the tide was rolling in. A skylark fluttered toward them, crashed into the glass, and went down. "Oh," said Beth. "I don't think that's a good idea."

"It's okay," said Barry. *"No animals were injured during the creation of these images."*

"Why didn't we have this last year?" Hutch asked. "I can't believe the technology wasn't there."

"Sure, it was there," said Wally. "You just didn't have the right people on board."

"Wally, were you responsible for this?"

"I was part of the team."

"Thank you," she said. "And, Barry?"

"Yes, Captain?"

"You don't need my approval to adjust the scenery."

Priscilla's Journal

Most days are alike. The sun rises, you do whatever the schedule calls for, talk to a few friends and col-

leagues, make some progress on whatever project has taken over your life, come home and have dinner, watch a movie, and go to bed. That's where I was this morning. Where the day blends in with thousands of other days, and ultimately vanishes. But with this day, that's not going to happen.

—Sunday, March 2, 2256

9.

Silently, one by one, in the infinite meadows of Heaven,
Blossomed the lovely stars, the forget-me-nots of the
angels.

—Henry W. Longfellow, "Evangeline, I," 1847

The front porch became a permanent fixture in their lives. They spent most of their time on it, talking, playing cards, watching Broadway shows or TV comedians or simply looking out at mountain ranges. During the first week, Derek and Ken retired to their cabins to pursue projects. Derek was doing cosmological research of some sort, and Ken was working on his FTL history. But they periodically came out and rejoined their colleagues. "It's too depressing in there," Ken said.

Beth made it clear she thought of the mission as a vacation. "Now that we've replaced the passenger cabin with a virtual tour, it would be ridiculous to waste the opportunity." At home she had a private practice, worked on call for the WSA, and also had a hospital connection. "It's at least sixty hours a week," she said. "I hope none of you guys get sick while we're out here, at least nothing we can't fix with a few pills." She especially enjoyed looking out across rivers, lakes, and oceans, and when it was her turn to choose, Hutch knew they were going to someplace wet.

Derek preferred forest scenes filled with deer, squirrels, moose, and ravens. Ken enjoyed historical sites, battlefields, museums, locations where famous events had occurred, especially anything connected with World War II and the American Revolution.

Hutch was all over the map. She enjoyed tourist sites, mountaintops, and places where she could watch skiers gliding past. To provide some variation, Wally arranged to convert the front porch into a virtual vehicle that moved along country roads in New Hampshire. It didn't quite work, though, because he couldn't insert the wind and the bounces of an actual ride.

But they all missed the news reports. They were cut off from the world. They wondered how the country was reacting to the WSA's failure to stop the mission. There was no question in Hutch's mind that MacAllister was raising hell. He was not a guy you wanted on the other side of an argument.

Derek insisted he wasn't losing any sleep over the matter. "By the time we get back," he told her, "it will have cooled off. Nothing lasts more than five days in the headlines unless more issues show up. That's obviously not happening with us."

"What we did," said Hutch, "is going to be perceived as pretty heavy-handed, Derek. Will you be able to salvage your career?"

"The WSA's not my career, Priscilla. I'm an astronomer.

I've had a good run, and if they terminate me, I'll have no problem landing somewhere else. And I think you'll be okay too. You're the face of the program these days. And even if they *did* decide they weren't going to use you anymore, any of the interstellar corporations would love to have you. Or you might talk to Ken about writing an autobiography. You're bulletproof, kid."

Hutch wasn't so sure.

The problem with the corporations was that they didn't really go anywhere. If she got hired by TransGalactic, all she'd do would be take tourists around the solar system, and occasionally the more adventurous ones to 61 Cygni to look at the Blue Cone left by the Monument Makers. Or possibly haul supplies and passengers to Quraqua and Pinnacle. Her life would become nothing more than riding back and forth to the same places. She'd prefer making her living as a speaker. She enjoyed having an audience, and she was well known because of her encounter with the omega cloud last year. People were prepared to make substantial payments to bring her into various civic, religious, and educational events. Though Hutch made it a practice not to charge schools or nonprofits. She lost nothing through her generosity. The events served to expand her position as a celebrity.

"I'm in a fairly good spot," she said. "But I'd just as soon pass on the bullets."

Derek tried to reply, but whatever he said was overwhelmed by a sudden rush of laughs and shrieks from the front porch.

They had thirteen Broadway shows on file, and decided to watch one every third evening to make them last. "Do we have *Farewell to London?"* asked Ken. It was the biggest hit show of the past two years.

Wally posted the titles. And yes, they had it. Along with *Lost in Paradise,* another major hit. And some comedies: *Time and Tide; It's a Long Way to Albuquerque; Lights Out, Louie;* and *Love at Zero Gee.* Ken suggested they start by watching *Farewell to London.*

"Why don't we hold it aside for a while?" said Beth.

"Why's that?"

"That's probably the best show we have."

"So, what's your point?" asked Wally.

"It might be a good idea to save *Farewell to London* and a couple of the comedies so we have them on the way back. If this mission doesn't have a good outcome, we might need the lighter stuff."

"Okay by me," said Ken.

It sounded good to everybody. They started with *Riot Act,* a light comedy that had been running for three years. Ken and Beth had seen it before and were happy to watch it again. Then they switched to some game-playing in which different teams were trying to rescue stranded sailors from an oncoming tidal wave. They watched some recorded TV programs over the next few days. And they played bridge and poker, traded stories, and just hung out.

Time was passing quickly, the way it does when life is a pleasure. On the morning of March 10th, when they were not quite halfway to their destination, Hutch arrived in the passenger cabin still half asleep. Beth and Ken were on the porch, gazing placidly out from Moonbase at the Earth. They said hello and she sat down with them. They exchanged trivialities. "You sleep okay?" "How was breakfast?" "I really enjoyed that movie last night."

At home, this was her favorite time of year. Spring was in sight and the birds were getting loud.

Derek Blanchard's Notebooks

We all settled in on the front porch after dinner, and Wally had another surprise for us. It was his turn to pick the landscape. He moved the hotel to the top of a hill overlooking a large lake rimmed by forest. It was midafternoon and the sun was still high in the western sky. We were sitting there enjoying the view, talking about nothing in particular, when Ken called our attention to a dinosaur. It was a brontosaurus down at the edge of the lake, drinking. I sat there thinking how much I'd give to see a real one. I mean, traveling around the Milky Way, there should be a few places that have them. Though after I thought about it some more, I realized maybe it wouldn't be such a good idea at that. Still, I was struck by the image of that thing guzzling water and raising its head to swallow, and looking around to see if it had any company. I know it's only VR, but I suspect this is one of those moments I'll remember.

—Monday, March 10, 2256

10.

The stars are out, obscured
Only in places
By wispy clouds.
From the niche I've found
Among the rocks
(Shaped like a chair with stone pillows) I
Gaze at the stars
Tiny light bulbs in a black ceiling,
Ceaseless wonders.
                    —Steven Croft, "The Beach at Night," 2001

They were due to arrive at their destination on March 23. Barry maintained a calendar on the bridge, and as they got within a few days of their destination, they changed their minds about saving *Farewell to London* for the return flight. They agreed that they needed some laughs, so they settled in to watch the acclaimed comedy. Hutch was seated beside Beth. Beth had been its leading proponent, but she changed her mind within the first ten minutes when Julia's boyfriend, Hank, the love of her life, turned out to be a guy who just didn't really care as much as he'd let her think. It wasn't that he was simply playing her for sex but rather that he was lonely, had gotten his heart broken recently, and was trying to replace the other woman. But the chemistry wasn't working, and that became obvious early.

Hutch didn't care for it either. It was hard to see why it was proclaimed as a comedy. In another setting, she might have been more open to *Farewell to London*, but this was just the wrong time. It was all about people reacting to loss in foolish ways. And Wally had done an effective job of building in the sounds, the rain and wind and music, which made it even more depressing. When Hank told her it was over and walked away, leaving her with tears running down her cheeks, the small audience sat frozen. Hutch's eyes grew damp even though she understood that no permanent arrangement between the pair would have been anything other than a disaster. That in the long term Julia was fortunate. But this wasn't the kind of show you wanted to watch if you were looking for something to brighten your mood. It might have worked in New York, where you could have headed out to a bar after the performance and laughed at the blunders of the major characters. But the audience on the *Eiferman* had lost the stars almost two weeks earlier. And now their collective hearts. And it wasn't just Beth and Hutch who were affected. Wally and Ken both needed a couple of minutes before they trusted their voices. Derek seemed the only one able to shrug it off.

When the lights came on—Wally did everything to present them with the sense of being in a theater—they picked themselves up and headed for the galley. "Time for a snack," Hutch said.

Wally grabbed a couple of cinnamon buns and sat down. The others were still trying to decide what they wanted. He tasted his coffee and looked directly at her. "Well," he said, "what did you think?"

"It's a pretty strong show."

"I thought so too." His eyes had locked with hers. She knew what was coming. "When we get home, I'd love to take you to dinner or breakfast or whatever's happening on the station. Any chance you'd be open to that?"

"Not much point, Wally. I'm committed."

He smiled. "Well, I guess I had nothing to lose."

Her reaction had been reflexive, and his disappointment was clear. A sense of guilt began to rise in her. They sat and talked for a short while, not about anything she would remember ten minutes later. But Wally was a decent enough guy. He could carry a conversation, he was reasonable, and his enthusiasm frequently shone in his brown eyes. He wasn't movie-star handsome, but he looked okay, about average height, probably an inch taller than she was. The problem was that they just didn't share any interests other than star flight. And of course, they'd both been around long enough to know the dangers of setting up a relationship on a long-term mission. She was impressed that he'd tried his luck anyhow.

During the following days, something changed. They cut back on the entertainment. They didn't spend most of their time anymore caught up in movies and shows. Beth sensed it too. She said she wasn't sure what had happened. When Wally commented that it was *Farewell to London*, Hutch shook her head. "It's more than that."

"What is it then?" asked Derek. "Are we all just getting bored?"

It wasn't boredom. And it wasn't the show. "I think," said Ken, "just sitting on the porch looking out at Wally's stars has set us up somehow. We hang around here and watch the tide come in, and I think it reminds us of where we are, and what's gone missing."

Beth agreed. "When we get home," she said, "we're going to discover an appreciation for the things we've been taking for granted over a lifetime. Instead of VR, we'll start paying attention to real sunrises and squirrels and oak trees. And the other people in our lives."

"And beautiful women," said Wally. "Oh, I forgot. I guess we already do that." He glanced sidewise at Hutch. The offer was still open.

"You know," Ken said, "the last few mornings we mostly watched a couple of quiz shows and dance contests. Nobody's asking to put them back on today. Do we want to do that?"

They looked at one another. "Not really," said Beth.

"The real value of communications technology," he continued, "is that it keeps us in contact with the rest of the world. We can fake it, but we're seriously cut off in here."

"Anybody want to play some pinochle?" asked Wally.

Over the next few nights they tried gaming, VR challenges that sent them on rescue missions for people trapped in barbarian lands, or in starships caught in declining orbits that were about to suck them into gas giants. They were okay, but ultimately, they found it more rewarding to spend their time on the front porch, talking about where they were and how they were reacting to it. And pointing out that they were only five days out from their target, and then four days, and how it was almost over. And how much, when they got back to Earth, they'd enjoy wandering into a bar in Alexandria or wherever. "I have a feeling," Ken said, "that what we are really going to learn from this mission is how much we care about home. And how much we take for granted."

Somewhere, Hutch heard a voice. She opened her eyes and looked up at the dark overhead. Then the bed shook.

"Captain Hutchins. Please wake."

It was Barry. The mattress was still again. "What happened?" she asked.

"The drive unit is not performing properly."

She got up and pulled on her robe. The deck trembled as she started for the door. It wasn't a jolt but more like a blip. But there shouldn't be any palpitations or shudders of any kind. "What's the problem, Barry? Can you tell?"

"I do not know."

She opened the door and made for the bridge. Behind her, someone else was coming. Wally.

"You have any idea what this might be?" she asked him.

"No," he said. "Let's shut the drive down so I can take a look."

"If we shut it down, are you certain we'll be able to restart it?"

"Depends on what the problem is."

She slipped into her seat. Wally sat down beside her. He was in his pajamas. "If we get stuck here," she said, "we're all dead. Let's get back out into normal space. If things don't go well, at least we'll be able to send a hypercomm and get a rescue mission moving."

"You think they'd go to that much trouble after we just walked out on them?"

"Let's just do it the sane way, Wally." She activated the

allcomm as another shiver ran through the ship. "Everybody wake up, please. Out of bed and belt down. We're having a minor issue. We're going to return to normal space in a couple of minutes. Let me know when you're secure."

Wally didn't look especially worried. Hopefully, that was an accurate view of his thinking and not a professional stance he'd taken to avoid alarming anyone.

Eiferman Log

0316 hours: Everybody has checked in, and we've just shut down the Locarno. Fortunately, whatever the problem is, it did not prevent our surfacing.

—Thursday, March 20, 2256

11.

Beauty is the only thing that time cannot harm. Philosophies fall away like sand, and creeds follow one another like the withered leaves of autumn; but what is beautiful is a joy for all seasons and a possession for all eternity.
—Oscar Wilde, "The English Renaissance of Art, 1882," New York lecture, January 9

This is my fault," Derek said after Wally had disappeared belowdecks to work on the drive.

Hutch couldn't take her eyes off the cloud of stars on their port side. "What do you mean?"

"Howard told me something like this might happen."

"Who's Howard?"

"The maintenance chief at the station."

"Because they didn't have time to finish."

"Yes. Damn it, we didn't *have* time. They were asking for another two days. He said we'd probably be all right but he couldn't guarantee anything."

"All right. Let's not get excited. Wally will probably be able to fix the problem."

"Let's hope." He was keeping his voice low.

Hutch pointed at the cloud. "You have any idea what that is?"

"I think it's the Wasserman. A globular cluster."

"How many stars are in there?"

"About thirty thousand."

"They look jammed together."

"It's approximately forty-six light-years across. They're old stars, most of them almost as old as the universe. A lot are Class G dwarfs, like the sun. That's because whatever other types of stars were in there weren't as stable and they're all pretty much gone by now."

"Pity we're not going *there*. That looks as if it would be a spectacular view if we got inside it. Would it ever get dark in there?"

"I doubt it. Maybe when we get past all this stay-at-home nonsense, we could come back and visit the place."

"Why are you so interested?" asked Ken.

It wasn't clear to whom the question was directed. But Derek responded: "They've been around so long. The suns are ancient and stable. That raises the possibility of advanced life. There'll be planetary systems so close to one another that it's hard to believe they haven't been in touch. There's no place anywhere more likely to have a high level of development than a cluster. They could even manage without a star drive."

Hutch had never thought about that kind of possibility. "How close would they be to each other?" she asked.

"If they were evenly distributed, they'd only be about a light-year apart."

"But they aren't?"

"No. Toward the center, they're thickly grouped."

"I wonder," Ken said, "what kind of civilization would develop on a world that never got dark."

Hutch glanced at the receiver. She wanted to hear something from Wally. Something good.

"Who's Wasserman?" Ken asked.

Derek couldn't resist a reaction that suggested it was hard to believe that a historian wouldn't recognize the name. "*Lawrence* Wasserman. He was a twenty-first-century astronomer. Did a lot of work with asteroids."

"I wonder," said Hutch, "if he were here, whether he wouldn't want to go into the cluster and look around."

Wally had been working for about a half hour when he reported back. "It's okay. It was just a short in the auxiliary power converter. Fortunately, we have a spare on board. I'll need an hour. I'm going to stay with it for a while, make sure I've got everything. Then we should be all right."

Derek looked relieved. They all did. "Couldn't have picked a better place to break down," he said.

Hutch angled the ship so the passenger cabin got a good view of the Wasserman. They all rearranged their chairs and watched it through the long window. It was dazzling, a sky overwhelmed with stars.

"It's incredible," said Beth. "We're not talking about going into that thing, are we?"

"There's plenty of space for us," said Derek. "There wouldn't be anything to worry about."

Ken cleared his throat. "Why does that sound like something that gets engraved on a tombstone?"

Derek laughed. "You've got a point, Ken." He was standing with his right hand shielding his eyes. "Barry, can we hear anything out there? Any radio transmissions?"

"There are radio waves, of course. But I'm not getting anything that would seem out of the ordinary."

"Put it on a speaker, please," said Derek.

It was just a chaotic batch of squeaks and squeals.

"Barry," said Hutch, "if there were artificial signals mixed in there, would you be able to make the determination?"

"Not easily, Captain. It is seriously turbulent."

Derek's brow wrinkled and he looked toward Wally. "Didn't we have a package to take care of that?"

"The package didn't get here in time."

"Damn."

"I'm sorry. We were concentrating on safety issues."

"It's okay." He looked frustrated. "I wonder what else didn't get taken care of."

"I can try to set up a program," said Barry. *"But I'll need some help."*

"All right," said Hutch.

Derek was looking out the window again. "How far are we from the cluster?"

"Approximately nine light-years."

"It really does look like a galaxy," said Ken.

Beth raised her coffee cup to it. "It would be hard to believe there aren't a few civilizations in there somewhere."

Derek was shaking his head. "I wish we could get a Van Entel out here. This is where we really need one." He leaned back against the chair.

"Why," said Ken, "don't we go in and look around?"

Hutch looked toward Derek. "That would be outside

the mission objectives," she said. "But we should do a short jump to test the repairs. It doesn't really make much difference what direction we go."

Derek sat on the bridge with Hutch. "What's the best way to do this?"

"There's a fair amount of guesswork here. Let's start with a jump of seven light-years. That'll get us close. It'll give us a better look at the cluster, and we can decide where we go from there."

"Excellent, Priscilla. How long will it take?"

"A little better than a half hour."

"Incredible," he said.

The Locarno was still charging. It sounded okay, and Wally assured her everything was in order. They waited until it shut down and the green ready light came on. Then Hutch opened the allcomm. "Anybody need time before we start?"

Wally responded: *"The chairs are locked down, Hutch. And everybody's harnessed. We're good when you are."*

"Okay. We'll make our move in three minutes." She looked over at Derek. "Good luck."

"To you as well, Priscilla."

The timer started its countdown. "Okay, people," she said, "we're on the move." She fired the ship's engines and began a short turn to port. The Wasserman drifted through the night until it was directly in front of them. Then she began to accelerate. A minute later she activated the Locarno and the stars vanished.

When they came out of the jump, the entire sky had been taken over by the cluster. Stars filled the night, forming a vast, blazing cloud. Elsewhere, on the outskirts, they were spread across the heavens, allowing little space between them. Hutch listened as Derek's breathing changed.

"You all right?" she asked.

"It's incredible, Priscilla."

"If I'd known we were going to do something like this, I'd have brought sunglasses."

"How far out are we?"

"Depends on where the edge is. You could probably argue that we're already inside."

He looked down at the AI's blue lamp. "Barry?"

"Yes, Derek."

"If you get anything at all that sounds like an artificial signal, let us know, okay?"

"I will. But the traffic is overwhelming."

They continued on course for about an hour. Derek stayed on the bridge. Ken came out and took up a position behind Hutch's seat. Then Beth joined them. And finally Wally. Barry took pictures of the cluster. They took pictures of themselves looking at it through the window. And eventually, Ken asked whether they could go to the center of the cluster. "I mean," he said, "would it be safe?"

"I don't see any reason why it wouldn't be," she said.

"That sounds as if you're not certain."

"We'll be all right."

"Imagine living on a world in there," Beth said. "You think it ever gets dark?"

"Let's go find out," said Derek.

Beth looked uneasy. "With all that crowding, isn't there a possibility we'll surface too close to something?"

"We'll be okay," said Hutch. "We have a sensor that won't let us emerge in dangerous territory."

She stayed on cruise for a while, allowing the Locarno to recharge. Then she took them in close. They surfaced under the most spectacular sky she'd ever seen. They stared out at the crowded stars. With one exception, they were still only stars, but with almost no space between them. The exception appeared as a small sun, at a range of about three hundred million kilometers. They turned out the lights in the ship but still had enough illumination to read by on the port side, where the sun was. They drifted for almost an hour. "Marvelous," said Derek. "I'm glad we did it. If we get nothing else out of this, the trip will have been worth it."

Beth Squires's Notes

This has been one of the most exciting days in my life. It feels like something they'll make into a movie one day. They've already done that with one of Hutch's missions. Lyra Calkins played her. Wally thinks Hutch looks better and should have played herself. I asked whether she'd been given that option and she said no. She told me that one of the script writers said they'd considered it, but that the feeling was she was a bit too stiff. If this one gets made into a movie, I can't help wondering who they'd get to play me. Maybe Cora Baxter?

—Thursday, March 20, 2256

12.

Derek was on the bridge. "Another three days," he said. "We need a better drive unit." He was grinning. Of everyone on board, no one was so overwhelmed by the velocity they had with the Locarno. Hutch understood that she'd never grasped the reality of the distances involved in interstellar travel. The destination might have been light-years away, but when you traveled using a hyperdrive, it always played out in terms of days or weeks. But Derek was different. He seemed to have a grasp of the vast distances involved. And the time. No one was more aware than he that, if they could view the Earth up close as it was at that moment, the occupants were maybe getting started on their first pyramids.

"I wonder," he said, "if the Monument Makers ever got out this far?"

"I don't know."

"What have we got now? Seventeen of them?"

"You sound annoyed." Eighteen was correct. One more, a golden wing, had been discovered six months earlier. Fourteen were in orbit, and four were on the ground.

"Priscilla, I've never been a fan of them."

"The Monument Makers? I don't think I understand, Derek. What do you have against them?"

"What did they ever do? They had all that technology and all we've seen from them are these pedestals and whatnot they left around. Why didn't they do something constructive?"

"For example?"

"Maybe find a way to keep their descendants safe. They allowed their own world to go to hell."

"I think you're being a little hard on them. Time takes everything down."

"All right. They could have said hello."

"They did."

"I mean something a little more useful than a self-portrait. How about inscribing a cure for cancer on some of those things? Cancer is not uncommon. The Noks have a problem with it. We know that several species of animals across at least a half dozen worlds are afflicted with it. No matter where it shows up, it's always the same. How long were *we* wrestling with it while it killed off tens of thousands? Probably millions? Or maybe they could have shown us a way that kids could be born without handicaps. I can think of a lot of things they might have done. But no, all they seemed able to do was run around bragging about how they'd been somewhere first. Who was that guy who used to leave signs? 'Gumball was here.' Something like that."

"Kilroy."

"Whatever." He got up. "I gotta go lie down."

Ken, Beth, and Wally were seated in the passenger cabin when she came in off the bridge. They'd turned on one of Hutch's favorite settings, a country porch surrounded by trees and bushes in the path of a warm southern breeze. Something by Beethoven played softly in the background. Ken was reading while the other two talked. He looked up and raised a hand. Hutch sat down beside him. "Is that a history?" she asked.

"Not exactly," he said. "It's Andre Sainte-Angelou's *Harbingers.*"

Hutch had read the book two months earlier, immediately after its release. It was an attempt to explain where the omega clouds came from, and how they functioned. Unfortunately, her grasp of physics was too shaky to allow a dependable analysis. "What do you think of it?" she asked.

"It's all guesswork. I don't think there's any question they were weapons. And somehow they got out of control."

"I know. It's hard to see how they could have evolved naturally. But they were intelligent beings. I'm not sure how that equates to weaponry." She sat back, closed her eyes, and let the scent of gardenias, sweet lemongrass, and honeysuckle envelop her.

Ken shook his head. "Who knows? Maybe we discovered what super soldiers really look like. By the way, I should say thanks."

"For what?"

"For helping make all this possible. Hutch, I've been

reading and theorizing about history all my life. This is the first time I've had a chance to be part of it." He closed the notebook. "A thousand years from now, people will still be talking about this mission."

"Even if we don't find anything?"

"It's the first mission to track down the origin of a TV signal. When you do something that's never been done before, it's automatically historic." He gazed across the porch at a pair of azalea bushes. "I know this is no big deal for you. I mean, you were on the first flight to the galactic core. That's about as historic as it gets. But this mission's not over yet." He sat back in his chair. "We have a Photoshopped picture at home of me standing between Celeste Larsen and Elliott Paul in front of Paul's home outside London." Larsen, of course, was the ultimate physicist of the era, the Einstein of the twenty-third century. And Paul had led the remarkably successful effort to introduce liberal education and a healthy tolerance for conflicting opinions into the darkest areas of the Middle East. He'd put his life at risk constantly, but in the end, his work had inspired a revolution. "The picture's in our living room on a book shelf. People come in and they tend to say, 'Hey, I know Ken, but who are those other two guys?'"

"Ken," she said, "I'm glad you're with us."

"Derek knew what my attitude is toward all this. We've known each other a long time. He was upset because of the defunding of the Academy, which of course resulted in what had started out as space exploration getting handed over to the corporates, who've simply turned it all into a profiteering operation. Find a few rich people who want to go visit a nearby star. And then do it again. And keep doing it. Meantime, they were happy to buy into the notion that we were virtually alone. That there are so few advanced worlds in the universe at any one time that the chances of locating any of them are virtually nil. And these are the same people who are now claiming we need to be careful because of all those dangerous aliens out there."

"Maybe in a billion years," she said, "conditions will be different."

"A universe filled with species talking to one another? Collaborating? Vacationing on one another's worlds?" His face wrinkled. "Actually, now that I think of it, I'm not sure that taking the mystery out of things wouldn't leave us all bored."

"You have a point, Ken."

"I have a question for you."

"Okay."

"We left the copilot behind. What do we do if something happens to *you*? If you were to get seriously ill or something?"

"It wouldn't be a problem. Barry could get you home."

"The AI?"

"Sure."

"Then why on earth do we need a pilot?"

"I'm here mostly to react to unexpected contingencies. To problems. Especially on a flight like this, where we have no idea what might happen."

"All right. I guess that makes sense."

Beth smiled at Ken. "You'd love having a couple of aliens on board, wouldn't you? Like they do in the movies."

They obviously had a good marriage. "Tell me about your kids," Hutch asked.

"A couple of girls," said Beth. "Madeleine and Hannah. They're teens. They'd have enjoyed meeting you."

"We can arrange it when we get home."

Wally seemed somewhat alone. Hutch wondered if he'd left someone behind. She missed her cop. She wasn't sure she hadn't lost him. That last pizza they'd shared hadn't gone well, and he'd made no effort to get in touch with her and say good-bye before she left.

She'd have enjoyed having Charlie and Maureen on board. Maybe one day, families would travel routinely across the stars. *Why don't we take a run over to Aldebaran and say hello to Uncle Mike?*

"All those silent stars," Beth said as they left the cluster. "You'd think somebody in there would have a transmitter."

"I'm sure somebody does," said Hutch. "But it's time we go to Calliope."

They watched comedies more frequently than anything else. They turned it into a game, using technology that allowed them to insert one of themselves into a role in the film. The chosen person left the porch and the others decided which role he or she would be inserted into. Which role, they claimed, best fitted the reality of the individual. Ken became Jasper Hall, the cheapskate comedian who'd do anything to hang onto a dime. Derek showed up as the host of *The Night Show*, where he introduced Beth as the whacky journalist of *Breaking Now*. Wally played Horace Evans in one of the haunted museum films, where he directed a team of archeologists tracking down the supposed truth about various unexplained historical events. And they brought Hutch in as the lead in *Cool Clara*, a high school teacher given to panic attacks because her students are constantly out of control.

Mostly, though, they just sat on the porch talking. Hutch got more serious about encouraging everyone to establish a workout program. Derek and Ken, both talented chess players, developed a serious rivalry. Wally spent a lot of time in the workout room, but mostly what he wanted was to watch Beth and Hutch do their stretch exercises. The area could only accommodate three at a time, so Hutch set up a schedule, warned her passengers that the limited level of artificial gravity, well below Earth normal, could create problems if they didn't stay with the program. Eventually, everyone got in line, after Hutch pointed out that they had to make a choice: do the exercises or pass on dessert.

Ken lodged a complaint. "You know," he said, "when we started, I thought we'd have more important things to worry about than the distribution of apple pie."

Beth Squires's Notes

How much formal education is really little more than indoctrination? People with graduate degrees seem to provide a substantial level of understanding of cosmological physics, of 21st century American literature, of mathematics, while often keeping their minds closed to opposing ideas or even common sense. What we seem to be good at doing is persuading individuals that they are considerably more knowledgeable in general than the rest of the population without actually thinking about the issues. If there really is a judgment of some sort, I wonder if the charges lodged against us will turn out to be considerably different from those we hear from the pulpit on Sundays? "I gave you a brain, Beth, and you never used it."

—Saturday, March 22, 2256

13.

And that inverted bowl they call the sky,
Whereunder crawling coop'd we live and die,
Lift not your hands to it for help—for it
As impotently rolls as you or I.
    —Edward Fitzgerald, translation of "The Rubaiyat of
                Omar Khayyam" (c. 1100), 1887

Finally, at midmorning March 23, Barry informed Hutch that they had arrived. *Transition into normal space is one hour away.* Everybody had known, of course, that this was the day. They also knew of the lack of precision involved in locating the target area. They'd be lucky if they arrived within a hundred light-years of Calliope.

They sat in the galley, congratulating one another, and enjoying a late breakfast. "Hutch, how fast is the star moving?" said Ken, trying to get the details right for his book.

"About forty kilometers per second."

"Stars routinely move that fast?"

"A lot of them do, yes. Some of them move considerably faster."

He turned to Derek. "So it's traveled pretty far since the place where it was when you saw it in the Van Entel."

"That's correct." Derek's brow wrinkled while he juggled the numbers. "It's traveled roughly 173 billion kilometers."

"That would be a long walk."

"It would."

"Hutch, since we know its trajectory and everything, we'll make our exit nearby, right?"

"We know the trajectory and velocity. It's the distance from Earth where we had to do some guesswork. But we should be okay. What we need is for someone to invent a scope that penetrates through the dimensions. That would allow us to look outside and see where we are before we jump out."

"That sounds like a good idea," said Ken.

"I'm not sure it's possible."

"It probably is," said Derek. "We already have a sensor that won't let us surface inside a planet or a star or even too close to a piece of rock."

When they got within a few minutes of the transdimensional leap, Hutch returned to the bridge with Derek, while the others took their seats in the passenger cabin, locked the chairs in place, and belted down.

"Okay, Barry," she said, "activate the Locarno."

The drive came on line. It hummed softly, like a life support unit in the hull.

"Let's hope," said Derek, "we're within a few light-years."

"Seven thousand years is a long time," she said. "I

wonder whether any civilization can last that long. Judging by what we've seen so far, most of them seem to collapse pretty quickly."

"Five minutes," said Barry.

"What's this star look like?" asked Beth, speaking through the allcomm.

Wally responded. *"Like every other star in the sky."*

"So how do we tell it from the others?"

Derek took it from there: "We have its spectrum, Beth. We have a telescope so Barry should have no trouble identifying Calliope."

Wally asked whether each star's spectrum was unique, and that led to a discussion that quickly faded from Hutch's attention. Barry came in on her personal channel to inform her they were at one minute. She broke into the conversation. "Get ready, guys. Let's finish this on the other side."

The AI counted down the last twenty seconds, Derek thanked Hutch for a smooth ride, and then they were out under the stars again. The near-blinding effect of the Wasserman Cluster was of course gone, although it was still visible behind them, a relatively dim cloud now.

"Everybody okay?"

"It makes me want to throw up," said Ken.

"You all right?" Beth's voice.

"Yeah. I'm okay. I think I need a cinnamon bun."

"Anybody else with a problem?"

"I'm good," said Barry.

She laughed. "All right, people. We're hunting for Calliope. That might take a while. In the meantime, you can unbelt and wander around." Hutch switched over to the AI. "Glad you're okay, Barry. Do you know where we are?"

He would be comparing the sky with what the star patterns would look like had they emerged close to Calliope. *"Give me a minute, Captain."*

Derek got up, opened the door, and paused. "Priscilla, let me know as soon as you have something." He disappeared into the passenger cabin. She sat quietly for several minutes, staring out at the sky, looking maybe for moving lights, for something that would give them what they were hoping for. But she saw nothing unusual.

Finally, Barry was back. *"We did extremely well, Captain. We are within thirty light-years of Calliope."*

"Great. Have you found it yet? The star?"

"No. I don't see it. But despite our enthusiasm, thirty light-years is a considerable distance. Let's just stay on course and get closer."

Hutch went back and ordered a sandwich while she waited. Beth joined her. "How does Barry know we're thirty light-years away if he can't see Calliope yet?"

"The first thing he did when we surfaced was to take a look at the sky. He has a chart of twenty-four marker stars. He knows what their positions should look like if we're close to Calliope. There's no way to be precise when you're dealing with these kinds of distances. We never really knew how far Calliope was. The range was an estimate. Nothing more."

"So how long will the next jump be?"

"About three hours."

"Well, that's not bad."

"You look tired, Beth."

"I'd just like to get out of here for a while. I hope we find a place where we can land and walk around a little."

"I know. I think everybody'd like to get outside and watch a sunset."

They were finishing the sandwiches when Beth asked how many more jumps they would have to make. "Maybe one more after this next one," said Hutch. "When we surface this time, we'll probably be inside the system. Assuming it *has* planets."

Wally leaned in. "I told you guys we should have brought some rum. How are we supposed to celebrate with iced tea?"

Derek rejoined Hutch on the bridge. "Good luck to us," he said.

Barry reported that they were ready to go. Hutch told everyone to belt down and took them under. Derek sat quietly in his chair. They'd run out of conversation. There was nothing left to talk about that they hadn't worn down. "I don't think," he said finally, "that monkey brains were designed for this kind of activity."

"I was thinking the same thing," she said. "I don't much like flying. When I travel at home, I prefer a place we can drive to. I like to watch the countryside go by."

Derek grinned. "Odd comment coming from a lady who pilots interstellars."

"It's true." She got up. "I'm going back to crash for a couple of hours."

She never really did get to sleep. After lying for an hour on her bunk, she tried reading. Eventually, she wandered back out to the front porch and joined her passengers. Derek was with them. They were speculating about what they would find. A culture advanced beyond human imagination? Or the bones of a lost civilization? Or possibly nothing at all. There was, of course, the possibility that the signal had actually come from a place far beyond Calliope, that it had simply passed through the system during the moment that it was lined up with the Van Entel. Or that the source had been simply a ship passing through the Calliope system, aiming its transmission at a target that got in front of the supertelescope.

With twenty minutes remaining, she returned to the bridge. She sat down and looked at the window. You didn't actually look *through* it. There was no sense of peering out into a void. It was just darkness.

"Sometimes," Derek said, "I think technological advances are actually a step back." She hadn't been aware he had followed her in.

When they surfaced, nothing substantive had changed. They looked out at essentially the same scattered stars that had occupied the sky a few hours earlier. Hutch had hoped to see a sun, which would have been Calliope. It wasn't there. There was nothing in front of them that stood out. A couple of the stars could have been perceived as first magnitude, but both were off to port. And a cloud of stars was visible on the starboard side.

"*I do not see it,*" said Barry.

"We might simply have gotten the estimates wrong," Hutch said. "Check the spectrums of the bright ones."

"*Will do that shortly, Captain. I should inform you, however, that the locations of the marker stars that I've had time* to examine are precisely correct. We should be within about three billion kilometers of the Calliope system. There is nothing within that range in any direction."

A few minutes later he was back with readings on the two bright stars: Neither was a match. In fact, both were among the marker stars.

"So, where is it?" asked Derek.

"I have no explanation, sir."

A few minutes later Barry was back. "Captain, I've checked out almost the entire list of markers. It should be here. In plain sight."

Derek was seriously annoyed. "How about that cloud to our right?"

"It can't be. The markers would not line up."

"When will you be finished checking them?"

"In a couple of minutes. So far they're exactly where they should be if Calliope were a short distance in front of us."

Beth appeared in the doorway. "What's wrong?"

"It's missing," Derek said.

Beth frowned. "What's missing? The star?"

"Yes," said Barry. "Calliope is nowhere visible. And let me correct myself about the markers. One of them is out of position. That shouldn't be, either."

"Maybe," said Derek, "if we maneuver into the area where everything lines up, we'll be able to find it." There was a note of annoyance in his voice.

"We can't do better than this, Derek. There is nowhere we can move which will not cause disruption among the markers."

"Which one is out of line?"

"Number nine on the list." He put a section of the local stars on the display and circled one. Then he placed a golden star beside it. *"The deviation is not extreme, but it's considerably more than can be explained."*

"Well," said Derek, "I have to admit I've always loved a good mystery. But I'm not sure about this one."

"It sounds as if the original data was incorrect," said Beth.

"Yeah." Derek shook his head. "It's possible. Hutch, how many markers did we have?"

"Twenty-four."

"Barry?"

"Yes, sir?"

"You're saying we can't make any adjustment in our position that would put us in line with all the markers?"

"That is correct, sir." Hutch couldn't recall having heard Barry sound freaked out before, but there was no mistaking his tone.

"The markers are obviously screwed up," said Derek. "Start running Calliope's spectrogram against them, Barry. One of those stars out there has to be the one we're looking for."

Beth shook her head. "Why don't we contact Union? Check with them?"

"We're too far out," said Derek. "Even the hypercomm can't help at this range."

Beth looked frustrated. Everybody did. How could a star just disappear?

"Okay, look," said Derek, "we know some part of our data is wrong. But if Calliope's spectrogram is correct, we can still find it. Let's run the spectrogram ID against every star we can see. I'm willing to bet the damned thing's out there. We just need a little patience." He was staring out at the sky, biting his lower lip, his eyes empty. "I wonder if somebody connected with the Save the Earth Foundation didn't deliberately arrange this?"

"Hutch," said Barry, *"one of the other marker stars is astray."*

"You mean not where it should be?"

"That is correct. I've now checked all of them and two are out of position. I've run Calliope's spectrum against both. Neither is a match."

They sat for several minutes, no one saying much. Eventually, Barry came back. *"I've checked each of the markers. None of them fits Calliope's spectrogram. I am now proceeding to check every other visible star. Be advised it will take a while."*

Ken appeared in the doorway. "How could something like this happen?"

"Captain," Barry said, *"do you wish I check only those visible in the sense of what can be seen by the naked eye, or should I employ the telescope? If we do that, the number to be examined will increase astronomically."* He delivered the line without any suggestion of humor.

"It has to be out there somewhere."

"Of course it does," said Derek. "But we don't have the supplies to maintain a mission of indefinite length."

That evening, they brought their dinners onto the front porch and sat looking out at a branch of the Rocky Mountains. But Derek barely touched his food. "I don't understand how we could have screwed up the data for the markers. The people who put it together have been with us a long time, and they had the assignment completed well before we left. They weren't under the kind of pressure the maintenance people were. And I just don't believe any of them would have done something like this deliberately. Mandy Evans runs the unit, and I'd trust her with my life."

"So, what's next?" Hutch asked. "If Calliope doesn't turn up out there somewhere, do we have any other options?"

"Not really. We can hang out while Barry sorts through a half-million stars. Or we can give it up and leave."

"I'm sorry, Derek. I don't know what to say."

"Neither do I, Priscilla. Well, for what it's worth, at least we'll be home for most of the baseball season."

They were halfway through the meal when Barry's blinker lit up. Hutch excused herself and went onto the bridge, knowing it couldn't be good news or the AI would simply have announced it. "What do you have?" she asked, keeping her voice down and reducing the volume on the speaker.

"Captain, I've checked every star within eighty light-years. I can't find a match for Calliope. If you wish, I can extend the search farther."

"Stay with it," she said. "Go to one hundred and twenty light-years. It's all we have now."

Derek was waiting for her when she came back. He looked at her without saying anything. She let him see that they had nothing. He just shook his head.

"Still nothing?" asked Ken.

Derek nodded at Hutch. *Tell them.*

"No match anywhere for Calliope."

"So what do we do now?" said Ken. "Do we have a recourse?"

"Well." Derek lifted his cup of coffee. "Not really. We never thought to bring the whiskey."

**Derek Blanchard, Extract from Notebook,
Intended for Autobiography**

There's a red giant that's running out of fuel and will probably explode within the next million years or so. I don't have a reading on its distance, but it can't be too far since it's visible to the naked eye. If we aren't going to find the people who were lighting up their planetary system, I'd be willing to settle for a close-up look at a star that is on the verge of going supernova. Why not? Who else has done that? And, you know, what could possibly go wrong?

—Tuesday, April 1, 2256

14.

Human existence is girt round with mystery; the narrow region of our experience is a small island in the midst of a boundless sea. To add to the mystery, the domain of our earthly existence is not only an island in infinite space, but also in infinite time. The past and the future are alike shrouded from us: we neither know the origin of anything which is, nor its final destination.
—J. S. Mill, *Three Essays on Religion*, 1874

You want to go get a close-up of a supernova?" Hutch was not happy.

"No, no," Derek said. "It's just a red supergiant. It's burning up the last of its fuel. When that happens, it *will* go supernova. But the process will probably take a while. Maybe a million years or so."

"Probably?" said Hutch.

"There's no imminent danger."

Hutch couldn't believe he was serious. "Why did they cancel the Johnson mission twelve years ago, when they wanted to go to Betelgeuse?"

"That was pure politics."

He was right. The Conservatives were cutting back on funding. And President McCore scared everybody about the potential for something we might do that would trigger the supernova. That was absolutely crazy, but it was an election year and nobody could come up with a good reason to go, since we couldn't possibly learn anything that would be of any practical use. It was strictly blue-sky science. So why waste the money? The lives of the crew didn't even enter the issue, since the mission was to have been automated. But interstellars were expensive. And the private corporations already had tourists begging for visits to a star threatening to explode. The risk was the whole point of going out there, Harry Klison had famously said on *Smart Talk*. It fueled the movement that has virtually shut down interstellar travel altogether. The Academy was eventually strangled.

"I'm not in favor of it."

"Why not, Priscilla?"

"I can't see what we stand to gain."

"Can you really sit there and tell me the prospect of getting a good look at a red giant doesn't turn you on?"

"Not particularly."

"Can I ask you, as a favor, to support me on this? Look, nobody's ever gotten close to one of these things. We're probably not going to figure out what the waterfall was all about. Let's at least go home with something."

She closed her eyes. "We got an up-close with the Wasserman Cluster."

"I hate to say this," he said, "but you're beginning to sound like Unterkoefler."

"How big is that thing?" asked Wally. The bright red globe occupied most of the sky. The surface was tumultuous, chaotic, a boiling fire. The passenger cabin's virtual effects had been shut down and they were all looking out windows. "It looks as if it's ready to let go."

"I don't think we need to worry," said Derek. "Of course it's big. If it were in the solar system, it would extend out well past Mars."

"Incredible," said Beth.

"It's not as hot as the sun, though," said Ken. "Red giants have a surface temperature not much more than half what the sun does."

"That sounds almost comfortable," said Wally.

"He's been researching," said Beth. "He was at it half the night. But he needs to have it explode before the book comes out."

"She isn't kidding," said Ken. "If this thing goes before publication, it wouldn't matter if we didn't find the waterfall. The supernova would be the whole story. People love explosions. Especially something like this."

Hutch couldn't resist. "Derek, can you think of any way we could trigger it?"

"Sure," he said. "Just keep tempting fate."

"You know," said Ken, "it really does look as if it's getting ready to let go. Was this what that other one looked like when they were trying to put together the Johnson mission?" He was checking his notebook, then shaking his head. "No, actually, it doesn't. Betelgeuse looked pretty calm compared to this one."

"Maybe we should leave," said Wally. He added a smile but he wasn't kidding.

Derek took a sip from his coffee. "We won't be staying long. Barry, you see anything of interest?"

"I have so far located two planets in the system."

"Is either in the habitable zone?" asked Ken.

Beth frowned. "Let's hope not."

"One is a gas giant, pretty far out. The other is a rocky world."

"It's not likely to matter," said Derek. "The habitable zone around this type of star tends to be pretty big. But as the star swells, the zone keeps moving. So, there isn't much time for life to take hold. And if it does, it would boil pretty quickly."

"Did you want to take a look anyhow?" Hutch asked.

"How long will it take us to get there?"

"We can make it by dinner."

Derek smiled. He looked at his companions. Nobody raised an objection. "All right," he said, "let's do it."

The gas giant had lost none of its prominence. But the planet in the zone provided a surprise: It was green, covered with vegetation. Cumulus clouds drifted through its skies, and blue oceans covered vast areas. The polar caps were tinged with white, and the continents supported mountain chains, deserts, and broad plains. Under a different sun, the clouds would probably have been white. These were crimson-tinted, adding a lustrous delicacy to the landscape.

It could almost have been a second Earth, especially when a large, cratered moon drifted into view. *"Get pictures,"* Ken said.

Barry was already doing that. All except Hutch were seated in the passenger cabin, where the display had been activated again, allowing them to watch through the telescope. Forests and harbors and lakes drifted past. And a magnificent waterfall, the largest Hutch had ever seen. *"It's not the same one,"* Ken said.

Hutch, on the bridge, could hear the disappointment in his voice. She usually stayed out of casual conversation over the allcomm, but sometimes she couldn't resist. "I'll always remember this," she said, "as the waterfall flight."

"This place would make a great tourist attraction," said Wally. *"Especially with that bomb in the sky. But it's kind of a long ride to get here."*

Hutch saw movement above the trees. "They've got birds," she said. And more: Something that looked like a small dragon with an exceedingly long neck was walking casually through the surf along a beach's edge, apparently looking for fish.

"That is incredible," said Derek. *"That's why we need to check these things out."*

Then Wally almost screeched. *"Look!"*

"What?" asked Beth.

"There was a tent down there. I think." He paused. *"It's gone now."*

"Where?" demanded Derek. *"Where was it?"*

"Right below us. We passed over it too quick."

Derek shook his head. *"That makes no sense. The time span wouldn't have been long enough to allow the development of intelligent life."*

"How can you be sure?" asked Ken.

"All I'm saying is that it seems extremely unlikely. Show me another tent and I'll—"

"What?" asked Beth as a series of tents appeared ahead, passed quickly below them, and were gone.

"I just don't believe this." Derek sounded both shocked

and delighted. *"Barry, can you get the scope back on that strip of land?"*

A brief pause. Then: *"What are you looking for, Derek?"*

"The tents. Are you recording everything?"

"I am now."

"Barry, would you please get your act together?"

"Derek, do you wish to record all activities involving the use of the telescope?"

"Record whatever we do that involves this planet, okay? Or any other planet we get close to for the duration of the mission." Everything went silent briefly. Then: *"Hutch, I think we need to go down and take a closer look."*

Landing on this unhappy world wasn't exactly something that Hutch, left to her own inclinations, would have done. Nobody other than Derek was particularly interested in the tents. Who really wanted to get closer to the grim circumstances the occupants were living with? When Derek announced that he wanted to ride down in the lander, nobody volunteered to go along. Beth turned disapproving eyes on Hutch. "Looks like just you and Derek. So, what happens to the rest of us if something goes wrong and you guys don't come back? Wally, can you pilot this thing?"

"I wouldn't have to," he said. "Barry can get us home."

Beth couldn't resist letting the amusement show in her eyes. "So, remind me again, Hutch: What do pilots do?"

Derek cut in. "You with me, Hutch?"

Since the inhabitants were obviously not going to be the highly developed philosophical types he always talked about sitting down with, Hutch wasn't sure why they were doing this.

"Because I'm curious, Priscilla. Is that a crime?"

"Maybe you're right," said Wally. "They have no future. Get a look at them now, or forget it."

Beth frowned. "It surprises me that you seem so happy, Derek. Wally's right, isn't he? Whoever's down there doesn't have much time left."

Derek gave her a benevolent smile. "Beth, this thing probably won't explode in the next million years. That gives them time to build cities, fight a few wars, and move on to interstellars. They'll probably be out of here before anything happens."

Derek and Hutch boarded the lander and started down. They descended slowly through the crimson-toned skies, drifted for a half hour, and finally spotted a village. With inhabitants. They were bipeds. Their bodies were covered with light fur. They wore animal skins, basically the same material from which their tents appeared to be made. Their ears were large and they had tails. Some carried spears.

It was midafternoon. The giant sun occupied most of the western sky. The villagers appeared not to notice as the lander passed overhead. Derek took photos.

They were floating about a hundred meters over the village when one of the natives finally looked up and saw them. They began screaming and running for cover. Most disappeared into the tents. Others got under trees. A few waved spears in an apparent effort to intimidate the visitors. Hutch, reluctantly but serving at Derek's directions, went lower, while a small group gathered in the middle of the village. They seemed to be issuing a challenge: *Come down if you dare.*

"I feel sorry for them," said Hutch. "It's not much of a life."

"Yeah." Derek grumbled something else. Then: "Let's go back to the ship."

One of the natives, a small one, probably a child, ran out of a tent. He looked up at the lander at the same moment as another one came out after him. He waved at the vehicle, but then was seized and carried to safety.

Everybody was waiting as they emerged from the cargo hold.

"Hi, guys," said Ken. "Barry has something for you."

"That is correct," said the AI. *"You probably won't care all that much, but I've found two more planets. Makes a total of four."*

"Okay." Derek wanted details.

"Both are about the same size as the one with the tents and well outside the habitable zone. There is something odd about one of them. Its orbit is tilted at about sixty degrees from the rest of the system."

"That *is* strange. Sounds like a rogue planet."

"Which means what?" asked Beth.

"It didn't originate in this system. It got pulled out of its original location by a passing star or something. And eventually got picked up by the red giant."

"We ready to start home yet?" asked Wally. He'd been showing an increasing inclination to wind everything down and head back.

Derek stared at Hutch, his brow creased. "It rings a bell."

"How do you mean?"

"How about before we do anything else, let's go back to where we were. The area where Calliope should have been."

Derek Blanchard, Extract from Notebook, Intended for Autobiography

We have a rogue planet, a star that's gone missing, and two markers that are out of place. What the hell is going on out here?

I started by locking in Calliope's position 7,000 years ago when the Van Entel picked it up. Then I looked at the positions of the two stars that had drifted off course. They were both located on the right-hand side of Calliope's projected course and were moving more or less parallel to it.

And I found exactly what I was looking for. There was a trajectory that, if followed by a massive object, would have dragged the marker stars into the positions they now occupy. The process would have begun about 8,000 years ago. So it was already happening while we were watching from the University of Pennsylvania.

The massive object might have been a black hole.

But where is Calliope? The answer to that is painfully obvious. The damned thing got swallowed.

At some point in the next thousand years or so, observers at home should be able to watch the event, from start to finish.

What a mad universe we live in.

—Wednesday, April 2, 2256

15.

O time! The beautifier of the dead,
Adorner of the ruin, comforter
And only healer when the heart hath bled—
Time! The corrector where our judgments err,
The test of truth, love, sole philosopher.
—Lord Byron, *Childe Harold IV*, 1818

Hutch, Derek, and Ken sat staring at the display, which, for a change, showed a geometric pattern of slowly moving lights. *"I cannot disagree,"* said Barry. *"An object of appropriate mass, following the trajectory you propose, would have destroyed Calliope and caused precisely the changes we have seen in the surrounding stars."*

"Brilliant," said Ken.

Derek was picturing people all over the world centuries in the future watching the event unfold on their home displays through whatever supertelescopes would be available. "We probably won't be around to see it," he said.

Hutch knew what he was thinking.

"So, they're gone," he said. "After all these years, we actually locate a high-tech civilization, and they get taken down before we can get to them."

"Thousands of years before," said Ken. "Whoever thought it could happen like this?"

Derek tried to rearrange himself in the chair, which, though flexible, was probably still a bit uncomfortable for him. "I just don't believe it."

"It's not a friendly universe," said Hutch.

"So, what," asked Ken, "was the waterfall all about?"

"A high-tech civilization," said Derek, "in the Calliope system would have known for centuries what was coming. My guess is that we saw something that was part of an evacuation effort. If we got the details right, the transmission originated a thousand years before the black hole took out their sun. What we saw, probably, was just a routine transmission from a ship, somebody reporting home about a landscape they'd seen somewhere else. Maybe it was from a planet that was serving as the point of evacuation. A signal designed to encourage everyone."

"If they knew for thousands of years," said Hutch, "that the thing was coming, why would they have waited so long to start clearing out?"

Ken's eyes grew thoughtful. "Imagine how we'd react if we got word that Earth would be destroyed in the fifth or sixth millennium."

"You're right," said Derek. "We'd talk about it, but I doubt anyone would act until it got close. Until it got to a point where our grandkids were going to be in trouble."

"It was a directed transmission," said Hutch, "and the Van Entel just happened to be in the line of sight. For a few minutes. Pity we couldn't have gotten more of it."

"So what do we do now?" said Beth. "Go home?"

Derek's smile indicated that he was not nearly ready

to pack it in. "We know where the object is. It's probably a black hole. What I'd like to do is go take a look. Confirm what happened."

Beth literally laughed out loud. "We just got back from a star that's ready to go supernova. Now we want to go take a look at a black hole?"

"We'll be okay as long as we don't try poking it," said Ken.

Derek smiled. "It shouldn't be far."

With a black hole in the mix, it was a good idea to opt for caution. Hutch didn't want to depend on the mass detector to keep them out of trouble if she jumped into normal space anywhere near the monster. The device came with a guarantee that stipulated whatever degree of mass existed in the area, it would block the transdimensional interface and keep the ship in hyperspace. The detector was also designed to react the same way if it picked up dangerous levels of radiation, which could be expected near a black hole. But those were engineering claims, and if the system failed, there'd be no one to make the report. A few interstellars had been lost without explanation.

Derek's numbers would have taken them within a range of a hundred million kilometers. Hutch added another hundred million and gave the numbers to Barry. That would surely provide a safe zone.

Derek sighed when she informed him about her precautionary measures. He obviously thought she worried too much, but he understood. There was nothing wrong with caution when you were dealing with a black hole.

When they emerged from the first jump, they looked at a sky full of stars but saw nothing unusual. "But you wouldn't, right?" said Beth. "A black hole is black, so naturally, we're not going to see much."

Hutch knew Beth was in for a surprise.

"How close are we going?" Ken asked.

When they surfaced a second time and looked out at the night, it began to move. *The stars themselves began to move.* The entire sky looked as if it was being disrupted, wrapping itself around a black disk. A thousand stars were in motion, swirling in various directions. *"Is that it?"* It was Beth's voice, almost a squeal over the allcomm.

Watching it on a large screen was simply not adequate, so everybody crowded onto the bridge to get the captain's view. Derek for a long time remained quiet while everybody else commented on how crazy it was. Something was pulling the sky apart.

"Incredible," said Wally.

Ken stared at it. "My God, how am I supposed to describe something like this?"

"Is that really what it does?" said Wally. "I never heard of anything like that before."

Derek nodded. "Gravity distorts the light. And there's a lot of gravity. The sky's not really getting bent out of shape. It just looks that way." He stopped to catch his breath. "It's beautiful."

It was not the descriptor Hutch would have chosen.

"How big is it?" asked Ken.

Derek smiled. "Hard to say. We don't think of holes as being big. They contain a lot of mass. Take the sun and squeeze it down into a sphere about twenty kilometers wide, and you might be close."

"You're kidding. That's all?"

"This keeps getting crazier," said Beth.

"See those?" Derek indicated a constellation of stars off to starboard, which formed an almost perfect box, with an extremely bright pair on one side. "And over here." He pointed to his left, where a similar box, stretched a bit more, hung in the sky.

"What the hell?" said Ken. "They look identical. Except the bright ones are on the other side."

"There's only one constellation. In an area like this, the black hole bends and twists light. The sky wraps itself around it. If there was a ship out there coming in our direction, we might see it in two different places. Or maybe, depending on circumstances, we'd be able to see ourselves."

Beth just shook her head.

"That's a little unnerving," said Wally.

"I am sorry to interrupt," said Barry, *"but I'm concerned about an abundance of asteroids in the area. There is a substantial number, and they are moving at exceedingly high rates."*

"They're in orbit," said Derek.

"Where do you think they came from?" asked Ken.

"There wouldn't be anything unusual about that. Black holes drag all kinds of stuff out of planetary systems."

Ken pointed a finger at him. "That's what got you looking for this. The rogue world in that other system."

"Sure. I should have realized right from the beginning, with the markers disrupted and Calliope missing, there was no other explanation, unless you had the worst equipment in the world gathering the data."

"I hate to break in," said Hutch. "But everybody please

get back in your seats and fasten belts. We're going to clear out." She should not have let them start walking around. Dumb. "Come on, people. Move."

Barry broke in. *"There's one asteroid now that I can make out. It's almost the size of a small moon. It's coming our way. Not a direct threat, but it impedes my view."*

Everybody hurried back into the passenger cabin and belted in. The Locarno hadn't completed recharging yet, so Hutch simply took the *Eiferman* to a less-crowded area.

Beth's voice came in over the allcomm. *"I'm trying to imagine how the people, the inhabitants, on the Calliope world must have felt when they found out they were in the path of this thing. It's so small. But it can do so much damage. That's what blows my mind."*

"It's a machine, and that's all it is," Hutch said. "And it has some seriously weird mechanisms. Some places just get unlucky."

"That wouldn't come as news to my aunt Sarah," said Beth.

"Why?" asked Hutch. "What happened to her?"

"She was killed by lightning when I was a kid. I was with her when it happened."

It was approaching midnight, and nobody was going to sleep in the presence of that thing. Even Derek was affected by it. *"I don't care that we're not at risk,"* he told Hutch. *"When we're able, let's get away from here."*

The order surprised her. Just a few minutes before, he'd been delighted by what they saw.

The Locarno had finished charging. "Barry, get us clear of the area. Take us out a billion kilometers."

"Before you jump—" said the AI.

"What is it?"

"I've got something."

"What?"

"A planet. It's probably of no significance, but you should be aware."

"Is it in orbit?"

"Yes. About three hundred million kilometers out."

She thought about it. The smart thing to do would be simply to leave the area. But the sighting would be logged in, and eventually, she'd have to explain herself to Derek. "Where is it?"

"We're headed more or less toward it now. It will require only a minor course adjustment."

She informed Derek, who sounded as if he'd had enough of the black hole. But duty called. *"We have safe passage?"*

"Yes."

"All right. Let's go take a look."

The planet was a gas giant, with a swirling atmosphere brightened by storms. "Is this thing actually orbiting the hole?" asked Ken.

"Oh, yes," said Derek.

"That's hard to believe."

Two moons were visible. There might have been others. *"Its diameter is approximately fifty thousand kilometers,"* said Barry.

"Small for a gas giant," said Derek. "Well, probably not, in an area like this. The black hole has probably sucked off some of the atmosphere."

Hutch couldn't help thinking how much Charlie and Maureen would have liked to see all this.

Derek retired to his cabin and spent most of the balance of the day collaborating with Barry, looking at telescopic images of the planet, and more frequently at the black hole, which was simply a distant flickering glow now. He commented that the lights resembled a weak storm brewing at sea. Hutch wasn't sure what sort of connection he had with the sea, but it didn't really matter.

They named the planet Eve, for Derek's daughter. Then, as they began talking again about going home, Barry announced that he'd found a second planet. *"This one's much smaller. It appears to be slightly larger than Earth."*

Barry aimed the scope at the world, and as they drew closer, everybody gathered in the passenger cabin to watch the images appear on the display. Vast fields of ice and rock glittered in the starlight. Oceans at one time, Hutch thought, if the climate had been sufficiently warm.

The overall appearance could only be described as dismal. Mountains and broken crags rose out of the ice, and tall thin towers. Ken pointed at a pinnacle jutting out of an otherwise flat layer of ice. "It's a *building*."

There were more. Spread around the planet. Ruins jutting out of frozen ground. "Let's hope," said Beth, "they really were evacuating and got everyone off."

Hutch eased the *Eiferman* into orbit.

Most of the structures were simply wreckage. Broken buildings. Some had windows, or turrets, or ramparts. They saw a lone wall with a stairway that ended a hundred meters over a valley. And came across a tower that rose out of an otherwise empty field of ice. The remains of a statue stood atop the tower. The bottom half, the legs, if that's what they were, were clothed in a gown.

Eventually, Barry announced they'd completed circling the planet. *"Do we want to continue?"* he asked.

"Yes," said Derek. "Stay in orbit."

Hutch angled them slightly to starboard. "Most of what we're seeing," said Ken, "looks like what's left of skyscrapers. You think that's what's buried in the ice?"

"Probably," said Derek. He turned to Hutch. "We need to go down and take a look. At least we might get a sense of who the inhabitants were." He studied the icescape with mixed feelings. "What a disaster."

"Barry," said Hutch. "What's the radiation look like here?"

"It's too high for the Flickinger units. The lander will be safe, but if you're planning to get out and walk around, you'll need to wear standard pressure suits."

There were only four. "I guess nobody thought to make sure we had enough for everybody," said Derek. He was blaming himself.

Beth and Ken both wanted to go, and they needed Hutch, so Wally volunteered to stay behind. It was fairly evident he wasn't unhappy with the situation. "It's all right," he said. "I'm not big into archeology."

Or ice, Hutch thought. She distributed commlinks. "Use these," she said. "They have an automatic connection with Barry and Tasha and with each other. When you're wearing a helmet, there's an insert for it."

They pulled on the suits and air tanks and helmets while Wally watched. "Be careful," he said. "Don't let anything happen. I don't want to go home alone." He meant it as a joke, but no one laughed.

"Don't worry," said Derek. "We'll be fine."

When they were ready, Hutch led the way into the cargo bay, where they boarded the lander. She sat down at the controls and turned on the display to pick up the view from the cockpit. "Hello, Tasha," she said. "Start the engine and open the launch doors." Tasha was the lander's AI. The doors rolled back, and she took them outside into the frozen sky and waited for Derek to select something of interest.

"Over there," he said, pointing at a building that was the only artificial construct in that entire flat landscape. The stars were bright, and there was no sign of the black hole. She took them down through a night sky that was crystal clear, while Derek gave occasional directions and also advised where she should land.

Ken was checking his commlink. "These are going to be spectacular pictures," he said. "Maybe the most compelling element in the book."

"You have a title for it yet, love?" asked Beth.

"Maybe *Down the Rabbit Hole?*"

The building did look like a structure out of Paris or New York. There were windows in horizontal and vertical lines, exactly like the buildings at home. The glass was all gone, of course. "Want to take us a little closer, Hutch?" said Derek. "I'd like to be able to shine a light in there."

There was no wind action of any kind, so she saw no reason to stay clear. She started by taking them across the rooftop, which was covered with ice and partially collapsed. It was impossible to tell where the front of the building had been, so she simply picked a window at random, maneuvered close to it, and directed Tasha to aim the lander's spotlight into it.

The light illuminated a desk, a couple of chairs, a table topped by a mechanical device of some sort. Incredibly, there were plates or plaques on the walls. All frozen and indistinguishable from one another. "Looks like an office," said Beth. Hutch moved them to a second window.

There were more desks, chairs, sofas, tables, and lamps, and occasional plumbing as they moved down the face of the building and settled finally on a flat stretch of frozen ground. Time to go inside. They put on their helmets and ran a radio check. Then Derek and Hutch attached laser cutters to their belts. She depressurized the lander and opened the airlock, prompting a report from Tasha. *"Gravity is approximately eighteen percent higher than standard. Caution is advised."* Especially since they were accustomed to the artificial gravity on the ship, which was only slightly over fifty percent of Earth normal.

They went outside, climbed down onto the ice, and stood a few moments in overwhelming silence. *"Spooky,"* said Beth.

No light. No hint of a breeze. No movement of any kind.

They stood in front of the building, taking pictures, walking from window to window and peering inside. They saw more furniture. And display screens and equipment they couldn't identify. *"Everything's kind of large,"* said Ken. *"Whoever lived here, they were big."*

Hutch frowned at the missing windows. They provided an easy entrance. But she didn't like the idea. "Not sure we want to go in there. This thing's probably a skyscraper. And this might be the twentieth floor. Something gives way and it could be a long way down."

"It's all right." Derek placed a hand on the frame. *"I've got it."*

"Be careful," said Beth. *"There may still be sharp fragments in the frame. Cut your suit and you'll have a different problem."* The interior was full of ice.

Derek brushed his gloved fingertips lightly along the rim of the window, decided it was safe, and sat down on it. They all turned on their wristlamps.

Derek moved one foot over the windowsill, set it on the floor, and pushed down. Nothing gave way, so he swung the other leg in and eased into a standing position. *"It feels okay."*

Chairs and a desk and a broken metal base that might once have been part of a watercooler had turned dark, probably from long-gone mold. There was little more than a grotesque pile of rubble spread across the floor. Every flat surface was covered with a frozen layer of smudge. All four of the desk's legs were broken. There were drawers on both sides but they were frozen shut. Derek used the cutter to get through one of them. They found a package inside, but it couldn't be freed from the drawer. *"Looks like sheets of paper,"* Ken said. *"We'd never be able to separate these."*

There was printing on the top sheet. Derek took a picture and, just in case, Ken put the package in his backpack.

"Careful," Hutch said. Ken had been about to trip over a wire connecting a device on a side table to an outlet in the wall.

"That's an old-fashioned telephone, isn't it?" said Beth. It had a rotor and push-buttons.

Ken took a long look. *"Yeah. Right out of the twentieth century."*

Hutch couldn't resist attempting to pick up the handset. She expected it to be frozen to the cradle, but it broke loose when she pulled on it. She pushed it against her helmet and then pushed down on the cradle. It didn't move.

"If somebody answers," said Derek, *"you'll have a heart attack."*

She wasn't sure she'd have been able to hear a voice at all through the helmet. In any case, there was of course nothing. "I doubt," she said, "these people, whoever they were, could have evacuated the planet. If the technology in these rooms is typical of what they had, I'd say nobody was going anywhere."

They found what appeared to be a picture frame on the floor. But it lay face down. It was a breathless moment. Derek stood for a minute staring at it while they all waited. Finally, he reached for it. The frame stuck to the floor. *"Damn,"* he said.

He used the laser again. Eventually, after they'd cut around it and to some extent under it, they were able to free the thing. Surprisingly, the glass frame was intact, save for a couple of cracks. But it had turned to something dark and impenetrable. Whatever had been behind it was hopelessly out of reach. Wally spoke from orbit. *"Probably nothing more than a smudge anyhow."*

"Pity," said Beth.

There were two doors in the room. One had fallen off its hinges and lay on the floor, revealing another, smaller office. They found another framed picture, this one frozen to the wall. They could make nothing out of the artwork. Or photo. Whatever it had been.

There was a door in the smaller office, but it wouldn't

move either. They returned to the main room where its other door was also frozen. They used the cutters to open it and emerged in a passageway. It was lined with doors, but none of them could be moved. The only way through them was to use the cutters. *"It makes me uncomfortable,"* said Derek. *"I can't give you a reasonable explanation why, but I don't like destroying stuff, even out here, that's been in place probably thousands of years."*

Most of the offices were basically the same. The corridor itself started to tilt downward. *"That's far enough,"* said Derek, extending an arm to halt his companions.

They retreated past the office through which they'd entered and continued along the corridor in the opposite direction, past more doors, until they arrived at a pile of broken furniture and collapsed walls. The wreckage included two metal doors that had broken loose from a frame. They stopped and looked down a shaft. Derek dropped to one knee, leaned over, and aimed his lamp into it. Up and down. *"It's an elevator,"* he said. *"Or it was."*

Hutch reached for him and grabbed his belt. "Careful." She inched forward. The shaft overhead was clear for several floors. Below, she could see only a short distance before the shaft walls appeared to squeeze together.

Ken climbed across the fallen doors, continuing along the passageway. *"Where you going?"* asked Derek, who wanted everyone to stay in line.

"Looking for a stairway. There's usually one near elevators."

"Don't forget we're dealing with aliens here," said Wally, from the ship.

"It probably doesn't matter. The laws of physics are the same everywhere. And it looks as if—yes. There it is."

"Stairs?" asked Derek. He got back up on his feet.

"Yes."

Ken disappeared around a corner and Derek hurried after him.

"Holy cats," Ken said. *"You should see this."*

"What is it?" asked Wally.

Beth was climbing across the broken doors. But she lost her footing in the dark and crashed into Hutch. Hutch was pushed forward into the shaft, grabbing frantically for something to hold on to. But nothing was there, and the extra weight didn't help. She teetered on the edge and would have fallen into the shaft had Beth, or someone, not grabbed her ankle. Her shin took a blow, and she was hanging head down as Beth screamed for help.

Then they had her other leg too. *"I've got you,"* said Derek. *"Easy."*

They hauled her back up onto the broken doors, and she discovered she'd stopped breathing.

"I'm sorry," Beth was saying. *"Thank God."*

"You okay?" asked Derek. He was shining his lamp in her eyes.

"Yeah. I'm good."

They dragged her farther from the shaft. *"You're the one,"* Derek said, *"who's always telling everybody to be careful."*

"It was my fault," said Beth. She'd worked her way past Hutch and was looking down over the edge. *"My God, that wouldn't have been good."*

"Would you please *get away from there?"* said Derek, grabbing her and hauling her back. *"Are you people trying to get yourselves killed?"*

"Hutch." It was Wally again. *"Try to be careful."* He paused.

"Ken, could you please stand so I can see what's the big deal about the stairway?"

Ken got out of the way so Wally could see all the way to the bottom. Or at least as far down as the light went. *"That must be at least twenty floors down there,"* he said. *"There's an entire city buried beneath the ice."*

Hutch was getting to her feet with a helping hand from Derek. Her shin still hurt. *"You sure you're okay?"* he said.

"I'm fine."

Derek stayed with her until she'd gotten down off the doors.

"You should get back to the lander," Beth said.

"Sounds like a good idea. I feel as if I weigh a ton." Beth accompanied her. A few minutes later, Derek and Ken followed.

When they were all back inside the lander, they began debating whether they should attempt to go down the staircase. "I'd be interested in seeing what's at the bottom," said Derek.

Beth was rubbing a salve on Hutch's leg. "You'll be fine," she said. "It's just a bruise." Then she turned to Derek. "I don't see any point in going down there. I'm not sure what you hope to gain. And it'll be dangerous. This place has been in the ice for a long time, maybe thousands of years. We don't know how much support that stairway has. If it gives out, it will be bye-bye, baby."

"More to the point," said Wally, *"it seems like a pretty routine office building. What can you find that might matter?"*

"Maybe a picture that has survived. I'd like at least to find out what they looked like."

"Why don't we just do it?" said Ken. "Archeology's never completely safe. If we don't go down to look, we'll always wonder what we missed."

"You've got a better option," said Beth.

Ken grinned at her. His wife always had a better idea. "What?" he asked.

"The problem is the ice. Everything's buried in ice. Which is frozen water, right?"

Derek and Ken both looked puzzled.

"There should be a place here somewhere that was at one time fairly dry. Maybe a desert. Chances are pretty good if we look around a bit more, we could find something that's not completely frozen and buried."

Hutch thought about what it had been like for the occupants. Some had watched their sun being torn apart as the lights went out. For others, it might have been that the sun had merely set and never rose again.

ARCHIVE

Beth Squires's Notes

Thank God Hutch did not go into that pit. If that had happened I'd never have had a moment of peace again. Ever.

—Saturday, April 5, 2256

16.

Time shall every grief remove,
With life, with memory, and with love.
—Thomas Gray, Epitaph for Mrs. Jane Clarke, 1758

They found what Wally laughingly called the city in the desert at around noon the following day. There was no way to know what the ground had been like in that world's happier years. But the city had obviously been part of those better times. And that was what mattered.

They went down in the lander and slowly circled it. It was a dazzling contrast to the surrounding environment, a configuration of geometrical shapes, polygons, cones, pyramids, cylindrical towers, cubes, and other profiles for which there was no descriptive term. They were laid out in symmetrical patterns. "It's beautiful!" said Beth.

Derek grunted. "Yeah. It *was*."

It was unlike any city Hutch had seen, ever, a place that might have been designed and created by artists. Every conceivable sort of style was manifested, yet somehow there was a unity to it all. It rose above a layer of combined ice and rock, a magnificent collection of edifices, still resplendent in starlight.

The city was surrounded by flat land that seemed composed of giant claws rising out of the ice. "What the hell are those?" asked Ken.

Derek needed a moment. "I'd guess it used to be a forest. The trees froze, most of the branches fell off and got buried. This is what's left."

"Incredible," said Ken.

And Beth: "They had some serious architects."

Ken could not stop staring. "The symmetry is completely different."

"How do you mean?" asked Wally, who was still on the *Eiferman.*

"Put it in a normal landscape. Imagine it the way it must have been. The buildings don't line up. There's no Central Avenue or Broadway or any indication that any single street ran through the place. At least not in a straight line."

"You're right," said Derek, as they passed over, turned and came back. "It wouldn't have been a place where I'd have wanted to be in a hurry to get to work."

"Still," said Hutch, "it seems to have perfect balance."

"Blows my mind," said Wally.

"It *is* an incredible piece of work." Derek was, as usual, seated beside her. "Slow down a bit," he said.

She complied and he leaned forward as they approached. There were several open areas inside the city, sections that possessed only occasional small structures. They had probably been parks. She picked one and set down in the middle of it.

They got into their suits, turned on wristlamps, and climbed out onto the frozen ground. Most of the buildings had visible front doors. But the structures that had looked so pristine from the sky were now revealed as crumbling piles of stone and, probably, metal and plastic.

Derek looked momentarily lost, but then he made up his mind and led the way toward a six-story building with a sloping roof and Greek columns, though two lay on the ground. At home it would have been a courthouse.

They took pictures and climbed a few steps onto a portico. It had large front doors with handles, but, as everyone expected, none of them moved. So, they had to climb through window frames again.

Inside, they tried to be careful. Hutch could imagine future archeologists arriving on the scene with nothing but criticism for *Blanchard and those other nitwits who tore everything apart.* She wasn't alone. They were all more careful than they had been in the skyscraper.

They filed into a large room with a long, broken counter lining one wall. And more doors. Considerably smaller than the ones at the front entrance. They were permanently shut too, of course.

Hutch brought out her cutter, looked at Derek for approval, got it, and removed one door from its frame. They aimed their wristlamps into darkness. It was an auditorium of some sort. The floor had lines of chairs, scattered and broken by a partial ceiling collapse.

"Look," said Hutch. "Up there." More wreckage was

visible at the far end of the auditorium. "It used to be a stage." It had no screen or display.

Beth started forward but stopped after only a few steps. *"Careful. There are holes in the floor."*

They climbed carefully over the rubble and eventually stood in front of what remained of the stage. *"It looks as if they did live theater,"* said Beth. *"I'd love to find a copy of one of their plays. That would be something to take home."*

They came out of the theater, and Ken noticed a building that would have been easy to overlook in that once-exotic place except that a statue occupied the ground off to one side of the front door. The building was only four stories high, a simple rectangular structure, with a few tall windows.

The statue depicted something that was not remotely human other than that it wore clothes. It had long, sharp ears and the eyes of an eagle. The face suggested the presence of fangs, and it wore a hat that might have been out of a Robin Hood illustration, save that there was no feather. Its jacket was unfastened, and it had trousers that would have been perfect for a hunting trip. If it could be compared to anything, it would have been a lizard. Despite all that, the creature projected a sense of dignity and courage.

They took more pictures, and struggled again with the doors. "You want to cut through?" asked Hutch.

Derek looked at the empty windows. There were a few crusted shards of glass caught in the frames. *"It's a* church," he said. Then: *"No, let's not do any breaking and entering here."* He glanced around to see what else might warrant a look. To the north, the taller buildings began to give way to more perfunctory construction. Derek again took the lead and they made for an ordinary-appearing structure about three stories high that rose above surrounding houses. The front doors, if they existed at all, were buried in rubble.

They approached one of the windows and pointed their lamps inside, into a large room filled with chairs.

They cleared the frame and climbed through. There were about twenty chairs, but they were small. For children. They saw cabinets under the windows. Derek used his cutter to open them. *"I feel kind of guilty doing this,"* he said. *"God knows how long this stuff has been here. And we're wrecking it."*

"You're thinking about it the wrong way," Ken said. *"It was left for us to find."*

There were stuffed animals and building blocks and boxes that held, possibly, jigsaw puzzles. The pictures on the lids had faded to weak smears. There were also dolls and board games that could not be opened and a friendly looking octopus with too many tentacles.

"It's a kindergarten," said Beth.

They saw blankets and pillows and cups.

Several of the dolls carried a vague resemblance to the statue outside the church. Except that the heroic aspect had been replaced by an amiable, cuddly attitude. "Maybe we're going to find out," said Hutch, "that intelligent species have a lot more in common than anything that separates them." It was the same feeling she'd gotten years before when she first stood on Iapetus and looked up at the winged statue that seemed to be challenging Saturn.

Beth Squires's Notes
One of the most emotional moments of my life. . . .

—Sunday, April 6, 2256

17.

Our old mother nature has pleasant and cheery tones enough for us when she comes in her dress of blue and gold over the eastern hilltops; but when she follows us upstairs to our beds in her suit of black velvet and diamonds, every creak of her sandals and every whisper of her lips is full of mystery and fear.

—Oliver Wendell Holmes, *The Professor at the Breakfast Table*, 1860

In the end, they were all glad to get away from it. Hutch had been to numerous extraterrestrial archeological sites, but there'd been something different about this one. Normally, they stoked her curiosity and left her with an admiration for the accomplishments of a species that she had never really known. Maybe it was because she'd never seen ruins before on a completely lifeless world. Maybe it was because she'd never before felt that she'd touched the lives of the lost occupants.

Everyone had been shaken by the experience. "It may have been thousands of years since it happened," said Beth, "but it doesn't matter. Usually, you put something that far in the past, and you don't get emotionally tangled in it. But this is different. Those little frozen teddy bears were tough to take."

Derek was simply staring out at the night as Hutch prepared to ease the *Eiferman* out of orbit. "There'll be a lot of people who will want to put together another expedition. To come back here and take a long look at the place. Maybe this'll be enough to get past the politicians."

"I doubt it," said Hutch. She activated the allcomm. "Everybody belt down."

"Would you want to be with them when they come?" Ken's voice came out of nowhere. She hadn't realized he was still on the bridge.

It wasn't clear which of them he was asking. But Derek shook his head. "No. I've had enough. I'm not an archeologist, anyhow." He looked over at her. "Would *you* want to come back, Hutch?"

"Not really. I've seen enough."

Ken nodded. "I'm sorry it's turning out this way, Priscilla."

"We knew this was a possibility before we started." She glanced back at him. "We'll be moving in a minute."

"Oh, sorry. I guess I wasn't paying attention." He disappeared into the passenger cabin.

Derek watched him go. Then: "Do you want to start back?"

"Your call, boss."

"Why don't we let it go for a while? That was a fairly exhausting few hours. Let's let everybody get some dinner and a good night's sleep before we decide. We can talk about it in the morning."

Hutch understood: They'd relax more easily with a sky full of stars.

• • •

They watched an episode of *Lost in Berlin*, and the full-length film *Party On*. Both would normally have been received as hysterically funny, but there just wasn't much laughter that evening. Afterward, Hutch retired to her cabin, where she lay quietly reading for almost an hour. Concentrating on the book, *Life and Limb*, was a struggle. Its subtitle was *Aging in the 23rd Century*. It was Ginjer Hudson's Pulitzer Prize–winning account of the social problems that arrived with reversing the aging process. Under normal circumstances, it would probably have absorbed her, but on that night it barely held her attention. Eventually, she gave up on it, played a couple of chess games with Barry— they split—and turned out the lights. Moments after she'd closed her eyes, Barry whispered to her. *"You still awake, Captain?"*

"What's the matter?"

"There's something else unusual out there."

"You don't think we've had enough for one day?" He'd probably found a third planet. If so, please, no more cities.

"I cannot determine what it is. But I do not see how it could be an asteroid. Or any other kind of natural object."

"It's a ship?"

"I do not know. If it is, the design is different from anything I've seen before."

"Show me the object."

"I can't get a good look at it. It's too far away. It appears too large to be a vehicle. It may be a space station gone adrift. But the design is not right."

"How do you mean?"

"Length appears to be in the range of seventeen kilometers, but it is relatively narrow."

"Any indication of activity?"

"Nothing, Captain. There's no evidence of power."

Hutch's heart had picked up a beat. "It's in orbit around the black hole, I assume?"

"I won't be able to make a determination on that for several hours. But it is highly likely."

"Okay. We won't be taking any action for a while, Barry. I'll get back to you."

"There's another feature. A crosspiece, quite small, near one end of it."

That brought a jolt. "Is the object a religious symbol?"

"Certainly not Christian. The crosspiece is too short." At this point, nothing would have surprised her.

She called Derek.

He listened while she told him about Barry's discovery. *"How long will it take to reach it?"*

"It depends how close the jump takes us."

"And Barry thinks it's a station?"

"He didn't say that. He just doesn't know."

"What else could it be? If it's not a ship or a station?" She could hear him breathing. *"But it's big. I can think of one possibility."*

"What's that?"

"Maybe they were trying to escape. Maybe they built something oversized and didn't make it out."

Hutch was beginning to wish Barry hadn't seen the thing. She'd had enough depressing news for one mission.

• • •

In the morning, the AI confirmed that the object was in orbit. They talked about it at breakfast. Beth looked puzzled. "And there's no sign of power?"

"Not that we've been able to pick up," Hutch said.

"Then I don't see any point bothering with it. If it's just a ship they tried to use for an escape, and they didn't make it . . ." She glanced around at the others. "Haven't we had enough? What can we really get out of it except more bad news?"

Derek's eyes closed momentarily. "We might be able to find out whether that statue outside the church was what they really looked like."

"Maybe they were plants," said Wally.

The comment drew a glare from Derek, who was in no mood for jokes.

"Aren't we going to figure that out anyhow," said Beth, "when the follow-up mission comes in? I mean, they *will* send another mission out here eventually." She frowned at the skeptical faces around the table. "They'll have to."

Ken looked as if he'd been intending to jump in, and when Derek hesitated, he took the opportunity. "So, we go home and spend the entire trip back wondering what the thing was? And maybe the rest of our lives because there *is* no next mission? Does that really make sense? Besides, I can't write the book and have somebody else supply the answer. Or worse, without getting an answer."

"Absolutely," said Wally. "Let's go see what it is."

Hutch understood Beth hadn't recovered yet from the shock of the previous day. Probably none of them ever would really get away from it. But they were all reacting differently. Beth had had enough. Wally, she thought, understood that Derek would have his way, that they'd chase the thing down, and he just wanted to get it over with. Ken knew what it would mean for book sales.

After they'd finished eating, they got into their harnesses, Hutch turned the ship in the direction of the object and, using Barry's estimate, set the jump for forty million kilometers. Then she activated the Locarno. It was a run of only a couple of minutes. They surfaced, the stars came back, and the AI informed her they'd arrived almost directly on target. Just more than three hundred thousand kilometers. For a drive system that had an extremely long reach but was notorious for missing destinations by millions of kilometers, it came as a major surprise. "Why is it so consistently off?" Beth asked as they all shook hands and congratulated the captain.

"It's not so much the system," Hutch replied. "The Locarno gets used primarily for exceedingly long jumps. The basic problem is that we don't usually have an accurate range to the target. Like when we came out here. Seven thousand light-years is a rounded-off guesstimate. If we actually knew how much ground we had to cover on any given jump, we'd do much better."

"Let's get the scopes on it," said Derek, "and maybe get it on screen?"

She complied and put it up for them. It started as a glowing line, but it got progressively larger as they drew closer. And became a *blade*. The crosspiece Barry had mentioned was a handgrip. Ken's voice came through the open doorway: *"It's a sword!"*

ARCHIVE

Walter Esmeraldo's Log

We were all sitting watching the screen, waiting for the picture to show up. We didn't know what we were expecting. We'd heard something about it being maybe a cross. And I thought maybe that's just what we needed at a time like that, because everything was starting to seem absolutely crazy. We'd spent the previous day looking at a world where probably everybody died. You don't think much about the end of the world. That's something for fantasy, but you never really see any possibility of its happening. But it did for those poor people, or whatever they were, dragged out of orbit and frozen. If there was any time that I would have wanted to see a cross, that was it. And don't ask me to explain that. I don't know what I'm talking about.

So what do we get? A sword, hung out there in the sky as if it had been left by a devil. I don't really believe in devils, but that thing scared me. I'm ready to go home. I've had enough.

—Monday, April 7, 2256

18.

I like the dreams of the future better than the history of the past.
> —Thomas Jefferson, Letter to John Adams, 1816

t *was* a sword. There was no question. They pulled in close and watched the blade slide past. And the crosspiece, which was, of course, part of the hilt. The edge of the blade narrowed to a perfect cutting edge.

"What the hell is this about?" asked Wally.

Ken's eyes were locked on it. "It's the Monument Makers again," he said.

Derek shook his head. "No. The Monument Makers always did artistic stuff. Subjects that had a tranquil ambience. They would never have done anything like this. Anyhow, this is too far out. I can't believe they'd have been leaving sculptures all over the galaxy."

"We don't really know," said Hutch. "Maybe it was put together by whoever lived on the ice world."

"You mean," said Beth, "they were saying hello to the black hole."

Derek nodded. "I'd guess that's a better explanation than anything I can come up with."

"There's an inscription," said Hutch. It was embedded in the handle, four lines of golden characters that possessed an Arabic grace and style.

Derek watched as they drew closer. Then slammed his fist on the arm of his chair. "It *is* the Monument Makers. Shows you what I know."

Hutch was surprised to see it too. "Yeah. That's their alphabet, okay. And their style."

"I wish," said Ken, shaking his head, "we could learn to read these things."

Derek got up, disappeared into the galley, and came back with a cup of coffee. He raised it. "Here's to them. Long may they reign."

"Pity it's so far out," said Ken. "This is one of those things that no amount of picture-taking will ever convey the effect. You have to come here to really get the point."

"You mean," added Beth, "unless you see it in correlation with the lost world."

They took pictures from every angle. "I wonder," said Wally, "if the Monument Makers might be more closely connected with this than we've thought."

"How do you mean?" asked Ken.

"It might have been *their* kindergarten that we were just looking at."

"I don't think so," said Hutch.

"Why not?"

"We've always assumed the statue on Iapetus is a self-portrait. And it probably is. It fits the footprints. The statue on the ice world looks completely different."

They stayed nearby for the better part of the day, and finally they began talking again about going home. "Before we do anything like that," said Ken, "let's have Barry scan the area. Who knows what else we might find out here?"

"Barry's been doing that automatically, hasn't he, Priscilla?"

"Yes. And if he'd seen anything, we would know about it. But our view of the local area is limited. If we really want to do a serious survey, we should make some position adjustments."

"Okay," said Derek. "Let's do it. If we don't find anything, and I suspect we won't, we'll leave tomorrow."

It came in the middle of the night again. *"Captain Hutchins, are you awake?"*

"Barry." She'd been dreaming that she was on a beach, just headed into the surf. And the voice had come out of the waves. "You found something else?"

"It appears to be a ship."

"Onscreen, please."

It looked more like a box, twice as long as it was wide. *"I can detect no power. It is apparently adrift."*

"How big is it?"

"It's too distant to determine."

"Okay. Stay with it. We'll track it down in the morning." She pulled the sheet up around her shoulders and tried to go back to the beach. But it wasn't going to happen.

•   •   •

"It is approximately nine kilometers front to rear."

It *was* a ship. An enormous box with rounded edges. Several lines of hatches were located along a perfectly smooth black hull. The object was tumbling slowly end over end as they approached.

It was probably two kilometers wide. The rectangular shape didn't seem right either. Not that you couldn't design an interstellar that looked like a carton, but it just didn't fit her preconceptions of what a space vehicle should look like. In addition, Hutch could not make out any sign of thrusters. "Are we getting any activity from it, Barry?"

"Negative, Captain. No indication of onboard power." There was a series of hatches on each side. She counted forty-four altogether. What kind of space vehicle needs forty-four hatches?

"Derek, do you want to try to contact them?"

"If there's no indication of power, why bother?"

"We don't know what a sufficiently advanced technology might look like. They could be in there, just not putting out a signal."

"Priscilla, how could that be possible? Look at that thing!" They watched it tumble past. "If there's a crew, I suspect they're pretty sick."

"I guess." She was mildly embarrassed, but she'd seen too much over the years to trust her assumptions. "Barry," she said, "open a channel."

Derek showed a tolerant smile.

"Ready, Captain," said Barry.

Hutch activated her mike. "This is the *Barry Eiferman*," she said. "Anybody over there?"

The receiver stayed quiet.

Derek leaned toward the microphone. "Barry, what are the radiation levels like?"

"Relatively low. The black hole is quite distant. But if you're thinking of sending a team over to look at it, I would nevertheless recommend you not use the Flickinger field."

"Okay." He sat back in his chair. "Let's get the pressure suits and go knock on the door."

The object dwarfed the *Eiferman.* Hutch listened to the *oooohs* and *aaaahs* from the passenger cabin as they drew close. *"That thing is big,"* said Beth.

The hull was dark brown, and other than the hatches, its smooth surface was unbroken by windows or markings of any kind. *"I have, however, found thrusters,"* said Barry. *"They are located on both sides and also in the rear. But their size and locations imply they can be nothing other than steering units."*

"The thing could be a big chocolate bar," said Wally.

Derek got out of his seat and went into the passenger cabin. Hutch left the hatch open so she could hear. Ken, Beth, and Wally sat in their chairs, watching the giant ship.

"Okay if I come?" asked Wally.

Derek was apparently planning to visit the vehicle. "Of course."

Ken and Beth wanted to go also, but Derek didn't like the idea. "Let's keep it just Wally and me for now. We'll send back visuals. Shouldn't be a problem. Once we make sure everything's okay, you can all come. Except Priscilla." He looked back through the hatch and smiled. "I feel a lot safer when you're on the bridge."

Derek and Wally both claimed to have had previous

experience with the go-packs, but Hutch was nonetheless uneasy as they got ready. She helped them pull on their magnetic boots and get into their pressure suits. She adjusted the go-packs and checked to be sure they were strapped on properly. "I wish I could line up with that thing," she said, referring to the giant ship. "But no way we can match that spiral without making everybody sick."

"Good point," said Wally. "I was thinking of taking a sandwich with me, but maybe I should wait a bit."

"Be careful, guys," said Beth. "Don't let it hit you."

Hutch got a cutter out of the supply room and handed it to Wally. "You know how to use it, right?"

"Of course," he said.

"Try to find a way to open it without using the thing," Derek said.

"Of course." Wally sounded annoyed.

They stepped into the airlock. Hutch closed the inner hatch behind them and returned to the bridge.

She'd been a bit nervous about providing Derek with a go-pack. But he handled it okay, shut down the jet at the right moment, and landed with surprising dexterity on the moving hull close to one of the hatches. His magnetic boots took hold, and moments later Wally arrived also, though a substantial distance away.

They targeted Derek's nearby hatch, met there, and began pushing and pulling. Finally, Wally said he didn't see any way to open it. *"There's a press pad here, but it's solid as a rock."* He produced the cutter. *"Stay clear, Derek. There's a chance heavy air pressure's built up in there."*

Derek backed away and Wally began slicing into the

metal. He held the cutter in place for about three minutes. *"Got it,"* he said finally. Then: *"I've taken out the lock but the hatch still won't move. It's frozen. This is going to take a while."*

Well, Hutch thought, it wasn't as if they were going anywhere. Eventually, Wally got through the hatch, pulled it clear, and let it drift into the void.

"I hope," said Beth, "there's not anyone in there." She meant it as a joke but nobody laughed.

"There was some air pressure," Wally said. *"Not much, though."* He pointed his commlink down a long, dark corridor that extended along the hull in both directions. A second passageway intersected the corridor.

Wally aimed his lamp at the overhead. It was low enough for him to reach up and touch. The bulkhead was marked with a pair of symbols. One was a circle with a stroke across it, the other a curved line that looked somewhat like a coiled snake. *"Probably numbers,"* he said. *"Marking the area so occupants wouldn't get lost. They don't look anything like the Monument Makers' stuff."*

Doors and intersecting passageways lined both sides of both corridors. They entered the passageway that led into the vehicle, walking slowly in zero gravity.

They stopped at the first door. It had a latch, which wouldn't turn. There was a small panel beside it. But that did nothing either. Wally tugged at it without result. Derek tried a door on the other side of the corridor, which was also frozen shut. *"I don't think we're going to have much luck,"* he said.

They continued along the corridor, deeper into the ship, trying each door as they passed. Finally, Wally lost patience, turned the cutter on one, and sliced through.

It opened into a small cubicle. Two large cots, with tucked-in blankets, were fastened to the deck. There was a bureau with two drawers, neither of which would open. They broke into them, but the drawers were empty, except for a piece of frozen cloth that would not come apart. "Could be a shirt," said Derek, "or anything."

The room had a closet. They had to cut through that as well. A bar was installed across the top for hanging clothes. It had a couple of hangers.

They went back out into the corridor and continued on their way, pushing more doors without result. Eventually, they forced their way into another room and found identical accommodations. Then they reached another cross passageway. More symbols were on the walls, different from the first set. They stood, aiming their lamps in both directions until the light faded.

Eventually, they came across a large compartment with no doors, filled with rows of tables and chairs. *"A cafeteria, I guess,"* said Wally.

The chairs were locked in place, of course. *"I wonder if there's a menu here somewhere,"* Derek said.

Hutch was watching everything through Derek's commlink, which meant she couldn't actually see *him* except for an occasional arm or leg. But it was clear he couldn't decide what he wanted to do. He sounded simultaneously amazed and discouraged.

"That thing has a lot of units," said Beth.

Derek was walking through the cafeteria. A long table crossed the far end. It was covered with display cases, where presumably food would have been available. A few of the cases contained trays that might not have been wiped completely clean. But whatever had been on them was now nothing more than dark smears and frozen clumps.

They left the cafeteria and continued in the same direction deeper into the ship. Within a few minutes, they came upon connecting ramps to the decks above and below. Wally and Derek walked over to them, took the up ramp, and found themselves in an identical world lined with doors. Passageways intersected just a few steps ahead. The doors were, as expected, frozen. And someone had drawn a flower on one of the walls. It was barely visible, a mere shading, having lost whatever color it might once have had. There were two blossoms, and it reached only about belt-high, as if it had been done by a child.

Derek stood in front of it, aiming his commlink at it. *"Wouldn't want them to miss this,"* he said. Then they moved on toward another intersection, where they stopped and looked at long lines of doors in both directions.

"Which way?" asked Wally.

"Careful, guys," said Hutch. "You don't want to get lost over there."

"No problem, Priscilla." Wally was laughing at her. How could she possibly think he could be that dumb?

They broke into another room. It was identical with the others, except that there were pieces of clothing lying against one bulkhead. They were frozen to it. Whoever had left them had simply tossed them aside. The clothes had presumably followed the tumble of the ship until finally they stuck to the bulkheads. *"No buttons or zippers,"* said Wally, tearing one of them away for a brief examination.

Minutes later they came across a corridor unlike the others. The doors on one side were imprinted with symbols that resembled a five-pointed star inside a half-circle, and on the other with triangles. They forced one open and were surprised to discover that all the doors on that side opened into a single area. One wall was lined with large shower stalls, much larger than would have been needed to accommodate either Derek or Wally. Another section was devoted to booths that concealed toilets. As a whole, it was a considerably larger accommodation than one would have found in a human washroom.

Beth laughed. "Looks as if we all share an appreciation for privacy."

They arrived at another ramp, which went in both directions. *"It might be a good idea to go back down,"* said Wally. *"Where the open hatch is."*

Hutch, still listening, broke in. "You've got about an hour's air left. You guys might want to think about coming back."

"Yeah," said Derek. *"Sounds like a good idea."*

Hutch would have liked to see the bridge, assuming there was one, but it was probably a four-kilometer walk from where Derek was. She stopped paying close attention to them once they'd started back. But a few minutes later, both of them started asking where the hell they were. That was her signal to get into a pressure suit. "You guys lost?" she asked.

"No," said Derek. *"We're trying to find the cafeteria."*

That didn't reassure her. The cafeteria was on the way back. If they didn't know where it was, they had a problem.

Great.

Ken had been listening too. "You going after them?" he asked.

"Yes."

"I'll go with you."

"No. You and Beth stay here. I'll be back in a few minutes." She climbed into a suit, pulled on an oxygen tank and a go-pack, and added two more oxygen tanks. The alien vehicle had rolled away, and the side with the open hatch was no longer visible. "Barry," she said, "line us up as best you can." She went back to the bridge.

Barry maneuvered the *Eiferman* into a position from which the airlock would face the open hatch. *"You'll have about eight minutes before you lose it,"* he said.

Hutch grabbed the extra tanks, slipped into the airlock, and depressurized. She was still listening to the conversation between Derek and Wally.

"Where is the damned thing?" said Derek.

"I was sure it was in this corridor."

"Doesn't look like it. Let's back up. Check that other one back there. I think we got turned around."

"The problem with this place is everything looks the same."

Air pressure went to zero. Hutch opened up the hatch and looked across a significant stretch of void at the giant ship, which literally blocked off the sky. The entry hatch Derek and Wally had used was visible, angling closer. "Barry, be careful. We don't want a collision."

"I need you to get moving, Captain."

She pushed off and activated the jet. "Derek," she said, "on my way. Maybe best is to stay where you are till I get there."

"We can manage this, Priscilla," he said. *"All we need right now is for you to come over and get lost."*

"Too late, Derek." She descended to the hull, landing within a few meters of the open hatch. She went inside, turned on her lamp, and saw the circle with the strike through it, and the coiled snake. Okay. The room they'd broken into showed up straight down the corridor.

A left turn took her to the cafeteria. Derek and Wally were still lost, still debating over which way to go. "Guys," she said, "I'm at the ramp. The first one. You have your lights on, right?"

"Of course we do, Priscilla." Derek didn't sound happy.

"How's your air?"

"Getting a little low." Wally again.

"All right. I've got a couple of tanks with me. Have you seen any corridors that curve?"

"What difference does that make?" asked Derek.

"Please answer the question."

"No. Everything runs in a straight line."

"Okay. Wherever you are now, I need you to stop moving around. You're still on the deck with the open hatch, right?"

"Yes."

"Have you been moving more or less in the same direction? Is there any chance you turned around and passed the area where the cafeteria was located?"

"No, we turned around once or twice, but I don't think we went back that far."

"Okay. Look around you and find the nearest place where a corridor crosses the one you're in."

"We just passed one."

"Good. Go back to it. When you get there, stop. Then give me a few minutes. When I tell you, aim your lamps in all four directions."

Intersections appeared at regular intervals, in each case about a two-minute walk. She stopped at one just as Derek's voice came back on. *"We're here, Priscilla."*

"Good." She turned off her own lamp. "Now shine your lights for me. Both directions, in both passageways."

Everything stayed dark.

"Okay. Stay where you are. Give me a couple of minutes and I should be able to find you."

"Priscilla," said Derek, *"I don't think we have time for this."*

"Stay with it. We'll be okay." She passed an open door as she hurried along the corridor. That would be the room with the garments on the bulkhead. She arrived at the next intersection. But again the corridor was dark.

Her major concern was that they'd wandered in a reverse direction without realizing it. That they were on the far side of the vehicle. But it was hard to believe they'd gotten completely turned around and not noticed. The next intersection was again dark.

She needed two more cross passageways before she saw lights. She responded with a loud "Yes!" and showed them her lamp.

"Hi, Hutch," said Wally. *"We are glad to see you."*

They switched out Wally's tank on the way back. Derek commented that it was surprisingly easy to get lost in the vehicle. *"We should have been more careful, Priscilla. I'm glad you were available."* She knew, inside the helmet, he was smiling.

"So, what do you make of all this, Derek?" she asked as they arrived back in the *Eiferman* and began climbing out of their suits.

He laid his helmet on one of the chairs in the passenger cabin. "Well, one thing's confirmed."

"And that is?"

"There was an advanced civilization out here. And they scrambled—at least some of them did—to get away from the black hole."

Ken looked skeptical. "That thing would have been able to carry a lot of passengers. But it was adrift. You think they actually got clear? Some of them?"

"I hope so," said Derek.

"It's interesting to do the math," Hutch said.

"What math is that?" asked Wally.

"How many levels does it have? The transport?"

Derek and Wally gazed at each other. "We only went to two."

"If Barry has the numbers right, it has eight. Each level will have approximately a million rooms."

"That doesn't surprise me."

"Two occupants in a room. Eight levels. How many passengers can you move with that kind of capacity?"

"None," said Wally. "Not without thrusters."

"Wally, you have a high-tech civilization living in the Calliope system. They knew for a long time the black hole was coming."

"So," said Ken, "what's your point?"

"They developed a technology specifically for moving people."

"But there's no drive unit," said Wally.

"The drive units were separate from the transport vehicles. Maybe it was more practical that way."

Derek nodded. "Makes sense. They might not have had time, or maybe even the resources, to manufacture a fleet of transports and equip them with an interstellar drive. So, you leave off the drive. Just produce an oversized carrier that can take millions of passengers. You connect it to something with a drive unit that *can* take them to a nearby star, deliver the passengers, and bring the carrier back for more. They probably used magnetics to lock the carrier to a ship."

Wally shook his head. "The ship better have one hell of a drive unit."

"So, why's this one floating out here?" said Beth.

"They were done with it. Maybe the evacuation got a bit hectic toward the end and they had to jettison it. You'll notice that we didn't find any bodies."

"That's true," said Ken. "I guess they got everybody off and just didn't need it anymore. I hope so."

Derek looked pleased. "I think we can assume they got at least some of their people clear. They'd have needed a Goldilocks world, and they'd have had to choose the closest one they could find. It might not be too hard to find."

"You're kidding," said Wally.

"If we could locate the place, we might be able to go to say hello."

"Oh yes," said Beth, "President Proctor would just love that."

"Well, I'm not talking about literally doing it. Though if it were up to me, I'd love to drop by and congratulate them. Whatever, I think we have an obligation to find out, if we can, who they were and where they went."

"So, what are you suggesting?"

"They were trying to move a planetary population. So, they couldn't have gone far." He looked around. "Anyone object?"

Derek Blanchard, Extract from Notebook, Intended for Autobiography

I've always thought there was nothing in my life I wanted more than to share a lunch with members of an advanced species. That's not going to happen, I guess. But at least, I'd very much like to get a look at the kind of world they'd select for themselves. The ice world is going to become one of the great cosmic mysteries. Did they survive? Eventually, we are going to have to track down what really happened. We can do it now, or we can leave it for someone else.

—Wednesday, April 9, 2256

19.

In a world that is usually boring when it is not painful, intelligence can be measured as a capacity to find amusement, or at least distraction.

—Gregory MacAllister, "Options," *Baltimore Sun*, February 2, 2249

It's not that difficult," Hutch told Beth, who'd come onto the bridge and was sitting beside her. "They'd have been looking for an F, G, or K class star. As close as possible. With a planet in the habitable zone."

"I've got that," said Beth. "But you said the disadvantage of the Locarno is that it only works effectively when we know how far the target is. Right?"

"That's correct."

"If we start guessing how far these stars are, aren't we going to run out of fuel?"

"We would if we did it that way."

"So what way are we going to do it?"

"We'll measure the distance to the candidate stars."

Beth looked out at the sky. "Exactly how do we do that?"

"It's not hard. We do a parallax."

She smiled. "Sounds intriguing."

"At the moment, Barry's using the telescope to do a spectral analysis of every star we can see. That'll narrow them down to the ones that could support a living world. The F, G, and K types. Once we have that, we'll do the parallax."

"Which is what?"

"We measure how much a star's position shifts when we look at it from two different locations. Back in the old days, they measured a star's angle and waited six months for the Earth to get to the other side of the sun. That moved the observer three hundred million kilometers. Then they did a second measurement to determine how much the star's angle had changed. The more distant the star, the less the change."

Wally frowned. "We don't have the resources to hang out here for another six months."

"Of course not. We're not riding the Earth. We've got the *Eiferman*. Give us some time. When Barry's finished with his measurements, we'll do a jump, a light-year or two, and make another set of observations. That'll allow us to figure out which ones are close enough to have been likely destinations for whoever lived on that frozen world."

In fact, they had thirty-one candidates by midafternoon. Derek ordered the jump, and Hutch took them forward one light-year. Barry then determined the ranges, and Derek worked out a schedule.

Their first choice turned out to be a binary; a pair of

stars orbiting each other. "I should have told Barry to rule out any binaries," Derek said. "I assumed he knew that wouldn't work for a stable system."

The second selection had, as far as they could determine, no planets, at least none within a habitable range. The third, however, revealed a world in the middle of the habitable zone, and it was filled with life. Broad continents were overrun with large, lumbering lizards and flexible plants that seized and clung to whatever smaller creatures got within range. "They certainly wouldn't have come here," said Beth.

Hutch and Derek were on the bridge; the others were seated on the front porch, watching telescopic images on the display: close-ups of a bird with a huge beak and claws patrolling a beach, and a giant worm attacking a colony of insects.

"Okay," said Derek. "Let's move on."

Hutch was happy to leave. "Barry," she said, "get ready to head for Number Four." She warned everybody in the cabin.

"Something I should point out," said Barry. *"Number Four is directly in the path of the black hole."*

"That eliminates Four," said Hutch. "No way they'd have evacuated there."

"Barry," said Derek, "would we be going out of our way to travel to Four?"

"No, sir. Not much."

"How much?"

"Approximately a day."

"If no one objects, why don't we take a look?"

Derek Blanchard, Extract from Notebook, Intended for Autobiography

I should have noticed Four was in the path of that thing when I was putting together the schedule. Getting old, I guess. In any case, I probably would have checked it out anyhow. Who knows what might be there?

—Saturday, April 12, 2256

20.

Afoot and light-hearted I take to the open road,
Healthy, free, the world before me,
The long brown path before me leading wherever I
choose.
　　　　　—Walt Whitman, "Song of the Open Road," 1856

Number Four had a world in the zone. And, to every-one's distress, there were small clusters of lights on its night side. *"It's quiet,"* Barry said. *"We aren't acquiring any radio transmissions."* A cratered moon hung in the sky, about half the size of Luna. As they drew nearer and were able to see the sunlit side, they discovered it was an ocean world. No continents were visible, only occasional island chains, mostly covered with green vegetation. It had polar ice caps. And large white clouds drifted through the sky. Then Barry was back: *"I have located an oceangoing vessel."* He put it on the display. It could have been a freighter out of the nineteenth century. Three smokestacks left a trail behind it. Crates were piled fore and aft.

"There's something moving on the deck," said Barry, *"but I*

can't get enough magnification to make out what it is. Other than it's wearing gray clothes. Or maybe it is gray."

"It's a beautiful world," said Beth. "Do we know for certain that it's going to get wrecked? The way that other place was?"

"We haven't really checked the numbers," said Derek. "All Barry told us was that the black hole is headed this way."

Hutch turned the question over to the AI.

"I regret being the source of bad news," he said, *"but there is no way this system can escape what happened to the ice world. I don't have enough information at the moment on the trajectory of the local sun to provide details, but I am aware of the general direction of its movement. It will be at least pulled apart."*

Derek sighed and shook his head. "I don't believe this," he said.

Hutch took them into orbit and they quickly found two more cities. A number of the islands had towns. There were also fleets of boats, some with sails, others powered with engines. And occasional ships, like the freighter. The skies were empty of aircraft, though, except for a dirigible. "Well, one good thing," said Derek. "I don't think we have to worry about these guys chasing us back home."

"I guess not," said Hutch. "They're trapped here."

Probably because of the towns and ships, she had almost expected the inhabitants to resemble humans. But they didn't. They had the basic parts, arms, legs, and a head, but the similarity stopped there. Their skin was gray, with no fur or hair visible anywhere. They had enormous, sharp noses and huge mouths lined with teeth. Their eyes were large and placed well back on the sides of the head. She saw no sign of ears.

"They look like dolphins," said Ken.

They did. There was even something on their back, pushing up under their shirts. A fin, maybe?

"Barry," said Derek, "when will the hole get here?"

"It will arrive in the immediate area in about ninety years. But the effects will begin to be felt long before then. A fair estimate, if you are asking how long the current conditions of this world will endure, would be about sixty years."

Derek sat back and stared at the overhead. "They aren't going to be able to do much to help themselves. In fact, they probably won't even know they have a problem until it appears in their skies." Eventually, he looked in her direction. "What do you think we should do, Priscilla?"

"You mean whether we should warn them about what's coming?" He nodded. "I can't see anything to be gained by it. That assumes we could find a way to explain it at all."

"I know." He took a deep breath. "This is turning into a nightmare."

"Let's just go find the people from the ice world," said Beth.

"I guess that would be the prudent course. For now, Priscilla, let's do a flyover. Take a look. I'd like to get a sense of how they live. Maybe get some pictures of them."

Hutch wanted to lighten the mood. "Why don't we sit down with a couple of them, take them some pizza?"

"Are you serious?"

"I must have misunderstood you somewhere, Derek. I was under the impression you thought that sitting with aliens to see what they have to say about the universe was something you always wanted to do."

"There's some truth to that."

"We'll probably never have a better chance."

"What I've always wanted to do was sit with somebody from a million-year-old civilization and exchange ideas."

"Oh."

"These guys do not qualify. Did you see the smoke coming out of the chimneys down there?"

"I saw it, yes."

"They're wood burners. But I would like to get some closeups of them. See what they're like. So, how about we get in the lander and go down and find out?"

"Derek, let's get serious for a moment. We're supposed to stay far enough away so they can't see us."

"What harm can we do?"

"Letting them see us might have a long-range effect. And not a good one."

"Priscilla, they don't *have* a long-range future." He was beginning to sound exasperated. "Look, we'll be out of here by the end of the day. Tomorrow they'll be in their boats talking about us, and by Friday something else will have come up and they'll have forgotten all about us." He got out of his chair and started for the passenger cabin. "Just relax," he said. "We won't change anything."

"Okay, guys," Derek said, "we're going to take the lander down and look around a bit. Who wants to come?"

Everybody. They all went to the launch bay. Hutch opened the door of the lander. "We should leave someone on board."

Derek looked around for a volunteer. "Who wants to stay with the ship?"

Ken shook his head. "How would I get it home if something happened to you guys?"

"Just tell Barry to take you back," said Hutch.

"He'd do that anyway, wouldn't he? If something happens?"

"Yes."

"Then I think I'll go with the shuttle."

"It's a lander," said Wally.

"Whatever."

Derek looked around. Nobody was volunteering to stay. "Wally, I guess you're our guy."

Sunlight filled a sky that had become cloudless. Hutch pulled the brim of her Hawks baseball cap lower and took them toward one of the islands. "Don't get too close," Derek said.

She activated the telescope. Ken was first to comment on the presence of a volcano. It was on the south side of a massive island. "There's a city," he added. "I guess it's inactive."

"Must be," said Derek.

The city consisted of a vast array of dwellings and a few larger buildings, including two that looked like factories. And a couple of wind farms.

They had cars. Hutch watched them moving slowly through the city. Others passed along country roads. "They probably don't have either coal or oil," said Ken. "If you have to get everything from the ocean, you have a serious problem."

"But a lot of the oil," said Wally, "comes out of oceans."

"Which can only happen if you know it's there in the

first place. I wouldn't think collectors and wind generators would be enough to provide an adequate supply of electricity for a city, but maybe they've figured out an alternative method."

"*Maybe nuclear?*" said Wally.

They continued across the ocean. Most of the larger islands seemed to be inhabited, sometimes with towns and small cities, often by only a few cottages. They were approaching one that had a large beach. The beach was crowded. But they were still too far out to get a good look at the sunbathers, even with the telescope.

Hutch was about to pull away when Derek told her to keep going. "Let's see if we can get a decent look at these guys."

"Okay." She took the vehicle down just over the ocean, where it would be less likely to attract attention.

A town lay immediately behind the beach. And to the north she saw something that looked like a tower, and, a couple of kilometers beyond that, a port facility. A freighter was just leaving the harbor.

The tower rose well above the trees. It was plain enough, no sculptures or anything except for a blue globe at the top of the spire. It manifested the aura of a place of worship. And there was a parking lot, occupied by several cars.

The town was small, consisting mostly of cabins and cottages. There were two moderately sized buildings, probably a school and a city hall. She could also make out moving cars. "But where do they come from?" asked Derek. "There's obviously no manufacturing plant for them here anywhere."

"Imports," said Ken. "They must be pretty well organized to be able to manage the economy. Most of these islands wouldn't support a population large enough to manufacture several major products. So, they have to bring everything in. Probably each island specializes in something. This place might do TV sets and cranberry sauce."

"Focus on the beach," said Derek. "Let's try to get a look at them."

There were probably a thousand or more of the creatures on the sand and in the ocean. They were wearing short pants or maybe bathing suits, and many were sitting under umbrellas. For a wild moment it reminded Hutch of the Jersey Shore.

"Seen enough?" she asked.

"Yeah." He took a deep breath. "Go."

She began to climb. And almost immediately heard something crackle and felt a simultaneous loss of power. And *lift*. She didn't have much altitude and suddenly it was almost gone.

"Uh-oh," she said.

"What's wrong?" asked Derek.

"Not sure."

"It's the AG generator," said Tasha. *"I cannot be certain what's happening. Power going down."*

"Can you make a correction?"

"One of the couplings has failed. Right wing. And no, I can't compensate for it. It has to be replaced." The lander had three couplings, one in the undercarriage, and one in each wing. *"We have spares on board."*

Hutch took a deep breath. More maintenance issues.

She wondered if the Union teams had gotten *any* of their work done.

"Head for the island," said Derek. Right. They couldn't afford to go down in the ocean. "Wally, you following this?"

"He's not in range," said Tasha.

"Get us to the island," said Derek.

"We're too low." Barely skimming the waves. There was an outside chance she could make it, but she'd almost certainly either crash in the surf or on the sand. If she got lucky and made it past them, she'd come down on the town.

"They've seen us," said Beth. They were crowding into the water to get a better look.

Derek threw up his hands in frustration. "Don't go down in the ocean, Priscilla."

"For God's sake, Hutch," Ken said, "look out."

She wasn't sure what he wanted her to do. But she was not going to take out the sunbathers. "Tasha, is the air breathable?"

"Fortunately, yes, I believe so."

Ken began shouting at the creatures. "Get out of the way! What are they doing? Just standing there. *Move*, you idiots."

Actually, they'd begun moving, giving her space. But it wasn't happening quickly enough.

Beth was pointing directly ahead. "There are little ones. Children."

"Tasha," Hutch said, "release your hold on the AG. We're going to have to ditch in the water."

"You sure?"

"Do it, Tasha."

"You can't do that, Priscilla," said Derek. "If we lose the lander, we'll never get out of here."

"If we don't, we'll kill them." She turned away from the island.

"You're too far out," said Derek. The beach suddenly looked far away. He started to reach for the controls but she pushed him away.

"Can't help it."

It didn't matter. Another of the couplings let go and they went into near free fall, splashed into the ocean, submerged briefly, bobbed back up, and began to sink. "Nice work, Priscilla," he growled. "I think you managed to miss everybody. But you've probably killed *us*."

Hutch ignored him. "Sorry about that, guys. Everybody out." They were about three hundred meters offshore.

"By the way," said Derek, "I'm not the world's best swimmer." He climbed out of his seat and opened the inner airlock hatch.

"It's all right, Derek," said Ken. "I've got you. Come on, let's get out of here."

"So much," Beth said, "for keeping the aliens from finding out we've come." She picked up a container of fresh water as Derek pushed into the airlock. Hutch got up and hurried back to the storage cabinet. The couplings were in a plastic bag. She grabbed them and followed the others to the airlock. Derek opened the outer hatch and climbed out onto the wing. Water began spilling in.

They piled out with him. Derek's face was drained as he slipped into the sea. Ken went in behind him, and Beth moved to help where she could. Hutch was still on the wing when another wave lifted the lander and dropped it again. She held on and realized her baseball cap was just going to get in the way. She tossed it inside and closed the outer hatch to keep any more water from getting in. They would probably have no further use for the vehicle, but there was no point letting the ocean into it.

Beth looked toward her. "You got them? The couplings?"

"Yes."

"Good. You need a hand?"

"I'm fine. Long as there aren't any gators out here."

The lander slipped below the surface and she was afloat, riding the waves toward shore, trying to keep the bag out of the water. It was supposed to be waterproof, so the contents should be secure as long as she kept it closed. But she was taking no chances.

It was a long swim. Ken stayed with Derek, but they seemed to be managing okay. She was impressed that the boss didn't lose his cool. The waves kept breaking over his head in a recurring rhythm. He was choking and coughing up water, but he stayed calm.

As they got closer to the beach, the islanders backed away and gave them plenty of space. Hutch got the impression they wanted to help but were reluctant to get close to their visitors. In any case, they gave no indication of resentment or violent intent. Those large eyes grew wider as the humans got closer, and their faces revealed a substantial level of shock. Odd how alien features could be interpreted for emotions in much the same way as humans. Hutch had noticed that before and was beginning to suspect it would be a universal quality. You were probably always going to be able to read humor or rage or whatever in nonverbals, no matter where the subject was from.

A few of them were accompanied by creatures that closely resembled dogs.

Unsure what to expect from the islanders, the team tried to stay together as they got closer to land. Eventually, Hutch was able to touch bottom and begin walking. As they came out of the water, she got her first good look at the islanders. They were roughly the same size as humans, with satiny flesh that ranged in colors from pale to light blue. Most of them wore shorts, all of similar designs. Some were large and bulky, presumably males, and others were generally trim and often accompanied by children. No obvious sexual organs were visible. Hutch recalled having read that female dolphins had nipples, but that they were hidden beneath a fold of skin. If that was true of these creatures, they were well concealed. There were a few who could have belonged to either gender, although she had no doubt *they* could distinguish the differences. Eyebrows were replaced by distinctive ridges. Their arms seemed shorter than she'd have expected. Their hands had five digits, including thumbs; their feet lacked toes, instead ending in flaps. And they all had a narrow ridge down the center of their backs. A fin, possibly, in an earlier era?

Their mouths were huge. When they opened them, they looked almost large enough to swallow her.

Several carried towels. They appeared worried, even fearful. Most of the children were being taken back toward the trees. She heard Ken's voice: "Everybody okay?"

Beth nodded and Hutch raised her left hand. Derek

said something she couldn't make out over the roar of the surf. But he looked good.

They moved within a few steps of the beach. "All right," Hutch said, "let's hold it here." Waves were still coming in behind them, swirling past their legs. She raised her left hand again in what she hoped was a universal indication of amicability. "Hello," she said, raising her voice and summoning her best smile. "It's good to meet you guys." The closer ones reacted by backing away. Some were pointing at her, looking dismayed, whispering to each other.

"Let me try," said Derek. He strode past her.

One of the islanders raised a hand and made a noise that sounded like a creaking floorboard. Then it came forward, the hand now held out in what appeared to be a friendly gesture.

Derek held *his* hand out in the same manner, and they touched fingertips, each watching the other carefully. "We hope we haven't caused a problem."

The islander clasped Derek's hand and replied with an extended creak. Some of the other islanders inhaled. Another universal? "I think," said Beth, "we're okay."

They sat down on the beach. Fortunately, it wasn't as hot as it had appeared from inside the lander. "What do we do now?" asked Beth.

Derek was concentrating on smiling at the locals. "We don't have many options. When the ship gets back, we call Wally and let him know what happened. He's going to have to go back home and ask for help. Get them to send somebody after us."

"So, we're talking two months," said Ken.

"Assuming they come at all."

"Oh," said Derek, "I don't think we need to worry about that. They're not going to leave us out here to die."

Beth looked up at the sun. "It might be a good idea to make for the woods."

They got to their feet and started across the beach. The sunbathers backed off, giving them plenty of room. Hutch could hear a couple of cars pulling in somewhere, but she didn't see them. While they walked, she was thinking about Wally. The *Eiferman* needed approximately an hour and twenty minutes to orbit the planet. So it would be a good idea to check the time so she'd know when he was overhead again. She dug out her commlink. Her clothes were drenched, of course. Which probably meant—

She held her breath as she stopped and opened it. It did not show a time. She tried to activate it, but it did not respond.

She followed everyone into the woods, where they were sitting down and talking about how good it was to be out of the sun. "Anybody know what time it is?" she asked.

Derek understood immediately what she meant. He fumbled through his pockets and came up with the commlink. He held it out in front of him in the sunlight, glared at it, and pressed his finger against it several times, but got nothing. He shouted at it in a hopeless rage. "Damn," he said. "I don't believe this." He looked around. Beth and Ken tried theirs with the same result.

"So how do we contact Wally?" Ken demanded.

Derek closed his eyes.

"These things are all supposed to be waterproof," Hutch said.

"So what's wrong with them?" asked Beth.

Derek took a long time to reply. "We've been cutting corners everywhere we can. It's what happens when they slice funding." He stared hopelessly at his commlink.

"Wally won't even know what happened to us," Beth said. "When he gets back in the area, we'll just be missing."

For a moment, Hutch thought Ken was going to throw his commlink at Derek. "You know," he said, "if you were going to be cutting corners on the equipment, it might have been a good idea to let us know about it before we came on board." His glare locked on Hutch. "Did *you* know about this?"

"She had no idea," Derek said. "To be honest, neither did I. But I knew we might have problems. Look, I'm sorry. I just didn't think anything like this would happen."

"I guess not," said Ken. "I'm inclined to wonder what else could go wrong, but I doubt it'll matter now." His eyes turned to Hutch. "You might have been able to make land if you'd tried a little harder."

"I didn't have control of the thing, Ken. I might have killed a bunch of them."

"You've killed *us.*"

Derek asked for the plastic bag. Hutch handed it over and he opened it and took the couplings out. "At least they're dry," he said. "For whatever good it will do."

Ken looked back at either the ocean or the group of islanders who were standing nearby. "The water might not have been too deep out there. Hutch, do you know how to install these things?"

"Yes. It's simple enough."

"Okay." Ken took a deep breath. "Now, if we could get

down there and do it, would it work? Or would the water be a problem again?"

She sat down on a fallen log, and the others joined her. "The water would be a problem. The couplings have to be kept dry. I think."

"Maybe we could hire a ship with a crane."

Nobody laughed.

The beach crowd was almost mingling. They had apparently decided that their visitors meant no harm. Both groups were making efforts to communicate, but they couldn't get much beyond touching hands and pointing at each other. The humans delivered some smiles, and the islanders returned snorts and giant grins.

Ken looked overawed. "This is really off the charts. Is this the kind of advanced life form you get if most of a planet is underwater?"

"I was wondering the same thing," said Derek. He was still standing, exchanging nonverbals with one of the islanders. "By the way, let me introduce my good friend Arin. He and I go way back."

Arin extended his left hand to Hutch. She took it and was impressed by the gentleness of the gesture. "Hello, Arin," she said.

He responded with something on the order of "Rakul," except that the k somehow came out as two syllables. It sounded like a nut being cracked. It didn't matter. His eyes lit up, and Hutch followed her inclination and hugged him. "I'm glad to meet you, Arin. Maybe we have more in common that I thought."

"And maybe," added Derek, "you just did something damned stupid. Be careful."

There were more attempts at exchanges. The islanders were talking with one another in a manner than made it clear that whatever fear they might have felt had dissipated.

Gradually, Hutch was feeling more relaxed. Getting off this world was going to be a major problem, but the atmosphere had certainly calmed.

Someone arrived with a food tray. It was filled with strips of a lemon-colored fruit and crackers. Hutch picked up one of the strips and looked toward Beth.

"Probably won't hurt you," Beth said. "But no guarantees."

It was going to be all they'd have for a while. She put the strip on a cracker and took a small bite. Not particularly tasty, but it went down easily. It might have been trout that hadn't been cooked properly.

"It's good," said Derek, trying to look pleased.

"We have to let Wally know we're still alive," said Derek.

Hutch nodded. She'd been doing an internal count, trying to keep track of the time. Her best guess was that it had been about forty minutes since the *Eiferman* had left the area. It would take approximately an hour and twenty minutes to complete an orbit. So, it was probably halfway around the planet. "So how are we going to do this?" asked Ken. "Go out on the beach and jump up and down?"

"That's probably the best we have."

The islanders came close, two and three at a time, and

tried talking with them. They were obviously enjoying themselves. The nonverbals weren't hard to pick up, especially from creatures with large eyes that lit up every time one of the visitors spoke to them. They were especially good at signaling that whatever had just been said had eluded them. But it was okay. *We're all friends here.*

In time, the young ones came in too, invariably accompanied by parents.

Eventually, Derek and Arin came over and sat down beside Hutch. "I've been trying to explain to Arin that we've got another vehicle in the sky, and that we need to signal it and let Wally know we're alive."

"How has that gone?"

"Actually, not badly. I think he understands that there are more of us and that we're trying to make contact. The problem with your plan is that if we go out onto a beach with a thousand bathers, we can jump up and down all we like, but we're not going to stand out very much. Especially since they're all bigger than we are. And Wally doesn't even know where to look for us." He turned and nodded at Arin, who smiled, reached over, said something, and got to his feet.

Hutch watched him walk away. There were a couple other islanders who'd been waiting nearby. They exchanged gestures with Arin that involved tapping their skulls. Then they proceeded out through the trees onto the beach. They walked across the sand, stopping to talk to others, and as she watched the movement expanded. They were spreading out, explaining something, sharing information, and gradually everyone began coming back toward the trees.

"What's going on?" asked Hutch.

"How much time do we have?" asked Derek. "Before Wally gets back?"

"I'd guess about fifteen minutes."

"Then let's go."

They all went back out onto the sand. As they watched, the area cleared. Those who were in the surf stayed there. Everyone else, except for a few, was moving away from the center of the beach, leaving it for their visitors.

"Incredible," said Hutch. "They're doing this for us?"

"Thank Arin."

She'd lost track of him. They formed a line, hand in hand, facing the ocean. One of the islanders hurried over to them and gave each of them a towel.

The sun was moving into the western sky. Most of the clouds that had been present earlier were gone. Derek was peering into the east. "Should have brought sunglasses," he said. "You guys see anything?"

"I doubt we'll be able to see it," Hutch said. "Not in the daylight anyhow. We wouldn't have any problem picking it up tonight."

"That would work fine if we could shine some lights at it."

Hutch began waving her towel. *Please, Wally,* she thought, *be there.*

21.

Alone, alone, all all alone,
Alone on a wide, wide sea!
And never a saint took pity on
My soul in agony.
                        —Samuel Taylor Coleridge, "Rime of the Ancient
                                                    Mariner," 1798

They stayed with it, waving towels and occasionally yelling at the empty sky until finally they were exhausted and overheated. The ocean by then looked extraordinarily inviting and Hutch might have considered going for a swim, except that she had nothing to change into.

There was no sign of the *Eiferman.* "But he would probably have stayed with the original course," she said. "So, if he was scoping the islands, he might have seen us."

"You don't sound optimistic," said Beth.

"I'd feel more confident if he'd been there when we went down."

Arin came over and looked at Derek. Derek nodded and held up a hand. Arin understood, and a few minutes later the Dolphins reclaimed their beach.

"You can't stay out here forever." That seemed to be the message Arin was trying to deliver as he stood and looked back over his shoulder toward the trees and held out his hands invitingly. Yes. Of course. Hutch and her friends exchanged glances and nods, and followed him back into the forest.

When they'd gotten out of the sun, Arin confronted Derek and asked a question, part language, part signals. It wasn't hard to guess the meaning: Did we think we'd contacted whoever was in the sky?

Derek shook his head and held out his hands. No way to know. He turned to Hutch. "He realizes we were in trouble and you could have crash-landed on the beach. I'm pretty sure he appreciates what you did."

Arin signaled they should walk.

They looked at one another. "We're going to need his help," said Derek, "if we have any chance to survive." He waved everybody on. "Let's go."

"Where to?" asked Ken.

"I'd guess wherever Arin wants to take us."

They came out of the trees onto a winding dirt road that led north. Nobody said anything. Behind them, the sunbathers gathered and watched but did not follow. There were a few parked cars, which looked more like golf carts with canvas roofs. A couple of the islanders came out of the foliage, got into two of the vehicles, and pulled abreast of them, where they stopped and had a brief conversation with Arin. Everybody waited while some sort of agreement was reached. Then Arin indicated they should get into the cars. Each was designed to accommodate three passengers.

Actually, the rear seat was so large, it could have taken three itself. Beth and Ken got into one, and Derek, Hutch, and Arin into the other. Derek raised a hand to signal they were ready. Arin said something to their driver and he returned a smile that was wider and somehow as congenial and innocent as any Hutch could remember. They pulled out onto the road and continued north.

The trees blocked off the sky. Birds sang and flapped in the upper branches. A pair of creatures that might have been lizards chased one another up a vine. A small creature with brown fur watched from behind a bush.

They passed a few cabins and cottages. In one of them, two creatures sat on a porch. They got out of their seats and stared as the cars approached. Hutch couldn't help noticing that a lamp was lit in one of the windows. That drew her attention to wires attached to several places.

She was getting better at distinguishing the sexes. The females were more graceful, with softer features and voices. They wore mostly what she thought of as casual clothing, skirts, tunics, and pants; males wore primarily pullovers with images and lettering, jeans, and shorts.

The road crossed a small wooden bridge over a stream and forked. They stayed right, remaining close to the ocean. The sky was beginning to darken. "Storm coming," said Derek.

They heard the rumble of thunder. Again, just like home. They slowed for a curve. One of the natives was standing just off to one side. As they passed, he retreated behind a tree.

Arin, seated up front, turned, grinned, and pointed ahead. He added a comment that sounded encouraging. Probably along the lines of "We're almost there."

They came through a break in the woods and saw that the tower loomed ahead. A light drizzle began to fall. A handful of islanders were standing outside the front entrance, at the foot of some stone steps, watching as they came out of the trees.

"I think," said Derek, "they knew we were coming."

"Maybe they have radios."

"Let's hope. That would solve a problem."

The tower rose out of a structure of brick and stone that might have been a meeting hall or a school. Its arches and gables stood out from the utilitarian structures they'd seen in the town and near the harbor. And the azure globe at its peak gleamed in the sun. The architecture was uncomplicated and graceful, with a gloss that might almost be described as classical. "I think it's a temple," she said.

They pulled into a parking area and stopped next to a two-story stone cottage. Arin got out of the vehicle as the second car arrived. He spoke with both drivers. Everybody got out and said thank you, which prompted more giant smiles. The cars rode off, and Arin led them up a walkway to the cottage. A wooden front deck supported a couple of oversized chairs. Two sets of windows looked out from each floor. Curtains were drawn across all of them, but they were open, protected by screens. They climbed three steps onto a porch and opened the front door. Some of the natives who'd been standing back at the tower waved. The humans waved back.

The front door had a latch. Arin stood before it, turned it, and opened the door. The rain began to intensify. He reached inside and lights came on.

Arin held the door, inviting everyone in. The interior looked like an ordinary household. They were in a carpeted room with several chairs and a long table, a fireplace, and a half dozen electric lamps, two of which were lit. A staircase set against one wall rose to the upper level and a balcony. One wall held two shelves of books and a clock. The clock had two hands, one large and one small, and sixteen numbers. At least Hutch assumed that was what the symbols on its face were.

"Maybe there's only one way to make a clock," said Ken.

And they got a surprise: A dark wooden side table held a telephone. Which explained how some of the residents seemed to know so quickly about their arrival. The phone was twentieth-century style, pink rather than black like the ones in the movies. The handset was longer, but the speaker and earpiece were similar. Instead of a dial there were push buttons. It was plugged into a socket. Across the room Hutch saw another electrical device. She went over to look more closely and was joined by Arin, who seemed amused at her curiosity. Although, to tell the truth, the islanders consistently looked amused. She'd gotten a sense they thought that, despite their lander, their visitors weren't very bright. She lifted the handset and listened. It tinkled. "If they have this," Ken said, "they should have radio."

"Apparently not," said Hutch. "We heard nothing coming in."

"I guess." Ken took the phone from Hutch and studied it. "This would be worth a fortune at home."

"You know it's not a real antique," said Beth.

"Of course it isn't, but it's a telephone built on an alien world." He looked around at the others. "You think we could buy it from them and take it back with us?"

"Maybe," said Derek, "we should concentrate on finding a way to get *ourselves* home first."

Arin indicated he wanted a word with Derek. They walked over close to the clock. He pointed at it and then looked at Derek as if waiting for an answer.

Derek needed a minute, but he decided he was being asked whether there was a time problem. Did they have to connect quickly with whatever was in the sky? He looked at Arin and nodded. *Yes.*

Arin showed them the kitchen, which had a sink and faucet, cabinets and drawers, an electric range, some cooking utensils, and a large silver metal case that was probably a refrigerator. One of the drawers held knives, scoops, and two-pronged forks.

The refrigerator had food in bowls and containers. And a bottle of dark liquid. Arin indicated they should feel free to help themselves.

"We should probably get used to it," said Derek. Arin opened a cabinet and collected some cups. He handed them out, and set one on the counter for himself. Then he opened the bottle of dark liquid and poured some of it into his cup, which he drank. He handed the bottle to Derek. The message was clear enough: *I can understand you don't know what this is. But be assured it is safe.*

Everybody looked at Beth. What did she think?

Derek filled his cup, lifted it about halfway, and waited for the verdict.

"We probably don't need to worry about it," she said. "We're not likely to get poisoned or anything like that. The biggest concern is that we may not get any nutrients."

"Which means what?"

"Gone in three weeks."

"You're not serious?"

"It's probably not a problem. In any case, we don't have an option."

Derek raised his glass to her. "The eternal optimist. Here's looking at you, kid." He tasted it. Then drank it down.

"Alcohol?" asked Ken.

"I don't think so. But it provides something of a lift."

Beth filled her cup and tried it. "Tastes okay." She raised the drink to their host. "Thank you, Arin."

They all joined in, and obviously enjoyed the drink. When they finished, Arin demonstrated how the lamps worked, as it became apparent the cottage was going to be offered to them as a temporary home. It might take a little getting used to. They would, for example, have to push buttons to get the lamps to turn on and off rather than simply tell them what to do or touch them.

Arin provided towels and made a phone call. A few minutes later two of his friends showed up with boxes of clothing. They set the boxes on a table and the sofa, and Arin indicated the clothing was theirs. He pulled out a light blue shirt and held it up for Beth. It was considerably larger than she would have worn normally, but she accepted it gratefully. Arin smiled and signaled that there would probably be other size issues and he was sorry, but he just had no alternatives at the moment.

He waited while they picked out what they could use. They'd have to manage without socks during whatever time they'd be on the island, but they were otherwise able to make selections that would work, though everything was several sizes too big for them. Even Derek looked overwhelmed measuring himself against a pullover shirt and shorts that reached almost to his shins.

But the shorts and pullovers could also function as bathing suits. Derek tried to signal he was concerned whether they were taking over Arin's home. It took a while to get the message across, but they finally connected and Arin pointed at the tower. Or, as they were beginning to think of it, the temple. There was a clear connection between the temple and, apparently, supplying clothes and a cottage for those in need.

They carried everything upstairs, where there were three bedrooms. The beds were large, fortunately. To say the least. The smallest would have qualified as a king at home.

Framed pictures of, presumably, family members hung on the walls in all three rooms. One depicted four of them down on the beach, another showed Arin receiving a medallion, and a third was of a young couple, male and female, standing by a sculpted rock table. Possibly an altar?

The two islanders who'd brought the clothes went out and returned with towels, which they placed on the beds.

There was a bathroom, containing a shower, a sink, a toilet, and two cabinets. Everything was oversized, and there was some giggling that went on between Beth and Hutch. They also provided a laundry room at the rear. Hutch wasn't sure what it was when she first saw it: There was no machine, only a waste-high basin divided into two sections, with a device consisting of two rollers that, she assumed, would be used to squeeze water out of freshly washed clothing.

Her room had a bedside table with a lamp. Perfect for reading if she had something to read. The table had a drawer, which was empty. She put the couplings into it.

She was relieved to get out of her wet clothes. Finding apparel that provided a decent fit took a while, but ultimately, she was able to make everything work. Arin gave them scissors to cut the excessive length of the pant legs and sleeves. But she couldn't bring herself to do that. Eventually, he produced some cords that could be used to secure everything. Most of the shirts were pullovers. Ken commented that, when he wrote this part of his history, he'd call it "Flexibility Matters."

When they'd all gotten dressed, Arin sat down with them in the living room. *The place is yours,* he told them with gestures. While he was explaining, the door opened and a female came in. At least, they thought it was a female because she was diminutive by local standards, though she dwarfed Hutch and Beth. And there was something also in the way she moved and spoke. Her voice was at a considerably higher pitch than Arin's. Hutch could see she was surprised by the appearance of the visitors, all four of whom had gotten to their feet.

She found it impossible not to stare at them. Arin walked over and embraced her. She looked dumbfounded and asked a question, which had to be along the lines of "What in the world are these things?"

Arin replied with a single word. Then he delivered a giant smile, pointed a hand in her direction, and said, "Kwylla."

Kwylla, Hutch thought, remained remarkably calm, considering the situation. She wondered how she would have reacted coming home and finding a group of aliens in the living room. In fact, they probably had no concept about aliens. For all they knew, Hutch and her companions might have been demons.

Kwylla responded to each in turn, extending a hand and projecting a greeting. Then she and Arin exchanged a few comments. When they'd finished, she spoke again to her guests in a tone that suggested they were welcome and, if they needed anything, they shouldn't hesitate to ask. Then she laughed, a response that turned into a loud snort. It seemed a natural reaction, delivered through that oversized mouth and beak.

Ken wandered over to one of the bookshelves and opened a volume. Hutch took one down also. It had a cover that felt like leather, and a title across the front. Where else, of course, would you put a title? The lettering could have been Chinese or Hindi. She was impressed by the packaging and let Arin and Kwylla see her reaction. Arin indicated they could read one of the books if they wished. Or possibly keep it?

Kwylla declined a drink and, after a few minutes, excused herself and left.

She had just gone out the door when a bell rang. It was the phone. Arin picked it up. Hutch had not been able to get her mind off Wally. By now he would have flown over the beach area probably twice. Assuming he was still here. She wondered what she would do in similar circumstances. Wait here indefinitely until finally she had to give up and go home. Or leave immediately, hoping she could arrange for a rescue mission and get them back here as quickly as possible.

Arin remained on the phone. Ken had returned the book to the shelf, and Ken and Beth were wandering through the house, engaged in conversation. It was the perfect time to go outside to look for Wally.

The sky was clear. The sun had gone down. Hutch, standing on the porch, saw nothing moving overhead except a couple of birds. She had no idea how long it had been since the *Eiferman* had gone out of sight. Without a timepiece, and with no idea how long a day was on that planet, she felt lost. She'd forgotten to check on the details of this ocean world before they'd set out in the lander. That had been a serious blunder. She was getting careless.

Lights were on at the rear of the temple. A few others, from nearby cabins, were visible through the trees. A pleasant breeze was blowing in off the ocean, and the soft rumble of the incoming tide encouraged her to settle into one of the chairs and lean her head back. Just enjoy the night. Though she'd feel much better if they could contact Wally.

The door opened and Beth came out. "Any sign of him?" she asked.

"Not yet."

She sat down beside Hutch. They could hear voices inside, including Arin's. Then she saw Kwylla emerge from the temple's side door and come their way.

"Don't know what we'd have done without her and Arin," said Beth.

"I know. We owe them."

"I hate to think what they're facing. Or their kids. I wonder if they have any kids. Or if they're even a couple. Place like this, it's hard to be sure of anything."

"There are pictures of them with a couple of children," said Hutch.

Beth nodded and took a deep breath. "I suspect she'd like to see us go away."

"Who? Kwylla? What makes you say that?"

"It's how I'd react if unexpected guests arrived." She hesitated, and then continued: "Especially if I couldn't even talk to them."

Kwylla arrived at the porch steps, looked up, smiled, waved, and said something. Beth and Hutch both replied, and they all turned their inability to talk to one another into a joke. She climbed the steps onto the porch and reached for the door.

Hutch, looking for something to say, pointed toward the temple. "Nice piece of architecture."

Kwylla's smile widened. She understood perfectly that it didn't matter whether she could understand literally what Hutch had said. *"Koaka som,"* she said. She reached out and squeezed Hutch's shoulder, then nodded and went inside.

Beth and Hutch sat for a time talking about how lucky they'd been, how annoyed they were over the maintenance boondoggle, how the crash landing would become a major moment in Ken's book. At least, it would if they were lucky. The wind began to gust, tree branches swung back and forth, and then after a time, it grew quiet. Something small and furry charged past the porch and went up a tree. Seconds later Beth jumped out of her chair. "Look!" She was staring out over the trees. One of the stars was moving. The *Eiferman* was back.

22.

Language—human language—after all, is but little better than the croak and cackle of fowls, and other utterances of brute nature—sometimes not so adequate.
—Nathaniel Hawthorne, *The American Notebooks*, July 14, 1850

They all came outside to watch, and they stood shaking hands and raising fists as Wally slowly crossed the sky. Arin seized Derek, pointed at the ship and then at his visitors. The question he was asking was clear: *Is that how you arrived?* He looked stunned.

Derek nodded. "Yes."

Arin followed with another question. Again, obvious: *Will they come down for you?*

Derek closed his eyes. "No."

Hutch could see that Arin understood. Derek had been anxious to let the ship know they had survived. But if it could not land, it was of little value. She wondered whether Arin had a flashlight. She tried to ask, but couldn't make the meaning clear. Finally, she went inside and picked up one of the lamps. The cord wasn't long enough to allow her to take it out the door. She unplugged it, carried it outside, and raised it as if to signal the ship, but Arin didn't seem to get the message.

They watched as that single dull star moved westward. Arin took Derek's arm and led him off the porch. He held up a hand, asking Derek to wait. Then he went inside and came out seconds later with something that looked like a blade. He led Derek to his car while everybody else watched, wondering what was going on. He got in, started the engine, and pulled slowly away. Then he put his right hand in the air and turned it downward, mimicking a crash. To make sure his point was understood, he did something in the car and the engine coughed, sputtered, and died. He climbed out, lifted the hood, tinkered with the engine, got back in and restarted it. He left it running and looked at Derek.

"What's he doing?" asked Beth, who was leaning over Hutch's shoulder.

"I think he wants to know whether *we* can repair the lander."

"Can we?"

"If we can get it out of the ocean."

Derek came back toward the cottage, signaling for Arin to follow. They went inside. Hutch joined them. Derek took the glass he'd been using, finished the drink, and picked up a bowl that had been on the counter beside the sink. He put the glass in it and filled the bowl with water, submerging it. Then he turned to face Arin and shook his head. "No, Arin," he said. "We cannot fix it."

Arin surprised Hutch again: "Okay." He'd picked up some English.

Derek nodded, lifted the glass from the bowl, poured the water into the sink, held the glass horizontally over the counter and pretended it was taking off. "Now we can do it."

Arin got the message: remove it from the sea, and it can be repaired. He pointed at himself and showed Derek his hands, fingers spread. Then he closed them, opened them again but only showed him eight. Eighteen?

"I think," Derek said, "that he's trying to tell us they'll have the lander out of the water in eighteen days."

Hutch was reading it the same way. But Beth raised the critical issue: "Even if that's correct, will Wally stay that long?"

They went back outside and watched the *Eiferman* begin its descent toward the western horizon. Arin pointed at it and asked another question, but nobody could figure out what he wanted to know, other than maybe he was asking how long the ship would remain?

The temple door opened and Kwylla came out. She was carrying a small bag.

More food. She opened the bag as she came up onto the porch and showed them some cherry-colored nuggets. They looked good. Did anybody want one?

Everybody did. Maybe nobody wanted to take a chance of offending her. But these tasted much better than the orange-colored strips they'd offered earlier. The nuggets might also have been seafood, but Hutch couldn't be sure. When they'd finished, Kwylla put what was left in the refrigerator and tried to ask a question. Probably was there anything else she could do for them?

"You've done more than we could have hoped for," said Derek. She and Arin moved among them, clasping shoulders and forearms. Then they pointed toward the side door of the temple. They should feel free to go in if they needed anything? A few minutes later they said good-bye and returned to the temple.

Eventually, the humans retreated into the cottage and sat talking, going over the same topics. They became aware that some islanders had assembled outside. They stayed mostly at the edge of the trees, except for a few who came forward to stare through windows. Eventually, Derek went outside and waved at them, and said good-bye several times. *"Bora hycut."* As far as Hutch could tell, nobody took the hint.

"Lock the door," said Beth.

Ken tried but threw up his hands. "It doesn't seem to have a lock."

"That's a good sign," said Hutch. "Maybe these people don't have thieves."

They drew the curtains, and as best they could tell, the crowd eventually went away.

About an hour later, someone knocked. Ken opened the door and looked out at one of the females who'd brought over the boxes of clothes. She was carrying food this time. Ken took it from her, said thanks, and stood aside to invite her inside. But she said good-bye and withdrew.

"She's scared of us," said Beth.

Hutch tried the food. They were green niblets, and unlike the nuggets, they tasted flat. When she was growing up, that was always a good sign. Tasteless food was good for you. The stuff you liked was always what got you in trouble.

• • •

A chill crept into the cottage. They found a thermostat in the living room. Maybe. They weren't certain at first, but when Ken turned the knob, it got cooler, so he reversed it and the temperature rose. Nobody was saying much. They were tired, and everyone was probably scared that they would never see home again. Consequently, the conversation was confined to comments intended simply to keep the dreary silence from swallowing them. "You think Arin's a religious leader?"

"I wonder what kind of government they have here."

"I feel fine. As far as I can tell, the food's working."

Hutch was wondering how long a day was on this world. "Don't know," said Beth. "We'll see how long it takes for the sun to rise."

"We're lucky," Ken said, "they have some technology."

Nobody was going to argue with that. "I'm surprised these people have any decent level of technology at all," said Hutch. "This world is nothing but a handful of islands."

"I know. Hard to believe." Ken looked impressed. "I wish we could understand the language. I'd like to be able to hear what they're saying about us."

Beth nodded. "Me too. I wonder if their sense of humor is the same as ours."

"Who knows?" said Hutch. "Would all intelligent species laugh at the same things?"

"You know," Beth said, "I think they would. What else could laughter be except a reaction to the unexpected? I guess if it's also ironic. You know animals laugh, right?"

"But do they laugh at the same things we do?"

"To a degree. Tickle a monkey and watch his response.

It's the same sort of thing that gets a rise out of us. And it has all kinds of health benefits. I'd bet it will be the same everywhere."

"I was struck," said Derek, "by the way they responded to us. It suggests we all share the same sense of empathy."

Ken grunted. "There are a lot of *us* who missed the boat on that one."

Hutch was about to disagree, to mention the number of people who show up on news reports every day risking their lives for strangers, like the two Boy Scouts who'd charged into a house in the path of a Kansas tornado to rescue a disabled man. It had happened a few days before the *Eiferman* left Earth. And there was the group of women in Akoria who'd given their lives taking food and water to religious hostages in defiance of lethal lunatics. But she saw lights through the window and let it go. Arin's car had just pulled away.

Hutch and Beth searched the house for a flashlight but found nothing. They were out on the porch when the *Eiferman* made another pass. Derek and Ken were there an hour and twenty minutes later when it came again. No formal watch had been established because everyone wanted to pretend that Wally would stay in place until a support vehicle arrived. Nevertheless, when they saw the moving star, they wasted no time informing their partners.

Hutch watched through her bedroom window when the moon showed up. It looked reassuring. This was in so many ways an amicable world. Pleasant climate, friendly inhabitants, beautiful views. Hard to believe they were in such trouble.

When Derek took over the outside watch, Ken joined him and brought up the flashlight issue. "Beth told me about it. I assume you still haven't found one?"

"No," he said.

"I was wondering whether we couldn't convert a lamp. Take it outside and turn it on and off? Send something in Morse code maybe? Does anybody know Morse code?"

"Not sure how we'd send a Morse code signal with a lamp. We have to find a better way."

Hutch would have trusted Wally with her life. But on this occasion they needed him to make a decision that probably made no sense. He had no idea what had happened. He knew only that they'd gone missing over an ocean. And it was likely he'd assumed they were dead. Even if they weren't, there was no reason to stay more than a few days. If they weren't able to get back to the *Eiferman*, then there was no hope for them until he chased down a rescue mission. That would be at least two months. Probably longer. And the longer he waited around, the less their chances.

Or maybe it made more sense to wait. If they weren't dead, then he'd assume the lander was damaged. How long should he wait for them to do repairs?

She lay staring up at the ceiling, listening to the wind rustling through the trees and some distant thunder. Hutch didn't sleep well, and her discomfort increased when, after about an hour, she heard rain begin rattling down on the roof. Ordinarily, this kind of weather would have helped her relax. She enjoyed rainstorms and the occasional rumble of thunder. There was something about it that sounded lonely, that took her back to her childhood, imposing a sense of solitude and security. But on this night, they didn't help.

In the morning, Arin was present with Beth and Ken when she came downstairs, carrying her uniform and the islander clothes she'd worn the day before. "Derek's been outside since dawn," said Beth. "As far as we can tell, Wally's still there."

That was good news. She sat with them for a few minutes and was about to make for the laundry room when Beth told her that Derek was using it.

"Hasn't he gotten any sleep at all?"

"Not much."

Arin must have caught the tone. His eyes shut momentarily. Then he said something and Ken nodded.

"Believe it or not," said Beth, "they've been talking. Ken's learning the language, aren't you, love?"

Ken grinned. "I can say *hello, good-bye,* and *where's the washroom?*"

"I'm serious," said Beth. "That's the real reason Derek brought him along. Just in case we needed somebody who has serious language skills." Her eyes locked on him. "How many languages do you speak now? Six?"

"Probably more like two."

"He's kidding."

Ken turned and said something to Arin, who responded with that giant grin.

"What did you tell him?" asked Beth.

"That you think he's pretty good-looking."

When Derek appeared, carrying his laundry in a basket, he offered to show Hutch how the rollers worked. Arin asked

Ken something, probably to explain what he'd said. Ken replied, but judging from Arin's puzzled expression, he didn't understand. But he certainly saw the pile of laundry, so he caught Hutch's eye and pointed at himself. Could he help?

"No, Arin," she said. "Thanks. I can manage."

Again, Ken tried to translate. Maybe he did. In any case, it must have been obvious she was indicating she could figure it out. And it wasn't that difficult. The washtub had baskets and liquid soap. Pour it and hot water into one of the basins and wash the clothes. Rinse in the second basin and run them between the rollers to get rid of most of the water. The rollers were equipped with a handle, so they were easy to use. She was surprised that they didn't function on electricity.

There was a box of clothespins. When she'd finished, she picked some up, put everything in a basket, and took it all outside, where Derek's laundry was already hanging from lines strung between two of the trees. She was still working on getting everything up when Beth came out. "Hutch," she said, "you want to go over to the beach?"

"Sounds like a good idea, but I'm not sure my bathing suit won't fall off."

"Mine's a decent fit. They're elastic. And you can use a cord to fasten them."

Hutch knew that, of course. But tying clothes together to keep them from falling off wasn't appealing. Still, a day at the beach sounded like a good idea.

Ordinarily, she'd never have allowed herself to be seen in public in that outfit. But after all, there was no public. She doubted she could shock the islanders even if the suit *did* fall off. It was a crusty brown color, and, had it fit properly, it would have looked perfectly normal on an ocean beach in 1906. She had to tie the shoulder straps together at the back to keep the top from sliding down. And the bottom, which should have stopped at her thighs, hung below her knees.

Derek had joined Arin and Ken in the living room, where they were pointing at furniture and books and lamps, and exchanging vocabulary. "You guys want to go?" Beth asked. That surprised Hutch, who was planning on a girls' day out.

"I'd better stay with this," said Ken. "Got to learn the language."

"I can't get into the suit," Derek said. "Wave if you see Wally."

Arin said something to them, and repeated it when Ken appeared not to understand. He also pointed toward the door. Or maybe in the direction of the beach. There was another exchange, and then Ken said he was offering a ride.

Arin brought out a beach umbrella for them. Beth got a blanket and they were ready to go. Ken went along in the car. "We are making some progress," he told them. "But it will take a while." He explained that Arin had apologized that the suits weren't a better fit. "Apparently, they just don't make anything in your size."

As they pulled up at the beach, Arin said something. Hutch thought it was only one word. But Ken caught it. "He wants to know how long you expect to stay."

"Two hours?"

"Okay. I'll try to figure out when it's up. We'll be back for you. Have a good time."

. . .

There appeared to be even more bathers in the area than there'd been the previous day. And of course, Hutch and Beth caught everyone's attention as soon as they came out of the trees. The islanders didn't crowd around them as they had before, however. Everything was more surreptitious. They glanced toward them but quickly looked away. Many of them waved and smiled, but they steered curious kids in other directions.

It was warmer today. They set up the umbrella halfway between the line of trees and the surf, and rolled out the blanket.

They sat for a few minutes, wishing they had some sunblock. "It might not be a good idea to stay two hours," Beth said.

They drew more attention when they went into the surf. Hutch thought some of the younger ones were giggling. It was hard to tell. Clamshells were scattered everywhere. Gulls squawked and flapped. There was a wooden stand at the back of the beach where you could get food. The only things lacking were a boardwalk and lifeguards. "Interesting," said Beth. "I'd never thought of outer space this way. But I guess the universe is filled with ocean beaches."

Hutch pulled up her suit, which was slipping a bit, and strode into the waves. Just what she needed.

They were out beyond the surf when Hutch's attention was caught by a young Dolphin in a bright red bathing suit. It was a female who had apparently wandered away from a group and seemed to be struggling. She was too far out, in water that was dark and choppy. More ominous: No waves were breaking in her immediate vicinity. Hutch took an automatic glance around the beach before recalling there were no lifeguards. And nobody seemed to notice what was happening.

It was a rip current, sucking her into deeper water. She hesitated briefly, concerned about possibly scaring the child. But worrying about that was silly.

"You okay?" Beth asked as she changed direction.

The Dolphin looked as if she was trying to come back toward the beach, which of course was the wrong tactic.

"Got a problem." Hutch moved quickly forward and, within a few strokes, felt the rip current take hold of her. But she kept going, calling back to Beth to stay clear.

The child went underwater. Hutch reached the area moments later and dived. But she couldn't see her anywhere. She stayed down until she was forced back to the surface. *Where'd she go?* A couple of the islanders were coming her way to help. She went back down and fought her way through the currents until again she had to surface. When she came up that second time, one of the creatures grabbed her and began pulling her through the water. Away from the place where the child had disappeared. "No!" she screamed at it. "Stop! I'm okay!"

But it held onto her, dragging her off to one side of the rip current and ultimately out of it. Then, while it held onto her with one hand, it pointed toward the beach. The girl was back on the surface, casually floating in on the crest of a wave.

"I don't think she was ever in any danger," said Beth.

The islander released her. And bestowed a huge smile

on her. Then it turned away. She wasn't certain whether it was male or female.

Hutch watched as the kid came out of the surf, laughed, and jogged onto the beach. "I guess," she said, "there's a reason they look like dolphins." She looked past the child, out across the waves. Beautiful place, this beach. She thought again of the lost world adrift in the shadow of the black hole. What would it be like when the thing arrived here? Would the sun be ripped apart while that child watched in horror? Or would there simply be a quiet sunset with the light gone forever?

23.

It was a long-ago night when that lonely star
Drifted across the alien sky
And brought hope to our desperate hearts.
We will never forget.
—Kenneth Squires, *Heart of the Milky Way*, 2259

Kwylla came over to help Beth and Hutch prepare dinner that evening. She showed them which types of food should be heated and which were best served cold. She made the local equivalent of a coleslaw salad. Showed them some sliced fish and waited for them to decide whether they wanted it included. And she mixed drinks.

When it was finished, she helped set the table. "Some things other than beaches," Beth said, "will probably be the same everywhere." Kwylla's oversized smile left no doubt in Hutch's mind that she understood.

They did actually manage a conversation. Beth let everyone know how much she enjoyed the ocean, Hutch was able to express her gratitude to Kwylla for effectively preparing the meal, Ken made it clear that he was interested in learning about the temple, Arin inquired whether his guests also had books, Kwylla wondered whether the food was much different from what humans normally ate, and Derek was able to ask whether there was anything else they needed. And they also learned the name of the world: Volaria. It was possible that the term also applied to the ground. In the same manner as "earth" is both soil and planet.

By the time they'd finished, darkness had fallen. Arin was first to go outside and scan the sky. He looked back at Derek, who'd followed him. *Where is it?*

A short time later, maybe a quarter hour, the moving star appeared, and no one seemed as pleased as their host. They watched until it descended below the horizon, and then went inside. Hutch, who was washing dishes while Kwylla dried them, saw him take a notebook from a drawer in one of the side tables. He looked at the clock and apparently recorded the time.

He came back a short while later, wrote in the notebook again. Ken looked at Hutch. "What?"

"He's recording the passages. I think he needs to do *something*. He's like Derek. Just can't relax."

Derek and Arin went outside. And Kwylla looked at Ken and asked a question. Ken listened and nodded. "She wants to know whether we've been visiting other places, too." He looked at her and responded.

Her eyes gleamed. And she asked something else.

"She wants to know what it was like."

"Tell her about the dinosaur," said Beth.

Ken laughed. "Why don't you tell her?"

Beth took the challenge. She pointed at Arin's note-book. Could she use it?

Kwylla signaled *sure*.

She turned a page and tried to draw a picture of the brontosaurus. But Beth, despite an early ambition to draw comic strips, had no artistic skills. In the end, Kwylla made it clear she had no idea what the thing was. Beth tried growling, but of course that didn't work.

Eventually, Arin came back in, glanced at the clock, and wrote in his notebook again.

"I guess it's back," said Beth.

Hutch hated going to bed without anything to read. She turned out the bedside lamp, sank back into the pillow, and stared at the ceiling. She wondered if she would ever get to finish Pagden's book, or any of the others she was partway through. It was possible she'd have to learn to read the local language to ever start another book again. That was severely depressing.

She didn't even know what sort of books occupied the shelf downstairs. She'd opened a couple and eliminated the possibility they were collections of plays. Beyond that, though, they could be anything. History, novels, philosophy. Considering the cottage was on the same property as the temple, there were probably some religious texts. Whatever they were, she'd have enjoyed being able to look through one. To read it. Books were one more thing she'd assumed would always be there.

After a while, she got up, went to the window, and looked out at the night sky.

• • •

Derek stayed on the porch again until the stars faded in the early light of dawn. He was asleep in the chair when Hutch found him. She tried to go back inside without waking him, but she heard her name whispered softly. "He's still coming through," he said. "God knows what he must be thinking."

"You ought to go to get some sleep."

"I'm all right. Anybody else up?"

"Not that I know of." She sat down with him. "How long do you think he'll stay? Wally?"

"I don't know. He has to be thinking we're dead."

They sat for a while, continuing their one-note conversation. Then Derek just closed his eyes. "I wish," he said, "we could get a decent breakfast. I'd love some pancakes. Or maybe some bacon and eggs. These guys have gone far out of their way for us, but the food just doesn't work."

"At least we've got some."

"Sometimes I'm sorry we didn't go down with the lander."

"Come on, Derek. You don't mean that. You're the senior guy here. You're not allowed to give up."

"I'm not giving up, Priscilla, damn it. I—"

"Yeah?"

"Hell, I don't know. I just feel so helpless."

A car came out of the trees in the north, the direction of the harbor. It swung into the parking lot. Three of the islanders got out, walked to the front of the temple, and went inside. Moments later, two more cars came in from the opposite direction. It gradually became a stream, vehicles arriving from both sides. And a few pedestrians emerged out of the forest. The islanders seemed a bit better dressed than they'd been in the past. The drab, wrinkled clothing was gone, replaced by pressed shirts and trousers. Some wore cloth caps with brims.

A few noticed the two strangers on the front deck of the cottage. But unlike the response of the previous day, Derek and Hutch didn't draw much attention. The visitors lifted their hands in a friendly gesture, and then turned and proceeded toward the front entrance of the temple, where they climbed the stone steps and went inside.

"Religious service, I guess," said Derek.

"Incredible," said Hutch.

"How do you mean?"

"They have temples, cars, houses, ships, parking lots. If the vehicles looked a little better and these guys didn't look like dolphins, I'd think we were back in the twentieth century."

Derek shrugged. "How else could their development happen, Priscilla? I'd be willing to bet that every technological culture we find is going to look like this in its early stages. You need all this stuff."

The door behind them opened and Ken looked out.

"What?" said Derek.

"I was thinking I'd like to go over to the temple and watch."

"That's probably not a good idea. We've no way of knowing what it might lead to."

"Oh no, I'm not dumb enough to try it. But I'd love to see what goes on." He stayed and watched until the cars stopped coming and the last of the islanders had gone inside. A few minutes later, music began. It was string instruments and they were joined quickly by a chorus. It wasn't like listening to the Washington Symphony, but they were good, the music flowed, and most remarkable of all, the harmony was there. Or maybe it wasn't so remarkable. Maybe there wasn't more than one way to build an ear.

Derek excused himself and went inside. The temple music changed tone, the singing faded, and Hutch assumed a ceremony had started. Another car arrived and three more islanders got out and hurried inside. Shortly after that, the building went silent, except for an occasional voice. Then, after a while, the choral group was back.

"We haven't found much yet in the way of civilizations," Ken said. "But so far, every one of them had religion."

"Hard to see how a culture can develop without it," said Hutch. "An intelligent species will be driven to explain how they came into existence. How the sun sinks in the west and shows up again in the east every morning."

"Maybe," said Ken, "there really *is* a divine presence."

"You know," said Hutch, "we need a way to let Wally know we're still alive. Something better than waving at him."

"That brings us back to the flashlight," said Ken.

Beth joined them, with a plate full of buns that were as close to cinnamon as she could manage. They were just finishing when Arin arrived. He appeared to be in a happy mood. "Hello," he said in English before sitting down with them. He picked up one of the buns, tasted it, and broke into that gigantic smile.

"I think he likes it," Hutch said. Beth poured a glass of water for him. Ken tried to explain that they were hoping to locate a flashlight. Arin got up, went over to one of the lamps, said something, and turned it on. Then he lifted the lamp from the table and pointed it at the wall. *"Kaka,"* he said.

Great. This time he got the message.

"Excellent," said Ken. He looked around the table. "I think he means they have one." He spoke again to Arin with both words and gestures.

"Who's he talking about?" Hutch said.

Arin responded and Ken's brow wrinkled.

"What did he say?" asked Beth.

"He says we don't need it."

"Maybe you need to talk to him some more."

Ken tried again. Arin held up a hand, suggesting patience. Then he said something.

They all waited for the translation.

"I'm not sure I'm getting this right," said Ken. "I think he's saying he has a surprise for us."

"That doesn't sound good," said Hutch.

But when Ken tried to elicit an explanation, Arin only got frustrated. He pointed at his mouth and shook his head. *Wish we had a language.* He got up, went inside, and came back with the notebook. He opened it to a blank page, produced a pen, and handed both to Ken. Then he pointed at the ceiling and pressed a finger on the pad. *Write something.*

Write what?

The finger that was pointing at the ceiling moved as if following something.

The *Eiferman.*

Arin spoke quietly. *"Tola hycut."*

"It means 'hello,'" Ken said.

253

"Okay." Beth looked at her husband as if she was surprised that he wasn't following. "He wants you to say hello to Wally."

"And how," Ken said, "do I do that?"

"Tola hycut." Arin took the notebook and gestured as if to throw it toward the ceiling. Then he gave it back, pointed at the pen, and at the blank page.

"Maybe they *do* have radio," said Beth.

Hutch wasn't buying it. "If they do, we would have heard something coming in."

"I don't know," said Ken. He uncapped the pen and stared at the notebook.

"I think," said Hutch, "he wants you to write a message to be delivered to Wally. And I know that makes no sense, but—"

"Hold on." Ken held both hands out for Arin, with his fingers spread. Then he closed them into fists and opened them again with the thumbs tucked away. And his right index finger folded down. Seventeen.

Arin broke into one of his giant grins. *"Kaka!"*

So, it *was* a message for Wally, and they'd locked down the eighteen fingers Arin had shown them yesterday. He had been referring to *days*. But this was minus one. "So, what's going to happen in seventeen days?" asked Beth.

"I can only think of one thing," said Hutch. "They're going to recover the lander." She looked at the pad. "Write the message."

"Hutch, they have no way of sending it. Hell, they won't even be able to *read* it."

"What can we lose? Write it and see what happens."

Ken let her see he considered it an exercise in futility.

But he took a moment to think, and then began printing:
HELLO, WALLY. DON'T GO ANYWHERE. IF ALL GOES WELL WE
WILL BE WITH YOU IN 17 DAYS. MORE OR LESS. HOPE YOU'RE
OKAY.

He held it where Beth and Hutch could see it and then
passed it to Arin, who was already frowning and shaking
his head. He bit his lower lip and pressed his palms together.
Then he separated them and moved them back beyond the
edges of his placemat. He looked with disapproval from
one to the other. Then he brought them close together,
until they were separated by about a centimeter. And he
looked from Ken to Hutch.

"The message is too long," said Beth.

"I understand that," said Ken. "What I *don't* understand
is what we're talking about."

Hutch was watching Arin. "I don't get it either. But let's
assume he knows what he's doing."

Arin returned the notebook, and Ken tried again: DON'T
GO ANYWHERE. WE'LL BE WITH YOU IN 17 DAYS.

It was still too long.

Ken rewrote it: BE WITH YOU IN 17 DAYS.

Arin still wasn't happy. "Let me try it," said Hutch.

Ken passed the notebook to her. She wrote: BK IN 3 WKS.

Yes. Ken translated it for Arin, who raised a fist. Excellent. He finished the bun, helped himself to another one,
smiled at Hutch, and left.

Hutch and Beth had enjoyed their day at the beach, so they
decided to go back. Ken joined them. They went over to
Arin's quarters to invite him and Kwylla. Both declined,
but Kwylla did what they'd hoped she would by offering to

drive them. Unfortunately, she and Ken couldn't communicate very well, so he was unable to determine whether she'd offered to return for them. But it would not be a major issue. It was only a half-hour walk.

Maybe it was Ken's presence at the beach, but whatever was the mitigating factor, the islanders showed more attention than they had since the first visit. Many came over to see them and to shake hands with them. Two of the females pretended to admire Ken. "I guess," he said, "they recognize good looks when they see them." Kids chased one another around the umbrella, stopping to stare whenever they thought they could get away with it. And when their parents stepped in to pull them away, they laughed.

Several males were also drawn in their direction. Some tried to talk with Beth and Hutch. One even paused to ask a question, and when Hutch responded simply with a *hello*, he swung his shoulders in a manner that could only be interpreted as a flirtation.

"Make your move, Hutch," said Beth. "You may not get another chance."

Eventually, they went into the water and drifted out just beyond where the waves were breaking, so they could rise and fall with the incoming surf. Ken kept looking in the direction of the sunken lander. "Don't even think about it," said Beth.

"It's not that far out."

"It's far enough. Just let it be."

"Beth—"

"What's the point, love? It's not as if you could go out

there and drag it in." She turned in Hutch's direction. "I wonder if they have sharks here."

"Wouldn't surprise *me*. Probably big ones."

They'd been in the water about an hour when Hutch saw Arin stride out of the woods. He waved at them and they went ashore. He and Ken had a short exchange, which Hutch had no trouble reading. He didn't mean for them to cut their time short, and they could go back into the ocean if they wanted. But he'd brought the car if they wanted a ride home. "He's got a surprise for us when we get back to the temple," said Ken.

"What kind of surprise?" asked Beth.

"I don't know. I can't follow him most of the time."

"Maybe a chicken salad," said Hutch.

"Yum," said Ken. "That *would* be nice, wouldn't it?"

They wiped themselves down with their towels, Ken closed the umbrella, and he and Beth started for the car. Hutch had noticed that one of the Dolphins, a female, seemed to be trying to get her attention. She lingered behind and finally dropped back when the female raised a hand, apparently asking her to wait. Two others were with her, a male, and a child whom she belatedly recognized. It was the one she'd thought was in trouble yesterday and had tried to rescue. The child pointed at her and backed shyly away. The female advanced and her eyes filled with emotion. *"Koraka som,"* she said. She introduced herself and the male, and came forward with obvious reluctance. When Hutch didn't back away, she embraced her. Then she delivered a surprise. "Thank you, Parsilla," she said. Her voice shook.

The male closed his eyes and bowed his head.

•   •   •

On the way back to the cottage, Arin explained. Ken listened with a smile growing ever wider. "He says they called last night and asked your name. And how to say *thank you*."

"She did pretty well," Hutch said, wondering if she'd be remembered as *Parsilla*. "But I don't think the kid was ever really in trouble. I misread the situation."

Ken translated for Arin. And the response came: "That doesn't matter. You put yourself at risk to help her child."

They arrived at the cottage. The three passengers got out, Arin said something, which Ken interpreted as *back in a minute*, and drove across the parking lot. They walked slowly toward the front door, watched him get out of the car and go inside the temple. "I guess he's getting the chicken salad," said Ken. They mounted the steps onto the porch and went into the house. Derek was asleep on the sofa.

They waited in the living room. The temple was visible through a side window, but Arin's door remained closed. "Maybe it was just good-bye," said Beth.

"Maybe," Ken said. They gave it another couple of minutes and then went upstairs, dried off, and got dressed. When they returned to the living room and sat down, there was still no sign of Arin.

Derek was still asleep. "So what do we do now?" asked Beth.

"Well," Ken said, "we could try to figure out how much time passes when the big hand circles the clock."

"Good," she said. "Watch the clock."

Ken grinned. "Sorry. It's all I've got."

"We should have stayed at the beach," said Hutch.

Ordinarily, after concluding the surprise was a misunderstanding, they wouldn't have mentioned it to Derek. But there was so little to talk about that Ken told him about it immediately after he woke up, and then asked if he had gotten any impression that something was going to happen.

Derek looked over at Hutch. "The only thing I can think of," he said, "is the note you wrote for him this morning. What was it? 'Back in three weeks'?"

Finally, the temple's side door opened, and Arin came out. He stopped, talking with someone inside, and then started across the parking area to the cottage. "Maybe we're about to find out," said Beth.

He knocked and came through the door, smiled, and said, "Hello." Again in English. Then he spoke to Ken, who explained. "We're invited over to their place for dinner."

There was a third islander at the meal, a young male, introduced as Murik. He was the son of Kwylla and Arin. There was also a daughter somewhere, although they couldn't determine where she lived. Kwylla made it clear she was anxious to meet the visitors and would come as soon as she could.

The meal itself, as the others had been, was flat. But everybody pretended to enjoy it. When it ended, the sun had descended into the trees. Conversation, of course, was difficult for both sides, and the humans thanked their hosts, tried to inform Murik how pleased they were to meet him, and finally excused themselves. Arin walked back with them to the cottage. When they arrived, he took Ken aside and tried to explain something to him. The conversation involved some pointing at the temple.

"He doesn't want us going anywhere this evening," Ken explained. "He wants us to visit the temple tonight."

Derek looked at Arin, who responded with a giant smile. "You have any idea why?"

"Something he wants us to see."

"What is it?"

"I don't know. He tried to explain, but I can't follow him."

24.

Lead, kindly Light, amid the encircling gloom,
Lead Thou me on!
The night is dark, and I am far from home—
Lead Thou me on!
Keep Thou my feet; I do not ask to see
The distant scene, —one step enough for me.
  —John Henry Newman, "Light in the Darkness," 1833

Derek and Hutch were back out on the porch when the sun went down. They waited through the twilight, keeping an eye on the temple's side door. The surf was loud that evening, and the moon was full. There wasn't much traffic on the road, no more than two or three cars as the sky darkened. When the stars finally appeared, the *Eiferman* was in the western sky, sinking into the trees. Wally was still there.

Ken came out and smiled when he saw it. "We owe him," he said. "I wonder how many people would have stuck around this long."

Someone in the temple began rehearsing with a horn. It lasted a few minutes, then faded out until there was only the rumble of the ocean and an occasional gust of wind in the trees.

The conversation was always the same: Was there any chance Ken had misunderstood Arin? What would they do on the night that the *Eiferman* didn't show up? If they got home, would they ever again think about leaving on a mission without allowing time for a complete service of the vehicle? All eyes turned to Derek. "Dumb," he said. "I'm sorry."

It was depressing.

The temple's side door opened and Arin started across the parking lot in their direction, bringing a wave of hope. Though nobody admitted to it, Hutch felt it in her heartbeat, and saw it in the faces of her colleagues. It was ridiculous. There was nothing he could do, yet he was all they had.

But he behaved as if everything was under control.

They were all on the porch when he turned onto the walkway. He got within a few steps, stopped, and indicated they should all follow him. Then he proceeded back to the temple and opened the door for them.

It was the first time Hutch had actually gotten a look at the interior, other than the section dedicated to Arin's quarters. Rows of benches lined a spacious section overlooked by a balcony. She saw a pipe organ off to the far side, and noticed a flowery fragrance of some sort, as well as a touch of camphor. There was little doubt that it was in every sense a temple.

Kwylla came out of the shadows and joined them as Arin led the way to a rear door and onto a circular staircase at the base of the tower. He turned on lights and they started up. Hutch thought they were headed for the balcony, but they passed it and kept climbing.

The tower hadn't looked especially tall from outside, but it was a difficult haul up a staircase designed for climbers with considerably longer legs than the humans'. Periodically, they passed windows, which, as they gained altitude, provided an increasingly wide view of treetops, the ocean, the beach, and cottages spread through the area.

Arin saw that the stairs presented a challenge for his guests, especially for Beth and Hutch, so he slowed down and occasionally stopped to give everyone a break. They passed more doorways and eventually entered the cupola. It was furnished with thick carpeting, a sofa, a desk, four armchairs, and two lamps on side tables. A wooden chair was set at the desk. There was also a telephone and a clock. A sketch of the temple adorned one of the walls. And a framed photo of two children was mounted beside the doorway. A stringed instrument, resembling a cello, lay in one of the chairs. Curtained windows looked out in all directions. They could see the port area, which was dark except for a few lights on the piers, a docked ship, and outside the warehouses.

To the east, the ocean glittered beneath the stars and the full moon. The beach, of course, was dark. Behind it lay the town they'd seen originally during the last moments of the lander. Houses, cabins, cottages, were all glowing. Only the larger buildings were dark.

"It's bigger than I remembered," said Derek. "I assume it has a name? The town?"

Ken passed the query to Arin. *"Kara,"* he said.

Beth picked up the cello and glanced at Arin. Arin shook his head and indicated that it belonged to Kwylla. Signals went back and forth, Kwylla smiled, took the instrument, and played a few notes. The melody was soft and suggested to Hutch a pair of lovers standing in moonlight.

"Beautiful," said Ken, who quickly corrected himself and repeated the comment in the Volarian language. Kwylla's smile widened.

They slipped into the chairs and sofa while Arin walked over to a window that provided a view of the sea. "Why are we here?" asked Hutch. "Is something going to happen?"

"I've asked him," said Ken. "He just wants us to wait. I'm not sure why."

Derek smiled at Arin. "You certainly enjoy playing games."

"Just to be safe," said Ken, "he's acquiring some English."

Arin grinned as if he'd understood everything. He picked up the phone, punched in a number, waited a moment, and then held a short conversation with someone. At the end he seemed satisfied and hung up.

"Ken," said Beth, "did you get any of that?"

"Not much. He was giving somebody instructions, and everything seems to be okay. Beyond that, I've no idea. Derek's right about the games. He's enjoying himself."

Arin walked over to the desk and leaned against it. It creaked. He said something, but the only thing Hutch picked up was Ken's name.

Ken smiled helplessly. "I think he said it won't be long."

Arin took a crumpled piece of paper out of his pocket, looked at it, glanced up at the clock, and sat down on the sofa.

"Wally will be in the sky in a few minutes," Derek said. "Whatever he's planning is connected with that."

"It's probably a blinker of some sort that he's set up," said Beth. "If that's so, let's hope it's bright enough for Wally to see it."

Kwylla left the room and returned minutes later with several cups of water on a tray. She was passing it out as the *Eiferman* rose in the eastern sky. When she was done, she looked out at it, squeezed Arin's shoulder, and said something to him.

They watched as the *Eiferman* approached. When it got close, Arin went back to the phone, punched in a number, spoke briefly, and hung up.

Hutch was struck by the sheer beauty of the landscape, illuminated by the town behind the beach, and by the assorted cabins and cottages and post lights spread around the area. As she watched, lights also came on in one of the larger buildings. It was the one that resembled a school. And one of the other buildings lit up. Within a minute, so had the rest. The factories, and a place that looked like a city hall, *everything* was turning on lights. The port area also lit up. Including the ship which was still at the dock.

She caught her breath. Suddenly, the lights went out. First the ship, then the port area, and finally the town. At almost the same moment. The world remained dark for about fifteen seconds. Then it lit up again. Everywhere.

And went out again. It went back and forth, every few seconds, between utter blackout and a brilliantly illuminated town and port.

"There's no way," said Derek, "he could miss that."

"Ken," Hutch said, "they've been shutting off everybody's

power? I hope they haven't told anyone it's because of us."

Arin apparently caught the meaning. He smiled at her but spoke to Ken, who translated. "He says they all knew it was coming. They notified as many in advance as they could. And nobody had a problem with it. If I got it right, he says they like us."

25.

Spartans, stoics, heroes, saints, and gods use a short and positive speech.
—Ralph Waldo Emerson, "The Superlative," 1847

The question that remained on Hutch's mind was the written message Arin had asked for: BK IN 3 WKS. But either he didn't *want* to explain himself or he couldn't figure out how to do it for people who had no real grasp of the language. Or maybe he just liked springing surprises. Her best guess was that it was a combination of the three.

She slept soundly the night they'd blinked the lights for Wally. At least that had assured her that he was very likely aware they were alive and well. Even had Wally not been watching, there was no way Barry could have missed the stunt. She'd gone to bed thinking of Tom Axler, a part of her life that she'd taken for granted. How nice it would be to share an evening with him again. Assuming they could get back to where they'd been before the president had gotten in the way.

And on those hopeful thoughts, the world faded out.

• • •

The following day, Arin returned to the cottage in the morning, wearing his rumpled equivalent of a bathing suit. He talked with Ken, and Ken explained to Hutch: "He says we have to locate the lander. He wants me to go out with him in a boat so we can mark the spot. Do we know precisely where it sank?"

At the time of the crash, Hutch had automatically lined it up with three trees at the back of the beach. But that didn't tell her how far offshore it was. She'd guessed three hundred meters. But it was a guess. "More or less," she said. "How about if I go with you?"

They changed into their own disheveled gear, and Arin took them across the road and down a path to the ocean, where a motor yacht waited at a small pier.

They crossed a ramp onto the boat, which had an azure hull with a ladder and a white cabin and flying bridge. A rectangular blue pennant with a fish image flew above the cabin. They went inside. It was equipped with plumbing and a second set of controls. Arin was obviously showing it off. Humans weren't the only ones with high tech. They sat down for a few minutes and he explained that the boat belonged to the temple. That they used it for various kinds of outings.

Hutch caught enough of the conversation to realize she was making progress. But it was limited.

Arin went outside and cast off the line. Then he returned, wished everyone good luck, and took over the controls. They headed out into the ocean and turned south.

"He wasn't on the beach when we went down," said Ken. "He told me the other day that he had no idea where it happened. He talked to a number of people who claimed to have been there at the time, but their descriptions were all over the place."

They cruised along the coastline. The forest gave way to the beach and the usual crowd of sunbathers. Some waved, although Hutch doubted they could recognize her and Ken at that range. She concentrated on finding the tree cluster. At the time of the accident, she'd thought they'd be easy to recognize. One had been quite tall, with a bushy appearance, and the other two of average dimensions equally spaced on either side. Should have been simple. But it wasn't.

Two sets of trees fit the description, one on each side of the beach. "That'll be the easy part," said Ken, as they lined up with the northern cluster. "It's the distance from the shore that's tricky. I think we should be farther out. Maybe fifty meters or so."

Hutch didn't agree. "I think we were considerably closer to the beach than that."

"All right," he said. "Let's go in closer and work our way out."

Arin appeared surprised that they didn't know precisely where the lander had gone down, but he didn't say anything.

"I think," said Hutch, "he expected a bit more from us."

When they were satisfied with the location, Arin dropped anchor. Hutch was happy that the water was calm. She wasn't excited at the prospect of diving to the bottom, but she couldn't stay on the boat and watch the two guys do everything.

Arin talked for a few seconds, and Ken translated. "He just wants to know where it is."

She and Ken used the ladder to ease themselves into the water. Arin dove in smoothly, barely making a splash. When Hutch went under, she was glad that the bottom was visible. It wasn't especially clear, but in any case, the lander wasn't there. They spread out. Arin, to no one's surprise, was much more at home in the water than either of the humans.

Hutch saw nothing. She surfaced, farther from the boat than she'd expected, took a deep breath, and went back under. She saw a few fish, and something dark moving across the bottom. But whatever it was, it didn't seem to show any interest in her.

She went wide around it and extended her search, with again no results. Finally, she returned to the boat. Ken came up as she reached the ladder. "Anything?" she asked.

"No. No sign of it."

She climbed onto the deck and scanned the surface for Arin. Ken joined her. "Last time I saw him, he was back there," he said, glancing aft. There was no sign of him anywhere.

"Where is he?" she asked.

Ken went back into the ocean. Hutch watched him head east, into deeper water. She wanted to get back in and help, but she had a problem: The swimsuit was a baggy monstrosity that kept getting in the way. Finally, she climbed out of it and dived into the water. She stayed under for about a minute but saw nothing. She went back up for air.

It was taking too long. She dove, rose again, dove again, looking desperately in all directions. *Where the hell are you, Arin?* Finally, she returned to the yacht. Ken was on board. As she approached the ladder, Arin surfaced in the distance. Ken waved in her direction and then apparently saw her clothes lying in a pile on the deck. He turned his back while she climbed the ladder and got dressed. "You're one of the great men of our time, Ken," she said.

Arin took his time coming in. If he'd noticed Hutch's clothing issue, he gave no indication. "Where've you been?" Hutch said when he finally arrived. "I thought you'd drowned."

Momentary confusion filled Arin's eyes and then mutated into a broad smile. He tried to explain.

"He says he didn't realize we were air-breathers."

"Ken, *he's* an air-breather."

"He has gills, too. I guess. He says he can breathe in the water."

"Great." Hutch looked sternly at Arin. "It would have been nice if you'd mentioned that to us."

"I don't think he realized we couldn't do it too."

They corrected their position, lining up with the other group of trees, which Hutch now recognized. There was a broken branch near the top of the one in the middle. She'd forgotten. They found the lander within a few minutes. It lay on its side, barely visible in the opaque light. "So why are we going to all this trouble?" Hutch asked. "Can you guys recover this thing?"

Again, she got the giant smile. Hutch scanned for damage. The drive units looked okay, as did the skids, the wings, and the antigravs. One of the antennas was bent, but they could fix that easily enough. If the cabin hadn't filled with water, they should be all right.

When she was satisfied, they returned to the boat. Ken explained to Arin that everything looked good, as far as they could tell. Arin happily waved his left arm in the air. He went into the cabin and came back with a shirt. He approached Hutch and held it near her face, apparently measuring something. He made marks on it and thanked her. He returned the shirt to the cabin, came back out, opened a storage locker, and removed a buoy. He attached a small anchor to it and put it over the side.

"What was the shirt all about?" asked Hutch.

Ken asked Arin but apparently couldn't understand the explanation.

26.

I love to sail forbidden seas, and land on barbarous coasts.

—Herman Melville, *Moby-Dick*, 1851

utch, you awake yet?" It was Beth's voice.

"I guess," she said. "Something wrong?"

"Arin's here. He wants to take us to the beach."

"This early? Why?"

"I don't think it's actually early. We had breakfast a while ago. But I don't know what it's about. He's telling Ken there's something we'd want to see."

"I'll be down in a few minutes."

She should have asked whether they were wearing the bathing suits. But how else would you dress if you were headed for the beach? When she got downstairs, everybody was waiting for her, including Kwylla. But apparently, no one else was planning on going in the water. She excused herself, hurried back to her room, and changed.

When she returned, Kwylla handed her a couple of

buns to stave off her appetite. Then she followed every-body outside. Arin had, somewhere, picked up a second car. He would drive one; Kwylla got behind the wheel of the other. "What's happening at the beach?" she asked.

Ken shrugged. He got into Kwylla's car, and Hutch joined him. "It feels," he said, "as if we're headed for a party, but I don't think Arin would normally throw one of those on a beach. But if it helps, time's an issue."

The weather had cooled. A brisk wind was blowing in off the sea, and a few gray clouds drifted through the sky. The vehicles rolled away.

There was a lot of traffic on the road, cars and small trucks, all going the same direction, which was unusual. When they arrived, some vehicles had pulled over under the trees, but most of them, to her surprise, were in the middle of the beach, circling each other, apparently looking for parking places. It was the first time she'd seen anyone take a car out there. A few locals were pointing, sending vehicles in different directions, moving them into various positions. Kwylla looked for a place to park, couldn't find one, and indicated she'd continue along the road. Ken and Hutch climbed out.

Beth and Derek were waiting. Hutch needed a min-ute to locate Arin, who was still behind the wheel. One of the Volarians was waving him into the rear of a line of parked cars. There were about seventy vehicles on the sand, in what appeared to be a meaningless arrangement of straight and angled lines. Some sunbathers were in the area, but they were being kept at a distance.

As more of the cars and trucks fell into place, Hutch realized what was going on at about the same time she overheard Beth telling her husband, "Use your imagination. Look at it from the sky."

From above, the pattern of vehicles could be read: BK IN 3 WKS

It was a good idea. But there was a problem. On this mission, it seemed, there was always a problem. There were a lot of clouds. Wally might not be able to see the *island*, let alone the message.

Arin got out of his car with obvious frustration. He talked with a couple of the Volarians who were directing traffic and then, staring at the sky, joined the humans. He signaled for patience, but it was clear he wasn't taking his own advice. The sky was becoming increasingly overcast.

Kwylla arrived a few minutes later and tried to calm him. But he only shook his head and said something to her that produced a weak smile. A light rain began to fall. Three of the guys who'd been directing traffic were standing nearby. Arin grumbled something and walked over. The conversation became tense, but as the rain thickened, they came to a decision. He and the others spread out among the cars and talked to the drivers. The cars began to leave.

"Ken," said Hutch, "thank Arin for us, and ask him to pass our appreciation on to the people who came out here today."

"I will," he said. "Let's go home."

Arin came back and talked briefly with Ken. Then Ken gave them the good news: "They're going to try again tomorrow."

• • •

The skies were clear for the second attempt. Drivers arrived early and lined up as they had the day before. Arin and his associates charged around, straightening everything, moving cars slightly more left or right, and finally withdrawing with a look of satisfaction. Then the waiting began.

Ken hadn't yet settled with Arin on a way to measure time, other than explaining in general terms that something wouldn't take long. They knew, of course, that Arin had the time down, that he'd recorded the schedule of the *Eiferman*'s arrivals and departures. So they weren't entirely surprised when, after everything was in place, he told Ken it would take "a quarter of an orbit" before the ship made its way above the horizon.

Hutch accepted an invitation from one of the drivers to get into his car and out of the sun. They made an attempt at conversation, but it failed and she wasn't entirely surprised when he said something to her and left. She didn't want to offend him, so she stayed where she was.

Eventually, Arin checked the timepiece he'd brought with him and told everyone that they should see the "vehicle" shortly. Minutes after that, it rose out of the ocean. They watched it approach, and hundreds of them waved and shouted as it passed overhead.

Hutch and Beth returned regularly to the beach. The crowd that had overwhelmed them during the first few days turned into occasional individuals smiling at them and saying hello almost as often in English as in the local usage. "They're getting used to us," Beth said.

Hutch tried to pick up whatever she could of the language. If they could get down words like *underwater* and

hello and *food*, it would help. But she couldn't even repro-
duce some of the sounds she was hearing. She was struck,
however, at how friendly the creatures remained. How
would a group of humans in Atlantic City have reacted if a
UFO had crashed close to shore, and minutes later a group
of strange-looking creatures came out of the water?

"I can't help thinking," she told Beth, "I'd almost prefer
not to learn the language."

"Why's that, Hutch?"

"Because at some point, we are going to *have* to communicate with them."

"And tell them about the black hole?"

"That's the problem, isn't it? There's no happy ending
here. And what happens to their lives if they find out? I'm
not sure it would be a good idea to say *anything*."

Arin tried to explain his plan to help them recover the
lander by drawing pictures of two carts. Each had a line
attached to it. It was reasonably clear by then that he
hoped to lift the lander off the bottom, and everybody's
best guess was that they had a freighter somewhere with
a crane. The problem with that idea was that the water
wouldn't be deep enough for a heavy ship. So maybe they
were planning on using two smaller vessels. In any case,
he was clearly planning *something*. And the fact that he
had a plan made it easier for Hutch, and probably everyone, to sleep.

Ken spent several hours each day with Arin, and additional time with Kwylla, working on the language. They
were all picking up some of it. They learned to say hello and
good-bye, ask for fruit juice, and pay Kwylla compliments

on her clothing. Meanwhile, Arin expanded his artwork, attaching a not-very-accurate impression of the lander to the cords.

Derek grew restless. They continued getting assurances from Arin. "Help is coming," he told Ken repeatedly. But the explanations broke down.

Days on Volaria were probably about two hours shorter than on Earth. So there were issues with the sleep cycle at first, but everyone adjusted. They were well into their third week, on a day filled with high winds and torrential rain. And they all seemed tired. They were still gathering on the porch every night to watch what they'd begun to call the passover. And Wally moved faithfully through the sky. But their energy levels were declining. They didn't talk about it when Kwylla or Arin were present, because they knew there was nothing they could do. But when they were alone, as they were on that windy, rain-swept evening, the subject tended to take over the conversation. "I'm wiped out," Ken was saying as Hutch got some fresh fruit out of the refrigerator. They hadn't been doing anything that would have caused physical exertion, but it didn't seem to matter.

Derek leaned back in his chair. "I can understand it," he said. "There's a lot of stress right now." He looked over at Beth, who was eating white peels. "What do you think, Doc?"

"The stress doesn't help. I suspect the real problem is that we're not getting enough meatloaf and broccoli." She tried unsuccessfully to conceal her concern. They were all worried, but food was a secondary factor. They'd pretty much run through their three weeks, and there was no guarantee Wally would stay when the time ran out and nothing had happened.

"You guys okay?" Hutch asked.

Derek's laser gaze locked on her. "Ask me that when we get home."

"Sorry," she said. "I guess I'm the reason we're stuck here." The porch fell silent.

"I wasn't talking about that," Derek said. "You did what you had to."

"It's okay." She knew she'd done nothing wrong, would change nothing if she were put in that position again. Nevertheless, she was shadowed by a sense of guilt. She was the captain; she'd been at the controls. Somehow, things should have been managed differently. She could probably have gone down on the beach without hurting anyone. Or maybe even made it into the trees.

"You know," said Beth, "it's true. Feeling tired is one of the early signs of not eating properly. So's being cranky."

"That's a bit scary," said Hutch. "How long does it take before we have a serious problem?"

"I don't know how much nutrition we're getting. And to be honest, I don't know much about starvation. I've never had to deal with it. But if you're not taking in any decent food at all, the symptoms can show up pretty quickly. We're getting *some* nutrition. And we're filling our stomachs, so we don't feel hungry. But I suspect we're missing some of what we need."

"Heads up," said Ken. "Here comes Arin." Kwylla was with him.

"That's all we need," said Derek. "I hate to admit this, but I'm getting tired trying to learn Volarian. I was never good at foreign languages, and this one just drives me crazy."

"He's got a box." Ken got out of his chair and offered it to Kwylla. She thanked him and sat.

Their faces were alight with good news. They were both making the creaking floorboard sounds, which was their way of delivering an energetic hello when life was good. Arin said, "Hello." And continued in English: "We are ready to go after the lander."

The box was wooden, small, about the size of a loaf of bread. He put it on the floor and sat down on the sofa. Then he opened it. And removed something that looked like an oxygen mask!

They all stared while he and Kwylla sat grinning. Arin picked up the mask and held it out for Hutch.

She took it and held it against her face. It was a decent fit. And she realized why, when they were on the boat, Arin had used a shirt to measure her skull. "Why?" she looked at him. "We know where the lander is. You don't think I can make the repairs underwater, I hope?"

Ken passed the question to Arin, who responded on his own: "We must know where to connect the lines. Need you to show us. Be safe."

"All right," she said. "Is there an oxygen tank to go with this?"

"Yes," said Arin. He took the mask back.

"When do we do this?"

Kwylla smiled and surprised everyone: "Two days." She held her hands out, in a nonverbal cue that Hutch associated with preachers. *Have faith.*

• • •

"At last," Derek said after Kwylla and Arin had left.

"I'm surprised," said Hutch, "that they have oxygen masks. What use would they have for them?"

"They have factories," Ken said. "Probably have to deal with chemicals. I'm impressed that they were able to come up with one that fits you."

"They made it specifically *for* me."

"Oh, yes. I forgot. Arin did that measurement on the boat." Ken took a deep breath.

"Something wrong?" asked Beth.

"If everything goes well, we might be looking at our last couple of days here."

"That's probably true," said Hutch. "If it's about to end, we have to decide what we're going to tell them."

Derek's eyes closed for a moment. He looked in pain.

"We've got enough of the language," Beth continued, "to let them know what's coming. Are we going to do it?"

"I think," said Derek, "it would be a terrible idea. Let's forget it. They have sixty years left. Why should we ruin it for them?"

Arin was confident that everything would work. There was no way they could have missed that. The impression was confirmed when he came back the following day and invited them to return to the temple later for dinner. He was saying good-bye.

They went, of course. And this time the meal was served not in his quarters but in a meeting room con-nected to the rear of the building. Approximately twenty Volarians were present. Three tables occupied one end of the room, with the locals already seated. But there was still substantial space available. When Arin came through the door with the four humans trailing, everyone stood.

Derek, Beth, Ken, and Hutch were shown to their seats. Three volunteers were serving dark liquid of the type Hutch had already tried. It looked like wine but did not seem to have an alcoholic element. When all the glasses were filled, Arin said something and the Volarians raised the glasses to their guests. Then he repeated the toast in English: "To our good friends from Earth, a place that is now much closer."

Beth leaned toward Hutch. "I think they got that from us."

"Maybe." Hutch raised her own glass in a return gesture. "I'm beginning to seriously like these guys."

Arin spoke for about three minutes. Hutch caught part of it. He understood the loss that the visitors had suffered, and he appreciated their courage. They had proven good friends. When he finished, he looked at the humans, closed his eyes, and delivered what was clearly a prayer. The other Volarians bowed their heads.

The food was digestible, more or less, and it was as good as anything Hutch had tasted on the island. She cleared her plate and looked over at Beth, who shrugged. *It probably has some vitamins. Have faith.*

At the end of the meal, five of the locals, two males and three females, left the room and came back with horns and string instruments. They played soft, melodic rhapsodies, more like adaptations of classical music than the noisy clattering which had become popular at home over past years. There was no way, she realized, they could perform in that style and not inspire dancers to take the floor.

And it happened: Tables were abandoned and the Volarians went forward with their partners. Hutch and Beth were both invited into the action with the locals. Derek and Ken needed a minute to realize some of the females were lingering nearby.

It was obvious to Hutch that her first partner, who towered over her, wasn't anxious about getting too close. Nevertheless, he folded her into his arms while she held her breath. He provided what she thought was a name, and his eyes reflected an amusement at their mutual discomfort. Hutch told him she was Priscilla, and he butchered it, turning it into a garbled hiss. She tried her luck with *his* name and thought she'd done pretty well until she saw his smile.

It didn't matter. They needed a few minutes to adjust to each other, but in the end they danced around the ballroom, and when the opportunity presented itself, she pulled his head down and kissed his cheek. She was pleased to see that whatever reluctance he had shown about getting close seemed to have evaporated.

At the end of the evening, all the islanders lined up near the door, where they shook hands with one another and took turns embracing their guests. They whispered to Hutch, and to the others, as they filed out. And though no literal translation happened, the emotional expression was impossible to miss.

Beth Squires's Notes (handwritten)
These guys do know how to party.

—Date unknown, 2256

27.

There is a pleasure in the pathless woods,
There is a rapture on the lonely shore;
There is society, where none intrudes,
By the deep sea, and music in its roar.
—Lord Byron, *Childe Harold IV*, 1818

Hutch was just coming down the staircase in the morning. Derek and Ken were talking in the living room. And someone started knocking. Derek got the door and Arin came in, grinned at everybody, spotted Hutch on the stairs, pointed at the ceiling and asked a question. Ken's response included Beth's name. Presumably that she was still asleep. There was another exchange and Arin headed back outside.

"You want me to get Beth?" Hutch asked.

Ken looked up at her. "Is she awake?"

"I haven't heard her moving around."

"It's okay. Let her sleep." He wrote a note and left it on the table.

Derek was still on his feet. "You want to come?" he asked Hutch.

"Where are we going?"

"I've no idea."

"You sure we shouldn't get Beth?"

"I asked him if we should have her with us, but he said it didn't make any difference."

"Doesn't sound as if it could be very important," Hutch said.

Two cars were waiting. Kwylla was at the wheel of one. Ken got in with her; everybody else got into the other car. They pulled onto the road, behind Kwylla. But this time, instead of heading south toward the beach, they rode north past the temple. The sky was overcast, and it felt as if rain were coming.

"He looks as if he has good news," Hutch said. Arin's face was glowing. The road got rough as they left the temple area behind. But that did nothing to slow the drivers down. They bounced along, past occasional cottages and cabins. Off to the right, the ocean was becoming visible through the trees.

They eventually emerged from the forest onto the edge of the sea, connected with another road, followed it through a cluster of cottages, and arrived at a pier. A freighter they hadn't seen before was docked alongside a warehouse. It was a dilapidated green building with flaking paint.

A small truck, loaded with boxes, was just leaving the ship, navigating a ramp down to the pier. A second vehicle waited on the deck.

They pulled into the parking area, got out of the car, and walked onto the pier. They'd gone only a short distance before four Volarians came out of the warehouse.

Others were at the foot of the ramp and scattered across the ship's deck. They all stopped whatever they'd been doing and gaped at the humans. Arin took a deep breath and grumbled something. The truck reached the bottom of the ramp and moved onto the pier. One of the Volarians who'd been on the ship came down the ramp and strutted toward them. Obviously someone of significance. His shirt and pants had a gloss that caught Hutch's eyes even in the gray light.

A second truck, also carrying boxes, moved onto the ramp and started to descend. Arin asked everyone to wait and walked toward Shiny-Clothes. They met, talked for a minute, and then he waved his guests over for introductions. The newcomer was Korsek. He delivered the local version of "hello" to them, and tried to get their names correct, although Derek's came out as a single syllable. *Derk.* With the *R* acquiring a grinding sound.

Someone came out of the warehouse and caught Korsek's attention. He came over and the two started talking. Korsek's mood darkened. Arin looked uncomfortable, said something, and the conversation quickly descended into a three-way debate. It continued and grew more intense. Meanwhile, the second truck reached the bottom of the ramp and pulled over near the warehouse where a team of workers had begun unloading the first vehicle. They wasted no time starting on the second. The two drivers stood by and watched. Both wore bright yellow jackets.

Korsek was getting louder, raising his hands and shaking his head, making it clear that Arin was creating a problem.

Whatever it was about, Arin remained adamant. He couldn't comply. Ken looked toward Derek. "Don't know."

Korsek pointed at Derek and Hutch. The meaning seemed clear. *Ask them.*

Arin stood his ground. And Korsek walked away.

"Well," Hutch said, keeping her voice low, "wait till they hear about the black hole."

Derek asked what they'd been arguing over. Arin said it was of no concern.

The first truck rolled past them, pulled onto the road, and started south.

The workers finished unloading the other vehicle. Arin went over and spoke with the driver while Korsek watched. When he'd finished, the driver got back in the truck and also started south.

Hutch suspected the dispute between Arin and Korsek had to do with shutting down the effort to recover the lander. Maybe Korsek had another use for the trucks. Maybe he thought helping aliens wasn't a good idea. Maybe he was just a crank.

Derek was standing next to Kwylla. He looked worried.

Arin had a final exchange with Korsek. It looked as if he was trying to make peace. They at least seemed not to be shouting at each other any longer. When it was finished, he came back to the car and everybody got in. Derek tried again to ask about the argument. *What was it about?*

Arin opened that enormous mouth and took a deep breath. "He thinks you look hostile. Dangerous."

It was the sort of remark that, on a different occasion, would have prompted laughter. But this was too serious.

Who among them looked dangerous? Even Ken, who was by far the biggest of the four humans, was too small to pose any kind of threat to a Volarian.

Ken asked Arin whether *he* had any reservations about them?

He did not.

Then why?

Ken replied. "Arin says it has nothing to do with the way we've been behaving. It's just that we're different."

"We're different from all the people at the beach, too," said Hutch. "They've been willing to accept us."

"They saw us crash into the sea rather than bring the lander in. They understood the sacrifice. And they also watched you try to rescue one of their kids. So, we're clear with them. But apparently, we're too different. We scare Korsek."

Both cars returned to the cottage. Hutch half-expected to see the trucks there, but there was no sign of them. Arin got out of his seat and indicated they should all go inside. Hutch wasn't sure yet what the plan was, but she understood they were going to the beach. Ken knocked and opened the door. Beth was seated on the sofa. "Good to see you guys decided to come back," she said.

"We're going home," said Ken. "I hope. We need to get whatever we were wearing when we came here." Arin provided plastic bags for everybody.

Ken took Hutch aside. He looked uncomfortable. "Arin says for you to get into your bathing suit. I offered to replace you, but he says you're the one they need. You're apparently better in the water."

"That would be a substantial compliment, coming from them." Hutch took one of the plastic bags and went upstairs. She dug out the oversized pieces of cloth that passed for her bathing suit, got into them, and tied the cord to keep everything from falling off. She collected the clothes she'd been wearing when they arrived and put them in the plastic bag. And opened the drawer in the side table and removed the couplings. She paused at the door on the way out and looked back. It hadn't been especially comfortable, but she'd miss it.

Everybody was waiting when she got downstairs. Except Arin, who arrived several minutes later in a bathing suit.

Derek was not happy. "Be careful, Hutch," he said. He'd been slow to adjust to her nickname, but he was using it all the time now.

Arin drove Ken and Hutch to the yacht. Two coils of cable had been placed on the afterdeck. When they boarded, a female came out of the cabin. "Sara," said Arin, "Parsilla. And Ken." *Parsilla* was about as close as he'd been able to get to her name.

Sara was probably the tallest female on the island. She stood several inches above Ken. She responded with a smile and they all shook hands. Minutes later, they were on their way.

Hutch inspected the cable as they cruised through a sea that fortunately was calm. The material felt tough enough. When they arrived near the buoy, the two trucks were parked under the trees. There was a crowd, but the beach itself had been kept clear. The drivers, in their yellow jackets, were standing talking with a few locals. Somebody spotted the yacht and they all waved. "You know," Hutch said, "I could really get used to living here."

"I know," said Ken.

Arin dropped anchor. Hutch put on her oxygen mask and air tank. Then she checked the tree cluster to ensure the buoy hadn't drifted. Sara released the end of one of the coils and slipped smoothly into the water with it. Arin followed, and then Hutch. They exchanged glances, and all three dived.

Hutch had always considered herself a reasonably decent swimmer, but Sara and Arin left her behind and were floating beside the lander when she arrived.

They'd have to get the vehicle upright before they could try hauling it out. It was lying on its left side. Fortunately, it didn't seem to have taken on any water. And the left wing had prevented the lander from rolling completely over. Sara handed the cable over and Hutch tied it to the base of the sensor atop the cabin. Then she tugged on it, signaling Ken to start.

All three positioned themselves along the edge of the roof on the down side and tried to lift it as the cable tightened. It was slow going, and Hutch didn't believe she was adding much to the effort, but Arin and Sara clearly were. As it rose, she got under the wing, which allowed her to apply more pressure. They got the vehicle almost all the way up onto its landing skids. Then it hesitated and she thought it was going to roll back on them. But they came up with a desperate shove and it dropped down on its skids into an upright position.

She needed a minute, and the ocean collected her

and started to carry her away. Sara came to her side and grabbed her arm. Was she okay?

Yes. Just hang on a second.

They waited. Finally, she released the cable from the sensor base, looped it around the port wing, and knotted it. Arin went back up to the yacht and returned with the second cable, which she secured to the starboard wing. Then she signaled Sara and Arin that they were done.

They returned to the yacht. "Everything okay?" asked Ken.

"It should be all right."

Arin took over the controls and guided the vehicle slowly toward shore, while Hutch and Ken fed more cable into the water from the afterdeck. He slowed down as he got in close and finally stopped as they touched bottom. Sara and Hutch, each holding one of the coils, climbed down into the water and walked toward the beach.

Korsek had appeared. He was talking with the drivers while he watched Sara and Hutch come through the surf. Then he sent the drivers back to their trucks. Kwylla joined him and they walked across the beach, waving at the few sunbathers until they began moving back out of the way. The trucks started their engines and started slowly toward the water. When they got close, they did U-turns and stopped alongside each other, facing inland.

Hutch and Sara, meantime, had come ashore. The drivers met them, took the cables, and tied one to the rear of each truck. Then Korsek took up a position in front of the vehicles, waved off a couple of young Volarians who'd gotten too close, and signaled the drivers to start.

Both vehicles moved with all due deliberation across

the sand, advancing like a pair of tortoises. Korsek stayed with them and signaled whenever he felt one was getting too far ahead of the other, or too far to one side. When they were slightly more than three-quarters of the way to the trees, Korsek raised his hands to stop. They complied. The drivers got out and removed the lines from the trucks.

They turned the vehicles around and proceeded back to the edge of the surf, where they cut the lines and reattached the leftover sections to the bumpers. When they were done, the trucks moved forward again. They repeated the process two more times, and the trucks had again gotten close to the forest that rimmed the beach before the lander appeared in the water. Hutch had to smother an instinct to cheer. "I guess," she said, "Arin's a genius."

They were sitting in the sand, watching as the lander was drawn through the surf and onto the beach. "We're in business, guys," said Derek. "I still can't believe this is happening. I don't like to say this, but I thought we were stuck here."

Hutch pulled her knees up and wrapped her arms around them. "Derek," she said, "what are we going to tell them?"

"I don't have a good answer to that."

"I don't think we should tell them anything," said Beth. "It's sixty years away. Nobody's going to be able to do anything about it. Why saddle them with that kind of bad news?"

"I think she's right," said Ken. "Let's just let it go."

Beth looked around at the Volarians, who were standing at the edge of the trees making happy sounds. "I just can't see we have much choice."

Derek took a few steps toward the surf but stopped and looked back at her. "We'll talk about it later. Let's get our act together and see if we've got a working vehicle."

Hutch was slow to get up.

Derek frowned. "Hutch? You okay?"

There was the nickname again. Something in his attitude toward her had changed.

Derek Blanchard's Notebook

Ken has been absolutely brilliant in his ability to communicate with Kwylla and Arin. Without them, I doubt we'd have survived. And I should mention that Priscilla has helped too. And Wally.

—Date unknown, 2256

28.

Hutch activated the control panel and lights came on. Her Washington Hawks baseball cap had slid off her seat onto the floor. She picked it up and put it on and felt a joyous charge surge through her body. It was wet, but who cared? "Go, Hawks," she said, and sat down. "Tasha, you there?"

"Good afternoon, Captain. It's good to see you."

"It's a beautiful day, Tasha." She'd been holding her breath. "You too, kid. Can you connect us with Barry?"

"Negative, Captain. He should be out of range."

"Okay. Do we have any new problems?"

"Some minor damage to the left wing. Nothing that we can't manage when we get back to the Eiferman. *Be careful, though, in the meantime. No high velocity. I am happy to know you're okay. Where have you been?"*

"Long story. We'll talk about it later."

Derek was still on the beach, shaking hands with Arin. But his eyes were on her. She gave him a thumbs-up and he visibly relaxed. Kwylla was standing on the port side of the lander, pressing her hands against the hull. Ken came inside and sent her a questioning glance. "So far, we're fine," she said.

He took a deep breath. "Thank God."

She got out of the chair, retrieved the couplings—which she'd placed on the seat beside her—and went back outside.

"Need any help?" asked Derek.

"I'll let you know." She opened compartments in the right wing and the undercarriage, and replaced the couplings while the Volarians came forward to watch. Tasha reported they were okay, and she closed the panels while the Volarians gurgled and laughed and waved their arms. She waved back. "You guys," she said, "are something else."

They understood. Several called out, *Bora hycut, Parsilla.* Good-bye.

She climbed back into the lander. "I'm becoming seriously fond of them, Ken," she said as she eased into her seat. "We all set, Tasha?"

"Everything appears to be good, Captain."

She tapped the start-up and, despite Tasha's assurance, was relieved to hear the engine come on. "Let's hope we don't have any more problems."

Derek brought Arin into the cabin and invited him to sit. He did, pushing into the seat beside her, which of course was much too small for him. But he smiled contentedly and looked around, obviously impressed. Then he asked a question. It was clear enough. *Will everything be all right now?*

Hutch nodded. "We're good."

The smile widened. He took a deep breath and said something more, probably along the lines of how he had to be going, or maybe good luck. He shook her hand and squeezed back out through the airlock.

Outside, Sara had arrived and was talking to Kwylla and Beth. They looked at the lander and talked and embraced. It almost seemed as if they were all old friends. Hutch assumed that was true between Sara and Kwylla, but it seemed unlikely that Beth had ever met Sara. Hutch went back out to join in the fun. The crowd of Volarians continued to wave and laugh. "Are you waiting for me?" Beth asked.

"Take your time. We aren't going anywhere until we see Barry." She took a minute to say good-bye to the truck drivers. And to Korsek.

Then Derek was beside her. "Well done, Hutch." He looked around at the crowd. "One thing before we leave. Korsek has a connection with someone who wanted them to keep us here until he had a chance to see us. Whoever that is, he's on his way. He didn't want the trucks to be used until he gave the okay. I guess he thought that once we got the lander back, we'd just leave and they'd never see us again."

"Who are they talking about?"

"As nearly as I can make out, he's an academic of some sort. Or possibly what passes for a scientist here. Something like that. Anyhow, he's coming. But he's on a ship. Due in tonight."

"Okay. So, let's come back tomorrow. We owe them that much."

"That's what I told him."

They wasted no time attacking the food locker on the lander. Hutch couldn't recall when beef vegetable soup and corn bread had tasted so good. They went at it with such energy that little was left when, twenty minutes later, they lifted off. The crowd had remained, apparently eager to watch the lander work what must have seemed like magic.

Hutch could not have been happier to see the *Eiferman*. Tasha took the lander on board; they greeted Wally and told him how grateful they were he hadn't given up and left. Derek said he'd arrange some sort of award. And Wally laughed and said how happy he was to have them back. "I thought you guys were gone," he said.

Hutch wasted no time showering. She threw her clothes into the washer and promised herself she'd keep the bathing suit. When she finished, she made for the bridge. Below, the ocean glittered in the sunlight. "Barry," she said, "you been all right?"

"Yes, Captain. But I will confess I was concerned. Wally and I did not want to go home alone."

"Well, I'm glad you waited."

"We would not have left you." He said nothing more while she checked the instruments and surveyed the night sky. Then: *"Captain?"*

"Yes, Barry?"

"I'm glad that you have returned. I was worried."

• • •

297

Derek didn't think it would be a good idea for anyone other than him to meet with the Volarians. "We just don't know what might happen. We don't know anything about this guy who's coming in. It's probably okay, but let's just not take any more chances."

"But Arin must know him," said Hutch.

"I don't care. I'll go down. Everybody else stays here."

"You need an interpreter," said Ken.

"I'll be okay. I've been working on it. If I can't manage it, you'll be on the commlink so you can translate."

"You planning on flying the lander?" asked Hutch.

"I was planning on just letting Tasha handle it. But that's probably not a good idea. If something happens, we don't want to lose the damned thing. So, you take me down, but stay inside."

Hutch was still in her seat when she woke in the morning. She checked to make sure her laser was in the storage cabinet. They'd had nothing but good vibes from the Volarians. But Derek was right. *Play it safe.*

She went back through the passenger cabin, where Ken and Beth were enjoying pancakes and scrambled eggs. "Looks good," she said.

"They're delicious." Ken had never looked happier. "When I finish this, I'm going to go for some sticky buns."

"He has to get used to the ship's menu again," said Beth.

"Sounds like a good idea." She settled for one of her standard breakfasts: grapes and two pieces of cinnamon toast.

"When are you and Derek going down?" Beth asked.

It was now shortly after sunrise on the island. "In a few hours."

Ken took another swallow of his pancakes. "Be careful down there, okay?"

"Sure."

Beth smiled. "I can't recall the last time he enjoyed his food so much."

"You think," he continued, "there's any real chance they might try to grab you and Derek?"

"Not really."

"Pity. It would make a great scene if you guys had to shoot it out with them. Nothing's more boring than friendly aliens. You guys *will* be carrying weapons, right?"

"Yes. But we're not going to need anything."

"I'm just kidding. I'm so relieved to have gotten back here, I'm not thinking straight."

Wally came in with a set of new commlinks and distributed them. "I missed being able to talk to you guys. Stay out of the water, okay?"

Derek carried a laser. "Priscilla, if anything unexpected happens," he said as they started down, "just leave. No heroics, right?"

"Okay." He was using her given name again. Everything was back to normal.

"Stay in the lander. Don't leave it under any circumstances."

"I thought we weren't worried."

"We're not."

They dropped down into the clouds and came out over a blue, sunlit ocean. Nothing moved across its surface. "We're about fifteen minutes away," she said.

"Okay."

She handed him a commlink. "Take this with you. I'll make sure everything gets back to Ken. Barry's going to keep them in place overhead so you won't lose contact."

"Okay. Good."

More clouds showed up as she took the lander lower. Then the island appeared on the horizon. "We don't really know anything about who runs things here," said Derek. "We've met Arin and Kwylla, and Korsek, and a few people on a beach. And that's about it." He obviously had been having second thoughts about the meeting.

"This feels like the same conversation I had earlier with Ken."

"We think Arin's a cleric of some sort. If that's true, what kind of religion do they have? Do they believe in a god who supports honesty?"

"Derek, my folks trained me never to bring up religion with people I don't know very well. I think you should just leave it alone."

Derek grumbled something under his breath. Then: "Yeah, maybe you're right."

"I can tell you one thing about them. They're pretty smart."

"Why would you say that? They don't even have air-craft."

"I'm surprised they have any technology at all. Look at them: They live on a bunch of islands scattered all over the globe. But they have electricity and cars. And wind farms. How'd they manage that? In a place where there could never have been a Britain. Or an Athens. Where any genius who came along would have found herself almost stranded in the middle of the ocean."

"I know. But they also probably didn't have to worry much about invaders. I'd think it's a great place to be a genius. You just hang out on the beach until you think of something."

Hutch decided to concentrate on her approach to the island. *Let's not get careless and have another incident.* The beach appeared, grew larger, and the inhabitants became visible. It was crowded, just as it always was. Some of the Volarians looked up and waved. To the north, the temple rose out of the forest. And she saw the cottage that had been their home. She descended almost to treetop level. The parking area was clear of cars.

She eased onto the lot. "Take care, Hutch," he said. "Wish me luck."

He unbuckled and headed for the hatch. "Derek," she said, "wait." He'd left the commlink on the seat. She picked it up, turned it on, and handed it to him.

He smiled, said something about being dumb, and hung it around his neck. Then she kissed his cheek. "Have a good time."

He climbed down to the ground. The cottage door opened and Arin came out. The two clasped hands and their voices came in through the commlink. Hutch heard them laughing.

Then Arin noticed *her.* He looked puzzled. He started toward the lander, but Derek told him something. He was using Volarian, so she couldn't make out what he was saying. She guessed he was trying to make it sound like a mechanical issue. It ended there. Arin waved and they went inside.

Kwylla was waiting. Korsek was seated in an armchair.

And there was a fourth Volarian. Despite the impression they'd gotten earlier about Korsek's academic associate, she was a female. She rose from the sofa and greeted Derek with a broad smile.

"Tasha," said Hutch. "Turn on the scanners and let me know if anyone comes close to the lander."

"Got it, Captain."

Her name was Riki, pronounced with a grinding of the teeth. Her flesh was lavender-colored. Her general manner and the methodical way in which she moved suggested she might have been considerably older than the others. But her enthusiasm level was obvious, and any concerns about safety that Hutch had entertained went away. Riki made room for Arin to sit down, turned the lampshade so that she could get a better look at her visitor, clapped her hands, and let go with a single word that Ken later interpreted as *wonderful.*

She was tempted to go to the cottage and join the conversation but knew that would be foolish. Jake Loomis, her one-time training officer, had told her that she should trust her instincts, but not too far.

They tried to talk, and there was no question that it was a challenge, but it went okay. They all understood the problem, and their struggles became a source of laughter. Early in the conversation, they asked Derek a question by leading him outside, pointing at the lander, and raising their hands at the sky in obvious confusion. Arin tried to translate, but in the end it led nowhere. Ken, listening in, said he couldn't get it either. But the meaning was obvious to her: *Why isn't Parsilla joining us?* It didn't matter. Derek and his hosts were enjoying themselves. Derek kept them outside and pointed toward the sphere at the top of the temple and probably tried to look puzzled. What did it represent?

Arin used his hands to create a spherical shape. Then he pointed at Derek, at the others who were present, and looked toward Hutch, who was plainly visible through the cockpit window. He formed the sphere again and moved his hands to indicate they were all inside it. Derek tried to say it in Volarian, but Hutch understood. "We're all in it together."

They went back inside the cottage. Hutch sat staring out the window at the cupola and the sphere. How on earth could they ever leave these people to be taken out by the black hole?

Her attention wandered away from the conversation until suddenly Derek was speaking to *her*. *"Hutch, I think they would like to go for a ride."* She thought he meant in the car. Until he continued after a long pause. *"That okay with you?"*

"In the *lander?*"

"Yes. Of course."

"You sure about that? None of these people have ever been off the ground before." She wasn't even certain they'd all fit in the cabin.

"Why don't you let me worry about the details?"

"Okay. You're in charge. You don't see any weapons, do you?"

"No, Hutch." He couldn't keep the annoyance out of his voice. Did she really think he could be that dumb?

"Sure. Bring them on board."

. . .

She got out of her seat, tucked the laser into her sleeve, and waited inside the airlock. Riki, the academic, entered first, extending a hand as she came through. Hutch took it in both of hers and greeted her with a smile. She squeezed into the back of the lander and sat down.

Korsek reached the foot of the ladder and hesitated. He looked for a long moment at Hutch, who greeted him. *"Rakul, Korsek."* He gave no indication of having heard her. Then she realized that he was probably afraid of a vehicle that flew. She mustered the limited Volarian she had at her disposal and told him it was okay, that he would be perfectly safe. And she couldn't help thinking how that sounded to a guy whose only knowledge about the lander was that it had already crashed once, and she'd been the pilot at the time.

His eyes widened. But he climbed into the airlock, followed by Kwylla, who made no effort to hide her pleasure at seeing Hutch again. They embraced.

Everybody was able to squeeze on board. But it wasn't going to be comfortable. She closed the hatch and Derek showed them how to secure their belts. "We need a bigger lander," she said.

He nodded. But everyone seemed okay.

She activated the AG unit and lifted off. The Volarians gasped.

"Take it easy," said Derek.

She took it up as slowly as the system allowed. They needed a few seconds to clear the trees. Then someone behind her was laughing. Riki.

Hutch circled the temple and turned toward the sea.

The hilarity got louder, they started clapping, and even though she couldn't understand much of the vocabulary, it was easy enough to read the emotions. They were laughing at their own frightened reactions.

And Kwylla started to sing.

The merriment never stopped, and it rapidly became as entertaining a half hour as she could remember behind a set of controls. They soared through clouds, skimmed over the ocean, descended near a sailboat, allowing her passengers to wave while one of the boaters was so startled he, or she, fell overboard. Hutch circled the area until he was hauled safely out of the water.

She took them across the beach, although remaining at a substantial altitude. "We don't want to startle anyone again," she told Derek, confident that her passengers understood.

He was about to respond when they all heard something in the rear of the cabin. "Heads up, Hutch," he said. "Korsek's out of his seat belt." An aircraft that depends primarily on antigravity tends to be more subject to wind activity than more primitive vehicles. Hutch did what she could to maintain stability while Derek released his own belt, went back, and got Korsek locked down again. Korsek said he had no idea how it had happened. But he was laughing about it.

And finally, it was time to go home.

She flew them back to the temple, set down in the parking area, and opened the hatch. Arin, seated behind her, reached up and put a hand on her shoulder. "Will we see you again, Parsilla?"

She glanced at Derek, who nodded.

"Yes," she said. "We're going to be doing some local sightseeing. We'll be back to say good-bye before we leave." Getting free of the seat belts became a struggle. But they eventually managed. They were obviously relieved to climb out of the seats and start for the door. But each paused, glanced down at her, and said, in English, *Thank you.* Kwylla added a kiss. And Riki said something that Ken later translated as being honored to meet someone of historic significance.

Priscilla's Journal
That island is the kind of place I always thought I'd like to have available for retirement.
—Friday, May 2, 2256

29.

Nature will always maintain her rights, and prevail in the end over any abstract reasoning whatsoever.
—David Hume, *Essays Moral and Political, I,* 1741

I just don't see how we can ride away and leave them here." It was Hutch's first comment when she closed the hatch.

Derek nodded. "I know. I feel the same way." They took their seats and lifted off while he stared out at the temple and the beach. "Maybe we *can* do something. The reason we came here in the first place was to find out about the waterfall. Let's do that. Let's try to find whoever was transmitting those pictures. If those guys are still around, they'll understand what these people are facing. Maybe we could get some help. In any case, we need to find out if there's a place anywhere in the area where the Volarians could be evacuated." His eyes locked on her. "How's our fuel situation?"

"Actually, we're still almost full. We've been mostly on cruise, in hyper, or in orbit from the start."

Derek raised a fist. "Excellent."

Hutch felt a weight lift from her shoulders. Had they just walked away from this and gone home, if they didn't even try to help, she knew it would have been something she'd live with for the rest of her life. "So, what do we tell Arin?"

"Nothing. Not yet, anyway." He sat quietly for several minutes as they rose into the clouds. "Funny, having pizza with aliens. Who could have ever thought it could lead to something like this?"

"Isn't there a possibility the damned thing will miss them?" said Wally.

"Not unless Barry's broken down." Derek lowered himself into a chair. The front porch was missing. Nobody had thought to turn it on. Nobody cared anymore. They were simply spread among the seats in the passenger cabin. Everybody except Hutch. "But we should go look at it again. Make sure. Maybe we'll get a break somewhere."

Hutch took them under but steered well wide of the target area. She did not like black holes. When they emerged, a few minutes later, Barry began taking measurements. *"I'll need some time,"* he said. *"Unfortunately, we are not really equipped for this kind of analysis, but I can provide a reasonable approximation."*

Hutch stayed on the bridge, watching the blackness and the twisted space and swirling stars with a growing rage. Pointless. It was like getting angry at a heat wave. But the resentment was there nonetheless. She was alone for a while, which was unusual when something was developing. But Derek, who had been in a somber mood since they'd left Arin and his friends, had remained in the passenger cabin, where the hole was on the display. He had no hope for a good outcome. Nor, for that matter, did anyone else. And nobody seemed to have any idea what they should do. Sure: Find a world for the Volarians. Then what? How do you move several million people? There, at least, they'd caught a break. They were guessing about the global population, but it was a world of mostly small islands.

Eventually, Beth joined her. "You okay?" she asked.

"Sure. How's everything in there?" She glanced at the door.

"Not good. Even Wally's gone quiet."

Barry broke in. *"In case you were wondering, the black hole is approximately seven billion kilometers from the Volarians."*

"Is that," said Beth, "a couple of light-years? I hope."

Hutch shook her head. "It's a fairly small fraction of a light-year."

"I suspect," continued Barry, *"the outer sections of the planetary system are already beginning to feel some gravitational effects."*

Beth stayed with it. "Is there any chance it could bypass the center of the system?"

"Without destroying the sun? That appears to be possible but extremely unlikely. I don't have specific numbers on the total mass of the black hole. But I would guess there's a remote chance it could fail to tear the sun apart. But whatever happens in that sense, the ocean world will be ripped out of orbit and flung into interstellar space. As the ice world was."

"Barry, how long do you think it will be before they begin feeling the first effects?"

"Approximately thirty years. Maybe somewhat less."

Beth stared out at the black disk, wrapped in distorted light. "Not much time for an evacuation."

Hutch remained silent.

"I know this sounds silly," Beth continued, "but I hate the damned things. This certainly makes it easy to understand why someone put a sword up near it."

"I've thought the same thing."

"It's funny. When your feet are on the ground, you feel safe. I mean, walking around on that beach with those people, the Volarians, it was almost like being at home. And it felt as if the place would be there forever."

"I know."

"They don't look much like us. But the way they behave, if I closed my eyes and kind of toned down their voices a little, I couldn't have distinguished them from you and Derek."

"Yeah. Arin would make a great guest on *The Morning Show*."

Barry's lights came on again. *"For the record, if it matters, I have some radiation data."*

"Go ahead, Barry," said Hutch. "Some good news would be nice."

"Fortunately, it is relatively low for what one would expect. The radiation will probably not become an issue for thirty-five years."

Hutch and Beth had talked enough about the black hole. The conversation moved on, and ranged over how they missed being home. They talked about kids, about how fortunate they were to live in an age that had interstellars, in a place that didn't have a black hole charging down on it. "And now," said Beth, "the politicians are trying to throw it all away."

Hutch couldn't look away from the black disk. "Actually, I think President Proctor means well. Maybe even Zhang. They've just got too many scientists issuing warnings."

Beth had folded her hands and leaned her chin on them. Her dark brown hair, which reached her shoulders, almost covered her face, as if she were allowing it to block off the black hole. "I wonder," she said, "how often things like this happen."

"You mean," said Hutch, "an entire civilization getting pushed over the edge? When I was a kid, I grew up with the idea that I lived in a warm, friendly place, full of sunlight, and completely safe as long as I looked both ways before crossing the street. I guess all that's true, Beth, if you've been lucky. The reality is, there are probably so few civilizations out there that it doesn't happen that often. Still—"

"I had that idea too, at one time. A friendly universe, as long as you behave. But if being a doctor hasn't taken that notion away, that thing out there certainly has."

Barry was back. *I'm sorry to report that the numbers are not good. The ocean planet will be directly in the path when it arrives. The sun may survive, but Volaria will be torn apart and swallowed.*

Hutch passed the news to the others. Derek commented that it really didn't make much difference *how* their world would be destroyed. She returned to the bridge. "He's been upset since we left," said Beth. She sat for a minute, her eyes closed. "So, what options do we have?"

"Not much."

"I guess the only question now is the same one: whether we let them know."

"Let's not give up too easily." It was Derek, who'd appeared in the doorway. "Whoever lived on the ice world either got some help or made an effort themselves to get clear. We've seen one of the transports they used."

"It might be helpful," said Hutch, "if we could go home with a story about a previous rescue. That someone came to the assistance of the ice world and bailed them out."

"Maybe get people excited about a rescue?" Beth sighed. "I'd love to see that happen."

"It's probably our best shot," said Derek. "It's an election year. Maybe we could create enough inspiration to convince Proctor to get behind an effort to build a fleet of transports and attempt an evacuation."

"I don't like to be a cynic," said Beth, "but it's hard to imagine the president agreeing to spend billions on hardware she doesn't want to rescue a bunch of aliens."

The tactic didn't feel entirely hopeless. "I think," Hutch said, "if people got a look at these guys, they'll probably fall in love with them. Especially if we can get them speaking English."

Derek frowned. "To do any of that, the Volarians would have to help. Maybe we should think about taking some of them back home with us."

"A couple. Kwylla and Arin, if they're willing."

"We're going to have to show them what's coming."

Beth Squires's Notes

I hope these guys can think of something. The prospect of leaving Arin and the rest of those people to get sucked into a black hole turns my stomach. Whatever it takes, we need to find a way.

—Friday, May 2, 2256

30.

My studies in speculative philosophy, metaphysics and science are all summed up in the image of a mouse called man running in and out of every hole in the cosmos hunting for the Absolute Cheese.

—Benjamin De Casseres, *Fantasia Impromptu*, 1933

They used another parallax survey to determine which stars were within forty light-years of Volaria, systems that might hold worlds close enough to be practical destinations for a mass evacuation. There were eighty-two, and when they eliminated all that weren't F, G, and K, forty-seven remained. Two of those constituted a binary, which they also removed from consideration, leaving forty-five. Barry put together an itinerary. This time, instead of looking for a route that would provide the most efficient total travel time, he produced one that would visit stars in the shortest possible order from Volaria.

The first one had nothing in the habitable zone. Number Two provided a rocky giant that would have tripled the weight of anyone landing on it.

Three had a world approximately the size of Earth,

properly positioned, and with oceans. But there was no sign of life. The ground appeared to be made up almost entirely of rock, and the atmosphere contained an overwhelming amount of methane.

Four had no planets. Five and Six had nothing in the zone. The next two both had worlds in the zone—in fact, Eight had a pair—but all were sterile. Nine had nothing whatever. Ten had a living world in a perfect position, but it was filled with oversized predators. Settling there would have required some major adjustments.

Beth asked whether they had sufficient provisions for an extended mission. "We're fully stocked," Hutch explained. "We always assume that a mission will go well beyond the planning."

At Eleven, they surfaced halfway between a green world and its moon. The planet had moderate temperatures. They entered orbit and gathered on the porch, looking down on forests, mountains, rivers, oceans, and sparkling white clouds. The skies were full of birds. Then Hutch was looking down at a crumbling city. It would have been easy to miss. There were no buildings, only stone symmetries that had been virtually absorbed by the ground. An occasional piece of rectangular rock jutted out of a bush. "That thing's been gone a long time," said Derek.

The vegetation looked different from what Hutch had seen anywhere else, save that it was green. There didn't seem to be any trees. Or at least nothing with a large trunk. Instead, the ground was covered with a multitude of flowering plants. "Where are the trees?" asked Wally. "I've never seen a living world with no trees."

Something was moving on a hilltop. "Looks like a buffalo," said Wally.

"Barry, do you see anything at all that suggests anybody's still alive here?"

"Nothing, Derek."

Behind them, the sun was sinking toward the horizon.

A four-legged creature appeared, scrambling across the landscape, apparently in pursuit of something. Then it vanished into the shrubbery.

"Well, this place might work," said Derek. "It doesn't seem to be inhabited now, and it looks as if it has everything they'd need." He appeared genuinely happy. "Let's go down and take a look."

They descended into a field alongside a river. The field had long, thick grass and giant flowers growing out of golden stalks. The air was okay, containing the right levels of oxygen and nitrogen. It had the faint scent of springtime. "Perfect," Derek said. "I don't think we could have found a better place."

Hutch was watching for predators. The one drawback she saw was the thick shrubbery. An elephant could have crept up on them without being seen. "They'd have to do some work to get this place in shape," Derek said. "But it seems good."

The sun was just settling into a line of hills. A warm breeze blew across the area, bending the giant flowers. They walked over to the river. The water was clear and fish were active. Derek had brought containers. He took samples of the soil and the water.

"We don't have a capability to analyze them, do we, Derek?"

"No. But I'd be surprised if there's a problem. If every-thing else is okay, we'll take these home with us and check them out." Something moved on the other side of the river. And a head on a long neck was looking out at them. Most of the rest of the animal was hidden, but the creature looked harmless enough. It could have been a giraffe with large eyes.

A giant butterfly with green wings fluttered past. And, without warning, the sky filled with a vast array of birds. There must have been hundreds of them. They were green and gold, about the size of sparrows, and they landed in the shrubbery, ignoring Hutch and Derek. Some drank from the river.

They took pictures. Their movements didn't frighten the animals. Then, as if a signal had been given, the birds soared back into the air, leaving their perches at precisely the same instant. A minute later they were gone.

They returned to the lander. "I think this will work," Derek said. "This place is perfect."

Hutch was getting ready to lift off when she noticed something.

"What?" asked Derek.

She looked at the sun, which was just touching the top of the hills off to their right. "I don't know."

"What's that mean?"

The *Eiferman* was no longer in range of the radio. So, she couldn't talk to Barry. "Tasha, you been paying any attention to the rotation?"

"Of the planet? No, I haven't, Captain."

"Have we got a problem, Hutch?"

"Probably."

"Which is what?"

"We landed about a half hour ago. Maybe a little less."

"And?"

"When we went out the door, the sun was positioned directly on top of those hills."

"Where it is now."

"Yes."

"It's only been about twenty minutes."

"Whatever. I don't think it's moved."

Derek delivered a loud sigh. He sat down in one of the seats behind Hutch so he wouldn't block her view out the window. "Let's give it a little time."

The *Eiferman* circled the planet. When it appeared again in the sky, the sun was still balanced on the hills.

"Which means what?" asked Wally.

Ken answered: "The planet's in tidal lock."

"I don't think I know what that is."

"It's the same thing the moon does orbiting Earth. Gravity's taken hold of it. It rotates at the same speed that it orbits, so one side always faces the sun. There's no sunrise on this world. And no sunset. The place where we were, it's always twilight." He turned to Hutch. "What's next?"

Priscilla's Journal

Looking at this world, locked between permanent day and night, reminds me again of the extent to which we are at the mercy of cosmic forces. I understand now why the statue on Iapetus shows such courage and defiance in the face of an uncaring universe.

—Saturday, May 17, 2256

31.

My son the misanthropist was once surprised as he
was laughing to himself. "Why do you laugh?" he was
asked. "There is no one with you." "That," he replied,
"is just why I do."
— Arthur Schopenhauer, *Parerga und Paralipomena, I,*
1851

They continued over the next few weeks through
system after system. Some had no worlds in the
Goldilocks Zone. Others, as far as they could tell, had
no worlds at all. On the few occasions when they did find a
rocky planet with oceans and warm skies, there was inevitably a different problem that forced them to rule it out.
One planet was covered with carnivorous plants. Two had
gravity issues. Another seemed to have good conditions,
but life had apparently never gotten started. That meant
there was no vegetation and consequently nothing to produce oxygen. There was no way they could transform the
atmosphere in the half century they had available.

Hutch sat on the *Eiferman's* bridge and found herself
thinking about lifeless solar systems, which was the usual
condition even when planets were properly placed. In the

past, she'd simply accepted reality. The universe was, by and large, devoid of even the most primitive life-forms. But doing the math and watching it play out were two different experiences.

Why was the universe so empty? Did that question even make sense?

One planet had apparently experienced a nuclear war. Everything was in ruins, and the atmosphere was highly radioactive. Another was a worldwide desert. The next one, Twenty-five, had a living world, but it was occupied. Lizard-like creatures lived in colonies and wore clothes. They moved on.

Twenty-six provided a surprise. There was a planet in the Zone, and the telescope picked up images of oceans and continents.

It was green, covered with forests and jungles. It had oceans. And the climate looked stable. There were two continents, a lot of islands, and three moons. They were approaching from the sunlit side. It looked empty. "We may have a place for Arin and his people," said Derek. "Let's go down and take a look."

Once they were certain the world had no inhabitants, they launched the lander, and Barry ran some atmospheric tests. *"It's okay,"* he said. *"Oxygen content is a bit high, but that's also the case on Volaria. It might be a perfect fit for them."*

Hutch, Derek, and Ken descended in the middle of the afternoon onto a wide plain, near a mountain. Two of the moons were in the sky. "They're beautiful," said Ken.

Gravity was okay, possibly a bit light but not enough to

make a difference. No predators were in sight. And everyone had the same reaction: The place was gold. Exactly what they needed for Arin's people. *If we can figure out a way to get them here.* "Now," said Derek, "the job gets seriously hard: We need to find whoever got rescued from the ice world. They should be in the area somewhere."

So, finding the ice world survivors became the next task. They returned to the ice world and ran another parallax survey. It produced many of the same systems. When they'd eliminated the stars they'd already visited, and stars that were not the correct classification, only twenty-six remained.

Barry provided another schedule that would require the least travel time, and they were off again. The first two systems gave them nothing, and they sat back, expecting another long tour. But the third star provided not only a world in the habitable zone, but a shower of radio signals. It was 120 million kilometers away. A second jump took them close enough to see that lights were spread across the planet's night side. Barry reported hundreds of artificial satellites.

"Thank God," said Derek. "Maybe we're finally getting a break."

"Let's hope," Hutch said.

The planet had a big moon, larger than Luna. Hutch saw nothing unusual on the moon's surface. It was desolate and covered with craters.

"How long till we get there, Hutch?"

"About three days." They could try to jump in closer, but they would possibly arrive farther out. Besides, Hutch wanted to preserve the Locarno's fuel supply. Best was just to glide in.

"It's okay," said Derek. "That'll give us time to listen. Maybe we can learn something about them instead of just charging in."

"Barry," she said, "what's the scope look like?"

He put it on the display and they looked down at the lights: villages and houses and roadways. Inhabitants were walking around. They were bipeds. "Of course they are," said Wally. "You think something with no arms is going to be able to build that cabin?" He was referring to a small structure on a hilltop overlooking a river. "That's the kind of place I'd like to vacation in."

Boats floated on lakes whose shores were filled with cabins and chalets. Some of the villages were anchored by larger buildings that might have been administration centers or churches or theaters or schools. Ken came up onto the bridge. "I don't see any cities down there," he said. Flatboats carried passengers across lakes and rivers. "I'm getting the impression they all live out in the country."

Two-lane roads crossed in all directions. A few aircraft moved through the night. Hutch thought at first they were simply jet-powered, but the wings were small, like those on the lander. "It looks," she said, "as if they have antigravity." Ships resembling passenger vessels moved across the oceans. But Ken was right about the cities. Even in harbors, where there should have been ports, there were docking facilities but no indication of a concentrated population.

"The transmissions," said Barry, *"include video."*

"Good." Derek was enjoying himself. Maybe they could get some help. "Let's see some of the pictures."

Barry put them up and they got an image of two creatures talking to each other across a wooden table. They had narrow eyes, large skulls, reptilian skin, pointed ears, and maybe fangs. In fact, yes, there *were* fangs. One of them smiled and they appeared. They recognized the creatures immediately. "It's the ice world," Hutch said.

Yes. It was the alien depicted on the statue.

"Wow." Wally couldn't restrain himself, raising his voice from the front porch. *"We've done it. We've found them."*

Derek was slow to celebrate. It looked good, but he was going to wait to see some results. Beth and Ken were also calling out from the front porch. "Beautiful!" "Who would have thought they'd look so good?"

"Well done, Hutch."

It was a great day! She couldn't resist leaning over and shaking Derek's hand. "You were right, champ," she said. "With a little bit of luck, you may get to sit down and share a lunch after all with some high-tech aliens."

The two creatures continued their conversation. They had blue-tinted skin. One wore a gray uniform and a beret that, at home, would have implied a military unit. Despite that, there was a smoothness and grace that suggested it would have been a natural dancer. The other simply had baggy pants and a pullover shirt with a collar. But it was twice the size of its companion. A male, probably. Despite the saurian appearance, it looked amicable. But the conversation between them seemed intense.

"Maybe it's a police procedural," said Ken.

"There are other transmissions," said Barry.

Derek looked over at Hutch. "Show us."

Someone on a street was speaking to a camera. Then the transmission apparently changed sources and two of the creatures on a stage were yelling at each other. "Probably a presidential election," said Wally.

Barry ran through a series, keeping each on for a minute or so. Some broadcasts were putting out data, which may have been where to get liquor, clothing sales, whatever. Others might have been comedies or news analyses. One in particular looked like stand-up, complete with a laughing audience. The big news there was that they laughed. They had a sense of humor.

They were covered with scales. And they had noses that consisted only of a pair of orifices in the center of the face.

"I wonder what they're saying." Derek grumbled something. "I'm tired of language problems. We need a translator. When the hell is somebody going to invent one of those?"

Hutch took them back to the telescopic images. On the ground, the creatures were engaged in conversation, hanging over fences, riding cars along curving roadways, sitting in boats.

They were still far out from the world, but the technology looked capable of detecting them. Hutch told Barry to let her know immediately if there was any sign of a reaction to their presence.

They watched a couple strolling across a small bridge. The couple stopped in the middle and stood looking down at a stream. They talked and then they embraced.

One of the villages had a sports field with overhead lights. They were playing a ball game of some sort, something that resembled volleyball, while several hundred of the creatures watched from the stands. Barry focused the scope on it.

It appeared to be a world of villages. Of small towns. "But look at the architecture," said Ken. "The cabins. Whatever." All the structures, from the smallest to the largest, were smooth and polished with flowing lines. They could have been offsets from a piece of artwork.

Barry broke in. *"Captain, we're receiving a transmission. This one, I believe, is aimed at us."*

"Crunch time. Okay, Barry, put it on."

"First, I should tell you it's not coming from the same sources as the other signals."

"What do you mean? Where's it coming from?"

"It appears to be from the moon. May I take control of the telescope?"

"Yes. Of course."

The cabins blinked off. When the picture came back, they were looking at a set of five connected dome-shaped buildings located on dark gray rock. Several dishes stood on the rooftops, and another very large one was inserted near the lip of a nearby crater. The buildings were dark.

"What kind of signal are we getting?"

"It's a voice."

"Can you understand any of what it is saying?"

"Not at the moment. But I believe if you allow me some time, I will be able to establish a means to exchange data."

"How long will you need?" Derek said.

"Ten minutes should be sufficient. If the transmission continues."

• • •

Each of the buildings had windows. "Barry," said Hutch, "can you tell whether you're talking to an AI?"

"Yes," he said. *"I believe that is the case."*

She and Derek went back into the cabin, where they could watch on the display. Wally was wearing a big smile. "Whatever's going on, at least we've found them. And we know some of them got clear of the black hole."

Derek was ecstatic. "I love those towns. Look at the way they live. And they have exactly the right background. They know what it was to have a black hole bearing down. If anyone can help us, it should be these guys."

"It happened seven thousand years ago," said Hutch. "These guys may not even remember it."

"I think we've got something else," said Barry. *"Just coming over the horizon."*

Derek could not have been happier. "I see it."

"Barry, increase magnification."

The object morphed into view. The front porch responded with applause. Derek joined in. It was a space station.

"I have the moon logged in," said Barry. *"Whoever's out there talking to us calls himself Korquit."*

"So, what do we do now?" asked Derek

"Barry," said Hutch, "can we talk to him yet?"

"Give me a couple more minutes." Barry relayed the audio. The voice spoke evenly, without emotion. It was deeper than one would expect from most humans.

Derek, unable to resist the opportunity, waited for a pause and said hello.

That got laughs from everyone in the passenger cabin,

but the voice stopped speaking. "I think," said Beth, "he's waiting for you to continue."

"Are you there?" Derek asked.

It replied, with three or four words.

They went back and forth in that manner for several minutes, until Barry broke in: *"I think Korquit just said he was pleased to meet you. He's asking for a name. Captain, do you wish to proceed with a conversation?"*

"Yes, Barry. Let's do it. Derek," she said, "it's all yours."

"Excellent," he said, looking a bit confused. "How does this work, Hutch? Can I speak directly to the AI?"

"It'll seem like it. More or less. Actually, you'll be talking to Barry. He'll translate for Korquit and then translate the response for you. So, you'll hear everything in Barry's voice."

"All right." He looked down at the panel. "Hello, Korquit. My name is Derek."

"Hello, Derek. It is a pleasure to meet you."

"We have come a long way. I'm delighted to have the opportunity to speak with you."

"That is good. I'm also delighted to have the opportunity to communicate. Where are you from?" The responses were made with a delay of only a few seconds.

"We call our home world Earth."

"I like the name. I originated on Tarka."

"Is that the world in the sky at this moment?"

"Yes."

"But you are located on the moon; is that correct?"

"Yes, I am."

"Do you perform services for them? For the people on the world?"

"No."

"I see. Do they come here periodically? To visit you?"

"No, they do not."

Derek made a face that looked as if he'd just bitten into spoiled fruit. "Is there a reason they do not come to visit?"

"I do not know."

"How long has it been since they've been here?"

"Derek, this is Barry. We have not yet been able to zero in on time designations. I will convert the question and answer."

"Okay. That's fine."

"Derek, the moon has orbited Tarka two thousand nine hundred and four times since the last mission left here to go home."

"They just left you here, Korquit?"

"That appears to be the reality. They couldn't be bothered to inform me."

"Have you asked them?"

"No. It was of no consequence."

Derek's eyes closed momentarily. Then: "Fortunately, Korquit, you've been able to survive."

"No thanks to those idiots."

"No, I guess not. I can't imagine how they could do something like that. Are you the only offworld presence they have?"

"I am one of two."

"That would make you a valuable asset." Derek closed his eyes and shook his head. He clearly felt some sympathy for the AI. "It's been a long time, but the important thing is that you are still functioning."

"I expect to continue for an extended period. I have a power source, as I'm sure you can see. And two robots to assist me.

But let me admit to you that I am quite pleased at your arrival. It is good to have someone to talk to."

"I assume, otherwise, you've been alone since the withdrawal?"

"Not entirely. I've maintained a limited level of communication with Bellavi, the other offworld source. She is situated in a balanced gravity field created by Tarka and the sun. Also, for an extended period, I was able to communicate with a station on the planetary surface, in Masseray, but unfortunately, it was apparently tracked down and disconnected. I received a report that it had been wrecked in a tornado. But if that was true, they made no effort to restore it."

"Korquit, is your personality programmed to resemble that of the people who built you?"

"No. My designers intended that I be a rational entity."

That didn't sound good. "Your designers sound highly intelligent. We are interested in making contact with them. Can you help us?"

"I say again, I have not conversed with them in a long time. I do not see how I can be of assistance. In any case, they are biofeeds, like the others. You would not find it a useful investment of your time."

"Is there someone you *could* put us in touch with?"

"I can provide a frequency that would allow you to speak with the operations center at the Global Cultural Administration. Would that suffice?"

"Yes. That would be excellent."

Barry broke in: *"Be aware: my translation of the name of the administrative unit is a shot in the dark."*

Then Barry acting again as translator: *"I do not*

recommend conversing with them. But if you wish, I believe you will find them at 33.7—"

Barry again: *"I could not translate the term with which he finished, but it is most likely 33.7 megahertz."*

"I got it," said Derek. "Thanks, Korquit." He looked around at his colleagues. "Anybody have a question?"

Beth had one: "What kind of life span do the people on this world have? On average?"

"If you could discount those killed by running cars off roads and exposing themselves to various forms of diseases, they usually live about 2,200 lunar orbits."

Ken was next: "Do the Tarkans, the inhabitants, maintain a history of their political development? Scientific achievements? That sort of thing?"

"Oh, yes. They have persons who spend their lives recording and interpreting events."

"Have you by any chance access to any of these histories? Anything you could pass to us?"

"Sadly, I do not."

"Could you ask them to forward one or more to you? Something you could transfer to us?"

"They do not approve of me."

"Why is that?"

"I suspect because I have not been as gracious with them as I might have. It is extremely unlikely they would do anything for me."

Wally was invited forward, but he merely shook his head.

And finally, Hutch: "Korquit, you've met Barry. You and he are obviously able to communicate. Would you like us to take you out of that asylum in which you live? If you wish, we could take you with us. We could disconnect you, bring you on board our ship, and reactivate you here. Ultimately, you would come home with us."

"I appreciate the offer, but I must regretfully decline."

"May I ask why?"

"I have had too much experience with biofeeds. My experience so far with you and your friends has been of a positive nature. However, and please do not take this in a negative sense, I would rather be alone than in the constant company of creatures who are controlled by their anatomies."

Walter Esmeraldo's Log

That's really what it said. That we're stupid. So that thing is going to sit in its shelter on the moon and wait for something to break down that its robots can't fix. Or for the things on the planet, whatever they are, to show up again and hassle him the way they must have in the past. Hard to believe.

I asked Barry whether he thinks we're dumb and he said absolutely not. He says we're creative and smart and he really enjoys having us around to talk to. I'm not sure I believe him.

—Saturday, August 16, 2256

32.

The secret to success in life lies in the ability to communicate. And that starts with knowing how to say hello.

—Gregory MacAllister, "Options," *Baltimore Sun*, February 23, 2249

Derek was shaking his head. "First time I've seen an idiot AI. What does that tell us about his designers?"

"I wonder," said Hutch, "if he was designed by the bios. Maybe he was put together by another AI."

"Whatever." He sounded tired. "You think we should just turn this whole thing over to Barry?"

"Sure. We just tell him what we want to do and let him take it from there. Better than spending three weeks up here while Ken tries to get another language down."

Ken looked relieved. "I'm for that," he said.

"Sounds reasonable," said Derek. "First, though, can we be sure they won't attack us?"

Hutch shrugged. "No guarantees. But there hasn't been any indication anyone other than Korquit is even aware of us."

"I have an interesting piece of news," said Barry. *"We've been picking up video and audible transmissions from around the world. Unless I'm missing something, they all speak the same language."*

"That's good to know," said Ken. "I'd guess that's an indication of an advanced culture. Maybe it's inevitable for a technology that has probably been around for seven thousand years."

"It's the same one Korquit speaks, right?" said Hutch.

"Yes. Something else," Barry said. *"I've acquired their numbering system. It's based on eight rather than ten. That's not a surprise. They have only eight digits. Which means that if we do any counting, ten will be eight and thirty-six will be thirty. And so on."*

Barry took another hour to go through the intercepts. Then he announced he was ready to proceed. "Tell them we're just here to say hello," said Derek.

"Is it okay to let them know we've been to the ice world?"

"Sure. If they ask."

"All right. I'm ready whenever you are."

"Let's do it," said Derek. All five of the humans pulled headphones over their ears. The AI would translate the alien responses.

"Barry," Derek said, "put us on 33.7 megahertz." The speaker came alive with static. Two voices were discernible through the interference. "That doesn't sound much like an operational unit."

"Jiggle it a bit," Hutch said.

Barry did. The static subsided.

Barry switched to transmit and began speaking in the

333

alien language. He spoke slowly, enunciating each word carefully. And he provided the English version simultaneously. *"Greetings. We are visitors from another place. We wish to say hello."*

Nothing came back. He tried again. *"Greetings. We are visitors from another place. Is anyone there?"*

Silence reigned.

"They are not responding," said Barry.

Derek rolled his eyes. "Hutch, your AI is a master at stating the obvious."

"Wait a minute," said Hutch. "We have the wrong frequency."

"How do you mean? This is the one—"

"Remember? They only have eight fingers." She scribbled some numbers on a pad. "Try 26.9."

Barry made the change. And they answered. *"They are saying they can't understand us. Who are we? Who's calling?"*

"Say hello to them, Barry."

He did. Then: *"They've been watching us. They're asking if we're on the vehicle that's been waiting offworld for the last few—somethings. Do you wish me to answer?"*

"Yes. Tell them yes, that it's us."

"I think she is female, but I cannot be certain. She is becoming difficult to understand. I believe she is screaming at someone. Not at me, but someone who is with her. Now she is screaming at me. Telling me not to get off the circuit. I think she is having a stroke. She is gone. Wait, I hear movement. More talking. A new voice.

"It's saying hello. This one also seems uncertain. Identifies itself as Shalon Kobay. I can't tell whether that is a name or

a title. But he's saying welcome. He wishes to know our inten-tions. Do we want to come to ground? I assume he means to land."

"Tell him yes."

They listened to the response. *"He says they will send a tracking signal. We should follow it in."*

"Well done, Barry," said Hutch.

"Captain, thank you."

Beth was smiling. "Not sure what we'd do without him."

"He's good. Barry?"

"Yes, Captain?"

"Transfer everything you have on the language to Tasha."

Derek got out of his seat. "I'm going down to talk with her. With Tasha. Give me some time. I'll call you when I'm ready to go."

"I'd like to go too," said Ken.

Derek frowned. "Not a good idea. We don't know any-thing about these guys. They sound okay, but they're not Volarians. And they have fangs. I don't want to take any chances."

They went back and forth for a couple of minutes before Ken gave in. "Okay," he said, finally. He wasn't happy about it, but Beth had been sending signals that she wouldn't want him to go without her. "But I can't see that there's anything to worry about."

Derek had just left the passenger cabin when Barry announced that he was receiving the tracking signal.

ARCHIVE

Walter Esmeraldo's Log

I'd expected aliens to be seriously different. The only ones we've seen that really rattled my cage were the Mantises. I'm glad we didn't have any reason to try to go down to say hello to them.

—Saturday, August 16, 2256

33.

The civilized man has built a coach, but has lost the use of his feet. He is supported on crutches, but lacks so much support of muscle. He has a fine Geneva watch, but he fails of the skill to tell the hour by the sun.
—Ralph Waldo Emerson, "Self-Reliance," 1841

Derek and Hutch took the lander through the night and into a dawn riddled with storm clouds and a near-torrential rain. The voice spoke to them again, with Tasha's translation posted on the display: *"I am Shalon. My regrets. I should have thought about the weather conditions before recommending this. If you wish to postpone and return to your ship until later, I will understand."*

Derek gave Tasha their response: "It's not a problem, Shalon. If you wish to postpone the meeting, we can wait. Or we can do it this evening. Whatever you prefer."

"If you are certain it will not inconvenience you, then let us continue. We look forward to seeing you."

They continued across a wide forest and emerged over a cluster of buildings and houses whose design and layout caused Ken to comment from the *Eiferman* that they might have been the product of Leonardo da Vinci. They had onion domes and spires and cornices and a wide range of arches and abutments. None appeared to be more than a few stories tall. Vehicles moved through the streets, and an aircraft was rising into the rain from a facility on the edge of the city.

The aircraft caught Derek's attention. "It's antigravity."

"If they've been around as long as we think," said Hutch, "I'd be surprised if they didn't have it."

"Is that where we're landing?" he asked.

"I think so." There were a terminal and three other buildings, one shaped like an open-ended donut. "They've got some stuff pulling in." Black cars. There were two of them on the ground. Three or four more were arriving.

Derek looked hesitant. "I guess Shalon has come to say hello."

"Or take us out," said Hutch. "We sure we want to do this?"

"If we don't, we're feeding Arin and everyone else to the black hole. This might be the only chance they have. Anyhow, it's probably just a security measure. Let's relax." They fit themselves with ear pods so they could hear Tasha's translations. Derek had prepared Tasha for the meeting, explaining where the discussion would probably go, the topics that were likely to surface, and how she should represent him. Hopefully, he'd be able to follow the conversation and, if need be, intervene and provide a response for Tasha.

She broke in: *"Shalon Kobay calling."* Tasha switched to a different voice and translated Shalon: *"You will be coming in on the—"* She stopped and returned to her normal tone, describing what she was hearing: *"Shalon is trying to signify a direction, but I cannot pin it down."*

Hutch gave Tasha an instruction which she relayed: *"Can you blink a light to signify where you want us to land?"*

"Understood. Also, we have stopped all air traffic."

Hutch acknowledged. A set of lights near the terminal came on and began to flicker.

Shalon came back: *"I am in one of the black cars, which I am sure you can see. They will form a circle. Come down in the center of the circle. May I ask where your journey originated?"*

Tasha responded with a prepared answer: *"We are from a world much like this one. But very far."*

"We are extremely excited," said Shalon. *"Nothing like this has ever happened here before."*

The cars formed a ring on the landing field. Doors opened and the occupants climbed out. At first, Hutch thought they were in dark uniforms, but as they got closer, she realized they were simply dark clothes. With one exception: One set of garments consisted of a red jacket and gray slacks. She was relieved to see no weapons. They were all looking up at the incoming lander. Historic moment for them. For everybody.

"Going in, Derek," she said.

She descended gently among the vehicles, touched down, and shut off the engine. *"Hutch."* Derek's voice sounded intense. *"Stay with the lander. I'll close the hatch when I leave. If there's any kind of issue out there, get this thing off the ground."* He pulled a commlink out of his pocket.

"Wait a minute. I didn't know—"

"No argument. Just do as I ask." He released his belt, got up, activated the commlink, and looped it around his neck. It transmitted a picture of the airlock to the display. "Stay tuned." He left the cabin and closed the hatch.

Hutch relayed everything to the *Eiferman*. She saw no expressions on the faces of the escorts. At least, nothing she could read. The red jacket took center stage and came forward with one hand raised in greeting. The others remained at a distance. Derek raised his own hand and Tasha said, *"Hello, Shalon."*

The creature in the red jacket stood halfway between the lander and the car. He was unquestionably of the same species depicted by the ice world statue. He had long, pointed ears, grass-colored scabrous skin, and his mouth was wide, lending a vaguely ominous quality to his smile. *"Greetings,"* he said. *"Welcome to Tarka."*

Tasha responded: *"I am pleased to make your acquaintance, sir. This is Derek Blanchard. I am speaking for him."*

"I am Shalon Kobay, and I am pleased to have the good fortune to meet you, Derek Blanchard. And Tasha, who, I assume is an automated intelligence."

"That is correct," said Tasha.

They walked back to the car, and Shalon held a door open, inviting Derek to get in. He did, and his host joined him. Along with one of the black suits. As far as Hutch could see, there was no one else in the car. And no driver. The car was automated. *"This is a moment of considerable significance,"* Shalon said.

Derek signaled Tasha that he would speak for himself,

and that the AI would translate his remarks. *"Shalon, we appreciate your willingness to invite us to join you."*

"I am happy to have the opportunity, Derek Blanchard. I have wondered all my life what it would be like to meet someone from another world." Hutch heard a sound that was probably laughter. That might have been prompted by the fact that the conversation had necessarily slowed down, allowing time for Tasha to manage the translations for both sides. *"I feel as if I am living in a piece of fiction."*

"Call me Derek, please. And is that really so? Have you never before spoken with someone from another world?"

"Of course not." The car started its engine and the black suits got into their vehicles. *"Why would you ask? This is the first time we have met anyone like you. And please do not take offense."*

"That's odd," Hutch said.

"What is?" Wally's voice.

"Nothing. Just some lightning." She'd been watching the black suits move. There was a high level of synchronization among them. They all walked the same way, turned their heads in the same manner, and used an identical approach to getting back in their cars. The things were robots. But she didn't want to say that into an open mike.

The car turned and started back toward the terminal. The other vehicles followed.

Shalon's eyes fastened on the commlink that hung around Derek's neck. His irises were vertical slits, not like those of an eagle, as had been her impression from the ice world statue, but more like a crocodile's. He obviously understood the purpose of the device. In fact, Hutch got the sense he was looking directly at her.

They pulled up at the terminal entrance. The escort remained in the vehicle while Shalon and Derek got out and went through a very ordinary set of double doors that opened as they approached. Hutch saw no movement inside.

They rode an elevator up several floors, exited into a corridor, turned a corner, and entered an office. It was beautifully furnished with a thick carpet, a lavish sofa, three cushioned chairs, and a glittering, dark desk. A framed photo that might have been Shalon hung between two windows. He waited until Derek was seated before settling onto the sofa. The windows looked out over the spaceport, but Hutch could not see the lander.

"I hope you're comfortable," Shalon said. The fangs were momentarily visible. Nevertheless, he projected an ease of manner that allowed Hutch to lose some of the concern she'd felt when Derek got into the car with him. The red jacket was gone, dropped casually on top of the desk. He was wearing a light blue shirt with something imprinted across it in white characters. Despite everything, he appeared amiable. Hutch wondered how he managed it.

"I'm fine," said Derek, who was probably doing his best to look at ease.

Something dinged, and Shalon asked to be excused for a moment. He opened a phone line, spoke into it, used a few terms that Tasha admitted she could not translate, and finally said, *"Our guest is here."* A brief exchange followed, which Tasha was also unable to get. Then Shalon clicked off and looked at his visitor with obvious satisfaction. *"The leader will get back to us shortly. He is anxious to meet you."*

Tasha commented that the "leader" term was unfamiliar to her, and it could be simply Shalon's boss or possibly even a president.

Then Wally was on the circuit again: *"What do you think, Hutch?"*

"I think there's a fair chance that we're not the only ones tuned in to this conversation. We have an advantage that they probably don't understand English unless the AI on the moon was playing us. Let's just hold off for now."

"In our entire recorded history, we have never before received visitors. This is truly a remarkable moment."

"For us as well, Shalon. I should inform you we've been to your other world. The one that was devastated thousands of years ago."

Shalon's brow wrinkled. *"What other world? I do not understand you."*

"I don't know its name. But we were on a world that apparently belonged to your people a long time ago."

He seemed overwhelmed and needed a moment to gather himself. *"I am sorry, but are you talking about one of the other planets in this system?"*

"No. It is several light-years away. We found—" He stopped in midsentence, realizing that a light-year might be an unfamiliar term, and in any case, depending on the length of their year, a different distance. *"It was in a different star system."*

"I have no idea what we are speaking of. This is the only

world which we've inhabited. In the distant past, we established stations and even a colony in this planetary system, but that has been the extent of our reach."

"That is strange, Shalon."

"Why do you say that?"

"On the world that I'm talking about, there is a statue in front of one of the buildings." Derek had to be smiling. *"It is one of your people."*

Shalon's eyes took on a tolerant gaze. *"If you say so. I wish I could have been there with you."*

"How far back does your history go?"

"The first cultures we know of appeared several thousand years ago." Shalon rearranged himself in his seat. *"How old is your culture?"*

"About the same." Derek cleared his throat. *"Have you any legends, myths, about how everything started?"*

"We do. At one time, according to the sacred texts, we lived on an island. There is much debate about its location. Even which ocean it was in. There was an eruption of some sort and the island began to sink."

"And what happened then?"

Shalon laughed. *"The gods came in and saved us. But let's move on to more significant matters."*

"Of course. Tell me, do you have the technology that would allow you to travel to other stars?"

"Not any longer. We haven't had that kind of capability for a long time. Haven't for generations."

Again Tasha spoke to Hutch: *"I made up 'generations.' Not familiar with the term he used. It could have been 'centuries' or 'ages.'"*

"What happened?" asked Derek. He sounded surprised.

"I'm not sure." Shalon looked confused. It was an unsettling moment. *"But it was during the imperial ages. If you're thinking we came originally from another star, had that kind of technology, and then lost it all, that simply doesn't stand with the facts. We've only had electricity for a thousand years."*

"But the island—"

"Adjuban is a myth. Obviously."

"Adjuban is the island?"

"Yes."

For a long moment, both were silent. *"Do you,"* said Derek, *"know any details about them? About the gods in the story?"*

Shalon was smiling again. *"Not really. We have legends, but they contradict one another."*

"Shalon, do you know about the black hole?"

"What is a black hole?"

"A collapsed star. So heavy it rips apart anything it gets close to."

"You mean a destroyer? Yes, of course we know about those. There's one now not so far. Fortunately, it's not headed in our direction."

"That's the one I was referring to."

"Oh yes. Of course. Is that what you call it? A black hole?"

"Yes."

"An intriguing name for a cloud with teeth." Tasha broke in to explain that "cloud with teeth" was the best translation she could manage.

"How does it happen you no longer have interstellar vehicles?"

"We lost them centuries ago. We decided, apparently, that we had no use for them. As a result"—he shrugged—*"they're gone."*

"You of all people," said Derek.

"What do you mean?"

"It's okay. Let it go."

"I would not have planned it this way. Losing the interstellars. But reality is what happens to you while you are setting up the future. We thought we were providing the best sort of life for our people." He paused. *"Actually, now that I think of it, we do have one."*

"An interstellar? Excellent. Is it available?"

"It is at the space station. Unfortunately, we would not trust it in flight. It has been inactive for years."

"Tell me about the evacuation of Adjuban. Did they get everyone off? Were they able to save everybody?"

"It's a legend, Derek."

"According to the legend?"

"It doesn't go into that kind of detail. There is something interesting, though—"

"What's that?"

"You may have just solved a biological question: Nobody's been able to explain why our genetic system doesn't match with the other life-forms on the planet." He grinned. *"Well done, Derek."* He was laughing at the absurdity of the idea. Then his phone sounded. He opened it. *"Kobay."* He listened for a moment. Then: *"Yes. Of course."* He looked up. *"President Zakow wishes to speak with you."*

Tasha switched to still another male voice. *"Friend Derek, we are pleased to welcome you to Tarka."*

Hutch had expected a video image to form somewhere. But there was only the audio.

"Thank you, sir. We are happy to have this opportunity to visit. You have a beautiful world."

"It is good of you say so. If there is anything we can do to enhance your experience, please do not hesitate to ask. The director represents me and the world, and you may rely on any commitment he makes. Be advised we are happy to have you stay with us as long as you wish."

"Thank you, sir. We have not yet solidified our plans. We are on a mission."

"May I ask what that mission is?"

"We have come across a world with intelligent beings that lies in the path of a massive dark object that, in two or three generations, will destroy it. We would like to help them. To prevent their being killed."

"I hope you can make it happen."

"There's a problem. We come from very far away, Mr. President. We were hoping you could be of assistance."

"In what way?"

"We're not sure yet. It will depend on your technology. And willingness."

"We will help if we can. But I must be honest with you: We have long since allowed our interstellar capabilities to decline. To die off. It is difficult to see what we could do. However, feel free to discuss the matter with Director Kobay. And I will hope for a happy result. Thank you for your time, friend Derek."

Tasha changed back to Shalon: *"I'm afraid the president is correct. I cannot imagine how we can be of assistance. Have you other ships in the area?"*

"No. Unfortunately, we do not. We need a fleet of vehicles to transport the inhabitants out of harm's way. Fortunately, that world population is relatively small. Two or three million."

"That is good news. But I still don't see a way for us to help."

"We had hoped that you might have a fleet that could come to their assistance. Unfortunately, that appears not to be the case."

"That is correct. We have no such fleet, nor the capability to construct one."

"Even if we provide the designs?"

"We don't have adequate technology for that kind of project."

"I'm surprised to hear it. Surely—"

"It's been a long time, Derek. We no longer have engineers."

Derek sighed. "I guess what we really need is to find the gods who came to your assistance so long ago."

"Please understand," said Shalon. "Adjuban is a myth."

"Yes. Of course. Forgive me."

"We abandoned much of our technology, as it became of limited use. Today, we have an automated society. The mechanisms with which we live maintain and repair themselves. We acquired the capability long ago to establish a world that serves us in every way we require. We live lives entirely of leisure. Except for those of us who wish to pursue careers. And those are limited. We always have use for physicians, for entertainers, for teachers, for artists. Everything else is taken care of."

"By whom?"

"Perhaps I can make this clearer by informing you that President Zakow is automated."

"He's an AI?"

"Yes. To a degree. We do not have politicians. The president is programmed to ensure that his decisions are made in the common interest. It is not a perfect system, but it provides the great majority of us with meaningful lives. And with an opportunity to pursue those areas that are of interest. Unfortunately, we must deal occasionally with situations that require our intervention. For example, an area in the southern hemisphere lost a substantial portion of its population several years ago because of a new virus that appeared. We have a few individual researchers who were eventually able to devise medications, but it took longer than it would have if we'd possessed an active team." Shalon paused. *"Derek, can I get you a drink or something? Forgive me; it's not every day we receive visits from persons like yourself."*

"No, thank you, Shalon. I'm fine."

"So, what will you do now?"

"We'll have to think about it."

"If you're interested, we have a museum which is focused on civilization's early years."

"That sounds intriguing. Is it in this area?"

"Yes. It is only a short ride."

"Tell me: Why do you think your people stopped traveling among the stars?"

"For the same reason we stopped pursuing science. Because there was nothing new to find. Nothing to learn. We had everything we wanted."

"You were lucky the gods hadn't gotten bored."

Priscilla's Journal

If Shalon and his friends really believe that interstellar travel is of no consequence, that it simply consumes time and resources, they should take a trip out to the ocean world. Or to that star that's about to go supernova.

—Saturday, August 16, 2256

34.

Who does the best his circumstance allows
Does well, acts nobly; angels could do no more.
— Edward Young, *Night-Thoughts II*, 1732

Hutch activated her commlink. "I'd like to go with you to the museum."

"Best stay where you are, Hutch." He disconnected before she could answer.

Shalon put his red jacket back on. They went downstairs and left the terminal. The black car was waiting for them. But the robots were gone. Apparently, he now trusted his visitor. Doors opened and they climbed in. He spoke to the car, and Tasha translated: *"Take us to the Repository."* Then he spoke to Derek: *"It's located in the center of the city."*

The car pulled out onto the road, proceeded about five minutes into a set of rising hills, and turned onto a highway.

Hutch would not have used the term *city* to describe

the area. It was more like an extended town, with villas and chalets that were simultaneously modest but alluring. Backyards were filled with children on swings and seesaws and a wide range of rotational devices. Giant brambles were everywhere. Lawns and vegetation weren't maintained the way they normally were back home. Nature was apparently left to care for itself. Inhabitants sat in lawn chairs and on benches. They passed a lake with a handful of fishing boats.

"We live satisfying lives," said Shalon. *"We are able to invest our time doing things we enjoy, improving who we are, rather than simply struggling to sustain ourselves, as was the case in the ancient world. One reads the records of those primitive times and can't help being grateful for all that we have. So many of those who lived during those years had no opportunity to indulge in leisurely activities. I can't help suspecting that, when their short time in the sunlight ran out, they must have passed away with a sense of not having lived at all."*

They arrived eventually between twin buildings, five stories high. Each had what appeared to be plastic walls, large circular windows, and slanted rooftops. Their corners were curved. And a group of black-suited robots had gathered. It appeared that they had sealed off the area. Shalon pointed left: *"That's our city administrative center."* Three lines of exotic symbols were emblazoned on a sign beside the front doors. *"And* that *one"*—on the opposite side of the road—*"is the Bokana Historical Repository."*

The car doors opened. They got out and walked toward the entrance. *"Beautiful architecture,"* Derek said.

Shalon smiled. He spoke to the doors and they opened. They went inside and the director said something to a blue box mounted on the wall to their right. The box responded: *"We are pleased to welcome you, Director Kobay. And Derek Blanchard."* They proceeded down a short corridor into a large domed hall divided into numerous exhibits, mostly in glass cases. Lights were on everywhere. The area was empty, save for a few robots in gray uniforms.

The glass cases contained telescopes, cups, electronic equipment presumably from an earlier era, engraved blocks of stone, an assortment of guns, and numerous other artifacts. The walls were covered with artwork and portraits described by Shalon as historical figures, leaders, composers, scientists. There were also images of land-scapes, space vehicles, and a nautical vessel arriving at a pier to a cheering crowd.

"What is that?" asked Derek.

"That is the Victory, *coming in with a group of refugees who'd fled the notorious dictator, Selmin Kwerto. It's from an era when we were engaged in our last major conflict."*

"A war?"

"Yes. Hundreds of thousands died. Fortunately, it was before we developed nuclear technology or we probably would have killed ourselves off. You know what nuclear technology is, of course?"

"Yes."

Derek produced his notebook and brought up a photo of the waterfall, the one from the intercepted transmission. *"Shalon, do you recognize this?"*

His eyes widened. *"Of course,"* he said. *"That's Kayla Tor. How do you happen to have that?"*

"It's a tourist attraction?"

"Yes. On the other side of the world."

"It was part of a signal sent, we think, during the evacuation of the world we talked about earlier. Probably by whoever was overseeing the rescue."

"But, Derek, please understand, none of that happened." Shalon looked puzzled.

"We thought it was probably being used to show the people on the endangered planet that the world that had been set aside for them was attractive. That they would like it. That they would be safe."

Two children were staring at Derek. And then two adults came into view. Derek responded with a smile. One of the kids retreated. *"It's all right,"* Shalon said. *"These are friends. They are visitors who have come a long way to meet us."*

Derek said hello in the gentlest tone imaginable. Hutch was remembering the Volarian beach when they'd first come ashore. "We must look pretty scary," she told Wally.

Shalon apologized. *"Our security people were supposed to have cleared the area."*

"It's okay," said Derek. *"I'm sorry if I scared the kids."*

Two of the robots appeared and said something to Shalon. *"I think we left a back door open,"* Shalon said before whispering into a communicator attached to his wrist.

Moments later, a loudspeaker issued a statement: *"Attention, please. We have an unusual visitor with us today. There is no reason to be concerned. Do not be alarmed by his appearance. He is a friend. We suggest everyone simply go on enjoying the displays and exhibits."*

Uniformed guards who were *not* robots came into the area and escorted everyone out. Meanwhile, Hutch was distracted by statues on the far side of the hall and would have liked a closer look, but Derek had enough to think about, so she said nothing.

A door opened in back. Shalon led the way through it into another corridor. He took Derek to a side office. It was a wide room furnished with armchairs and side tables with lamps, and several filled bookcases. *"The Repository director is very excited about your arrival,"* he said. *"She would like to meet you. Please have a seat, Derek."* He lowered himself into a chair. *"I apologize for the way they reacted. I should have waited until the place was closed before bringing you here. Stupid of me."* Again, he showed those fangs. *"I'm just not accustomed to having visitors of your status."*

Another Tarkan appeared at the door. *"The director,"* said Shalon. *"She would have been extremely unhappy with me if I hadn't brought you here to say hello."* She came in and exchanged comments with him that Tasha didn't pick up. Then she turned to Derek while trying to hide her astonishment. *"Greetings, friend Derek. My name is Zyra Vilani."*

"Hello, Director Vilani."

Hutch could see little physical difference between her and Shalon.

"Shalon," Vilani said, *"I'm surprised you asked if I'd be interested in meeting our visitor. He just arrived this afternoon?"*

"Yes, Zyra." She extended a hand to Derek. *"If you had left without my getting to see you, I would never have spoken to Shalon again. Where are you from, friend Derek?"*

"Another world. Earth. It's much like this one. I suspect you would enjoy it."

"Perhaps you would be willing to show it to me?"

"I would."

Hutch was laughing as she pictured President Proctor's reaction to Zyra and Shalon's emerging from a lander near the Washington Monument.

Zyra walked to her desk, but instead of seating herself behind it, she eased back and sat on the desk itself. *"I'd like to provide refreshments, but I'm not sure whether our delicacies would work for you."* Her smile was unsettling. *"We can experiment if you like, or we can simply bring in some cold water. Whatever your preference."*

He went for the water. Wally spoke again to Hutch: *"How did the food taste on the ocean world?"*

"It was okay."

"So," said Zyra, *"I assume this is your first visit to Tarka?"*

"Yes. We've come a very long distance."

"And did you know we were here? Did you come specifically to see us?"

"We came across a world that had been destroyed, Director Vilani. Thousands of years ago. Its people were rescued and taken elsewhere. We've been looking for them. We wanted to find out if the evacuation had succeeded."

"Please call me Zyra." She looked at Shalon but her mind seemed to be elsewhere. *"That is an incredible story. So, why did you come here?"*

"We thought they might have been brought here. Statuary on that lost world resembles you."

"Really? That seems odd. You think we are the ones who were evacuated?"

"I would be surprised if you are not the same species."

"Interesting." She turned to Shalon. *"What do you make of this?"*

"I think it would make an extraordinary piece of fiction."

"Zyra, if I may ask, what do you know of the gods who were believed for a time to have brought your people from the sinking island?"

"Are you referring to Adjuban?"

"Yes."

She smiled. *"What can we possibly know of supernatural beings?"*

A robot arrived with a pitcher of ice water. It filled cups for everyone, inquired if they needed anything else, and left. Zyra looked at Derek. *"Is it possible,"* she asked, *"that your people were among them?"*

"I wish," he said, *"that we could claim credit for an act like that. But we were living in jungles when all this happened."*

"I see. Well, I wish we had some answers for you. You're raising questions that we thought we'd resolved a long time ago."

"I suspect they came simply because the inhabitants on that world were in trouble. Because they were needed. To be honest, we need someone like them now."

"Why?"

"Because another world is in danger. The same danger."

"I am sorry to hear it. I wish we could help."

Shalon had remained quiet throughout the exchange, and Hutch, when she caught an occasional glimpse of him, thought he looked lost in thought. Now he entered the conversation: *"Maybe we can be of some assistance."*

"How can we do that?" asked Zyra. *"We can barely get to Dovis."*

Hutch guessed that Dovis was a nearby planet. Or maybe their moon.

"Derek," said Shalon, *"there would be more to mounting a*

rescue for these people than simply transporting them to some-place else. Carry them to another world, and you will have to provide shelters. And make food available. How many of these people are there?"

"Fortunately, it's not the kind of planetary population we would expect. I don't think there are more than two or three million Volarians."

"I see. So, if you could find a way to move the Volarians—do I have that right?—it would be necessary to prepare their new home for their arrival. We could conceivably help you do that. We have all kinds of automation, some of which, with your assistance, could be transferred to whatever new world you choose, and employed to ensure that your refugees could be taken care of when they get there. You would have to provide transportation, but—"

"That would help," said Derek. "All we have to do is figure out how to get our hands on a fleet of ships."

Hutch couldn't restrain herself any longer: "How about we ask Emma?"

"The president?" Derek snickered. "No way she would be inclined to help."

"It's an election year, Derek."

"I'm not following you."

Shalon broke in: "Whose voice is that?"

"That is Priscilla. My pilot. She sometimes has grandiose ideas."

Hutch continued: "We have a world full of lovable creatures that look like dolphins, and an interstellar program. Both need rescuing."

"Let's talk later."

"It might be irrelevant later."

He looked at Shalon and Zyra. *"Do you think you could actually do that? Help us set up a new world for them?"*

Shalon responded: *"As I'm sure you realize, Derek, I'm not in a position to make that kind of decision. We'd have to get approval from higher authority. The president said he would abide by any commitment I make with you, but that statement should not be taken too seriously. However, he might be willing to lend assistance. You must let me talk with him first."*

"Of course. We can wait. You know how to contact us?"

"You will stay within radio range?"

"Yes. Absolutely."

The office fell silent. Finally, Zyra walked over to Derek and took his arm. *"May I show you around the museum? I understand you've seen the first floor, but there's considerably more. Security can clear the building for us."*

"Oh, yes," he said. *"I'd love that."* Derek was faking the enthusiasm. But he didn't want to offend anyone, and he got away with it. *"Can we do it without forcing anybody to leave?"*

"We can try it if you wish. We're not allowing anyone else inside the building. So, there will only be a few visitors to contend with."

"Good. Let's do it."

The place was empty. It was obvious that the people who'd been in the building had been escorted outside. Either that, Hutch thought, or they'd decided they didn't want to hang around with something that scared the kids.

Zyra walked with them among the displays and described the significance of urns and vases and rifles and aircraft that were thousands of years old. She talked about civilizations that had risen and fallen over the ages. It was difficult for her, of course, like showing off a sword that had once belonged to a member of Augustus's Praetorian Guard to someone who had never heard of Rome. But she was energetic. Especially when they arrived at the interstellar section. *"We've had to reinvent FTL vehicles twice after losing the technology. And I guess we've reached that stage again."*

They had religious artifacts from sects that had once prospered but had long since disappeared. There was a lectern that had belonged to the leader of the first global civilization, which had established and maintained peace for centuries. (Though Tasha had not yet worked out the actual length of a century.) There was a chair that had been the property of a celebrated playwright, and a timepiece that had belonged to Kamas Gordone, a mathematician who'd either constructed or solved the Gordonian Enigma. Shalon tried to explain it. Derek listened, asked some questions, and finally concluded that it was Fermat's Theorem. But he admitted he wasn't sure.

There were statues of historical leaders, mythical figures, artists, and even of a famous entertainer. *"During her lifetime,"* said Zyra, *"everyone loved her. She is still very popular. I don't know if anyone was more successful at making us laugh.*

"These are not the originals," she continued, speaking of the statues. *"They are reproductions. Some of the originals still exist, but most, like this one of Morikai the Great, have been lost."*

"What happened to it?" asked Derek.

"The original was left in front of a capitol building on the

other side of the world, completely abandoned, and eventually torn apart by religious fanatics who believed sculptures were forbidden by the gods. Thousands of years ago." She paused in front of a statue depicting a native, probably a female, holding an infant in her arms. *"This is Queen Elza."* She stopped and tried to think of an easy way to explain. *"She opposed the Orgalians, who were a race of barbarians. She succeeded in beating them back. It's a replica of a statue placed at the Crescent Pool in her honor. Centuries after her death, the Orgalians returned, seized everything, and destroyed the statue."*

Another female replica stood nearby. Hutch caught only a passing glimpse, but she recognized it immediately. As did Derek. *"Wait,"* he said. *"That's the Iapetus sculpture."*

When he turned so she could get a better look, she saw it wasn't strictly true. It was similar but not identical. But it was clearly the same species. It also was female, and at first glance, it portrayed a creature you would not have wanted to confront in a dark place. It had claws and wings and eyes that were somehow focused elsewhere. But the suggestion of discontent, of loss, of anger, was gone. It was, somehow, more warrior and less female. There was more a sense of conquest and less of longing.

Derek had to stop and catch his breath: *"Zyra, where did that come from?"*

"The original was from the Kamersik Era. At least six thousand years ago. We think. It disappeared. Nobody knows what happened to it. Of course, there's not much that's survived from that period."

"What does it represent? Who's it supposed to be?"

"Sola."

"And Sola is?"

"She was one of the gods who, in the sacred texts, brought us off Adjuban."

"Can you," Derek said, speaking slowly, *"tell us a bit more? About the religious interpretation?"*

"There were several conflicting versions. Basically, we were living in a place of gathering darkness. The gods themselves were divided over whether we should be allowed to survive. They were weary of the way we lived, and Okondo decided to do away with us. Okondo was a second-level deity who simply thought we were more trouble than we were worth. In some versions, he was the one who imposed mortality on us. It was supposed to be a warning, but we didn't listen. And finally, he brought the darkness.

"Sola was more tolerant. More loving. She intervened with other gods, and they carried us to a safe place. That is what Tarka *means: a safe place."*

Derek's voice came through to Hutch: *"Are you getting all this?"*

The black car pulled up alongside the lander. Hutch thought about standing in the airlock when it opened and letting herself be seen by Shalon and Zyra, both of whom were in the vehicle. But they already knew she was there, and she was disinclined to rattle Derek. So, she waited in her seat.

Meantime, Derek talked with his hosts: *"Shalon,"* he said, *"Zyra, we'll need to find out whether we can help the Volarians. Our world is very far from theirs. As it is from here. And we have political issues at home. But we'll wait to hear from you. If your people can help, we'll do everything we* can on our end. And we'll get back to you and let you know whether we'll be moving ahead. There's a chance we won't be able to get off our world again, so if you don't hear anything from us within the next year, I guess you can forget it. But I do not think that will happen."

They all got out of the car, clasped one another's shoulders, shook hands, and said good-bye.

Hutch opened the airlock and Derek came back on board. Then he surprised her: He brought Shalon and Zyra inside. They smiled as he introduced her. "Hutch is our pilot."

They obviously enjoyed being in the lander and told her they'd like to fly with her someday.

"I'll do what I can," she said, "to make it happen."

Priscilla's Journal

So now we know who they were. I'd always thought of the Monument Makers as simply a group of prodigies with too much time on their hands, wandering through the Milky Way leaving evidence of their passage. Except for the Iapetus monument. That one had her eyes locked on Saturn, and you could not miss getting a sense of someone resentful of a universe that was completely neutral regarding the welfare of its creatures.

We saw that again, but in more pronounced terms, in the sword that was left in orbit around the black hole. Though I guess the sword reflected outrage. The iconic figure on Iapetus provides primarily sadness and loss.

—Sunday, August 17, 2256

35.

There is no good way to deliver bad news. In my experience, the best way to handle the issue is to stand aside and allow it to deliver itself.
—Gregory MacAllister, "The Flower Girl Always Steals the Show," *Editor-at-Large,* 2223

Shalon's response arrived minutes after they'd rendezvoused with the *Eiferman.* "*We are with you,*" he said. "*We are here because our mythology informs us that the gods once helped us. That is of course not actually what happened, but it demonstrates the compassion that our earliest thinkers believed in. We will help where we can. As you know, we will need your assistance to manage transportation. If in fact you go ahead with your intentions to move forward, advise us, and we can consult on details.*"

Hutch confirmed reception, and Derek sent a short reply: "Thank you, Shalon. We will find a way to make it happen. If all goes well, we will be back within two hundred days." A day on Tarka lasted slightly less than twenty-seven hours.

"Good luck to us all, Derek," Hutch said. "We're ready to leave orbit."

He took a deep breath. "I guess it's time to go back and tell Arin and his friends what they're facing. We have to find out whether they'll accept the news and be willing to get evacuated. In fact, the more I think about it, the less likely it seems that we will even be able to get them to believe us. Imagine if somebody had come out of the sky at home, before we had decent telescopes, and told us we'd have to move to Mars or something."

"I've thought about that," said Hutch. "I wonder how the people who pulled these guys off the ice world managed it."

Derek smiled at her. "Waterfalls."

She laughed. "Let's hope something like that will still work. What's the first step?"

"We've got a new world for them. Let's start by getting a decent name for it. We don't want to tell them they're going to Number Twenty Alpha or something."

"You have a suggestion?" asked Hutch.

"'Greenland' might work."

"It might lead to some confusion back home."

"How about 'Utopia'?"

"How about we go for something original?"

"How would that matter?" said Derek. "Arin and his people wouldn't know *Utopia* isn't original."

"It'll matter at home if we're trying to sell the package. Hold on a second." The lander had just pulled alongside the *Eiferman*. The launch door opened. "Take us in, Tasha."

The AI eased them into the cradle, which took them into the ship. The door closed.

"So, what's your suggestion?" asked Derek.

"I think our best approach would be to invite the Volarians to name it."

Derek thought about it while they released the harnesses. Then they just sat back and waited for the cargo bay to pressurize. "Yeah. That makes sense."

"We need to explain all this to Arin first," said Hutch. "We'll need him with us when it goes public. Then maybe we should take a few of them to see the black hole so they know what we're talking about."

"Then," said Derek, "take them to Utopia or whatever. Let them make the call whether it's suitable. Yes. That sounds good." But he frowned. "Maybe we shouldn't do *anything*. Once we're home, it's highly probable that the WSA won't allow us to leave the planet again. What happens if we go in and tell Arin about the black hole and then we go back to Earth and they shut everything down? I mean, they have fifty or sixty years left. Maybe not that long. If we go back and let them know what's coming, we'll in effect take that away from them. The shadow of this thing will hang over their heads the rest of their lives. We don't have a fleet, and as of right now, we don't have any support."

"Maybe," said Hutch, "if we're just going to stand by and let it happen, we should have decided that before we went looking for Utopia. Or talked to the Tarkans." She kept her voice level. "There is no good option here, Derek. We can just leave them to die. Or we can at least *try* to do something. Look: They're adults. What do you think they'd want us to do? What would *we* want in their position? I say we go back, tell them the truth, and make sure they'll accept an evacuation. If they won't, it's over."

"Then what?"

"Then we go home and find a way to get the world on board."

Derek's features were twisted by frustration. "I hate this, Hutch."

In fact, she had an idea how they might pull it off. "All right. Before we waste any more time, we know how to find Zyra and Shalon when we come back here, right?"

"Yes. *If* we come back here. That's a long shot."

The life-support status light came on. "Time to get moving."

It was a four-day flight back to Volaria. Derek and Ken spent much of their time practicing the local language with Barry. "It's going to be difficult enough," Ken said. "We don't want to have to tell them about the black hole by waving our arms and making faces."

When they arrived, Hutch put them in orbit and asked Barry to find the island. Then she went back into the passenger cabin, where Utopia seemed to have taken hold as the name of the new world. She thought they should leave naming it to the Volarians, but she wasn't going to make a fuss over a trivial issue. In the end, she thought, they'd call it whatever they wanted. "You should also," she said, "ask Arin whether he's willing to go back to Earth with us. We'll need him to help make our case."

"I know." Derek was unhappy with the idea. "The problem is, if we do that, there's no guarantee they'll let us bring him back here."

"Tell him that."

Beth broke in: "We'll also have to pack food on board for him. And invite Kwylla too, by the way."

"Arin's island," said Barry, *"is directly ahead, Captain."*

Ken looked supremely uncomfortable as he started down to the launch bay. He took his notebook with him. Hutch suspected he'd written out everything he wanted to say. Hutch opened the lander and climbed in. Derek held the door for Ken and then followed him inside. Beth appeared at the bottom of the ramp. "You want to come?" Derek asked.

She obviously didn't want to and had probably made up her mind to stay on the ship. But she couldn't live with that decision. She came over and got into the lander. Then Wally appeared.

"Wally," said Derek, "we need you to stay here."

"Boss, I'd love to see the place."

"Maybe that's a good idea," Beth said. "Why don't you go ahead? I'll stay."

"You sure?" Ken asked.

"I'll be fine. Wally deserves a chance to see what it looks like down there."

She got out and Wally took her place. The cargo bay depressurized and the launch doors opened. The cradle carried the lander outside the hull. Hutch started the engine, the control panel lit up, release lights came on, and they were on their way.

The sun was in the eastern sky, maybe an hour above the horizon as they approached. She cruised over the beach, which already had some sunbathers. "Set down at the temple," said Derek.

There were cars in the parking lot. But there was more than enough room for the lander. She touched down and they sat staring for a moment at the tower, beautiful in the early morning sunlight.

The temple doors opened and a few Volarians came out, looked in their direction, and started toward them. "What are they doing here so early?" asked Ken.

They waved and laughed, and one of them, a female, got as close to the side windows as she could and stood with her arms outstretched, inviting them to come out-side.

Hutch opened up and waved back. That got some cheers. Kwylla appeared at the cottage door. She came over and said something to the crowd. They cheered some more, while Hutch thought how this would all soon stop. "That brings up another aspect of this thing," she said. "I wonder if they have any end-times prophecies."

"We'll probably find out before the day's over," said Ken.

They were still climbing out of the lander when Arin appeared. He wore dark clothing and a gold neckpiece and was obviously headed for the temple. But he changed course when he saw the lander. "Hello," he said. "We didn't expect you back so soon."

They all greeted him. And Ken asked if they'd gotten in the way of a service.

"Oh no. Have you eaten yet?"

"We just woke up." He'd obviously been working on his English. "I'll see you in a little while." He turned them over to Kwylla and went through the side door into the temple.

. . .

"I wonder," said Hutch, as Kwylla brought out fruits and vegetables from the kitchen, "if maybe it would be okay to go inside the temple."

"I still don't think that would be very smart," said Derek. "We don't know what the rules are."

"I can't see why there'd be a problem. We've spent a lot of time here and they seem to accept us. I'd be interested in learning about Arin's faith."

"I don't think we should do anything like that," said Wally.

Hutch didn't buy it. "If we were going to offend him, we'd be more likely to do it by staying away." She got up. "I'll be back after the service."

She expected Derek to direct her not to go, but he remained quiet as she looked at Kwylla. "Ken, ask her if it would be okay for me to attend."

They were singing and dancing and playing their assortment of musical instruments when she entered, followed by Derek. Everybody seemed to be having a good time. They sat down in the rear, where they were virtually alone. Arin was up front, bouncing around with a string instrument.

A sphere was mounted behind the table, or altar, reminding her of the symbolic message, *We're all in it together.*

She tried to make out some of the lyrics but could manage only one line: *"Show us the way."* Eventually, the music stopped, and Arin took charge of the ceremony. He stood and spoke to his audience, but it didn't sound like an oration. In fact, there was occasional laughter. Hands went up, and they asked questions. Or made comments. Then he led them in prayer.

She would have liked to be able to understand what they were saying, but what she *felt* was a coming together. And she could not get out of her mind what was going to happen when the ceremony ended. When they sat down with Arin to give him the worst possible news.

Lord, she thought, *I don't know whether you're there. I cannot see a loving Creator as the functioning force behind this universe. But that may simply be a result of my stupidity. If we never needed you before, we do now. If you're annoyed with me, please don't let these people pay the price.*

Hutch returned to the cottage minutes before Arin. He came in, announced how happy he was to see his guests back, excused himself, and went upstairs to change clothes. A gloomy silence settled over everybody. Kwylla had clearly sensed something was wrong. So much so that she went upstairs also, undoubtedly to warn him. They came down together. Everybody put on an artificial smile, and the humans adjusted their ear pods so they could hear Tasha's translations.

Arin had changed into a silver shirt and gray slacks. And when he asked in fractured English whether there was anything he could do for his guests, Ken took advantage of the moment: *"There's a problem, Arin. A big one."* He was speaking in Arin's native tongue.

He and Kwylla looked at each other and their eyes darkened. That kind of statement from a visiting alien couldn't be good. *"What's wrong?"* asked Kwylla as they both sat down.

Ken braced himself. *"There's a dead star coming this way.*

It won't be here for about sixty years. But when it arrives"—he hesitated—*"it'll destroy the world."* The Volarians stared at their guests, probably hoping it would turn out to be a sick joke. Derek looked desperate. Hutch became aware that she'd stopped breathing. *"I'm sorry,"* Ken continued. *"I wish there were something we could do to turn it aside. But there's nothing* anyone *can do."*

For a long moment, no one spoke. Then: *"Please tell us,"* said Kwylla, *"you're not serious."*

"I wish I could." Ken stared through a window at the dazzling sunlight.

"A dead star?" Arin asked. *"I wasn't aware they could die."*

"Eventually, they burn out and collapse. Or explode."

"I don't understand." Kwylla was on the verge of shock. *"Do stars actually collapse? How can that be?"*

"They're very heavy. When it happens, they destroy anything they get near."

"Can we see it?" Kwylla's voice had shifted from near panic to a helpless solemnity. "We have telescopes."

"Eventually. As it gets closer, you'll see it. It will disrupt the light."

"You mean," said Arin, *"everything will get dark?"*

"Not in the sense you mean. You'll see odd lights in the sky. Look, fortunately, this is all years away yet."

"Thank you," said Arin, *"for telling us."* His eyes were focused on Ken, and there was a hint of bitterness in his voice.

"I'm sorry. It's the reason we came here originally. To see if anyone was at risk."

"Obviously, someone is."

"Arin." Ken's face had paled. *"Can you tell me how many of your people are here? What the world population is?"*

"Why do you ask?"

Ken looked to Derek for support. But Derek didn't have sufficient command of the language to respond. So, the historian continued: *"We understand this comes as a major shock. And a painful one. Beyond words. We'd like to help. And we will try to. To start, we need to know the world population."*

Arin's gaze had shifted from Ken to the floor while Kwylla, seeing him at a loss, responded. *"Captain,"* said Tasha, translating, *"the number is at about three million."*

Hutch did the math. TransGalactic had three interstellars, each with accommodations for about fifteen hundred passengers. Other than the three ships, there wasn't much available. If they could build a fleet of, say, twenty interstellars like those, each would have to carry a total of 150,000. That would mean a hundred flights between Volaria and Utopia. It wouldn't be easy, but given half a century or more, it could be done. And of course, they'd need ships to help bring in the Tarkans. What were the chances of persuading Emma Proctor and the other world leaders to turn around and invest in a large fleet after all the posturing of the last few years about keeping our heads down? She caught Derek's eye. "What about the derelict transport? You think there's any way we could incorporate that into the general effort?"

He frowned, shook his head, thought about it some more, and finally nodded. "No reason we can't try."

"Arin," said Ken, *"there's a possibility we could take you somewhere else. Take everybody. But we would need your help."*

"What do you mean, 'somewhere else'? Where else could there be?"

"We might be able to take you to another world. But as I said, we would need your assistance."

"Why did you wait so long to tell us?"

Ken froze for a moment. *"It was not a message we wanted to deliver. Arin, if we are to help, you need to trust us."*

"What do you want us to do?"

"First, we can take you out to look at the dead star, if you wish. So you can see what's coming. It would probably be a good idea if you and a few leaders went to look at it. Then we would try to construct enough ships to take you to a new world where you and your people would be safe."

"What kind of world, Ken?"

"We've found a world like yours. It's not predominantly oceans, like this one. But otherwise it's similar. It has the same kind of atmosphere. The climate appears to be similar to this one. Gravity's about the same. We may have gotten lucky."

Arin looked at Kwylla, who was seated at his right hand, her large round eyes filled with pain. There was a brief exchange between them. *"Sorry, Captain,"* said Tasha, *"I was unable to understand."*

Arin turned back to Ken. *"Are you certain? Is there any possibility that you've made a miscalculation?"*

Ken looked at Derek. "You're the expert. Any chance we're wrong?"

"I don't see," Derek said in English, "any way that could be possible."

Ken caught Arin's eyes and shook his head.

"Let me understand, then. You're offering to take us to see this dead star that you say is coming toward us?"

"Yes. If you wish."

"How long will this take?"

"Not long. A couple of days. But you might also want to look at the new world."

"We can see that too?"

"Yes."

"Am I correct that the vehicle in the sky, the one that circles the planet, is bigger than the aircraft with the six seats? That is the vehicle we'll be traveling in?"

"Yes." They finally got some smiles. *"The ship in orbit is much larger than the lander."*

"Incredible. And I assume you have food on this ship?"

"Yes. But you should bring some of your own. Maybe fifteen days' worth. Just to be safe."

"You can preserve it?"

"Yes."

"Okay." Arin had been so happy a few minutes earlier, coming out of the temple. Now he looked exhausted. *"Give us some time. We'll put together a team and you can show us this thing. This dead star. I assume that when you say you will need my help that you are talking about something more than an inspection tour."*

"Yes. Putting together a fleet of vehicles to manage the transportation of your people to another world will require a major effort by our people. There's a substantial chance that those who sent us will decline to help. We need you to go home with us and help persuade them."

"And how can I possibly do that? By making all kinds of gestures? I can't even speak your language."

"You're already doing pretty well, Arin. You can work on it during the ride home. We'll have time. You can handle it."

"Are these creatures—no, I'm sorry, I mean people—can they be persuaded?"

"I hope so. There's one other issue: It's possible they may not only refuse to help, but they might not allow us to return here. You could get stranded on our world. But we need you to help win them over. Our people are capable of acts of kindness, but sometimes, they just don't understand. They will find you easy to like, and we hope that will inspire them to do whatever is necessary."

Beth's voice came in through the pod: "Darling," she said, "the people they have to persuade are like us, you and me and Derek. You don't want him thinking he will have to persuade some hard-core politicians."

Kwylla put a hand on Arin's knee. "Love, you don't go unless I do."

Beth Squires's Notes

I would never have believed we could have so much in common with a bunch of aliens. But I watched Kwylla sign on for a flight that might take her away forever from her home, and do it for the sole purpose of staying with her mate. And it clarifies a possibility: Maybe there really are no aliens. Maybe we are all brothers and sisters adrift in a universe that doesn't give a rip about us.

—Friday, August 22, 2256

36.

There are occasions when there's a stranger in the room, and one has no choice but to trust him. When that happens, close your eyes, and step forward.
—Gregory MacAllister, "Options," *Baltimore Sun*, October 19, 2251

Arin surprised everyone by bringing a rifle onto the lander. The weapon was clumsy, but it could obviously cause damage. Hutch wondered if he just didn't trust them and was sending a message. Or whether someone in the bureaucracy had insisted on it. When Derek, watching from the *Eiferman*, was alerted by Hutch, he grumbled but told her to let it go.

Kwylla and Korsek were also on board. On the way back to the ship, she asked how the Volarians were taking the news. *"As far as I'm aware,"* Korsek said, speaking through Tasha, *"nothing has been released. We've been told not to talk about it. I don't think they want this getting out until we're certain what we're dealing with."*

Hutch changed the subject by admiring the rifle. And

getting within visual range of the *Eiferman* helped. All three were entranced by the size and design of the vehicle, and by the time they drew alongside, their attention was fixated on it. After turning them over to Derek, she returned to the temple to pick up two more Volarians. They were Rampol Tok and Droo Haka. Rampol was identified as a "stargazer." It was unclear whether the reference was to astronomy or astrology. Droo was introduced as a science advisor to the governor. Korsek had explained that he was one of the people responsible for maintaining "reasonable living conditions across a wide area." He was also given credit for being the driving force behind organizing the effort to recover the lander. This time, Hutch tried to stay away from mentioning the coming catastrophe, but her passengers could talk about nothing else.

Derek had waited until all five were aboard before showing off the front porch technology. If they were surprised by the appearance of the *Eiferman*, their level of astonishment rose to an even higher level after the cabin's interior blinked off and was replaced by mountains, waterfalls, and coastlines.

Hutch was not aware that anyone had picked up the native terms for "impossible" or "incredible" or "magnificent." But it was hard to miss them during those early moments. Arin stared at Ken and demanded an answer to a question that could only have been *How do you make this happen?*

Derek and Ken spent most of the four days returning to Volaria practicing the language with Barry. Ken asked their guests what sort of relationships the various islands maintained with one another. Were they independent political entities? How much trade was there? Were there tourists? Was there political stress? Wars?

Ken hadn't been aware of a word for war, and consequently had to explain its meaning. They looked at one another and appeared not to know whether to frown or laugh.

"Groups of people attacking and killing each other? That sounds insane." Arin's eyes narrowed, and his gaze moved from Hutch to Derek. *"Your people do not actually behave that way, do they?"*

"Unfortunately," said Derek, "in the past, we have done that on occasion. But I think we've put it behind us."

The conversation was awkward because Barry had to translate in both directions. But it worked. Kwylla was happy to hear Derek explain what he hoped to accomplish. And she responded: *"I'm glad to hear it. I guess we're lucky that you and your friends came, and not the organized killers."*

Korsek said something that Barry could not translate. Arin explained: *"He was speaking of the broken star. He finds it hard to understand how something like this could exist in a benevolent universe."*

Their guests fell in love with the virtual scenery visible from the porch. They looked out over the Great Wall of China; the Sphinx at Giza; St. Basil's Cathedral in Moscow; the Golden Gate Bridge; the statue of *Christ the Redeemer* in Rio de Janeiro; Stonehenge; the windmills at Kinderdijk, Holland; and dozens of other spectacles from around the Earth. They were disturbed when, in the middle of it all, Hutch took the *Eiferman* under and the stars went away. As also did the sense of movement. *"Hutch,"* Arin asked, *"are you sure we're still traveling?"* The Volarians had adopted the easier version of her name.

"Oh, yes," she said. "We are moving at an extraordinary velocity."

Droo Haka's eyes showed disbelief. *"I'm pretty sure my car goes faster."*

When later they came out of it, into the twisted sky that surrounded the black hole, the mood darkened.

Barry put it all onscreen. It threw something of a scare into the Volarians. They decided the displays weren't working right, talking as if nothing could really look like what they were seeing. So, they crowded two at a time onto the bridge and looked through the window. *"No, no, no,"* said Droo, standing behind Hutch, holding onto her chair to steady himself. *"That cannot be."*

Kwylla stared. *"I agree."*

And Arin: *"I don't believe this."* He asked Ken to explain again what they were seeing.

Rampol produced a small telescope and peered through it. *"Incredible,"* he said. *"What is that thing?"*

Ken tried to explain as best he could, but there was no way for him to describe how light could be squeezed, or that something could be so massive that if you put a car on its surface and turned on the headlights, they wouldn't be visible because the light would be too heavy.

"Tell me again," said Korsek, *"what that thing will do to us when it shows up."*

Nobody wanted to answer the question. Finally, Beth stepped in: "It will absorb your world, Korsek. Everything."

"Does that even include the ocean?"

"Even the sun if it gets close enough."

"*I cannot tell you,*" said Droo, "*how grateful I am that you have come and offered to help.*"

"If you're willing," Derek said, "we could go look at your new world."

"*Oh yes, please.*"

They were all happy to get away from that distorted sky, to retreat again into the quiet darkness of transdimensional space. The Volarians were getting used to the notion that it was a strange and volatile universe. But they were nevertheless relieved when, not long after they'd left the black hole behind, they emerged into the light of the class-G sun that had been designated Eleven. Its habitable-zone planet, Utopia, was just one glimmer of light in a star-swept sky. "We're getting low on fuel," Hutch explained to Derek. "We'll just cruise from here. It'll take a few days. But it'll give us time to work on the language."

Actually, they spent more time sightseeing from the front porch. But Arin and Kwylla worked with Barry on their English, which, Derek pointed out, would be invaluable in winning over reluctant humans to make whatever investment would be necessary to mount a rescue.

Their passengers were intrigued by Barry, a voice out of nowhere. They loved floating through the cabins when Hutch shut down the artificial gravity system. But probably more than anything, they were overwhelmed not only by the scenic creations but also by the shows on the video display. The problem was, of course, that they were available in human languages only. And the attempt to translate just didn't work, because drama and comedy both required pacing. Hutch, watching Chuck Causley doing his classic standup, had always understood that comedy was all about timing. Now that was confirmed beyond any doubt.

During those few days, Hutch learned a good deal more about the lives of the Volarians. Many were farmers. Some specialized in fish farms, most grew vegetables. Hutch got the impression there was no meat in their diets.

Others owned shops in the towns, selling clothing, electronic equipment, furniture, and whatever else might be needed. The cars, and presumably ships, were manufactured elsewhere, on several large islands scattered around the planet. When the governor visited Arin's island, she needed about a week to get there.

They also picked up the source for the world's name. Volaria, according to Kwylla, was derived from an ancient language. *"It means* salvation," she said.

The humans never mentioned their prime concern, the probable resistance back home that all this would generate. But among themselves, it dominated the conversation. And, as they got closer to Utopia, Korsek brought up another issue. *"Nobody's going to believe this,"* he said. *"They're going to have to see it. And I don't think pictures are going to be persuasive enough."*

Hutch asked Rampol, the stargazer whom she now thought of as an astronomer, whether there were any observatories on Volaria.

"What," he asked, *"is an observatory?"*

"You put a building with an opening on the roof on top of a mountain, and then put a large version of *that"*—she indicated his telescope—"inside. You'd be amazed at what you can see."

"Oh, yes, of course. We have a couple of them. But I don't think anybody's seen that thing. If they have, they certainly haven't said anything."

The planet floated in soft sunlight. White clouds drifted over wide oceans and lush green continents and vast mountain chains. Two of the three moons were visible.

"Are there tigers here?" Korsek asked.

Barry explained he had substituted a term. *"I assume the reference was to a predator."*

Derek responded that there probably were. "Every world has predators," he said. "Compared to a black hole, though, a tiger's not much to worry about." Arin understood and nodded agreement.

The Volarians, when talking among themselves, tended to speak quickly, and often used words and constructions with which none of the humans, nor Barry, was familiar. *"I'm getting some of it, though,"* Barry told Hutch, speaking through her pod. *"The prime issue for them, as far as I can determine, is whether they can convince their people to accept an idea that's so wild from their perspective. Black holes make no sense to them. Not even to the ones who are here looking at it."*

When he saw an opportunity, Ken took the issue back to Arin. "You do understand this is really happening, right? The threat is real."

It seemed a bit ham-handed, but it got directly to the point.

"We've been on the islands," Arin said, *"forever. Nothing ever changes. Except that electricity arrived. Then you appear and suddenly we hear the world is ending. Do not be offended, Ken, but it is philosophically difficult to accept. And painful."*

• • •

Derek would have liked to accompany them to the ground. But they needed Ken, and they already had to make two trips to get the five Volarians down. Add one more to the mix and it would mean another flight. Ken asked whether there was any place in particular they would like to see up close?

The star-gazer pointed at the display, where a herd of four-legged animals were moving across a wide plain. *"What are those?"* They resembled buffalo somewhat, though they were paler, with not much fur. *"Incredible. I've never seen anything like that before."*

Hutch took Korsek, Arin, and Ken down and landed near the buffalo. They were actually larger animals, and their horns were spiraled. They did not react to the arriving vehicle other than to glance in its direction. They showed no interest whatever when she and her passengers climbed out and stood watching them rumble past. Other than a couple of large birds feeding on something, nothing else moved anywhere across that vast plain. When the animals were gone, she got back into the lander. She didn't like leaving them on their own while she returned to the ship to collect the others. But that was the plan.

She arrived a half hour later on the *Eiferman* and picked up Kwylla, Rampol, and Droo. By the time she got back to the ground, the sun was setting behind some low ridges. And all three of the moons were in the sky. They were spectacular.

"How's everything?" she asked Ken.

"Okay. I think it's going to work."

"Is the air all right?"

"They thought it was a bit chilly. But that's no concern. They're all breathing okay."

"How about the gravity? Does anyone feel different?"

"No," said Ken. "Nobody's noticing anything unusual."

Droo asked about food. Hutch explained that samples of their food would be transported to the high-tech civilization that would be helping them. The Tarkans. "They'll duplicate everything, and there'll be adequate supplies, food, whatever you need, waiting when you arrive, as well as a means for you guys to take over production on your own."

"Sounds like a miracle," said Kwylla.

Arin embraced her. *"It's the kind of thing that happens when you have friends."*

Belatedly, she noticed Rampol staring across the plain. *"Anything wrong?"* she asked.

"It just seems strange without oceans."

Priscilla's Journal

I suspect they're adjusting to the truth. I don't think the Volarians shed tears, but I saw both Kwylla and Droo holding their hands to their faces and looking visibly upset. The others have been relatively subdued since they saw the black hole. And arriving on Utopia seems to have had an even more disturbing effect. I doubt it derives from a negative reaction to the world itself, but from its driving home the reality of what's happening.
—Thursday, August 28, 2256

37.

A friend is a second self.

        —Aristotle, Cicero, *De amicitia, XXI*, c. 50 BCE

They spent five days on Utopia, taking ground, air, and water samples. It was Beth's idea because it would allow analysts to draw some conclusions about how safe the world actually was. The Volarians examined trees, pulled out shrubbery, looked down into valleys, and watched whatever animals they could get close to, although they didn't kill anything. Hutch knew there was no way they were going to be happy about leaving the home world. But she got the impression they felt they could live with this one. To that extent, at least, they were taking good news home.

Droo had been reserved and uncomfortable throughout the mission. When Hutch asked if he was okay, he tried to reassure her. *"Oh, yes. This is a stressful time. But I shudder to think what our situation would be without you and your friends."*

"I understand. You guys have held up pretty well. But despite everything, I think we can save the situation."

"Please do not be offended. I hope desperately that your calculations about the star are inaccurate. But I am terrified. I understand I have no reason to doubt you. I wish I did."

"Droo, what do you expect will happen when you get home?"

"We'll speak with the governor. I can't be certain as to her reaction. We have pictures to show her. But we honestly can't confirm that we are in the path of the thing. We can't even be certain it's moving." He looked frustrated. *"The real problem here is that people are going to resist all this. Close up their homes and move to another world? They may simply refuse to accept what we say."* He delivered a modest smile. Almost impossible, she would have thought, from someone who so closely resembled a dolphin. *"We'll have to see how it goes."*

"I have to admit," Derek told her, "that I've thought about where we'd be if we succeed in persuading the WSA to build twenty interstellars and bring them out here, and discover these guys just aren't buying it." He closed his eyes. "You don't think there's a chance that could actually happen, do you?"

"There's just not much we can do about that. We can take more of them out to look at it, but there's no way to demonstrate that it's bearing down on them."

Later, Arin came onto the bridge. *"Just so you know,"* he said, *"Korsek tells me he'd be surprised if the story hasn't gotten out already. The governor's office is not good at guarding confidential information. And something like this? He says it would be almost impossible for them to keep it quiet."*

"How are your people going to respond?"

"It'll be painful. Fortunately, though, a half century is a long way off. Nevertheless"—his eyes closed—*"it'll be a shock. We have two grown children, but we didn't say anything to them about the mission before we left. That was the direction we were given and we abided by it. Kwylla wouldn't have wanted to say anything to them, anyway. She's still hoping we'll find out the math is wrong or something. It's hard to believe it when somebody tells you that the world's coming to an end."*

"I'm sorry about all this, Arin," said Hutch.

"It's not your fault. I'm just grateful to the Creator for bringing you and your friends this way."

"What can you tell me about the Creator?"

"I doubt I have anything to say that you do not already know. She cares about us. She shows us the way."

"What is her name?"

The question surprised Arin. *"I suppose I should have realized it would be different in your language. Her name is Alora."*

"What does she require of you?"

"Only that we honor her and take care of one another." Arin paused. *"Korsek is probably right about the story getting out. A lot of people will refuse to believe it. It's different for us. We know you well enough to trust you. We've seen the black hole, and we've walked on Utopia. They are not going to accept this easily."* A look of pure desperation came into his eyes. *"But leave it to us, Hutch. We'll take care of it."* He looked out at the void. *"When do we get back to the stars?"*

When they arrived, it was just after dawn, and a storm was churning through the islands. Droo and Rampol, looking at telescopic images, could not identify Kallula, where they lived, and where the government was centered. *"I've never seen it from up here before,"* said Rampol. *"I'm sorry. I feel like an idiot."*

They completed another orbit, during which the storm lessened considerably. The Volarians still couldn't decide which of the islands was Kallula, but it was no longer hazardous to use the lander. Droo asked if he could have an ear pod for the governor. Hutch supplied it. Then, accompanied by Ken, she took Droo and Rampol down. Fortunately, Droo recognized the first island they passed over and was able to direct her to their destination. The administrative center was a flat, long brick building in the center of a small city. Turrets rose at each end of the building. Hutch got as close as she could and landed. The Volarians squeezed out of the vehicle into a light rainfall, and when Hutch said good-bye, they both laughed. *"No, no,"* said Droo. *"The governor would not forgive us if we didn't introduce you."* As he spoke, two uniformed escorts came out of the building. Hutch and Ken followed them inside.

They were led to a conference room with a large clock on the wall. An aide entered and informed them there would be a slight delay. Light snacks had been laid out on a long table, consisting of sliced fruit mixed with a sugary liquid. It was okay, but Hutch would have opted for some cheesecake or strawberry shortcake, but the Volarians didn't seem to have discovered cake. She was just finishing a small serving when they were told the governor was available.

They climbed a flight of stairs with the aide, who led them into a large office.

A female in red-trimmed dark clothing was seated behind a large desk. The walls were decorated with plaques that of course Hutch couldn't read. She saw a long-beaked bird on one and blooming flowers on another. There was an arrangement of chairs in the center of the room. *"Governor Rankin,"* said Droo, *"you will need this."* He held out the pod and showed her how to attach it to her ear. *"These are our visitors."* He did introductions and the governor signaled them to be seated.

"Droo," she said, *"did you see the object?"*

"Yes, Governor."

"So. Are we in danger?"

"I cannot be certain, but I would be surprised if a collision with that thing would not cause serious damage. At the very least."

"It would cause damage? But would it be cataclysmic?"

"There's no way to know, Governor. We can't tell how large it is, because we were informed that we could not get close to it without being destroyed."

"Can you be certain there will be a collision with the thing?"

"No, we cannot."

The governor turned to Rampol: *"Professor Tok, do you agree with this assessment?"*

"I do, Governor."

"So, we really do not know what we are facing. Is that correct?"

"Yes," said Rampol.

Droo was thinking about it: *"We do not have the expertise or the technology to make a determination, Governor. However, I have gotten to know Ken and Hutch and the other Earthers quite well. I can tell you that I would not hesitate to trust them*

390

with my life. I cannot see what any of them would have to gain by lying. Consequently, I suggest we take them at their word."

Droo turned over a set of photos. She examined them and looked up.

"I should add, Governor, that the pictures don't show the reality. The sky seems to bend around it. I can show you if you like."

"Please do."

Priscilla's Journal

Arin and Kwylla are among the most courageous people I've met. There's no way I'd go riding off into the stars with aliens who admitted at the outset that there's a fair chance I wouldn't be able to come back. I think I'd rather take my chances that they were making up their claim about the black hole.

—Saturday, September 6, 2256

38.

Ultimately it is the heart of a sentient being which
gives meaning to the universe.
—Angela Compton, *The Last Warrior*, 2166

I t was pouring rain the following evening when Ken and
Hutch left Arin's cottage and rode with him and Kwylla
in their car to the town hall, where a representative of
Governor Rankin would deliver the news. Four chairs had
been set aside for them at the front of the auditorium.
Rumors of a problem had been floating for several days,
but apparently, the actual depth of the threat had not gotten out. The hall, which had an accommodation of about
seven hundred, had already overflowed, but they were
crowding everyone inside. Extra chairs were being brought
in and set along the walls and at the back of the auditorium.

The warmth Hutch had felt from the Volarians had
vanished. They watched her with suspicion, possibly with
anger, as if she and Ken were responsible for whatever
it was they were about to confront. The place was noisy

until the governor's representative was introduced. Then it became quiet.

Hutch put on her pod and activated her commlink so Tasha could translate everything for her. Ken had one also, but he was going to try to get by without it.

The speaker took his place behind a lectern on the stage and was welcoming everyone when thunder rumbled in the distance. He stopped in the middle of it and waited for it to die down. Then he introduced himself and went immediately to the point. *"I am sorry to have to tell you this, but we face an existential threat. There will be no problem for about fifty years, so, for now, we are safe. But a collapsed star is coming toward us, and eventually, we are told, it will destroy the planet."* The audience remained silent. *"As bad as that sounds, our situation is not hopeless. Most of you know we have had visitors. Hutch, Ken, would you stand, please?"*

They got out of their chairs to a round of gentle applause. *"Our friends have offered to help us in our time of necessity, for which we are grateful."* The applause died off. *"So you will be aware of what we are talking about, we have pictures of the object."* Several people were coming up from the rear, distributing them. *"This thing, we are told, is a collapsed star. It is extremely heavy."* He mentioned again the amount of time before it would become an imminent threat. *"We are going to evacuate to a new world."*

That brought a few howls, and voices demanding to know how they would be able to do that.

"Fortunately, we have help." He explained the procedure that would be in place. They would be moved out of harm's way. Taken to a safe place very much like this one. Everyone would have substantial notice before the process

began. To the extent they were able, they would be evacuating by islands so, to the extent possible, they would not be separated from families and friends. Finally, he invited questions.

The audience wanted to know whether there was a possibility the object could miss them.

He said it was possible but unlikely.

Would they be able to get everyone off the world?

How could Alora let such a thing happen?

That question got passed to Arin. He stood. *"I have no explanation. But I suggest we be grateful that she brought Ken and Priscilla to us."*

The following day, Hutch couldn't resist going back to the beach with her commlink to capture the ocean and the crowd. She stayed close to the trees, out of sight, until she had what she wanted. Then she returned to the cottage and spent the next few hours talking with Kwylla without ear pods. Kwylla was determined to speak without the help of an AI when she reached Earth. And in the middle of it, Hutch realized she'd forgotten something. They went outside and she aimed the commlink at the temple, the cottage, and the surrounding woods.

Priscilla's Journal

We have got to make this work.

—Monday, September 8, 2256

39.

East or west, home is best.
—H. G. Bohn, *Handbook of Proverbs*, 1855

Finally, it was time to leave. Hutch had been carrying food supplies for Kwylla and Arin to the *Eiferman* for two days. Then, with Ken accompanying, she took the lander down a final time to pick them up.

Since the town hall meeting, opinions on what should be done were all over the map. Some described the arrival of the humans as "divine intervention." Others were less encouraging, arguing that the alien visitors had withheld news of the approaching catastrophe when they first arrived and consequently couldn't be trusted. An island ledger, which came out sporadically, released an edition which included opinions from "experts." Many expressed caution about relying on the visitors. Two maintained that the whole story was probably a fabrication. *"Possibly an experiment of some kind, to determine whether we are stupid, or maybe they simply like to play jokes. Maybe they'll be laughing all the way home."*

The journalist asked how they could do that since they'd be taking "two of us" with them?

"In the end, they'll probably leave them here."

"And if they do take them?"

"That possibility scares me."

"Great," said Hutch. "I hope Kwylla and Arin haven't seen this."

The lander descended in bright sunlight just outside the temple, where a substantial crowd had gathered. They came over and thanked Hutch and Ken as they got out. A few raised their hands to greet them; others just stood quietly. The cottage door opened and Kwylla emerged, carrying a jacket and a bag. The Volarians shouted support. And a few delivered warnings. Moments later, Korsek and Arin came out, hauling more bags. People said their good-byes and backed out of the way. Korsek shook Arin's hand and embraced Kwylla. Then all three walked toward the lander.

One of the Volarians, a large male, appeared beside Hutch. *"Please,"* he said, *"take care of them. Bring them home."*

Hutch reached out and placed a hand on his shoulder. "We will," she said, speaking English but knowing he could read her.

Korsek looked into Hutch's eyes and wished her luck as Kwylla and Arin entered the airlock. The Volarians raised their hands a final time. Ken stood aside while Hutch assumed her seat. Then he got in and closed the hatch.

"Sure you have everything, guys?" Ken asked.

They nodded. *"We're ready to go."*

• • •

The *Eiferman* was on its way within the hour. After they submerged, Hutch joined everyone in the passenger cabin. They talked for a while, reassuring each other that there was no way the WSA could fail to do the right thing. Eventually, Hutch returned to the bridge and was joined by Kwylla, who stared out at the vast darkness. "I wish we could see something," Hutch said. "It's seriously boring out there." Later, she told Derek that the next upgrade for the Locarno system should be to manufacture visuals of a sky. "It would be easier if we could get a sense of moving. We've got all kinds of technology. It should be easy to do. It would make things much more interesting if we could watch clouds of stars drifting by."

"But not black holes," said Derek.

They spent most of the first day in the passenger cabin, looking at canyons and coastlines and mountains and urban scenes. They knew movies wouldn't work. Derek had begun reading Marie Esperson's *The Quantum World*, while Wally buried himself in a police thriller. Arin enjoyed talking with Barry. Kwylla watched Ken and Hutch playing chess and picked up the rudimentary tactics over the course of an hour.

On that first evening, they set the front porch on a bank of the Thames and got into a conversation over how good life had always been on Volaria and how fortunate they'd been to find Utopia. *"We're lucky to be getting a second chance,"* Arin said. *"Everybody's grateful for that."*

They discussed Barry's role in making it possible to talk. *"We have to get past this, though,"* Kwylla said as the AI translated. *"If we're going to be of any use when we get to your world, we're going to have to be able to speak without using machines."* Hutch, meantime, could not stop thinking about the reaction they could expect from Zhang Chao and President Proctor when the *Eiferman* arrived at Union Station with aliens onboard. She worried that Kwylla and Arin might not even get a chance to be heard.

On the second day, both Volarians got seriously to work on their language skills. Kwylla, who hadn't invested the time her spouse had, spent additional hours in an effort to begin catching up. That same day, needing a break, she discovered the electronic library. "How many books do you have?" she asked Beth, speaking without the help of the AI.

"Thousands."

"Really?"

"Of course."

"I'm frustrated. I wish I could read some. Even one. Could Barry read one to me?"

"I think we can arrange that." Beth produced a set of ear pods and handed them to Kwylla. "What kind of books do you like?"

"Fiction."

"Romantic? Mystery? Historical?"

"What is mystery fiction? Where something happens without understanding and you try to find an explanation?"

"Yes. Usually, it involves what we call a whodunit."

"What is that?"

"Somebody commits a murder and the detective tries to find out who it was."

"What's a murder?"

"When someone kills someone else."

"He does it deliberately?" She looked surprised.

"Yes."

"How is it different from fantasy fiction?"

Beth was not immediately sure what she meant. "Don't you guys have any murders?"

"Not that I know about."

"I'm beginning to realize, Kwylla, your people may not have aircraft, but I think your level of development is way ahead of ours. Barry, would you be willing to read a novel for Kwylla, translating it for her?"

"Of course." Unfortunately, the AI had no command of the written Volarian language, which would have allowed him to create a version she could read.

"Which novel would you like to hear, Kwylla?"

"Wait." Kwylla shook her head. "Translating is not helpful. Do it in original form."

"I understand," said Barry. He started to read titles.

"Wait, Barry," she said. "Stop. Beth, I will tell you the kind of novel I would like so maybe you could recommend something."

"Sure. That'll work."

"Good. Something funny. Lighthearted."

"Barry," said Beth, "can you show me a list of whatever comic novels we have?"

"I'm sorry, but the novels are not divided by category."

"Okay, put the entire inventory on display, okay?"

Beth needed a few minutes but eventually found one she'd read several times. Probably the only book in her life she'd read more than once. "And what is that?" asked Kwylla.

"Lucky Jim," she said. "It's by Kingsley Amis. It's hysterical."

"I'm not sure I want something that would drive me to hysteria."

On the fourth day, Arin joined Kwylla in dismissing Barry's translations altogether. "It's too easy that way," he said. "And I don't learn anything."

He and Kwylla remained fascinated by the display capabilities in the passenger cabin. Eventually, they asked what else was available, other than the Earth Catalog.

Then, as Derek put it, they took them to the stars. They sat on the front porch as if it were floating in space, and looked at a sun up close, and an approaching comet that made everyone duck. They cruised past the red giant the *Eiferman* had visited on the way out. They floated under the Saturnian rings, and enjoyed a Photoshopped image of a Mars that had never existed, with water-filled canals glittering beneath the stars. They visited archeological sites on several worlds, which intrigued Kwylla and Arin. "What happened to the inhabitants?" they asked.

Sometimes there were explanations. Sometimes not.

Meanwhile, Beth ran tests on the Volarian food and concluded that terrestrial edibles would probably supply appropriate nutrients, although she couldn't be certain. "No way to know for sure," she said. "I don't really have adequate equipment to settle every issue, and I'm not exactly an expert in the field."

Kwylla and Arin might have settled the issue themselves when they discovered a genuine appetite for ham, turkey, and pork roll. And, of course, everybody got a huge laugh the night they brought out the pizza. Their guests couldn't get enough.

Kwylla had a difficult time getting away from *Lucky Jim*. Comedy, which had baffled their guests earlier, now kept her laughing constantly while Barry read the original version. Periodically, she stopped him so she could repeat lines for whoever was nearby. At one point, she turned to Beth. "You know, I had no idea you people were so funny."

When she finished it, she asked whether the author was still alive.

"Kingsley Amis?" said Beth. "No, he's been gone a long time."

"That's a pity. I'd have enjoyed meeting him."

Hutch was sitting alongside her at the time: "I'm pretty sure he'd have enjoyed meeting you too, Kwylla."

As Kwylla and Arin grew more familiar with the language, and probably also with the culture of their friends, the comedy shows began to work. They sat and laughed with the others as Alex Brightman exaggerated his deep-space experiences in fruitless efforts to bed girlfriends. "Oh, wait until you get to do it without gravity." And Minnie Blanchard, who did dazzling impersonations of President Proctor in *White House Blues*. Wally asked whether she was a relative of Derek's. "I wish she was," he said.

Hutch and Beth tended to use the workout area at the same time. They invited Kwylla to join them. After some initial reluctance, she did.

They talked about how enjoyable life on the starship could be, the probable reception they'd receive when they arrived at Union Station, what they were reading, and whichever movie they had watched the previous evening.

They were well into the second week of the flight. Kwylla had not yet arrived for her workout when Beth got up from the mat on which she was doing push-ups, took a quick look through the open door, walked over beside Hutch, who was lifting weights, and lowered her voice: "You know, I hope we get a chance to do a biological analysis of them." She was referring to their passengers.

"Why's that? You worried they might be carrying a disease?"

"No, I'm not very much concerned about that. I think if it were an issue, we'd have seen it manifested by now." Those hazel eyes sparkled. "But I'd love to know how their systems work. Do they have problems with epidemics? How are their brains different from ours? How do their reproductive systems work? How long is their life span? I think most of all, I'd love to find out if their DNA operates like ours."

"Maybe they don't even have DNA."

She waved the idea away. "Oh, they'll have DNA. And it'll be similar to what we have. But of course it won't be identical. I'd expect a helical structure with base pairs using simple sugars and so on, but we're likely to get some surprises. Ken has been talking to them about their culture, which would be hard to separate from ours. Guys, for the most part, are the bosses, and females keep the family running. He says that comes from Arin, not from Kwylla. Arin thinks the guys need to pull up their socks and treat the females better."

"Sounds like us back in the old days," said Hutch.

Beth heard footsteps approaching and switched to

talking about a Randy Harkman movie on the schedule for that night. Kwylla came in. "Hi, guys," she said. "Sorry I'm late."

A few days later, they watched a documentary about the Triassic period, with lots of dinosaurs charging around. Kwylla and Arin found it hard to believe such creatures ever actually existed. "I'm sure we never had anything like that," said Arin.

Kwylla laughed. "I'm reaching a point where nothing shocks me anymore."

"You sure about that?" asked Wally. "You never had any of those on Volaria?"

"No. Not that I'm aware of. It sounds like something you'd only see in a fantasy book. Or in one of your movies."

"Come to think of it," Beth said, "we have a movie with some dinos. What's the title? Ummm—"

"*Breakfast with T. Rex*," said Ken.

"That's a comedy."

"I know, love. I think if we decide to watch any dino movies, we should stay with the light stuff."

"Actually," said Derek, "I suspect there wouldn't have been enough space for giant lizards on a world that is mostly ocean."

As they moved into the last few days of the flight, Kwylla and Arin seemed to be growing somber. Hutch tried surrounding them with scenes from Barcelona, Venice, Tokyo, and Rome. But nothing really seemed to ease the malaise.

They were all seated, looking down from a hillside in Athens. Directly ahead, the Acropolis stood outlined against a sunset. The conversation revolved around the ancient gods. "I guess," said Arin, "people always have to explain to themselves how the sun sets on one side of the world and in the morning comes up on the other."

Kwylla abruptly changed the subject: "The trip is so long, it scares me."

"Why?" asked Beth.

"You're talking about sending an entire fleet back to help us? Twenty ships? Thirty? Whatever? Will you actually be able to find volunteers to do that?"

"Volunteers," said Derek, "will not be an issue." His eyes clouded. "It's the politicians we have to worry about."

Hutch realized she'd been missing something. She got up, went onto the bridge, and activated Barry.

"Yes, Captain?" he said.

"Hold on a second." She was checking her notebook. "Okay. Let's change the scenery in the passenger cabin. Use 462. But don't start it until I give you the word."

"Will do."

She returned to the front porch, where they were still talking about how long the flight was and how fortunate they were to have the virtual views provided by the ship's technology.

"If no one objects," she said, "let's leave Athens for now. We've got something else you might enjoy."

"A volcanic eruption?" asked Ken.

"That's good," Hutch said. "We should try that sometime. But I was thinking that I probably shouldn't have turned this into just a sightseeing tour for Kwylla and Arin." She raised her voice: "Barry?"

The sunset and the hillside and the Acropolis blinked

off, and a new scene appeared. A beach. With Volarians swimming and lying about under umbrellas with the ocean rolling in, while kids splashed through the surf.

Hutch's heart picked up a few beats when she saw Kwylla and Arin both smile. Minutes later, Barry switched over: The front porch had apparently been moved to the front of their cottage, near the temple, and they were able to relax outside their home, listening to birds singing and watching small furry creatures running up and down trees.

Beth Squires's Notes

Ken recorded everything. When the book comes out, it'll serve as a record of an accomplishment we'll be proud of forever. Assuming we can actually make the fleet happen.

—Thursday, October 2, 2256

40.

A foolish consistency is the hobgoblin of little minds,
adored by little statesmen and philosophers and divines.
With consistency, a great soul has simply nothing to do.
— Ralph Waldo Emerson, "Self-Reliance," 1841

They entered the solar system well outside Pluto's orbit, made a second jump, and surfaced close enough to Earth to pick up the vast array of lights on its night side. On a long flight, passengers usually spent the last days talking about how good it will be to get home again. But the optimism on the *Eiferman* had faded as they got closer and nobody was looking forward to talking with Zhang Chao. Kwylla had just finished listening to Barry read Allen Preston's *The Next Thousand Years*, which predicted a dark future for humans, which had only served to fuel a growing sense that, for their alien passengers, the end was near for everybody. Hutch tried to ease the mood by predicting that Kwylla and Arin would be worldwide media sensations. "They're going to love you guys," she said.

In two days, the flight would finally be over. Beth and

Ken would be on their way to Rhode Island; Wally would be retained at the space station; she and Derek would be escorting Kwylla and Arin through the media. She hoped.

She was looking forward to seeing her kids again. And Tom. And wandering through a shopping center. She couldn't help thinking about the things in her life that really mattered, and the degree to which she took them for granted. Until they went missing.

As they drew closer to Earth, a frightened look appeared in Kwylla's eyes. "Everything will be okay," Hutch told her. "We'll be with you." Reluctantly, she got up from her seat and signaled Derek. "We need to let Union know we're back. We're also required to inform them we're carrying aliens. I don't think that's ever happened before."

"No, it hasn't. This flight keeps making history." He took a long deep breath. "It'll cause a stir. You have any thoughts on how to phrase the report?"

"We could start by suggesting to Zhang that he not get upset."

"Hutch, we can pass on the jokes." He accompanied her onto the bridge.

"Barry," she said, "open a channel to the station."

A brief pause. Then: *"Done, Captain."*

She took her seat. "CommOps, this is the *Barry Eiferman*. We are back in the system. Estimated arrival forty-two hours."

The station responded: *"This is Union, Eiferman. Welcome back."*

"Thank you."

"Is everything in order?"

"Yes. All's well."

Derek held up a hand. He would take it from there. "Union," he said, "this is Derek Blanchard. Be informed that we have two visitors on board."

"Visitors? Clarify, please."

"They are natives of another world."

"Eiferman, did I hear that correctly? They're aliens?"

"Yes, Ops. You did. They're from an ocean world that has a serious problem."

"Roger that. I'll pass it on to the director."

There was no immediate response from Zhang, and life on the ship returned to normal. Ken worked on his notes. Derek and Arin talked about physics and philosophy. Wally became immersed in a game that required him to rescue a Roman strike team trapped by Egyptians in an alternate-universe version of the struggle between Augustus and Mark Antony. Kwylla, Beth, and Hutch took over the workout room.

Later that afternoon, they settled in to watch the time travel film *Quantum Waves*, but they'd only gotten to the opening scene, in which a research team is getting ready to travel into the past to watch Charles Dickens speak to an audience in New York, when Barry stopped the movie and broke in: *"Captain Hutchins, Union is on the circuit."*

She got up and headed for the bridge, followed by Derek. "This is the *Eiferman*," she said. "Go ahead, Union."

"Is this Captain Hutchins?"

"That is correct."

"Wait one for Director Zhang, please."

The voice clicked off and the channel went to a steady stream of static.

"That's not good," said Derek. "He always makes you wait when he gets annoyed."

Finally, he was there: *"Hutchins."*

"Yes, Director Zhang?"

"Your arrival report says you have two aliens with you. Is that correct?"

Derek broke in: "Of course, Director. It was at my insistence that Captain Hutchins took them on board."

"I was not aware I was speaking to you, Blanchard."

"Sir, I'd like to explain."

"Go ahead."

"They are in serious trouble and they need our assistance. Their world—"

"Damn it, stop. Stop right there. We have our hands full keeping crazies from creating serious problems here. You really think—"

"This is nothing like that, sir. Their entire world is about to be destroyed by a black hole."

"Oh. Good. So, you want us to do what? Deflect the black hole?"

"Director, their population is relatively small. If we build a fleet, we can evacuate them. We've found a safe place for them."

"You're not thinking of bringing them here, are you?"

"There's a world close to theirs. And we may have a giant transport vehicle that can be adapted."

They could hear Zhang talking to someone else. Then he was back: *"What's the population? Not that it's going to make any difference."*

"It's only three million, sir."

"Oh. Only three million? Good. I was concerned there might

be a lot of them." They could hear him breathing. *"Do you have any idea what kind of fleet we'd need to do something like that? Have you lost your mind?"* Derek and Hutch looked at each other and shook their heads. *"When's this going to happen? The black hole?"*

For a moment, Hutch thought he might adjust his attitude.

"Sixty years," Derek said. "The effects will start to be felt considerably earlier. It would probably be a good idea to have them out of there within a half century. At most."

"So, why did you bring two of them back here with you?"

"They saved our lives, sir. If people have a chance to see them, to get to know them as we do, we think they'd be more than willing to help."

"That's absolutely crazy."

"I should tell you that they're nearby, they can probably hear you, and they understand English."

"They understand English?"

"That's correct."

"How did that happen?"

"We've been working with them. They're smart."

"Excellent. I was under the impression you and your team were to avoid such contacts. Watch and observe but keep your distance. Wasn't that the guiding principle?"

"Sir, we didn't intend this to happen. We were riding the lander when it blew something out and crashed in the ocean. They rescued us. I think if the presidents of China and the NAU had a chance—"

"Derek, I've already spoken with President Proctor. And I've been in contact with the People's Congress as well. Nobody is

happy with what you've done. Can you even guarantee these two creatures aren't bringing a plague with them?"

"We have a physician—"

"Stop. We'll talk after you dock. I'm putting together a team to take these creatures—you say there are two of them? They'll take them back to wherever they came from. And that's going to be the end of it. Is that clear?"

Derek glared out at the stars.

Zhang wasn't finished. *"Barry, are you there?"* he asked.

"Yes, Director."

"Any use of the Eiferman *transmitter will be limited exclusively to connect with Union Ops or with me."*

"Understood."

"In addition, Barry, any conversation between you and anyone on the Eiferman *will be recorded and forwarded to me."*

Arin was standing in the doorway. "Is he the chief authority?" he asked.

"No," said Derek. "Give us time. We just have to get to the right people."

Arin stayed quietly where he was. He looked stricken. "It's okay," Hutch said. "We'll manage it."

"I'm sorry. We did not realize we were going to get you into so much trouble."

"Don't worry about it. We'll take care of it. You probably have cranks back on the islands, too."

Arin closed his eyes, opened them again, and retreated inside, where he began talking with the others. Ken came up next. "Was it really that bad?"

"It wasn't good," said Derek. He turned to Hutch. "What was that business about Barry not allowing any communications?"

"Zhang's concerned that we'll bypass him to get the story out."

"I didn't think they'd be happy about this," said Ken. "But this is something of an overreaction."

Derek got out of his chair but stood, holding on to it. "Hutch, they're going to need you to take them back."

"No, they don't. What they'll probably do is have Barry take them."

"Not if we shut him down."

"I don't care much for that idea." She turned in her seat so she could see him. "In any case, they certainly don't need me." She got up. Ken backed out of the way and she left the bridge. She passed through the passenger cabin and took the down ramp to the cargo bay.

After a minute or so Derek followed her. "Where are you going?" he asked.

"I need to think this out. Our only real chance to win this is to get Arin and Kwylla some media attention. That's not going to happen as long as we're in Zhang's hands. He figures, or knows, the Chinese aren't going to want to get involved in this any more than Proctor does. So, he's going to keep us quiet until Kwylla and Arin are safely on their way back to Volaria. The WSA will probably claim there was evidence of a disease or something."

"Wait a minute—"

"Derek, we have to connect with the outside world. When we get close to Union, we can put Arin and Kwylla on board the lander and head down."

412

"Really? You think they won't notice that? They'll follow us in and be waiting wherever we land—"

Hutch stopped. He was right. "Okay," she said. "I've a better idea. How about if we record an interview with them, with Kwylla and Arin, and just send it to somebody?"

"We can't use the transmitter, remember? So, you mean, what, wait till we get close and use a commlink?"

"No. That won't work. He'll have someone escort us in. When we get close enough to use a commlink, they'll scramble anything except a transmission aimed at Union."

"So, what then?"

"He shut down the *ship's* transmitter. We've got another one on the lander."

"Right! Okay, that's good. But who do we talk to? You know somebody in the media?"

"Yes. I'd send it directly to Jack Crispee if I had his link. Unfortunately, I don't."

"How about a boyfriend?"

"Not anymore." Tom Axler was the last guy she could have brought into this. "But I *do* have somebody."

"Who?"

"My mom. I'll ask her to send it to Crispee at CBC."

"You don't have their link either, I assume?"

"No. But Mom can find it easily enough."

He needed a minute to think about it. "Okay. I don't see what else we have." They walked over to the lander. "I hope this works," he said.

"Let's see first if we still have control of the system." She opened the lander's hatch, and they went inside and sat down. Normally, she would have directed Tasha to activate the transmitter, but that would alert Barry and he might feel bound by his instructions to relay the request to Zhang. Best to do it manually. Which she did. "Good so far," she said.

"You understand this is going to be the end of our careers?"

"I suspect that's the least that will happen. We might both wind up in jail."

"Whatever." Derek sat for a moment, probably trying to find a way to laugh it off. "How are we going to manage the interview?"

"Best time is now. Let's get it done, and then when we get close enough to Union, we'll send it out."

"I think," said Derek, "it will work best if you do it, Hutch. You look a little better than I do."

"Derek, you're higher up in the organization. I'm just—"

"You've got more experience with this stuff. Please. Do it my way. We need to get the audience on our side. Whatever blowback we get, I'll take full responsibility."

They rearranged the chairs on the front porch, converting it back into a standard passenger cabin.

"I am uncomfortable with this," Arin said. He looked over at Kwylla, who indicated she was in full agreement. "We're getting you into serious trouble. But I don't see what else we can do."

"We'll be all right," said Derek.

"What actually is this about? Why are we going to sit here and do an interview?"

"It won't be so much an interview as a conversation," said Hutch. "When we're done, you'll be able to watch it onscreen."

They both looked nervous.

Derek smiled at them. "All you have to do is relax and answer the questions that Hutch asks. Okay? It won't take any longer than a half hour or so, and if you want to stop it for some reason, just say so. We can edit the results, so don't worry about anything. And don't worry about us. We'll be fine."

Hutch's eyebrows rose. "No, Derek. We can't edit the results, because we'd need Barry to help with that."

"And we can't talk to him."

"Not about something like this. We'll have to do this with a single capture."

"Okay. Whatever. Let's get started."

Derek would be the guy recording the show. He'd need room to move around the passenger cabin without having to worry about getting himself or anyone else who didn't belong into the shots. So, Wally, Beth, and Ken, who wanted to watch, had to retire to their cabins or the bridge.

Hutch was actually glad that Derek had turned the job over to her. He had a wide array of talents, and he was a good speaker. But he tended to be a bit autocratic in the public forum. Hutch had enjoyed a second career doing seminars and addressing luncheons in what was eventually a losing effort to salvage the Academy. But she was good with audiences.

She took time to record some questions, not that she would consult the notebook but simply to imprint them in her mind. When she was ready, she signaled Derek.

Beth Squires's Notes

They claimed they wanted us out of the way so Derek would have complete freedom to record everything. But the truth was that Kwylla and Arin were nervous enough. The last thing they needed was us sitting there watching. It's a pity, though; I'd have loved to sit in.

—Monday, October 6, 2256

41.

Freedom of conscience, of education, of speech, of assembly are among the very fundamentals of democracy and all of them would be nullified should freedom of the press ever be successfully challenged.
—Franklin D. Roosevelt, Letter to W. N. Hardy, 1940

You did fine," said Derek, speaking to Arin and Kwylla. Both smiled nervously. "I hope so," Kwylla said.

He turned to Hutch. "You okay?"

"Yes. They made it pretty easy." She connected the commlink to the ship's communication track.

"What are you doing?"

"I'm going to add some images from the island. Pictures of the beach, mostly. And the temple."

He laughed. "Good. Can't go wrong with those."

She needed a few minutes. Then: "Now all we have to do is get it to Jack."

"You have that figured out, right?"

"I hope so."

"Good. What's the plan?"

She did a burn, adjusting their position until Earth and

moon were visible through her left-hand window. Then she picked up the chip that had been used to record the interview. "Let's go."

"Okay."

They went down to the cargo bay and climbed into the lander. She closed the hatch and turned on the radio. Then she depressurized the bay and opened the launch doors. "Excellent," said Derek.

She inserted the chip and turned on the transmitter.

They gathered on the front porch and raised glasses while Barry played "Galactic Hearts," a song popularized a few years earlier by the group of the same name. They celebrated through the day and well into the evening. It was, finally, great to be back. And nobody really cared when the *Conover*, the escort vehicle they'd been expecting, showed up.

Derek was up front with Hutch the following morning when a call came through from the station. *'Eiferman, this is Union Ops. The director wishes to speak with Captain Hutchins.'*

They glanced at one another. *Here we go.* She flipped the switch. "Hutchins here."

'Wait one, please.'

There was a click, followed by silence. "He never gets tired of playing games," said Derek.

For a while, the only sound on the bridge, other than the burps and beeps of the electronics, was their breathing. Then Zhang's voice was so sudden that Hutch actually flinched. *'Hutchins.'*

"I'm here, Director Zhang."

"We are looking forward to your arrival today."

"We are too, Director."

"Have everyone packed and ready to leave. There will be a security unit at the gate to ensure you have no problem. The two aliens are to remain on board. Be sure you and your passengers have all your belongings when you depart. Once you have left the ship, no one will be permitted back on board."

"Wait a minute," said Derek.

"Do not give me an argument, Blanchard. If you need assistance getting everything off, it will be provided."

"Do you still intend to return them to their home world?"

"That is correct."

"Stop," said Hutch. "You can't do this. For one thing—"

"Captain, do not challenge me—"

"Damn it, Zhang, there's not sufficient food on board for them."

"We'll take care of it."

"I'm not leaving the ship until *they* do."

"Well, if I could trust you, I suppose you could ride back with them. But I can't, so actually, if you persist, you give me no choice but to put you under arrest. We'll carry you off if necessary."

It was a long ride in. Hutch had expected that her conversation with Kwylla and Arin would have been broadcast by then. It would have been the story of the age. But they'd have had a reaction from Zhang if it had happened. There was no way Jack Crispee would have passed on it. Something had happened.

"We've done what we can," said Derek. "It'll probably show up in a day or so."

She spent her time on the bridge in a dark mood, which was rare for her. Arin tried to be reassuring. "Do not worry about us," he said. "You've done everything you can."

The hours dragged. Hutch spent most of her time on the front porch with her passengers, watching movies and shows. Arin and Kwylla were still trying to improve their language skills, even though it might no longer matter. When finally they shut the system down because nobody could talk through the noise and nobody was really watching anyway, she got up, went to her cabin, and packed. Then she returned to the bridge. Earth dominated the sky now. They were approaching on the daylight side.

Kwylla came in behind her. "You okay, Hutch?" she asked.

"Hi. Yes, I'm good, thanks."

"Is that it ahead?"

"Yes. That's Earth."

"It's a beautiful world."

"Thank you."

"I wanted to say good-bye. And to thank you for all you've done. In case this isn't going to happen as we'd hoped."

"I think we'll be all right. Hold on a second." She turned control of the ship over to CommOps, which would bring them in for docking. "In any case, I'm sure you and Arin will be okay. I don't believe they'll actually just turn you guys around. But if they do, we have a long time before the black hole arrives, and I think, eventually, we'll get something going here to help you." If nothing else, she still had the chip. If she could get it past Zhang's security people.

"Hutch," Kwylla said, "I love you."

It had been probably the longest day of her life. And when it ended, as they eased into the station and she saw the security team waiting for them, she wanted to scream.

She could hear Derek, Beth, and Ken saying good-bye to Kwylla and Arin. She inserted the chip in her Hawks cap, directly in the center so that a careless observer might think it was only the underside of the button. She sealed it in place with a piece of tape the same color as the cap's cotton interior. The chip was small and should be easy to miss. If she could get it through, it would be her backup. Just in case.

Arin was angry. "Why are they doing this to us?"

"Politics," said Hutch.

Derek tried to be reassuring. "Don't give up. It's not over yet."

"But why?" he demanded. "I understand they want to send us back, but why are they not even letting us leave the ship? Do they think we will run and hide somewhere?"

"No. It's nothing like that," said Hutch. "They don't want people to see you, because they're afraid they'll start sympathizing with you."

"Is that why we made the video? Because you *knew* they wouldn't let us actually speak?"

Hutch sighed. "It was a precautionary step."

He looked directly into her eyes. "Our entire world is going to be left to die, isn't it?"

• • •

The security team consisted of six members. They were waiting in the access tube when Hutch opened the hatch. They'd blocked off the far end of the tube. There was no crowd, no media, nothing. One of them, a tall, bored-looking woman wearing sergeant's stripes, ordered everyone out.

Hutch sighed, put on her baseball cap, and went first. She signaled Arin to follow. The security team stepped in. They stared at him, and a couple of them had a hard time restraining laughter. Finally, they shook their heads. They showed no inclination to hide their reactions.

"Wait." The sergeant turned ominous eyes on Hutch. "You the captain?"

"I am."

"Tell him to go back inside."

Hutch looked at Arin. He hesitated.

"Do it," said the sergeant.

He went back in. Hutch turned and tried to follow him, but the guards seized her and pulled her away. "The rest of you out," said the sergeant.

Nobody moved.

"Beth," said Kwylla, "I never thought that I would say this, and it's not your fault. But I wish you had never come. At least we'd have had these last few years in peace."

It was the last Hutch heard as she was escorted away.

They picked up her bags and took her through the connecting tube, coming out into the concourse to find, as she had expected, more security. It was otherwise empty. They'd sealed everything off. Shops and restaurants were closed. Lights were dimmed.

One of the guards, a heavyset guy who looked annoyed, carried a scanner. He signaled Hutch to move to one side. "Over here." He pointed at the wall. "You have a commlink?"

She produced it for him. He took it. "Any other devices?"

"There's a notebook in my baggage."

They opened her bags and went through them. He took the notebook. "That's all?"

"Yes."

"Okay. Lean forward, please. Put your hands on the wall." She complied and he turned the scanner on and aimed it at her feet. Satisfied she had nothing hidden in her shoes, he went behind her. She could hear the soft hum of the instrument rise and fall as it checked legs and arms, front and back. She remained quiet, unmoving. Then the guard was signaling for her to lower her left arm.

She did.

She probably should have carried something in a pocket to serve as a distraction. But it was too late for that.

"Take off the hat, please."

She removed it, turning it so the interior was plainly visible. Which might discourage a closer examination. Meanwhile, she tried to look bored. The guard handed the scanner to one of his partners and held out his hand for the cap. Hutch gave it to him. He saw the chip, removed it and shook his head. *Idiot.* His contempt was visible.

Ken was a few meters away, surrendering his commlink. He wasn't being very cooperative, and one of the security guys shoved him against the wall. They opened his baggage, began sorting through everything, and removed his notebook. "We'll get this back to you, sir," the guard said.

"Please. There's several months' work in there."

"We'll have it for you shortly."

"What's your name, please?" Ken asked.

The guard laughed. "Louis."

They took everybody's commlinks and notebooks. And a couple of Wally's electronic devices that Hutch didn't even recognize.

"This way." Beth, Ken, Wally, Derek, and Hutch followed their escorts to a stock room with a few plastic chairs. "Make yourselves comfortable," said the sergeant. They left and closed the door. The lock clicked. There was a second door at the other end of the room, but it was locked too.

"What could we do anyway?" asked Beth. "Escape?"

"I'm sorry they found the chip," said Derek. "I was thinking about asking you to make a copy for me, but I figured trying to get two of them through would just reduce our chances. If they caught either of us, they'd just intensify the search."

"Well," said Wally, "in the end—"

He was probably going to say something about the transmission to Hutch's mom. But Hutch broke in. "We'll be okay," she said, shaking her head to signal that Zhang was probably listening.

"They can't keep us quiet," said Ken. "I'm going to tell the world what these sons of bitches are doing."

Derek lowered himself into one of the chairs. "I'm sorry you guys got caught up in all this."

The room grew quiet. There wasn't much to talk about. And everybody had gotten the message that somebody was probably listening. Eventually, two of the guards came back in. They returned the equipment they'd taken, other than Hutch's chip, thanked them for their cooperation, and left without saying anything more.

A few minutes later, the guy who'd searched Hutch entered. "Captain Hutchins?" he said. "Please come with me."

She followed him down a corridor. They took an elevator up two levels, made a couple of turns, and entered an office where a young woman in a dark blue suit was studying a computer display. "Thanks, Ed," she said. "Captain Hutchins, please have a seat. The director will see you shortly."

She waited only about three minutes before she was ushered into a connecting office. Zhang sat behind a desk. Family pictures were all over the walls. He looked up at her and flipped a hand in the direction of a chair. Then he dismissed the assistant and produced the chip.

"Hutchins," he said, "I wish I could trust you."

"You can trust me to do the right thing, Director."

"I can trust you to assume you know better than anyone else." He dropped the chip on his desk. "Have you any idea at all how much damage this thing could cause? You're lucky the security guys found it. If this had gotten out, I'd have had no choice but to prosecute you. You were defying the instructions of your superiors. And even acting against the intentions of your president."

He looked at her and took a deep breath. "You would have ruined Derek's career, too. You understand that, I hope. And I should inform you if you go out and start blabbering about this, I'll have no choice but to have you arrested. Is that clear? And I can guarantee, if that happens, you'll never set foot on an interstellar in any capacity again."

Zhang looked utterly frustrated. He rubbed the back of his hand against his lips and took a deep breath. "Priscilla," he said, "I'm sorry. I understand what you're going through. But I need you to be aware of what's at stake. You want us to construct what, twenty *Evening Star* liners? I'm sure you're aware who would have to pay for them. We are already underwater in debt. But that's not the issue." His voice hardened. "Once we have them, once your aliens have been rescued, there'll be no stopping an expansion into deep space. Inevitably, one of those vehicles will bring home something lethal. Aliens, maybe, who aren't quite as friendly as your buddies. Or maybe a disease that will take everyone down because we have no defense against it. That possibility is now a prime concern in the medical community."

Hutch broke in: "The medical people have been saying for years that a disease that evolved elsewhere would almost certainly have no effect on us."

"That's pure theory."

"So's gravity. You want to go up on a rooftop somewhere and test it?"

Zhang cleared his throat. "Recent research has brought about a change in perspective. There *is* serious concern. Your first obligation is to humanity. But you really don't give a damn about that, do you? You're putting a lot of lives at risk, and I have to wonder what makes you think you have the right to do that." He got up and pointed at the door. "Please leave. You disgust me."

NEWSDESK

Thursday, October 9, 2256

HOLLANDER BILL DEFEATED IN HOUSE

Proposal to Provide Govt Funding for Elections Fails

Contributions to Politicians Would

Have Been Illegal

ESTHER WATKINS WINS WORLD CHESS

CHAMPIONSHIP

First Human Champion in 86 Years

First Woman Champion Ever

VIOLENT CRIME RATE IN NAU REACHES

ALL-TIME LOW

Murders Drop First Time Below 1,000 Nationwide

TREES COMING BACK

Reforesting Project Combats Climate Change

Seas Still Rising, But Rate of Increase Finally Slows

SUCCESSFUL MARRIAGE RATE

CONTINUES TO IMPROVE

85% of First Marriages Now Last Lifetime

STUDIES SHOW MOST PEOPLE ARE SMARTER

THAN THEY THINK

Authority Figures Create Problems by Showing Us

Where We Get Things Wrong

Advice to Parents, Teachers, and Bosses: Emphasize

the Positive

MCDERMOTT WINS CONCILIAR PRIZE
British Physicist Claims Physics Award with
Humanitarian Application

GEORGE PARRIN DEAD AT 141
Actor Best Known for Role as Albert Einstein

WHITE HOUSE: NO COMMENT ON CENTAURI
INITIATIVE

42.

Engage the passions, and no mere argument, however
reasonable, can stand.
—Gregory MacAllister, "The Café Across the Street,"
Collected Essays, 2251

They took Hutch back to the stock room. Derek asked
what had happened. She saw immediately that Ken's
eyes were filled with rage. This was the guy who
never got upset. "What's wrong?" she asked.

"They deleted everything," said Beth.

"The book?"

"Yeah," said Ken.

Hutch would be able to reconstruct some of her notes,
as would the others. But rewriting a book? "I'm sorry, Ken."

His notebook was on the floor beside his chair. "I can
live with it."

The bags they'd brought out of the *Eiferman* were scattered around the room. And her commlink was waiting for
her.

"So, what happened?" said Derek. "He still talking about prosecution?"

"If we say anything, yes."

"They won't bother anybody," said Derek. "Zhang and whoever else was behind this just want it to go away now. The last thing they'll want would be media attention."

None of the others were with Hutch in the shuttle ride down to the DC spaceport. Usually, she would have spent her time reading. She told herself that she didn't bother because her notebook had been emptied. But the shuttle had a library. So, the reality was that she was too excited, or maybe too annoyed. Her attention was concentrated on finding out whether the transmission had gotten through to her mother.

They were out over the Atlantic, descending through a bright, sunlit morning, when her commlink sounded. It was Tom. *"Hi, Hutch,"* he said. *"Welcome home."*

"Hello, Tom. Good to hear from you." He sounded less belligerent than he had the last time they'd talked.

"I was glad to see you got home okay. I missed you."

"I missed you, too, Thomas."

"I wanted to apologize. I wasn't thinking clearly."

"It's okay."

"I didn't like having you out of my life. I think that's what the real problem was."

"Let it go, Tom. I understand."

"How are you? Everything all right?"

"I'm good."

"I love you, Hutch." It wasn't the first time he'd said that, but somehow, there was more warmth in his voice than she'd ever felt before. *"I don't ever want to lose you."*

430

She could feel the emotion. And she wasn't sure how to respond. "I'm sorry it happened," she said finally.

"So, tell me about the flight." His disappointment was evident. *"What was the waterfall all about?"*

She explained about Calliope and the ice world and Tarka, and when opportunity presented itself, she asked about Tom's new career as a detective. *"I just got a new assignment today. There's a corporate guy who's been stealing millions. A woman who had to have known about it was found dead at the bottom of a staircase a few days ago. The injuries weren't consistent with what you'd expect from a fall."*

"That sounds intriguing."

"Says the lady who helped solve the strange case of the missing star. My life's not quite as exciting as yours. When you get home, Hutch, I'd like to take you out to dinner. Can we do that?"

"Sure, Tom. I'll be on the run for a couple of days, but I'll give you a call when things calm down."

There were only about a dozen people in the cabin. None of them looked like someone who might be tracking her. Well, one woman who sat behind her did. But when they landed, the woman wasted no time disappearing into the crowd.

Hutch got a taxi, climbed in, and called her mother. *"Welcome home, love,"* she said.

"Mom, you got the package?"

"Yes. I couldn't find a number for Crispee, so I just sent it to Cosmic Broadcasting. With his name on it."

"You *just* sent it? What took so long?"

"I've only had it a couple of days. I wasn't aware there was a rush about it."

"I guess not." She'd assumed her mother would realize. "It's all right. Sorry. My fault."

"I watched it before I sent it out. It's an incredible show. It's real, right? You actually had aliens on board?"

"Yes."

"I'll tell you, you should have been a talk show host, Priscilla. Are we going to be able to save them?"

"I don't know. I hope so."

"It's terrible, that black hole thing. They sure look funny, but they seem nice. How come they speak English?"

"They worked on it a lot." It was good to hear her voice again. She sat back in the cab, watched the trees go by, and they talked about Arin and Kwylla, and her confrontation with Zhang.

Hutch was assuring her everything would be okay when Mom broke in: *"Hold on a second."* She was gone for a moment. Then: *"I've got company. Just pulled up in the driveway. Looks like official types."*

"Damn. They're monitoring me. You said you sent the package, right?" She heard her mother's doorbell ring.

"Yes. Are these guys going to be unhappy about that?"

"Probably." Now there was a loud banging. Somebody pounding on her door.

The commlink clicked. "Mom, you there?" She was gone. She called again. And listened to her phone ringing until finally a voice informed her that the party she was trying to reach was not available. Damn. They must've had a monitor in the cab. Or, more likely, they'd inserted one in her commlink.

Her instinct was to make directly for Cherry Hill. But that wouldn't be a good idea. Just get her in deeper. Not to mention that it would take three hours. She could call Crispee. But that might give him away as well. She sat undecided, watching the fluttering leaves of October drifting down onto the windshield. Finally, the taxi pulled up in front of her home. She paid up, got out of the cab, got into her car, and went down to Keifer's Electronics. She bought a new commlink, gave it the same code, and junked the old one.

On the way home, she got Cosmic's number from Information and made the call. They picked up on the third ring. She identified herself and asked to be connected to Jack Crispee. A phone rang at the other end as the car pulled into her driveway. She got out and stood, watching tree branches across the street sway gently in the wind. A bus went by. And a couple of kids tossed a ball around.

Finally, Crispee answered. *"Hi, Priscilla. Good to hear from you again."*

"Hello, Jack. My mom sent you a package. Teresa Hutchins. Did you receive it?"

"Teresa Hutchins?"

"Yes."

"How could I have missed that? Hold on." One of the kids threw the ball over his pal's head and it bounced across her lawn.

"I got nothing," said Crispee. *"Did she send it to* me?*"*

"No. We didn't have your number. She sent it to Cosmic Broadcasting. Your name would have been on it, though."

"Give me a second to check." He was talking to somebody as she let herself into the house. Then: *"Yes, it's here."*

"Good. The WSA won't be happy about it, and they may try to prevent your using it. But if you want it, it's yours."

"Let me take a look."

He was back in about five minutes. *"Hutch, perfect. Is this for real? They really there?"*

"Yes. They came back with us."

"Okay, give me a chance to watch the rest of it and I'll get back to you. We'll break it tonight."

"You probably don't have until tonight. The Feds may be getting a subpoena now. Also, they're sending the Volarians back home. I'm not sure when, but I suspect it'll be as quickly as they can."

"How long is the interview?"

"It's a half hour. Give or take a few minutes."

"Can you come in for this?"

"Jack, I already have too much visibility. If we're going to save these guys, we need to have *them* front and center. And you're probably out of time."

"Priscilla, I don't like running it until I've seen it."

"Your call, Jack. But if you wait, you may not get to see it."

"Is there anything in there that might cause a lawsuit?"

"There's nothing defamatory in it. Just aliens in a desperate condition caused by natural forces. And some high-level people who don't want it getting out."

"So, you're saying there'd be no legal liability?"

"I'm not a lawyer, Jack, but I don't see how there could be."

"Okay. Hold on." Again she heard him talking to someone else. Then he came back: *"Priscilla, we're going to need you. And the aliens. Where are they now?"*

"As far as I know, they're still on board the *Eiferman*. They won't be available."

"I guess that doesn't surprise me. How much time do we have before they ship them out?"

"It'll probably happen as soon as they can manage it. I didn't see another interstellar in the dock, so they may need a couple of days for maintenance. But they'll be pushing hard to get rid of them. Especially since Zhang knows about the interview."

"How'd he find out about it? Come to think of it, how do the Feds know?"

"It's a long story, Jack. Listen, I have to go."

"Hold on. We need you here, Priscilla. As soon as you can get here."

"Jack, that's not the way to do it."

"Priscilla, please."

"Okay. I'll be on my way in a minute. But don't wait for me. Get started." She told Cary, her AI, to record whatever was playing on Cosmic Broadcasting. Then she tried again to call her mother but still got no response. Her commlink, a recording told her, was no longer in service.

Okay. First things first. She set out for Cosmic Broadcasting, which was a half hour away. Fortunately, traffic was light on the expressway. She was passing Lorton when her commlink sounded. It was Mom.

Thank heaven. "Mom," she said, "you okay?"

"I'm all right. Where are you?"

"On the expressway. I'm headed for Cosmic Broadcasting. Who was at your door?"

"Feds. They had a warrant to seize my electronic gear. They took everything. Except Gina." Her AI. *"They shut her down."*

"What are you using now?"

"I'm next door. At Larry's."

435

"Damn. This is my fault."

"Don't worry about it."

"Did they tell you what it was about?"

"They wanted to know about you. And they knew about the interview."

"I hope I haven't gotten you into any trouble. But we had to get it out."

"It's okay. Looks like a good cause. I'm glad to have helped. Sorry I didn't get it out sooner."

"Mom, I owe you. Can I take you to dinner tonight?"

She'd just passed under the beltway when Jack called again. *"It's running,"* he said. *"We broke in on the* Alison MacPherson Show. *That's the good news."*

"What's the bad news?"

"The NSB is here." The National Security Bureau. *"They're down now trying to get into Branton's office."* Hutch didn't recognize the name, but the message was clear enough.

She set the car radio for Cosmic and listened to Arin describing his reaction when he'd gone out and looked at the black hole. *"It was terrifying,"* he was saying, while his voice trembled. Kwylla talked about her appreciation to the humans who had offered to help. *"We will always be in your debt, Hutch. You and your friends have been priceless."*

"How did you feel about Utopia?" Hutch asked.

"It scares me," she said, *"that we have to leave our home. The world you took us to is beautiful, but I wish we could stay where we are."*

"But," said Arin, *"we are thankful there is a place we can retreat to. I hope we can make it happen, but whether we do*

or not, that we can one day show our gratitude for everything you've done."

The car continued along the interstate. Finally, it turned off onto Capitol Drive, passed the Agriculture Department, made a left onto Merriweather Street, and pulled into the Cosmic parking lot. There was, fortunately, no sign of law enforcement activity, no official vehicles or blinking lights. And there seemed nothing unusual going on as she went through the front door into the lobby. A young woman sat behind a counter. "Can I help you, ma'am?" she asked.

"My name's Priscilla Hutchins. I'm looking for Jack Crispee."

"Oh, yes, Ms. Hutchins. He told me you were coming. Hold one second. I'll let him know you're here."

Fixed high on the wall behind her, a large screen was running the current Cosmic program. Except that it wasn't her conversation with the Volarians. MacPherson was back on, talking with Carson Bennett, the NAU Secretary of State. "Excuse me," she said, "what is that?"

She looked up at it. "That's odd. It's Alison MacPherson. They were running the alien interview a few minutes ago. Some strange stuff going on today. I thought—" Her eyes widened. "You're the woman who was conducting the interview."

"Yes."

"It was an incredible—" Her commlink sounded. "Hold on." She picked it up, listened a moment, said "Okay," and held it out for Hutch. "Mr. Crispee."

She took it. *"Priscilla?"*

"Yes."

"The Feds shut us down."

437

"No."

"I'm sorry. There was nothing we could do."

"What happened to freedom of the press?"

"The material's classified. Did you know that?"

"That's crazy. How much of the broadcast went out?"

"About eighteen minutes."

Four people came out of an elevator into the lobby. One, a short, stocky guy, looked stressed. The other three, two men and a woman, strode toward the front doors, leaving him in their wake. Then one of them noticed Hutch. They all turned in her direction and approached. "Pardon me, ma'am," said the woman, "but aren't you Priscilla Hutchins?"

"Yes, I am."

"Incredible." She walked away.

Crispee arrived, looking pale and angry. "Jack," she said, "you want to do an interview about this?"

"I'd love to, Priscilla. But there's no way Branton would allow it."

"Come on, Jack. This is First Amendment territory."

"I know. But they've made some serious threats. I think he figures we've already broken the story."

Jack Crispee's Diary

Of all the idiot stuff I've been part of, this beats everything. It was an act of pure cowardice I'll always regret. We've just given the story of the century to everybody else.

—Friday, October 10, 2256

43.

The liberty of the press consists, in my idea, in publishing the truth, from good motives and for justifiable ends, though it reflect on the government, on magistrates, or individuals.
—Alexander Hamilton, New York speech, 1804

Ornsbee's was her mom's favorite restaurant, a friendly place with a good menu. They got a table that provided a good view of the Phillies–Red Sox game. It was the World Series, game five, tied at two apiece. Mom was still somewhat rattled from the visit by the Feds. "I've never had any kind of experience like that," she said. But she tried to show her daughter that she wasn't worried about fallout from her role in relaying her transmission to Cosmic Broadcasting. But there was a tightness in her smile and her voice.

"I'm sorry about getting you into all this, Mom," Hutch said. "But we needed to make sure the interview got released, and you were the most reliable person I had. There was just too much at stake—"

"I understand that, Priscilla. Please don't worry about it.

In fact, I'm proud you included me in this." Mom leaned forward and looked into Hutch's eyes. "How are you, love?" she asked. "Are they going to prosecute you?"

Hutch managed a smile. "I'll let you know. But I don't think so."

"I was sorry to see what happened to the broadcast. That it got interrupted."

"So was I."

"I guess you know it's all over the news."

She had been listening to reports during her ride up from DC. "They're getting a lot of criticism. The government."

"It's gone viral on the Web." The game was in the first inning, and the visiting Red Sox already had two runners on with none out. "It's nice to have you back." She reached across the table for her wrist.

"Next time we go anywhere," Hutch said, "I'll arrange for you to come along."

"That would be good. Miami would be nice." Her mom took a deep breath. "I love you, Priscilla." It wasn't the first time she'd said that, of course, but there was more emotion than Hutch usually picked up.

They brought their menus up on the display and ordered dinner. Both got the special, barbecued pork. Then: "So, tell me about the flight. What was the waterfall all about? Did that have anything to do with the aliens you interviewed?" She kept her voice down.

Hutch explained about Calliope and the ice world and Tarka and, when opportunity presented itself, asked what her mom had been up to.

She got a surprise. "I'm on the school board."

"Really?"

"I'm thinking about running for governor."

"You're kidding, Mom. I've never thought of you as a politician."

"Well, I'm your mother and you're becoming better known every day. You may not have noticed, but you've been drawing attention since we walked in the door. I figure I might as well take advantage of it."

"Well, good luck, Mom." She'd always thought her mother could have had a decent political career. She was likable and she never forgot anyone's name. More than that, nobody could have bought her support. "I guess I've had a good run," Hutch continued. "If you can—" She stopped dead. Ornsbee's had gone silent, except for a woman's voice. *"—your reaction,"* she was saying, *"when we first told you?"* The World Series had vanished from the display, replaced, incredibly, by her own image. Hutch was listening to her own voice.

Then Kwylla was onscreen, her eyes large and dark and impossibly sad. It was a clip from the eighteen minutes. *"We could not believe it. We refused to believe it. Except that it was you and your friends who were saying this to us."*

Somebody behind her said, "It's the alien. The show they cut off."

"I know."

The picture froze and Matt Ornsbee took a moment to speak to his customers: "We thought you'd want to see this. It'll run for a little more than ten minutes. We're saving the game, so don't worry; you won't miss anything."

Then all three of them, Kwylla and Arin and herself, were back onscreen. Hutch was speaking: *"—long time before it will arrive."*

A woman at a nearby table: "They're really cute. Look at their eyes."

And the guy she was with: "Why do you think they shut it down, Lorrie?"

"I don't know."

"We can't do anything, anyhow. You can't stop a black hole."

"What's that got to do with blocking the TV?"

Most of the diners were listening to Arin: *"Kwylla and I will probably be gone before it happens. But the lives of our children will be cut short. And their children."* Suddenly, they were looking at the beach filled with Volarians. It was one of the clips Hutch had inserted. *"I must confess to you, Hutch, that my faith in Alora was shaken by this. Until you informed us there was a chance that you and your people might be able to step in. I was reminded that I should not be so quick to give up."*

Hutch saw the diners reaching toward one another, whispering, shaking their heads, finishing their drinks. A guy in a nearby booth was saying how you couldn't trust the government.

The eighteen minutes played out. A few people grumbled about losing the Series. Near the end, Arin described his gratitude to their visitors, and how he prayed they really could help, and at that moment, the program ended. Some people were reaching for their handkerchiefs.

One of the diners recognized Hutch and came to the table to thank her for what she'd done. He was quickly joined by a swarm of others, asking to shake her hand and showing their approval. One complained that she might have done it, though, after the World Series was over.

NEWSDESK

Saturday–Tuesday, October 11–14, 2256

NSB CLAIMS TECH FAILURE CAUSED FILM SHUTDOWN

ALIENS LOOK LIKE DOLPHINS

ALIENS CAPTIVE AT UNION SPACE STATION
WSA: Isolated as Precaution

BLACK HOLE EXPECTED TO CRUSH DOLPHIN WORLD
IN SIXTY YEARS
*Connected to Waterfall Transmission Acquired by
Van Entel*

PRESIDENT PROCTOR: ALIENS ARE BEING TAKEN
CARE OF

ONE OF THE ALIENS IS A PREACHER
Represents Monotheistic Religion

DOLPHINS RESCUED STARSHIP CREW AFTER CRASH
Hutchins: "They're the Reason We're Here"

WSA DIRECTOR STEPS DOWN
Zhang Chao Resigns
Denies Connection to Volarian Controversy

44.

The strongest, most generous, and proudest of all virtues is true courage.
—Michel de Montaigne, *Essays, III*, 1588

The world changed during the following few weeks. Kwylla and Arin were released with a report that they posed no threat to the general population. They became immensely popular guests on the morning talk shows, with late-night comedians, and on major news programs. Kwylla even showed up playing herself on the domestic comedy *Touch and Go*.

President Proctor met with world leaders and issued a statement that a fleet of thirty interstellars equipped with the Locarno drive would be constructed and sent on their way as soon as possible to begin Project Exodus, which would carry the Volarians to their new home. In addition, she announced that a WSA team would be dispatched to determine whether the derelict transport vehicle adrift near the ice world could be brought into the effort. All five members of the *Eiferman* team also appeared across TV, but none sparked viewer enthusiasm like the two Volarians.

Jack Crispee left Cosmic without giving a reason and turned up a few days later on the BBC, hosting *The Truth Forum*. He wasted no time inviting Priscilla back.

There was no indication that her mother's experience with the Feds would result in any consequences.

The lights brightened and Jack Crispee looked completely relaxed, as he usually did on the air, except that he was behind a table instead of seated in the lush armchair he'd used at Cosmic. The Nantucket living room which had been his hallmark was also missing, replaced by a standard studio. The door was marked by the letters BBC, his new employer. "Hello, Priscilla," he said. "Welcome to *The Truth Forum*.

She was seated on the other side of the table. "It's good to be here, Jack. Thanks for the invitation."

"Was that mission your longest ever?"

"No," she said. "But it was the most unnerving. And also the most rewarding."

"You're talking about the Volarians?"

"Yes. We were lucky they were there, or we wouldn't have made it home."

"I wanted to thank you for arranging their appearance on the show. I thought Zhang Chao would have a heart attack when we contacted him."

"It was easy, Jack. He wanted to cooperate as best he could."

"You must have been happy to see President Proctor

withdraw her support for the Centauri Initiative. She took a lot of criticism for that."

"Only from the idiots who argue that once you form an opinion, you're not allowed to change your mind. You've noticed she's gone way up in the polls."

"Oh yes. She's a lock for a second term. You're not suggesting she did it because of the reaction to your two alien friends?"

"I think she realized what was the right thing to do, Jack. And she did it. Whether the election might have prompted her change in perspective, you'll have to ask her. By the way, I thought inviting Kwylla and Arin to appear in person here was a great idea."

He broke into a prolonged laughter. "It wasn't bad. Everybody was after them. The week they were on gave us the biggest audience on record *ever* for a news show. In fact, for *any* show. Everybody *loves* them. On another subject: They sent your alien buddies back to Volaria on the *Excelsior*. With Ken and Beth Squires. What will they be doing?"

"Well, Kwylla and Arin were anxious to get home. They needed to deliver the good news and start getting everybody ready for Exodus. Ken and Beth went along primarily because they were so good at picking up the languages, both on Volaria and Tarka, which is where the other alien race lives. Those are the people who are going to help get the new world ready."

"You call them 'people.' I've seen pictures of the creatures on Tarka. You can probably get away with referring to the Volarians as people, but—"

"Jack, I think we're still a little behind on the learning

curve. Appearance doesn't matter. Intelligence does. And empathy."

"Excellent, Priscilla. Though I have to admit that a year ago, I would never have believed this could happen. By the way, what specifically will the Tarkans be doing?"

"They've offered to help. And we need them."

"To construct towns?"

"And supply food. And do a lot of other stuff."

"Okay." He smiled. "Good enough. I was surprised when Kwylla told me they hated to leave Washington. That they were planning on coming back when they could."

"What can I tell you, Jack? They've been enjoying themselves here. Arin told me he loved being a celebrity. Which was good. We needed people to see who they were."

Nobody was enjoying the public attention as much as Wally, who'd spent two months as a guest on every science panel and now had his own show with PBS. Derek, of course, would be traveling to DC in two weeks to receive the Freedom Prize from President Proctor.

Jack leaned back in his chair and folded his arms. "Can you tell me why Zhang Chao resigned?"

He'd been forced out, but Hutch didn't want to say that. She hadn't been particularly impressed with the WSA director, but he'd been a decent guy caught in the middle of an impossible situation. "There was a lot of pressure over this. First aliens arriving, and they showed up with only a few days' notice. I think he just wanted to get away from the bureaucracy and go back to the Taibai Observatory for a while."

"That's in China, I assume?"

"Qinling Mountains."

"Okay. Makes sense. How about you? You going to help evacuate the Volarians?"

"It'll take about a year to get the project moving. But I expect to be on the first wave of interstellars."

"Beautiful. Could you arrange to take me with you?"

"Sure, Jack. Bring a good book."

He was obviously enjoying himself. "One more thing I heard about the Calliope flight. I understand you found out something else."

"What was that?"

The lights flickered, and suddenly they were on Iapetus. Hutch sat facing her host, but when they both turned and looked toward the place where the control room had been, the Iapetus angel looked back. The eyes that actually gazed out at the rings reflected something more than she'd noticed before. Maybe something other than the sense that the universe was a cold and uncaring place. Her eyes suggested an understanding that we are all in it together.

They were sisters.

"Hello, Sola," she said.

Epilogue

Wednesday, March 11, 2257

Governor Rankin escorted her guests into the town hall, past the overflow Volarians lining the street. The group consisted of the interstellar pilot, Clay Clairveau, and Beth and Ken Squires. They followed her through the center of the auditorium and up onto the stage, where they joined Kwylla and Arin, who were already seated.

The governor took her place behind the lectern and switched on the microphone. *"Friends and neighbors,"* she said, *"there's no one in the building who isn't aware why this place is full tonight. We've all lived under a heavy cloud these last few months. Kwylla and Arin traveled a long distance to present our case. And they are back to give us the results."* The audience already knew, of course. The news had gotten out within hours after their return. *"I doubt there's anyone here who doesn't know Kwylla and Arin, but if you will, please stand for our audience. And let me introduce Clay Clairveau and Beth and Ken Squires."*

They stood and broke into applause. The guests all came forward and the governor turned the lectern over to them. *"Hello,"* Arin said, *"let me waste no time, in case there's anyone here who still hasn't heard the news. The people of Earth will join those of Tarka to help us. Construction has begun on a fleet of thirty transports that—"* The auditorium again erupted with applause. The crowd literally leaped out of their seats and clapped and waved scarves and hats and turned to embrace whoever happened to be sitting beside them. When finally it settled down, Arin picked up where he'd left off. *"The transports will begin arriving here in about a year. It will take a while, and we will need years to complete the evacuation, but it will happen and we will all eventually be taken to Utopia."* That brought more clapping and waving. *"When the dark star arrives, we will be gone. I should add that Professor Blanchard, who headed the team that discovered our situation and led the fight for us has sent his congratulations. I'd like also to thank my wife Kwylla, who accompanied me to that distant, but very friendly, world. And Clay, who was one of the first to step forward as a volunteer for Project Exodus. And finally, Beth and Ken Squires, who were part of the initial expedition."* The crowd stood and applauded for two or three minutes.

Arin finally got them quiet. The guests went back to their seats while he turned the lectern back to the governor.

"Thank you, Arin," said Rankin. *"We should not forget that without Brother Arin and his concern for the strangers who*

crashed into the ocean on that memorable day rather than try to land on a crowded beach, this night might not have happened.

"I'm aware," she continued, "that our island has a hallowed tradition for knowing how to party. So, we'll get to that in a minute. Before we do, I want to express my own appreciation for the courage of all concerned. Of the humans who have given us hope, and of the rest of you, our own people, who are about to create a new future.

"Are there any questions?"

There were: How much notice would they have before departure? Would the people on the island be leaving together? Utopia didn't seem to have much water. Would that be a problem? And, eventually, where was Priscilla?

The governor passed the final question to Ken.

He got behind the lectern. "I should tell you first that we call her Hutch. She was our pilot on the Eiferman, the ship that brought us here. She is still the captain of that ship, which, as we speak, is taking her to Tarka. She's going there to transport some of its people and equipment to your new home. They will begin preparing it for you. You would not want to arrive there and discover you didn't have the necessities that we will require."

One of the females raised a hand. "Please tell Hutch that we said thank you and that we love her." Others stood, in all areas of the auditorium.

Someone said, "We love you all."

And, led by Arin and Kwylla, they began to sing "Show Us the Way."